SECOND
CHILD

JOHN SAUL

SECOND CHILD

BANTAM BOOKS
NEW YORK · TORONTO · LONDON · SYDNEY · AUCKLAND

SECOND CHILD
A Bantam Book / July 1990

All rights reserved.
Copyright © 1990 by John Saul.
Book design by Richard Oriola

No part of this book may be reproduced or transmitted
in any form or by any means, electronic or mechanical,
including photocopying, recording, or by any information
storage and retrieval system, without permission in
writing from the publisher.
For information address: Bantam Books.

Library of Congress Cataloging-in-Publication Data

Saul, John.
 Second child / John Saul.
  p.   cm.
 ISBN 0-553-05877-0
 I. Title.
PS3569.A787S4   1990
813'.54—dc20   89-77149
                                                            CIP

Published simultaneously in the United States and Canada

Bantam Books are published by Bantam Books, a division of Bantam Doubleday Dell
Publishing Group, Inc. Its trademark, consisting of the words "Bantam Books" and the
portrayal of a rooster, is Registered in U.S. Patent and Trademark Office and in other
countries. Marca Registrada. Bantam Books, 666 Fifth Avenue, New York, New York
10103.

PRINTED IN THE UNITED STATES OF AMERICA

BVG   0 9 8 7 6 5 4 3 2 1

For Helen, Alison, and Marya

SECOND CHILD

CHAPTER

1

When Polly MacIver awoke just before dawn that morning, she had not the slightest presentiment that she was about to die. As her mind swam lazily in the ebbing tide of sleep, she found herself giggling silently at the memory of the dream that had just roused her. It had been Thanksgiving Day in the dream, and the house was filled with people. Some of them were familiar to her. Tom was sprawled out on the floor, his big frame stretched in front of the fireplace as he studied a chessboard on which Teri had apparently trapped his queen. Teri herself was sitting cross-legged on the carpet, grinning impudently at her father's predicament. There were others scattered around the living room—more, indeed, than Polly would have thought the room could hold. But the dream had had a logic of its own, and it hadn't seemed to matter how many people, strange and familiar, had come in—the room seemed magically to expand for them. It was a happy occasion filled with good cheer until Polly had gone to the kitchen to inspect the dinner. There, disaster awaited her. She must have turned the oven too high, for curls of smoke were drifting up from the corners of the door. But as she bent over to open the oven door, she was not concerned, for exactly the same thing had happened too many times before. For Polly, cooking was an art she had never come close to mastering. She opened the door and, sure enough, thick smoke poured out into the kitchen, engulfing her, then rolling on through the small dining room and into the living room, where the coughing of her guests and the impatient yowl of her daughter finally jarred her awake.

The memory of the dream began to fade from her mind, and Polly stretched languidly, then rolled over to snuggle against the warmth of Tom's body. Outside, a summer storm was building, and just as she was about to drift back into sleep, a bolt of lightning slashed through the faint grayness of dawn, instantly followed by a thunderclap that jerked her fully awake. She sat straight up in bed, gasping in shock at the sharp retort.

Instantly, she was seized by a fit of coughing as smoke filled her lungs.

Her eyes widened with sudden fear. The smoke was real, not a vestige of the dream.

A split second later she heard the crackling of flames.

Throwing the covers back, Polly grabbed her husband's shoulder and shook him violently. "Tom! Tom!"

With what seemed like agonizing slowness, Tom rolled over, moaned, then reached out to her. She twisted away from him, fumbling for the lamp on her nightstand before she found the switch.

Nothing happened.

"Tom!" she screamed, her voice rising with the panic building inside her. "Wake up! The house is on fire!"

Tom came awake, instantly rising and shoving his arms into the sleeves of his bathrobe.

Polly, wearing nothing but her thin nylon negligee, ran to the door and grasped the knob, only to jerk her hand reflexively away from its searing heat. "Teri!" she moaned, her voice breaking as she spoke her daughter's name. "Oh, God, Tom. We have to get Teri out."

But Tom was already pushing her aside. Wrapped in one of the wool blankets from the bed, he covered the brass doorknob with one of its corners before trying to turn it. Finally he pulled the door open an inch.

Smoke poured through the gap, a penetrating cloud of searing fog that reached toward them with angry fingers, clutching at them, trying to draw them into its suffocating grasp.

Buried in the formless body of smoke was the glowing soul of the fire itself. Polly instinctively shrank away from the monster that had engulfed her home, and when Tom spoke to her, his shouted words seemed to echo dimly from afar.

"I'll get Teri. Go out the window!"

Frozen with terror, Polly saw the door open wider; a split second later her husband disappeared into the maw of the beast that had invaded her home.

The door slammed shut.

Polly wanted to go after him, to follow Tom into the fire, to hold onto him as they went after her daughter. Without thinking, she moved toward the door, but then his words resounded in her mind.

"Go out the window!"

A helpless moan strangling in her throat, she dragged herself across the room to the window and pulled it open. She breathed the fresh air outside, then looked down.

Fifteen feet below her lay the concrete driveway that connected the street in front to the garage behind the house. There was no ledge, no tree, not even a drainpipe to hang onto. If she jumped, surely she would break her legs.

She shrank back from the window and turned to the door once more. She had started across the smoke-filled room when her foot touched something soft.

The bedspread, lying in a heap at the foot of the bed. She snatched it up, wrapping it around her body, then, like Tom a few minutes earlier, used one of its corners to protect her fingers from the searing heat of the door. Drawing her breath in slowly, filtering the smoke through the thick padding of the spread, she filled her lungs with air.

At last, battling with the fear that threatened to overwhelm her, she pulled the door open.

The fire in the hall, instantly sucking in the fresh air from the open window, rose up in front of her, its crackle building into a vicious roar.

Time seemed to slow down, each second dragging itself out for an eternity.

Flames reached out to her, and Polly was helpless to pull herself away as panic clasped her in its paralyzing grip. She felt the burning heat against her face, even felt the blisters begin to form wherever her skin was exposed.

She heard a strange, soft sound, like the sizzling of oil in a hot skillet, and instinctively reached up to touch her hair.

Her hair was gone, devoured by the hungry fire, and she stared blankly for a moment at the ashy residue on her fingertips. What had been a thick mass of dark blond hair only a moment ago was now only an oddly greasy smudge on the blistered skin of her hand.

Her mind began closing down, rejecting what she saw, denying the searing heat that all but overwhelmed her.

She staggered backward, the bedspread tangling around her feet as if it had joined forces with the fire to destroy her.

Faintly, as if in the distance somewhere impossibly far beyond the confines of the house, she heard Tom's voice, calling out to Teri.

She heard vague thumpings, as if he might be pounding on a door somewhere.

Then nothing.

Nothing but the hiss and chatter of the flames, dancing before her, hypnotizing her.

Backing away, stumbling and tripping, she retreated from the fury of the fire.

She bumped into something, something hard and ungiving, and though her eyes remained fixed on the inferno that was already invading the bedroom, her hand groped behind her.

And felt nothing.

Panic seized her again, for suddenly the familiar space of the bedroom seemed to vanish, leaving her alone with the consuming flames.

Slowly, her mind assembling information piece by piece, she realized that she had reached the open window.

Whimpering, she sat down on the ledge and began to swing her legs through the gap between the sill and the open casement; her right leg first, then her left.

At last she was able to turn her back on the fire. Gripping the window frame, she stared out into the faintly graying dawn for a moment, then let her gaze shift downward toward the concrete below.

She steeled herself, and clinging to the bedspread, let herself slip over the ledge.

Just as she began to drop away from the window, the corner of the bedspread still inside the room caught on something. Polly felt the pull, found herself unreasonably speculating on what might have snagged it.

The handle of the radiator?

A stray nail that had worked loose from the floor molding?

Falling! Suddenly she was upside down, slipping out of the shroud of the bedspread.

Her fingers grasped at the material; it slipped away as if coated with oil.

She dropped toward the concrete headfirst, only beginning to raise her arms to break her fall as her skull crashed against the driveway.

She felt nothing; no pain at all.

There was only a momentary sense of surprise, and a small cracking sound from within her neck as her vertebrae shattered and crushed her spinal cord.

It had been no more than three minutes since she had awakened, laughing quietly, from her dream.

Now the quiet laughter was over, and Polly MacIver was dead.

Teri MacIver stood rooted on the lawn in front of the house, her right hand clutching at the lapels of her thin terry-cloth bathrobe with all the modesty of her nearly fifteen years. Her eyes were fixed on the blaze that now engulfed the small two-story house which had been her home for the last ten years. It was an old house, built fifty years earlier, when San Fernando had still been a small farming town in the California valley of the same name. Built entirely of wood, the house had baked in the sun for half a century, its wood slowly turning into tinder, and tonight, when the fire started, it had raced through the rooms with a speed that stunned Teri. It was as if one moment the house had been whole, and the next it had been swallowed by flames.

Teri was only vaguely aware of what was going on around her. In the distance a siren wailed, growing steadily louder, but she barely heard it. Her mind was filled with the roar of the fire and the crackling of the siding as it curled back upon itself and began to fall away from the framework of the house, venting the interior to the fresh air that fed the raging flames.

Her parents . . .

Where were they? Had they gotten out? Forcing her eyes away from the oddly hypnotic inferno, she glanced around. Down the block, someone was running toward her, but the figure was no more than a shadow in the breaking dawn.

Voices began to penetrate her consciousness then, people shouting to each other, asking what had happened.

Then, over the roar of the fire and the babble of voices, she heard a scream. It came from the house, seemingly unmuffled by the already crumbling walls. The sharp sound released Teri from her paralysis, and she ran around to the driveway, her eyes wide as she stared up to the second floor and her parents' bedroom.

She saw her mother, a dark silhouette against the glow of the fire. She was wrapped in something—a blanket, perhaps, or the bedspread. Teri watched as her mother's legs came over the windowsill, and a second later she saw her jump . . . then turn in the air as the bedspread tightened around her legs.

Her mother seemed to hang for a moment, suspended in midair. A scream built in Teri's throat, only to be cut off a second later as her mother slid free from the swaddles and plunged headfirst to the driveway below.

Had she heard the sound as her mother's head struck the concrete, or did she imagine it?

Teri began running then, but as if her feet were mired in mud, it seemed to take forever before she reached the spot where her mother lay crumpled and still on the driveway, one arm flung out as if reaching out to her daughter, as if even in death she were grasping for life.

"M-Mom?" Teri stammered, her hand falling away from her robe to tentatively touch her mother. Then her voice rose to an anguished wail. *"M-o-m!"*

There was no response, and as Teri became aware of someone running up the sidewalk, she threw herself on Polly's body, cradling her mother's head in her lap, stroking the blistered cheek of the woman who only a few hours ago had stroked her own before kissing her good night. "No," she whimpered, her eyes flooding with tears. "Oh, no. Please, God, don't let Mommy die." But even as she uttered the words, Teri already knew somewhere deep inside her that it was too late, that her mother was already gone.

She felt gentle hands on her shoulders and slowly looked up to see Lucy Barrow, from across the street. "She's dead." Teri's voice broke as she spoke the words. The admission seemed to release a tide of emotion that had been locked inside her. Covering her face with her hands, she began to sob, her body shaking.

Lucy, her own mind all but numbed by the sight of Polly MacIver's seared and broken body, pulled Teri to her feet and began leading her back down the driveway. "Your father . . ." she said. "Where's your father? Did he get out?"

Teri's hands dropped away from her face. For a moment her shocked eyes flickered with puzzlement. She started to speak, but before the words emerged from her mouth there was a sharp crack, followed instantly by a crash.

Lucy Barrow grasped Teri's arm tightly, pulling her down the driveway as the roof of the house collapsed into the fire and the flames shot up into the brightening sky.

Three fire trucks clogged the street in front of the MacIvers' house, and a tangle of hoses snaked along the sidewalk to the hydrant on the corner. An ambulance had taken Polly's body away more than an hour before, but as more and more neighbors arrived to gape in dazed horror at the smoldering ruins of the house, others would point with macabre fascination to the spot where Teri's mother had plunged to her death. The newcomers would stare at the driveway for a few seconds, visualizing the corpse and imagining, with a shudder, the panic Polly must have felt as she died.

Did she know, at least, that her daughter had survived the fire? No, of course not.

Heads shook sadly; tongues clucked with sympathy. Then the attention of the crowd shifted back to the smoking wreckage. Most of the beams still stood, and parts of the second floor had remained intact even when the roof collapsed. Now, as sunlight cast the ruins into sharp relief, the house looked like a desiccated, blackened skeleton.

Teri, who had spent the last two hours sitting mutely in the Barrows' living room, unable to pull her eyes away from the spectacle of the fire, finally emerged onto the porch. Next to her, Lucy Barrow hovered protectively, her voice trembling as she tried to convince Teri to go back inside.

"I can't," whispered Teri. "I have to find my father. He— He's—" Her voice broke off, but her eyes returned to the ruins across the street.

Lucy Barrow unconsciously bit her lip, as if to take some of Teri's pain onto herself. "He might have gotten out," she ventured, her quavering voice belying her words.

Teri said nothing, but started once more across the street, still clad in the bathrobe she'd worn when she escaped the inferno. An eerie silence fell over the block, the murmurs of the bystanders dying away as she moved steadily through the crowd, which parted silently to let her pass.

At last Teri came to the front yard of what had been her home. She stood still, staring at the charred wood of the house's framework and the blackened bricks of its still-standing chimney. She took a tentative step toward the remains of the front porch, then felt a firm hand on her arm.

"You can't go in there, miss."

Teri's breath caught, but she turned to look into the kindly gray eyes of one of the firemen. "M-My father—" she began.

"We're going in now," the fireman said. "If he's in there, we'll find him."

Without a word, Teri watched as two firefighters, clad in heavily padded overcoats, their hands protected by thick gloves, worked their way carefully into the wreckage. The front door had been chopped away, and inside, the base of the stairway was clearly visible. The men started up, testing each step before trusting it to hold their weight. After what seemed an eternity, they finally reached the second floor. They moved through the house, visible first through one window, then another. From one of the rooms an entire wall, along with most of the floor, had burned away. As the firemen gingerly moved from beam to beam, they appeared to be balanced on some kind of blackened scaffolding. At last they moved out of Teri's sight as they carefully worked their way toward her room at the back of the house.

Ten minutes later the fireman with the kind, gray eyes emerged from the front door and approached Teri, who stood waiting, her eyes fixed on him.

"I'm sorry," he said, his voice made gruff by the memory of the charred remains of Tom MacIver, which he had found in front of the still-closed door to Teri's bedroom at the back of the house. "He was trying to get you out. He didn't know you'd already gotten away." His large hand rested reassuringly on Teri's shoulder for a moment, but then he turned away and began issuing the orders for Tom MacIver's body to be removed from the ruins.

Teri stood where she was for a few more seconds. Her eyes remained fixed on the house as if she were still uncertain of the truth of what she had just been told. Finally Lucy Barrow's voice penetrated her thoughts.

"We have to call someone for you," Lucy said. "We have to call your family."

Teri turned away from the smoldering rubble. She stared blankly at Lucy. For a moment Lucy wasn't certain Teri had heard her, but then Teri spoke.

"My father," she breathed. "Will someone please call my father?"

Dear Lord, Lucy thought. She doesn't understand. She hasn't grasped what happened. She slipped her arms around Teri and held her close. "Oh, darling," she whispered. "He didn't get out. That's what the fireman was telling you. I—I'm sorry," she finished, wondering at the helpless inadequacy of the words. "I'm just so sorry."

Teri was motionless in her arms for a second, then pulled away, shaking her head.

"N-Not him," she said. "We need to call my real father." She wrenched away from Lucy's protective embrace, her gaze returning to the house, where three men were already working to retrieve Tom MacIver's body. "He was my stepfather," Teri said. "He adopted me when I was only four. Now we have to call my real father."

CHAPTER

2

Bright sunlight flooded the room. As Melissa Holloway's eyes opened, she instantly felt a pang of guilt—she'd overslept yet again. She started to fling the thin sheet aside, then remembered. It was all right to oversleep today. Today, this and all the other tiny sins she fell victim to every day of her life would be forgiven.

For today was her birthday.

And not just any birthday, either. Today was her thirteenth birthday, the first day of a whole new era. Finally, the eternity of being a child was over. She was a teenager.

She flopped back on the pillow, stretched luxuriantly, and tried to feel the difference between the Melissa who existed today and the Melissa who had endured all the other days of her life.

She felt nothing. No different at all.

Her feeling of well-being dimmed slightly, but then she decided it didn't matter that she didn't feel different. That would come later. The point was that she *was* different.

She sat up and glanced around the big room in which she'd spent every summer of her life. It would have to change now, she decided. It wasn't a teenager's room at all. It was a little girl's room, the shelves that lined its walls overflowing with her collection of dolls and stuffed animals, and a few favorite toys from her toddler years still tucked away in the corners. Next to the fireplace was her enormous Victorian dollhouse, which would certainly have to go. After all, dollhouses were for babies.

She frowned, already wondering if perhaps she should compromise on the dollhouse. After all, it wasn't as if it was just *any* dollhouse. It was big—so big that when she was very small she'd actually been able to crawl inside it—and it was furnished with perfect miniatures of Victorian furniture.

"What do you think, D'Arcy?" she asked out loud. "Don't you think we should keep it at least for a while?" Suddenly she clamped her hands over her mouth, remembering her promise to her father. Only last week Melissa had vowed that she would give up D'Arcy today.

After all, friends who existed in your imagination were only for children, too. When you grew up, you gave up the imaginary friends for real ones. Except that in Melissa's mind, D'Arcy wasn't really imaginary at all—she was almost as real as she herself was. She lived up in the attic here in Secret Cove, and never traveled to the city when they were in the apartment in Manhattan the rest of the time. Of course, besides Melissa, there weren't many people for D'Arcy to talk to—only Cora Peterson, the housekeeper—but that had never bothered D'Arcy at all.

Melissa thought that D'Arcy must be lonely when the house in Secret Cove was closed up for the winter, but years ago, during one of their long talks in the middle of the night when Melissa couldn't sleep, D'Arcy had told Melissa that she liked being all by herself. In fact, when Melissa had confessed to D'Arcy yesterday that she'd promised to stop talking to her, D'Arcy had agreed immediately. "But I won't stop thinking about you," Melissa had reassured her friend.

D'Arcy had said nothing, but Melissa had been certain that her friend knew exactly what she meant—that was the wonderful thing about D'Arcy. Even when no one else understood Melissa, D'Arcy always did.

Melissa sighed. It was going to be hard giving D'Arcy up, even harder than giving up the dollhouse. Well, maybe she'd sort of cheat. Maybe she'd keep the dollhouse and pretend when she was talking to D'Arcy that she was really talking to the tiny wooden figures that populated the house. Except that even if it fooled her parents and Cora, she herself would still know she'd been cheating.

"I'll tell you what," she said, unconsciously speaking out loud once again. "You can have the dollhouse. I'll move it up to the attic, and then come and visit it sometimes. And if you're there when I come, that's not my fault, is it?"

From far away, in the depths of her imagination, she was certain she heard D'Arcy laughing softly.

She turned away from the dollhouse and went to the window. It was a warm morning—even in Maine, July wasn't really cool— and the sky was clear and cloudless. Tag, Cora's fourteen-year-old grandson, had already mowed the broad lawn earlier that morning, and Melissa breathed in the green scent of fresh-cut grass. The lawn swept down toward the beach fifty yards away, where the waves that came into the cove from the open sea were gentle this morning. They broke with a soft whooshing sound, then threw a white coverlet of foam onto the sand, smoothing out the tracks of the birds that skittered in front of the advancing water.

Melissa's eyes wandered over the beach. It was just the way she liked it—all but deserted, with only a few people far off to the south, sunning themselves on the sand that fronted the Cove Club. Between here and the club, which perched on the southern point of the cove itself, there were only five other cottages, none of them quite as large as the Holloways', but all of them surrounded by equally well-manicured gardens and lawns. And since most of the other kids hung out at the club all the time, Melissa thought of the beach as belonging almost exclusively to herself.

She dressed quickly, pulling on a clean pair of jeans and a T-shirt she'd talked Tag into giving her last week, then went downstairs to find her father. The first thing they'd do today, she decided, was go for a long walk on the beach. They'd go north, away from the club, and maybe climb around the rocky point that cut Secret Cove off from the beach beyond. As she started down the stairs a few minutes later, she'd already made more plans for the day than she and her father could possibly carry out. Still, whatever they did would be fine with her. The important thing was that it was her birthday, and no matter how important his business was, her daddy would spend the day with her, even if her mother thought it was childish.

Melissa smiled as she remembered the conversation she'd over-heard last Sunday, before her father had gone back to New York for the three days before her birthday.

"She's going to be thirteen this year, Charles," her mother had said. "She's not a baby anymore, and it certainly isn't going to hurt her if you don't get back till Friday night."

Melissa had held her breath, waiting for her father's reply, and hadn't let it out until she heard the words. "It's her birthday, and it doesn't matter which one it is. I'll be here for her. She counts on it."

The conversation had gone on, but Melissa hadn't paid further attention, for she knew that once her father committed himself to something, even her mother couldn't change his mind. Which meant that today was all hers, and Daddy would do whatever she wanted, even if it were no more than flopping on the beach and making up stories about what the clouds looked like. That was just what they'd done last year, in fact, and her mother had stared at her at dinner that night as if she were crazy. Indeed, even after a whole year, she could still hear her mother's angry voice: "Well, you certainly managed to waste your father's valuable time today, didn't you? It was very inconsiderate of you to make him come all the way out here just to do the same *nothing* you do every day."

Melissa, stung, had felt tears well up in her eyes, but then Daddy had come to her defense. "I thought having nothing to do was the whole point of coming here," he'd said. "And if Melissa had as good a time as I did, I'd say the day was pretty damned close to perfect."

Out of the corner of her eye Melissa had watched her mother's lips tighten, but she'd said nothing. Still, the next day, after her father had gone back to the city . . .

She resolutely put the memory out of her mind. This year it was going to be different.

She found her father in the kitchen with Cora, and he grinned at her as she came in. "Ready for one of my special chocolate-blueberry waffles?"

Cora frowned her disapproval. "I swear to God, I don't know where you got the idea for those things. I certainly never fed them to you when you were a boy—"

"Want one?" Charles interrupted, cocking an eye at the elderly housekeeper, who pursed her lips, surveyed the counter full of dirty dishes her employer had created, then sighed in resigned defeat.

"Well, I suppose just one wouldn't hurt."

"Go get Tag," Charles told Melissa, winking. "Tell him he's not allowed to do anything on your birthday except goof off."

Melissa started toward the back door, but the phone jangled loudly and she paused as Cora picked it up. A moment later, her face pale and her hand trembling, Cora handed the receiver to Charles.

"It's Polly," Cora said, her voice quavering as her eyes filled with sudden tears. "She's—She and her husband . . . There was a fire . . ." She sank down onto a stool next to the sink as Charles snatched the phone from her hand.

Melissa stood next to the back door, trying to sort out the fragments of sentences she heard her father speak. When he finally hung up, his face was as pale as Cora's. "I'm afraid something's happened, baby," he said, his voice gentle, but choked with emotion. "I'm going to have to fly to Los Angeles this morning."

Melissa stared at him, her eyes wide.

"Polly and Tom MacIver have died," he went on. "There was a fire in their house this morning."

"Teri," Cora breathed, her eyes fixing on Charles. "What about Teri?"

Charles's own eyes closed for a second, and his right hand went to his forehead as if he'd been seized by a sudden headache. Then he managed a nod. "She's all right," he said. "She got out. From what they said, Tom didn't know she'd escaped. He was trying to rescue her. Polly tried to go out a window, but fell."

"Dear God," Cora whispered.

Melissa heard the words, even understood their meaning, but still she shook her head. "But . . . But it's my birthday—"

Charles came to her, put his arms around her and hugged her tight. "I know, baby," he whispered into her ear. "And I know what I promised. But it can't be helped. I'm Teri's father, too, and I have to go to her. She doesn't have anyone else. Can't you understand that?"

Melissa stood perfectly still for a moment, then nodded. As Charles released her, she managed an uncertain smile. "When you come back, will you bring Teri to live with us?"

Charles hesitated, not certain what Melissa might be thinking. "I guess I'll have to, won't I?" he asked. "She's my daughter, and there isn't any other place for her to live. And even if there were, don't you think she belongs here?"

Melissa hesitated, trying to sort out the mix of emotions inside her. Of course she was sorry about what had happened to Teri's mother and stepfather, but she'd never met them and didn't really know anything about them at all. And she didn't really know anything about Teri, either, except for two things.

Teri had been born right here in this house.

And Teri was her half sister.

A half sister was almost the same thing as a full sister, and for as long as she could remember, Melissa had wanted a sister more than anything in the world.

An older sister, someone who would be her friend and answer all the questions she couldn't ever ask her mother.

That, really, was what she'd always wanted D'Arcy to be. Except that D'Arcy wasn't real.

Teri MacIver was real.

Melissa's uncertain smile widened slightly. "It's all right, Daddy," she said. "I mean, I'm awfully sorry about what happened, but I'm finally getting something I always wanted. I'm going to have a sister, aren't I?"

Charles bit his lip sharply as his eyes flooded with tears. "Yes," he said, "I guess you are."

Melissa floated on her back, kicking her feet just enough to keep them from sinking, feeling the heat of the sun on her face. Her eyes were closed and all she could see was a faint pinkish haze through her lids. She concentrated hard, trying futilely to focus on the colors that swirled behind her eyelids, but then gave it up as a shadow passed over the sun. She opened her eyes and gazed up at the bank of clouds coming in from the sea, then rolled over in the water. A few feet away Tag was floating on his back, his eyes still closed. As silently as she could, Melissa drew an arm back, preparing to shoot a cascade of water over Tag's freckled face, but just as she was ready to make the splash, Tag suddenly came to life, flipping over and at the same time flailing his own arm so that it was Melissa's eyes that stung with salt.

"Got you!" he shouted, then began swimming toward shore as Melissa hurled herself after him.

A moment later she caught up and her hand closed around his left ankle. She pulled hard, felt him slide beneath her, then planted both her hands in the center of his back and shoved him farther under while maneuvering and kicking to escape his reach as he tried to grab hold of her, pulling her down with him.

The fight went on, each of them ducking the other, until at last they both gave up at once, swimming toward the beach, riding the gentle surf the last few yards. Laughing and gasping, Melissa dropped onto the sand, wrapping her arms protectively around her face as Blackie, the huge Labrador that only technically belonged to Tag, hurled himself upon her, his big tongue slurping affectionately at her. "Down!" she yelled at last. Obediently, Blackie dropped down onto the sand beside her, resting his large head on her lap. Melissa scratched at the dog's ears, then glanced over at Tag, sprawled a few feet away.

"What do you suppose she's like?"

Tag understood the question immediately. "You mean you wonder if she'll like you?"

Melissa flushed. "Maybe," she admitted. "But I mean, I wonder what she looks like?"

Tag grinned slyly at her. "Want to see some pictures of her?"

Melissa stared at him. Most of the day, ever since her father had left for the airport, she and Tag had been talking about Teri. Until now he'd never mentioned any pictures. "You mean you have some?" she demanded.

Tag's grin broadened. "Sure. Her mom sent one to Grandma every year. Grandma's got 'em all in a drawer."

Melissa scrambled to her feet. "How come you didn't tell me?"

"How come you didn't ask?" Tag teased, picking up his beach towel and slinging it around his neck. "Am I supposed to be able to read your mind or something?"

With Blackie trailing along behind, they crossed the beach, then started across the lawn toward the small cottage behind the pool house in which Cora Peterson had lived every summer for the last half century. They had almost reached the front door when Melissa heard her mother's voice calling from the master suite on the second floor of the main house. "Melissa! Where are you going?"

Melissa froze, her mind working quickly. "The pool!" she called back. "We're all covered with salt."

"Well, can't you just take showers?" Phyllis Holloway called back. "You know Tag shouldn't be using the pool."

Melissa reddened with embarrassment. Her mother could see that Tag was standing right there! And why shouldn't Tag use the pool? Then she remembered that she and Tag hadn't been planning to go swimming anyway. "All right," she called back. She started to turn away, but once more her mother's sharp voice cut through the quiet of the afternoon.

"I want you in the house in five minutes!"

"Yes, Mother," Melissa replied.

She quickened her step, catching up with Tag just as he disappeared around the corner of the pool house. Though he said nothing, Melissa could tell by his expression that he'd heard every word her mother had said.

"We can use the pool if we want to," she offered. "Daddy said we could."

"Sure," Tag replied sourly. "And right after we got done, she'd make me drain it and scrub it." His eyes rolled scornfully upward. "Us servants aren't too clean, you know."

Once more Melissa flushed with embarrassment. She wanted to deny that that was what her mother had meant, but what was the use? It was *exactly* what her mother had meant, and they both knew it. "You and Cora aren't servants," she said. "Cora's just like my grandmother, too."

Tag rolled his eyes. "Don't ever tell your mom that." They were at the front door to the little house now, and instinctively they both looked back. But from where they stood, Phyllis's window couldn't be seen. Feeling like conspirators, they slipped inside the house.

"They're in the drawer on the end table," Tag said. He tossed his beach towel at the foot of the stairs and moved into a living room sparsely furnished with a worn sofa and a pair of sagging easy chairs. A moment later he handed Melissa a small album.

Melissa stared at the album's cheap plastic cover for a moment, feeling a strange hesitancy about looking in it. Finally, she opened the book and studied the first picture.

It was of a toddler, no more than two years old, clutching the hand of an unseen man. The little girl wore a blue dress with white socks and patent-leather Mary Janes, and her pale blond hair was capped by a wide ribbon with a bow on one side.

The little girl in the picture didn't look much different from any other two-year-old, and Melissa, suddenly feeling better, flipped quickly through the album to the last picture.

Her heart sank.

She stared at the image of a tall and slender young lady whose hair, cut stylishly short to leave her perfect features unobstructed, was only a few shades darker than it had been when she was a baby. Her features themselves were elegant but delicate, and her blue eyes, spaced well apart, seemed to gaze out at Melissa with the kind of self-confidence Melissa herself had never felt.

Almost against her will, her eyes left the picture and went to the mirror that hung above the mantelpiece. She silently began comparing her own features to those of the girl in the photograph.

Her hair, an unremarkable brown, hung lankly down her back. She tried to tell herself that it was only because she'd just gone swimming, but knew it wasn't true—no matter how much she brushed her hair, it always seemed unwilling to come to shiny life.

Her own features seemed hopelessly plain—her nose just a little too large, her brown eyes, almost lashless, a little too close together.

And there was a slight puffiness about her face that she was positive, no matter what her father told her, was not merely baby fat.

"She—She's beautiful, isn't she?" Melissa managed to say.

Tag nodded. "Grandma says she looks just like her mother."

Melissa's eyes drifted back to the image in the album. She studied it carefully and began to think that maybe things weren't going to be so bad after all. Even though she'd never imagined that Teri would be so beautiful, she could also see that Teri knew how to dress and how to do her hair.

On Teri, clothes looked right.

On herself, they always looked as if they'd been bought for someone else.

Maybe Teri could teach her how to do her own hair, and how to pick out clothes that would look good on her.

And, she reminded herself, no matter how beautiful Teri was, she was still her sister.

But what if Teri didn't like her?

She put the thought out of her mind and handed the album back to Tag. "I—I better go back to the house. Mom said—"

Before she could finish, there was a loud rap at the front door, which instantly opened to reveal a glowering Phyllis Holloway.

"What are you doing in here, Melissa?" her mother demanded.

"I—Tag was just showing me something. . . ."

"Was he?" Phyllis asked, her accusing glare shifting to Tag. "I don't like your bringing Melissa in here," she went on. "I'll speak to Cora about it." Without waiting for Tag to reply, she took Melissa's arm and steered her out of the cottage. "What am I going to do with you?" she asked as she led her daughter back toward the main house. "I know Tag is your friend, and I certainly don't object to it. But you have to keep in mind that he is also a servant, and there are limits."

"But Mother—"

Abruptly, Phyllis dropped Melissa's arm and smiled at her. "No buts," she said. "And I don't think we ought to fight on your birthday. Besides, you have to get ready for your party."

Melissa stared at her mother in disbelief. "What party?" she asked. "I'm not having a party."

"But I am," Phyllis announced. "And believe me, it wasn't easy, putting a proper birthday celebration together at the last minute. But I knew how disappointed you were when your father had to leave, so I explained the situation to all your friends' mothers . . ."

Phyllis chattered on about the children she'd invited, but Melissa heard no more. With a sinking feeling, she realized what her mother had done.

The Cove Club.

Phyllis had called all her women friends at the Cove Club and insisted they send their children over to Maplecrest for Melissa's birthday. And, of course, after Phyllis had explained what had happened, and why Melissa's dad had suddenly left, everyone had felt sorry for her, and agreed that she should certainly have a party.

And they'd all show up, but they'd do the same thing here that they all did at the Cove Club.

They'd talk to each other, and ignore her.

"And it's going to be wonderful, darling," she heard her mother saying as they went into the house. "You can wear your pink organdy, and I've even hired a disk jockey so everyone can dance. It will be such fun for you. After all, you're a teenager now, and it's time you started doing more things with the crowd. What better time for you to start than on your birthday?"

Though she already felt faintly sick, Melissa knew there was no point in trying to argue with her mother.

Silently, she went up to her room and started getting ready for the party.

Melissa sneaked a look at the clock as she escaped into the small powder room under the main staircase and locked the door. It was only four, which meant that the party was going to go on for hours yet—the disk jockey hadn't even arrived, and the caterers from the club had just started setting up the buffet on the terrace around the pool. And yet to Melissa it seemed as if the afternoon had already gone on for an eternity.

She'd at least saved herself the humiliation of wearing the pink organdy dress her mother had picked out for her. She'd had it on, had even been ready to go downstairs, when she'd heard a car pull up in front of the house and seen Brett Van Arsdale arrive in the black Porsche he'd gotten for his sixteenth birthday two weeks earlier. There were six people crowded into the little car, and as they untangled themselves, Melissa had seen what they were wearing.

Tennis whites.

The boys' shirts were still soaked with sweat, and it had been obvious to Melissa that they'd come straight from the club, not even bothering to change first.

As she heard the door bell ring, immediately followed by her mother's voice commanding her to come downstairs, she'd rushed back to her room, wriggled out of the dress, and pulled on a pair of shorts and a blouse, which she realized as she fumbled with the buttons had fit fine last summer but was too tight now. She'd shoved her feet into a pair of sneakers and started downstairs, but had to stop to tie her laces when she tripped and almost fell the last ten steps. When she looked up from her shoes, the kids were already in the foyer, staring up at her.

Among them was Jeff Barnstable, on whom Melissa had had a secret crush for the last two summers. Next to him—holding his hand—was Ellen Stevens.

"We already played tennis," Ellen said, pointedly staring at Melissa's shoes. "We thought we'd take a swim now."

Without waiting for a reply, the kids had trooped through the house and out to the pool, where they'd found bathing suits in the pool house. By the time Melissa had gone upstairs to change, a game of water polo was in progress.

Melissa had stood silently at the edge of the pool, waiting for one of the teams to invite her to join them.

Neither had.

When her mother had come out to watch a few minutes later, and asked Melissa why she wasn't playing, Melissa had insisted she didn't want to.

But she could see clearly that her mother knew the truth.

The next two hours had been more of the same. Now, Melissa wondered how long she could stay in the powder room. It wouldn't be long, she knew, before her mother would come looking for her.

Suddenly she saw the doorknob turn, the impatient rattling immediately followed by the sound of Ellen Stevens's voice: "Well, is this dismal, or what? First we have to come over here for a mercy party, and now you can't even get into the bathroom."

"Let's go upstairs," Cyndi Miller replied. "Maybe I can find one of Melissa's lipsticks."

The powder room echoed with Ellen's sharp laughter. "Melissa's? Even if she has one, it'll be some terrible color. Why don't we just leave?"

"We can't," Cyndi answered. "My mother said we have to stay until at least nine, no matter how bad it is. Otherwise she'll have to listen to Mrs. Holloway talking about how rude we were to her precious little daughter."

Suddenly Melissa had enough. She pulled the door open and stared at the two girls, willing her tears not to overflow and run down her cheeks. "You don't have to stay," she said in a low voice. "I never wanted you to come in the first place."

The two girls, only a year or so older than Melissa, glanced at each other. It was Cyndi who finally spoke. "You shouldn't have been in there listening to us," she said.

Melissa felt her self-control slipping away. She hadn't done anything to them, hadn't tried to hear what they were saying. But they'd just stood there, talking about her. Why was it her fault? And then she saw her mother coming down the stairs, stopping to look at her.

"Is something wrong?" Phyllis asked.

Melissa started to shake her head but was too late.

"I think we'd better go home, Mrs. Holloway," Ellen Stevens said as if she were trying to find a nice way to handle the situation. "Melissa just told us she didn't want us here."

Seeing the look of cold anger that flashed into her mother's eyes, Melissa fled up the stairs to her room. She flopped onto the bed, her body wracked with sobs, her fists pounding the pillow with frustration.

But soon her sobs subsided and her anger toward Cyndi and Ellen and the rest of the kids died away.

After all, it wasn't their fault—they hadn't wanted to come any more than she had wanted them to. And they wouldn't have, if her mother hadn't called their mothers and begged.

So the anger dissipated, only to be replaced by fear. For after what had happened this afternoon, she was certain that sometime tonight, sometime after Cora had gone to bed for the night, her mother would come into her room.

Come into her room, for one of her little "talks."

CHAPTER

3

Charles Holloway had the same feeling of vague disorientation that always came over him when he arrived in Los Angeles. Part of his confusion was caused by the fact that all the freeways seemed to run north and south, even when they crossed at right angles. But at last he'd worked his way out into the vast suburban morass of the San Fernando Valley, turning onto the block where the MacIvers lived only a little more than an hour and a half after leaving the airport in his rented car. It was the first time he'd ever seen this part of the valley, and he knew immediately why it had attracted Polly.

The houses in this area all had a feeling of permanence to them, their yards dotted with large shade trees, their gardens having the look of being carefully tended for decades. Nowhere here did he see the too-bright green of freshly laid sod or the patches of "beauty bark" with which the newer subdivisions were littered. No, this particular area had a look of stability to it, a certain middle-class solidity that would have appealed to Polly.

To himself, of course, it simply looked dull, like a California version of all the small towns in the East that he had always found unutterably boring, but to which Polly had always been drawn like an iron filing to a magnet. "At least they're real," she'd said over and over again in those first few months of their marriage, when he'd still hoped it was going to work out. "I just can't stand the idea of raising children in Manhattan and Secret Cove—it's so horribly insular!"

In a way, of course, Charles had understood what she meant. Certainly, both of them had grown up with a lifestyle greatly different from that of the vast majority of people. Charles had always simply accepted it, and when he'd married Polly, he'd assumed that she had, too. But the truth, he'd soon found out, was that Polly had resented both the wealth and position of her birth. Not that the Porters were as wealthy as the Holloways. They weren't, and never had been. Nor had they thought the same way as the Holloways and most of the rest of the "Secret Cove Crowd"—as they tended to think of themselves, complete with quotation marks—though Charles hadn't really been aware of it when he'd married Polly. Oh, he'd known Polly had gone off to Berkeley when the rest of them had headed for Harvard, Yale, Bennington, and Vassar, but he hadn't realized how much she'd been affected by the West Coast until long after they'd married.

"But if you didn't like the way we lived, why did you marry me?" he'd asked her after the divorce had become final.

"Because it was expected of me," she replied. "Good God, Charles—we both knew we'd get married from the day we were born! And I really thought it would be all right! But after Berkeley, the whole thing just seems so unreal! I mean, Lenore Van Arsdale not only doesn't know what's going on outside of Secret Cove, she doesn't even care!"

Charles's mouth dropped open. "Lenore is your best friend! You grew up with her."

Polly had smiled ironically. "I know. But I grew away from her, and you, and everything else in Secret Cove. I can't spend my life planning parties that cost three times as much as the money they raise for whatever cause the Crowd has fastened on each year. I can't keep spending piles and piles of money on clothes when I know how many people can barely afford clothes at all."

"So what are you going to do?" Charles had finally demanded. "Give it all away?"

To his shock, that was exactly what Polly had intended and exactly what she had done. After the divorce she'd set up a foundation, picked a board of trustees that hadn't included a single member of the Secret Cove Crowd, and then turned over every asset she had to the foundation. There'd been no one to stop her—her parents had died in a skiing accident three years earlier, and though Charles had considered at least fighting her over custody of the infant Teri, in the end he hadn't. Polly, after all, had never been anything but a devoted mother, and Charles was less willing to put his tiny daughter through a protracted legal battle than to allow Polly to raise her as she saw fit. Indeed, he'd even approved of the adoption after Polly had married Tom MacIver and moved west, where both Polly and Tom had built careers in the university system.

He, on the rebound from the divorce, had promptly married Phyllis, whom Polly herself had first brought into their life as Teri's nurse. Though not born into the Secret Cove Crowd, Phyllis had at least respected its values; and the marriage, if far from perfect, had allowed him to continue the lifestyle he'd grown up with and hoped to die with. Only a few months after the marriage, Phyllis presented him with a baby girl who had quickly filled the void left by the loss of Teri. For all of them, things had worked out.

But now, as he gazed at the charred remains of the MacIvers' house, he knew that everything had changed once more. Teri was about to be transported across the country and thrust into an unfamiliar environment, filled with unfamiliar people. And he suspected that Polly had never prepared her daughter for what life would be like in the East. After all, why should she have?

He turned away from the blackened pile of rubble and crossed the street to the house bearing the address he'd scrawled on a scrap of paper earlier that morning. It was no different from the rest of the houses on the block—a small frame structure, modest, but substantial-looking. As he mounted the short flight of steps to its front porch, he found himself wondering if it would burn as fast as Polly's house had.

He suspected it would.

Charles pressed the button next to the front door and heard a soft chime sound inside. A moment later the door opened and a plump woman peered out at him. "Mrs. Barrow?" he said through the screen door. "I'm Charles Holloway. Teri's father."

Instantly, the door opened wider, and Lucy Barrow pushed the screen door open, too. "Mr. Holloway," she breathed, her relief apparent in her voice. "Thank God—I just don't know what to say. It's all been so terrible, and when Teri told me to call you—" She broke off and stood almost still for a moment, her fluttering hands betraying her confusion. "I—Well, I'm afraid none of us even knew you existed. I mean, Polly and Tom never told us—" Once again she fell silent.

Charles reached out to take her arm, gently guiding her toward her own living room. "It's all right, Mrs. Barrow," he told her. "I understand what you must have thought. It's . . ." And then his own words died in his throat as they stepped over the threshold and he saw Teri, huddled in a corner of the couch, her thin robe wrapped tightly around her slender body. Her eyes, wide and uncertain, were fixed on him, and she seemed to be holding her breath, as if she had been waiting to see if he would actually come for her.

For a long moment neither of them said a word. Then Teri stirred on the couch and got uncertainly to her feet. Her mouth opened, and when at last she spoke, her voice was rough, as though she'd spent most of the day crying. "F-Father?"

Choking with emotion, Charles strode across the room in three quick steps and slipped his arms around the girl. She stiffened for a moment, but then seemed to relax, her face resting against his chest. He clumsily stroked her hair, then tipped her face up so he could look into it. "It's all right, Teri," he whispered. "I'm here, and you're not alone, and I'm going to make everything better for you." He held her close again, and though he couldn't see her face as she pressed it once more against his chest, he imagined he could feel a tiny smile breaking through her grief.

Until this moment, he knew, she must have felt totally alone in the world.

Alone and terrified.

Melissa sat at the small vanity that stood between the two large windows of her bedroom, toying with the supper that Cora had brought her an hour ago. Try as she would, she had managed to eat no more than half of it, and even that was lying like a lead weight in the pit of her stomach. She stared disconsolately at the plate, wishing she could summon up the appetite to finish the food. Cora had made all her favorites for her birthday supper—a small steak cooked just the way she liked it, with corn on the cob (the white kind, which didn't even seem to get caught in your teeth) and sugar snap beans she herself had helped Tag plant last spring in Cora's little garden behind the garage. And she should have been hungry—she'd barely eaten anything all day.

She heard a footstep in the hall outside her room and quickly picked up her knife and fork, certain it was her mother coming to check on her. But when the door opened, it was only Cora, and Melissa felt herself relax. Then she flushed with guilt as the housekeeper eyed the half-filled plate. "I—I'm sorry, Cora," she said. "I just couldn't eat much tonight."

"Now don't you worry about it, Missy," Cora replied, using the nickname that Phyllis Holloway had long ago forbidden. "You just eat what you want, and save a little room for this." She set a thick wedge of chocolate cake on the vanity, nodding with satisfaction as she saw a smile break through Melissa's gloom. "The way I look at it," she went on, "what happened at the party's just as well. None of those kids would have appreciated my cake half as much as you do, and this way we got a lot left over. Tomorrow, you and Tag can poke away at it all day long."

Abandoning the remains of the steak, Melissa picked up her fork and plunged it into the moist bulk of the cake. But just as she was about to put the morsel into her mouth, her mother appeared in the doorway.

"Now, Melissa," Phyllis said. "You know we don't have dessert until we've finished our dinner."

The brief flicker of eagerness died in Melissa's eyes, and she obediently put her fork back on the plate. "I—I guess I'm too full, Cora," she said, her eyes pleading with the housekeeper not to argue with her mother. "Maybe I'll be able to eat some tomorrow."

Cora, her own eyes carefully avoiding Phyllis, picked up the plates containing the remains of Melissa's dinner and slipped out the door.

Without another word to her daughter, Phyllis followed the housekeeper out, firmly closing the door behind her.

Melissa, left alone once more, moved back to the bed, where she huddled, waiting for the inevitable.

She picked up a book, tried to read it, but found herself going over and over the same page, her eyes taking in the print, but her mind refusing to absorb the sense of the words. The minutes ticked by, and finally, when the sound of Cora's voice calling out to Blackie signaled that the old woman was on her way back to her own house for the night, Melissa put the book aside. Five minutes later her bedroom door opened once more and her mother stepped inside. Wordlessly, Phyllis went to the windows and closed them. At last she turned to face her daughter.

"How dare you?" she asked, her voice quivering with the indignation she'd been nursing all afternoon. "Doesn't anything matter to you at all? Do you have no appreciation for everything I try to do for you?"

Melissa shrank back on the bed, her knees drawn defensively up against her chest. Her eyes fixed on her mother, and in her mind she began whispering silently to D'Arcy.

What did I do, D'Arcy? What? I didn't do anything to anyone. Why can't Mama understand that they don't like me?

"Your dress, Melissa?" Phyllis suddenly demanded. "Where is it?"

Melissa was silent for a split second, but as her mother took a step toward her, she forced herself to speak through her constricted throat. "The closet," she whispered.

Her eyes narrowing, Phyllis turned and moved to the closet, hurling the door open with enough force to make it bang loudly against the wall. The pink organdy dress lay crumpled on the floor where it had lain since slipping off the hanger Melissa had hastily put it on earlier. Phyllis snatched it up, then turned to face her daughter. "Is this the way you treat your clothes?" she demanded. She grasped the dress in both hands, then jerked hard. There was a tearing sound that made Melissa want to sob.

Then, as if brought back to life by the violence of Phyllis's action, Melissa jumped off the bed and rushed toward her mother. "Don't!" she cried. "Don't tear my dress!" She reached for the dress but stopped as her mother's hand snaked out and slapped her sharply across the cheek.

Melissa gasped, and staggered back toward the bed. As Phyllis followed her, the torn dress clutched in one hand while the other tightened into a fist, Melissa cowered back against the headboard.

Help me! she silently cried out to the room that was empty except for herself and her mother. *Please, D'Arcy, help me. Don't let her hit me again!* As her mother came closer, Melissa's eyes darted around the room, as if searching for someplace to hide or for someone to come to her aid.

And then, in the corner of the room, she saw the familiar shadow. Barely visible at first, the diaphanous form quickly took on the shape of a girl and moved soundlessly toward the bed.

Stop her, Melissa whispered silently to the strange form she alone could see. *Oh, please—tell her I didn't do anything. Don't let her punish me!* And then D'Arcy was beside her, whispering softly, directly, into her mind.

Sleep, Melissa. I'm here now, and I'll take care of you. Just go to sleep . . .

As her mother came to the bedside, Melissa felt the soft warmth of D'Arcy's arms slip around her, cradling her. She closed her eyes and listened only to the sound of D'Arcy's musical voice, crooning to her. Her mother's angry words died away, and then the familiar darkness of sleep began to close around her. She drifted away, leaving D'Arcy alone to absorb her mother's wrath.

Phyllis's hand closed on Melissa's arm and jerked her upright. "Why shouldn't I rip up the dress?" she demanded. "Did you pay for it? Do you even take care of it? Will you even wear it? Of course not!" She shook Melissa then, pushing her back onto the pillows. Methodically, she tore the dress into two pieces, then ripped it again, jerking the sleeves from the shoulder seams and flinging them in Melissa's face.

"I don't know what to do with you!" she grated, glaring at her daughter. "Do you know how hard it was to get those children here today? Do you think they wanted to come? And how do you show your appreciation? You insult them, that's how!"

Her right hand closed on Melissa's shoulder again and jerked her around. Melissa flopped to the side but made no sound, nor did her arms move up to ward off her mother's anger. Her eyes,

wide open, stared straight ahead as Phyllis began shaking her
violently, flinging her against the headboard.

Through it all Melissa remained silent, saying nothing, not even
crying out at the sharp stabs of pain in her neck or the hard crack
when her head struck the headboard.

And her eyes, still wide open, seemed to stare sightlessly straight
ahead as her mother's fury finally spent itself.

Panting with her own exertions, Phyllis released Melissa's shoulders and let her drop back onto the bed. Then she picked up the
torn remnants that had been the pink party dress and flung them
once more toward Melissa. "By tomorrow," she said, her voice
low and dangerous, "I'll expect the dress to be mended and back
in the closet."

Glowering darkly at her daughter, she turned and stalked from
the room.

As soon as the door closed, Melissa rose from the bed and
moved over to the vanity. Cocking her head in a faintly curious
manner, she gazed into the mirror with blank and empty eyes.
Her own image stared back at her, but in the reflection it seemed
somehow different. Her face seemed thinner, the layer of fat
peeled away to expose her bone structure, and her features had
softened. Tentatively, she reached up to touch her hair, pushing it
back and away from her face, then let her fingers caress her
stinging ears, still sore from the blows they had received from her
mother. At last, turning from the mirror, she picked up the pieces
of the dress and moved to the door. Switching off the lights in her
room, she stepped out into the darkness of the hall. She paused,
listening, but the house was silent now.

Carrying the ruined dress with her, she moved down the long
hallway until she came to the steep flight of stairs that led to
the attic. Once more she paused, then went on, carefully climbing
the stairs until she came to the closed door that led to the attic
itself.

She slipped inside and closed the door behind her. The attic
was almost pitch-dark, lit only by a pale glow of moonlight that
penetrated the small dormer windows in the roof. But Melissa,
her eyes never wavering, moved easily through the gloom, threading her way through the piles of boxes, the ancient steamer

trunks, and the old furniture that had been consigned to the attic over the years.

Unconscious of her surroundings, she didn't pause as she trod the attic floor, finally coming to a small room tucked beneath the sloping roof. Inside there was a worn sofa and a chest of drawers. On a small table in front of the sofa there was an oil lamp, and Melissa, putting the tatters of the dress on the sofa for a moment, struck a match and carefully lit the lamp.

The tiny room glowed with a soft orange light.

She moved to the dresser, and from the bottom drawer took an old wooden box filled with an assortment of needles, thread, thimbles, and pins. Carrying the box with her, she returned to the sofa, sat down, and opened the box. Carefully, she chose a shade of thread that nearly matched the dress.

Pulling off a length of thread, she expertly slid its end through the eye of a needle, then began to work.

Her fingers moving quickly, she began to reset the right sleeve into the body of the dress. The needle flashed up and down, each stitch tiny and perfectly even.

Oblivious to her surroundings, she worked steadily and silently in the flickering light of the oil lamp.

The hours passed, but her fingers never tired, and her arms never ached from holding the material.

For it was not truly Melissa who worked through those endless hours. Not Melissa, but some other child, who sewed steadily in the silence of the night until the first rays of sun began to creep up out of the sea. Then, her work completed, she allowed herself to sleep.

Cora Peterson woke promptly at five-thirty the next morning, just as she had nearly every day of her life. She dressed, then made her bed, glancing uneasily out her bedroom window every now and then, looking across the yard and up at the closed windows of Melissa's room. She thought about breaking her normal routine and going directly to the main house to see if Melissa was all right.

Certainly, she hadn't looked all right last night, when she'd been unable to finish her supper. The poor child's nerves had been strung tight as a violin string, and her face had looked positively drawn. But perhaps she'd simply been tired, Cora thought, and forgotten to reopen her windows when she'd gone to bed. After all, there hadn't been any trouble at all so far this summer, and so the housekeeper decided not to worry about it.

She finished making her bed, and rapped sharply on Tag's door before going downstairs to fix their breakfast. Of course, it would be a lot easier for her to make their breakfasts in the big kitchen of the main house, but the second Mrs. Holloway—she still thought of Phyllis that way, even after all these years—had her rules, and one was that the staff cooked for themselves.

"The staff," Cora snorted to herself as she began scrambling half a dozen eggs. Just like there were a lot of footmen and maids, and maybe even a butler around. Well, that had been a couple of generations back, and even Cora, at seventy-three, could barely remember those days. Now it was nothing more than a weekly cleaning crew coming in, with she herself making do from one day to the next. Still, she didn't mind. After all, she'd been taking care of Charles Holloway since the day he was born, and she'd go on taking care of him and his children as long as she had a breath left in her.

Thinking about Charles brought back Polly, and for a moment Cora thought she might cry. But that wouldn't do any good at all, and if there was one thing Cora prided herself on, it was her own practicality. No, she mustn't dwell on Polly at all. Instead, she would start thinking about Teri coming home.

A bedroom would have to be chosen for her—maybe the nice sunny one at the northeast corner, which looked straight out over the cove.

She paused. What was she thinking of? It wasn't a baby who was coming back to Secret Cove in a few days. It was a teenage girl. A girl who would certainly want to decide for herself which room she wanted.

Her thoughts were interrupted as Tag, wearing only a pair of worn-out cutoff jeans, loped into the kitchen and sprawled on the chair. Cora eyed his clothes archly. "You planning to take another day off?" she asked.

Tag shook his head. "I'm gonna work in the vegetable garden. Mrs. Holloway won't even see me."

Cora grunted, and put a plate of food in front of her grandson, wondering, not for the first time, where his personality had come from. Certainly not from her son, who had spent almost every day of his childhood wiggling out of whatever task she assigned him. And not from his mother, either, who, as far as Cora had been able to tell, had spent most of her time in the tavern where Kirk Peterson had met her. The two of them had taken off while Tag was still an infant, leaving the baby with her "for a couple of weeks." The weeks had stretched into months, and then years. So she'd raised Tag herself, and been pleased to find that her grandson was turning out exactly the way her son hadn't. He worked hard, never seemed to get angry at anybody, and regarded the world with a sunny disposition that Cora thought he must have invented himself, since he hadn't gotten it from anywhere else. Now, putting her own plate on the table, she glanced again at his disreputable cutoffs. "Well, if she tells you to change into pants and a shirt, don't say I didn't warn you."

Tag grinned impishly. "Come on, Grandma. You really think Mrs. H would show up in the vegetable garden? I bet she doesn't even know where it is."

Cora's brows rose slightly. She thought she should say something about respect for their employer, but changed her mind. After all, Tag was right. Ever since she'd married Charles Holloway, Phyllis Martin had carefully avoided any reminder of her own humble origins; a farm somewhere in Pennsylvania, Cora believed. A farm, as far as Cora could tell, was nothing but an oversized vegetable garden, and certainly the high and mighty Mrs. Holloway wouldn't go anywhere near it. "Well, all right, but if she catches you dressed like that, don't say I didn't warn you."

"I won't," Tag promised, then picked up his plate and took it to the sink, where he began washing the dishes. Cora stacked her own breakfast dishes on the sink, gave Tag a quick hug, then headed toward the main house to start her day. But as she crossed the lawn, she once more noticed Melissa's closed bedroom windows. Entering the house, she didn't even stop at the kitchen, but went directly to the second floor and opened Melissa's door without knocking.

As she'd feared, Melissa was not in her bed.

Cora climbed the stairs to the attic slowly, joints aching as she pulled herself up the steep flight and paused at the top to catch her breath. The attic gloom was only partially relieved by the sunlight filtering in through the dormers. She wove through the clutter, pausing at the door to the tiny room beneath one of the gables. At last, taking a deep breath, she pushed the door open.

Curled up on the dusty sofa, sound asleep, was Melissa. "Oh, baby," Cora whispered almost silently. "Not again."

She went to the sofa, lowered herself down, and gently began waking Melissa, taking care not to startle her. At last Melissa's eyes fluttered slightly, then opened. For a moment she smiled up at Cora, but then the smile faded as she realized where she was.

Gasping, she sat up straight, her eyes darting around the tiny room. Finally she faced Cora, her face pale with fear. "Don't tell Mother," she begged. "Please?"

Cora took Melissa's hand gently in her own. "Now, Missy, you know I have to tell your mother. If you're going to be walking in your sleep again, she has to know. You could hurt yourself."

"But I've only done it once this summer," Melissa pleaded. "I won't do it again—I promise! Please don't tell Mama. Please?"

Cora rose to her feet, drawing Melissa along with her. "Well, now, let's just get you back to your bed, and we'll think about this later, all right?"

Melissa bit her lip but nodded, and let Cora lead her back through the jumble of castoffs that cluttered the attic floor. A few moments later she was back in her own room and Cora was tucking her in bed. "Now you sleep for a couple more hours," the housekeeper told her. "You just get your rest and don't worry about anything. What happened wasn't your fault, and your mother won't blame you. She just wants to help you."

Cora gently kissed Melissa's forehead, then, before leaving, opened the windows to let the room fill with the fresh morning air.

When she was alone, Melissa lay in bed trying to remember what had happened last night. Slowly, it came back to her.

Her mother had come in and been angry with her. In fact, she'd been so angry that she'd torn up her pink organdy dress. And then she'd slapped her. After that Melissa didn't remember anything at all.

For after that, D'Arcy had come to help her, as D'Arcy always came to help when her mother was angry at her.

She lay in bed for a few more moments, and her mind went back to the dress. She got up and went to the closet, hesitating only a second before pulling the door open.

The dress was hanging neatly on a hanger.

Melissa stared at it for a moment. Had she been wrong? Had her mother not come in at all? Had she imagined the whole thing?

At last, her hands trembling, she reached out and took the dress off the hanger. Turning the seams inside out, she examined them carefully.

Some of them looked perfectly normal. But others—the ones that held the sleeves on, and the one up the bodice—were different.

The stitches were tiny and perfect, but the thread was a few shades different from the dress itself.

She smiled, then glanced up at the ceiling. "Thank you, D'Arcy," she whispered. "Thank you for mending it for me."

CHAPTER

4

"For heaven's sake, Cora! What are you doing?" Phyllis Holloway's sharp voice startled the housekeeper, and the paring knife in her hand clattered into the sink.

Her eyes automatically flicked to the large clock on the wall: it was only nine-thirty, at least half an hour before Mrs. Holloway made her usual appearance in the kitchen. She picked up the knife, set it on the drain board, then turned to face her employer. "I thought I'd make an apple pie," she offered. "You know how Melissa loves my pies."

Phyllis's lips tightened. "After her behavior yesterday, I hardly think she deserves a treat, does she?" Cora, knowing the question was purely rhetorical, said nothing. "And you have better things to do than make pies today, don't you?" Phyllis went on.

Cora's brows rose and she quickly reviewed what she'd already done that morning. Melissa's breakfast had already been finished and the dishes washed, and Mrs. Holloway's pot of coffee had been waiting in her room as usual. Downstairs, the last of the mess from the party had been cleared away, and every room thoroughly dusted. Then she thought she understood. "I was holding off on the vacuuming," she explained. "I didn't want to disturb you."

"And that was very considerate of you," Phyllis replied, relenting slightly. "But it was Teri I was thinking of. It seems to me we ought to start getting her room ready."

Cora felt a wave of relief flow over her as she realized she was going to be spared one of her employer's tirades over some minor detail she had overlooked. "I've been thinking about that," she said. "I thought maybe the corner room in the east wing . . ." Her voice trailed off as she saw the dark look that immediately came into Phyllis's eyes.

"The east wing?" Phyllis repeated. "But that's the guest wing, with all the best views. No, I was thinking about the room next to Melissa's."

Cora's brows knit in puzzlement. Melissa's room was in the corner of the south wing, and there was nothing next to it except the small nurse's room, connected to it by a bath. "Well, I don't know," Cora began. "It's awfully small—"

But Phyllis didn't let her finish. "We'll go up and take a look at it."

"Yes, ma'am," Cora murmured. She wiped her hands on a dish towel, then followed Phyllis through the butler's pantry and dining room into the large foyer. Upstairs, they turned to the right, and a moment later stepped into the small chamber that adjoined Melissa's large and airy room. Cora looked around doubtfully. The room was sparsely furnished with only a small daybed, a worn bureau against one wall, a table in front of its single window, and an old wooden rocking chair. Covering the hardwood floor was a threadbare oriental rug that Cora knew had originally been in one of the guest rooms, but which had been consigned to this room when it had been deemed too frayed for further use.

Except in the servants' quarters.

"It—Well, it's kinda small, isn't it?" Cora asked, then regretted the question as Phyllis's impatient eyes fastened on her.

"This was my room once, Cora," she reminded the housekeeper. "I don't recall complaining about its size at all."

And you didn't stay in it long, either, Cora thought darkly to herself. When she spoke, she was careful to keep her voice neutral. "I was just thinking that for a teenager, with all her clothes and things, maybe we ought to look for something bigger."

Once again Phyllis's temper flashed. "Don't be silly, Cora," she said sharply. "I talked to Mr. Holloway this morning, and Teri has nothing—she barely got out of the house alive. Now, doesn't it seem silly to put her in some enormous room with empty closets and dressers? And," she added, "I think we have to remember her background. We want to make her feel comfortable here, and how is she going to feel rattling around a room that's the size of the entire house she grew up in?

"There's a lot we can do to make this room more cheerful," she continued. "In fact, I think in a way you're right. I always hated the furniture in here. I can't believe there aren't some things up in the attic we can bring down. Call Tag, and we'll go up and take a look."

Twenty minutes later, with both Melissa and Tag following along, Phyllis led Cora up the stairs to the attic. She opened the door, stepped inside, then stopped short.

Illuminated by a brilliant beam of sunlight, there were clear footprints in the thick layer of dust that covered the attic floor. Phyllis stared at them, then turned back to face her daughter. "Melissa, is there something you want to tell me?"

Melissa's eyes widened in sudden fear as she saw the incriminating footprints in the dust. Instantly, she turned to Cora in a silent plea for help.

"Were you walking in your sleep again last night?" Phyllis asked.

Melissa bit her lip but said nothing, and it was finally Cora who answered. "She was just upset from the party yesterday," she suggested. "It's the first time it's happened this summer—"

Phyllis's eyes narrowed slightly. "Is it? Or is it simply that no one's told me about it before?" She gazed steadily at her daughter, and when she spoke, her voice betrayed nothing of what she might be feeling. "Tell me, Melissa. *Is* this the first time this summer?"

Melissa felt a knot of fear forming in her stomach, and wished her father were here to help her. What should she say? Why was it that with her mother there never seemed to be a right answer? But as her mother's eyes remained fixed on her, she knew she had to say something. "I—I don't know, Mama," she murmured. "I don't remember doing it at all."

Phyllis took a deep breath, then slowly let it out, finally turning back to Cora. "Very well," she said. "If she doesn't remember, perhaps you can tell me what happened, Cora."

As briefly as she could, Cora told Phyllis what had happened. "But she was perfectly all right," she finished. "She just went into the little room at the back, the one right above her bedroom. She was sound asleep when I found her."

Phyllis's eyes bored into Melissa once again. "I want you to look around up here," she said, her gaze never leaving her daughter, though her words were directed to Cora. "See if you can find anything Teri might like. I'm afraid I have to talk to Melissa now."

Grasping Melissa's arm, she marched her down the stairs and along the wide corridor toward her room. A moment later, as they heard Melissa's door close, Tag looked uneasily at his grandmother.

"What's going to happen, Grandma? What's she going to do to Melissa?"

Cora was silent for a few seconds, then shook her head. "I don't know," she said. "I just don't know."

In Melissa's room, Phyllis closed the door, her eyes fixing on her daughter, who stood near the fireplace, her back against the wall, her hands held defensively behind her back. Phyllis said nothing, but simply stared at Melissa until, cheeks scarlet with shame, Melissa turned away. At last Phyllis moved across to the closet and pulled open the door. The pink organdy dress hung on its hanger where Melissa had left it.

Phyllis lifted the hanger off the rod and took the dress to the window, where she began carefully inspecting its seams. At last her gaze shifted back to Melissa.

"This is very good," she said. Melissa relaxed ever so slightly, but her wary eyes remained on her mother. "Did you do this?"

Melissa hesitated, then finally shook her head.

"If you didn't do it," Phyllis asked, her voice deceptively low, "then who did?"

The question seemed to hang in the air while Melissa groped in her mind for an answer that would satisfy her mother. But in the end she decided simply to tell the truth. "D-D'Arcy," she breathed, her voice barely audible.

Phyllis's eyes narrowed. "Who?" she demanded.

Melissa cowered back. "D'Arcy," she said, a little louder. "I'm not very good at sewing, so D'Arcy came and helped me."

Phyllis's hands tightened on the gauzy pink material, and for an agonizing moment Melissa thought she was going to tear it up again. But then her mother flung the dress onto the bed. "But D'Arcy doesn't exist, does she?" Phyllis demanded, her voice rising.

Melissa shrank back against the wall, but managed to shake her head.

Phyllis moved across the room once more. Her hands clamped onto Melissa's shoulders, her fingers digging into the girl's flesh until Melissa thought she would cry out from the pain. When she spoke again, Phyllis's voice had dropped to a furious hiss. "Melissa, we've been over this again and again. D'Arcy doesn't exist. You made her up in your head. Do you understand?"

Too terrified to speak, Melissa managed to nod.

"You're thirteen years old now, Melissa," Phyllis went on, her grip never loosening. "You're far too old to be making up people who don't exist. And you're old enough to start taking responsibility for the things you've done. Do you understand what I'm saying?"

Once more Melissa forced a small nod.

"Now, why did you walk in your sleep last night?"

Once again Melissa's head swam. She wanted to tell her mother the truth, that D'Arcy had come to help her last night, that D'Arcy must have taken her up in the attic to work on the dress and that she'd simply fallen asleep there. But she didn't really remember it at all. All she remembered was D'Arcy coming to help her. After that, everything was a blank until Cora had awakened her this morning. But now, at least, she knew what her mother wanted her to say. "I—I was upset about what happened at the party yesterday. And when I get upset, I walk in my sleep."

Her mother's hands relaxed, and the sharp pain in Melissa's shoulders eased off to a gnawing ache.

"And why were you upset about the party?" Phyllis pressed.

Melissa closed her eyes tight and summoned up the proper answer. "Because I was rude to everyone. It was a very nice party, and I ruined it for everyone. It was my fault, Mama."

At last Phyllis's hands dropped away from Melissa's shoulders. Her expression softened into a smile. "That's right," she said. "What happened yesterday was your fault, and it was your own guilty conscience that made you walk in your sleep."

Melissa nodded numbly, then looked pleadingly up at her mother. "Is it all right now?" she asked.

Phyllis's smile remained in place, but a cold look came into her eyes that renewed Melissa's terror. "We'll see," she said. "We'll see what happens for the rest of today."

At a little past noon Phyllis pulled her Mercedes into the parking lot of the Cove Club and flipped the visor down to examine her hair and makeup in its illuminated mirror. A single strand of her pale blond hair had escaped the severe French twist at the back of her head, and she carefully worked it back into place, then applied a touch of gloss to her lips. At last she got out of the car, acknowledged the valet's friendly greeting with a curt nod, and walked into the foyer of the club, pausing for a moment, as always, to admire the view of the open Atlantic from the picture windows that comprised the entire eastern wall of the building's main lounge. She glanced around, almost nervously, then chided herself for falling victim once more to the uneasy sense that even after thirteen years she still didn't quite feel as if she belonged here. She glanced into one of the full-length mirrors that covered the huge pillars supporting the roof, and reassured herself that she was dressed perfectly—the emerald-green suit was made of pure silk, as was the cream-colored blouse beneath it. Her stockings, with their fashionably patterned seams, were free of snags, and though her shoes weren't quite comfortable, they went perfectly with the suit. As the maitre d' approached, Phyllis smiled at him with just enough coolness to keep him gently in his place.

"I hope I'm not the first," she said. "I always hate sitting by myself."

"Not at all," André replied smoothly. "The rest of the ladies have just begun their drinks." He turned, leading Phyllis into the main dining room where, in the far corner, she could see the other three members of the club's Social Committee already seated at Lenore Van Arsdale's usual table.

And then, as she approached the table, her blood froze.

Lenore, and the two other women, too, were all wearing warm-up suits, their feet clad in tennis shoes or sandals. None of them wore even a hint of makeup. As André held Phyllis's chair out for her, Lenore smiled with what might have been sympathy. Phyllis was certain it was a look of amusement.

"I'm so sorry," Lenore apologized. "I should have called and let you know some us were having a game of tennis this morning and we'd decided not to dress. But you look wonderful! I'd never have the nerve to wear that color so early in the day—I always save the really bright things for big parties where I want to be sure Harry can keep track of me."

Phyllis felt herself flush with humiliation, and hoped the color in her face wouldn't show under her makeup. So they'd played tennis but hadn't invited her. And how dumb did Lenore Van Arsdale think she was, coyly suggesting her clothes were wrong? Why *shouldn't* she wear this suit at lunch? Yet as she nervously glanced around the dining room, she realized Lenore was right— all the women in the room were dressed in soft pastels—simple cotton skirts with expensively casual knit tops. How could she have been so stupid? At the last meeting—

And then she remembered. At the last meeting all the other women had been going on to a large cocktail party.

A cocktail party to which she herself had not been invited.

She came out of her reverie as she felt Kay Fielding squeeze her arm, and realized that though Kay had spoken to her, she hadn't heard a word the woman had said. "I'm sorry," she apologized. "I'm afraid my mind drifted."

"Well, I certainly can't blame you," Kay said, her voice filled with sympathy. "After what's happened . . ."

Once again Phyllis flushed. "I can't tell you how sorry I am," she said. "I can't imagine what got into Melissa. I suppose it was the disappointment of her father having to leave, but she asked me to apologize to everyone."

Kay's smile faltered. "Apologize? For what?"

Phyllis swallowed. "The—The party yesterday. I'm afraid Melissa behaved abominably, and I want you all to know I've spoken to her about it."

Lenore Van Arsdale's tinkling laughter rippled across the table. "Oh, for goodness sakes, Phyllis—what's a child's birthday party without a disaster? And who can blame Melissa for being upset—we all know how she feels about her father!" Then her expression turned serious and she leaned forward, her voice dropping. "Kay was talking about poor Polly. It's just ghastly. How on earth could such a terrible thing happen?"

Suddenly the other three women were leaning forward, too, their gazes fixed on Phyllis. And for once, she realized, they truly wanted to hear what she had to say. Doing her best to remember every word Charles had told her on the phone that morning, she described what had happened.

When she was done, Lenore Van Arsdale sat back in her chair, sighing heavily. "It's horrible," she said. "Well, thank God at least Teri got out. But what's going to happen to her now?"

Once again every eye at the table fixed on Phyllis Holloway. "Why, she's coming to live with us, of course," she said. "After all, she *is* Charles's daughter. Where else would she go?"

Kay Fielding's perfectly manicured fingers toyed nervously with her fork. "We were simply thinking—well, we all know about Melissa's . . ." Her voice trailed off for a second as she searched for the right word. ". . . well, her *problems*, Phyllis. She's always been such a high-strung child."

Phyllis felt her face burning, but forced a calm smile. "Actually, I think it will be good for her to have Teri here," she said. "Sometimes I think a lot of Melissa's problems are simply a function of her being an only child."

"Perhaps you're right," Kay Fielding replied, though her voice clearly indicated she doubted her own words. Then she brightened. "And certainly Teri has all the right genes. After all, she's a Holloway on one side and a Porter on the other. You can't really beat that, can you?"

Eleanor Stevens spoke for the first time. "Polly certainly managed to," she observed archly. "I mean, can you imagine, giving away every cent she had? Her parents must still be spinning in their graves." She shook her head sympathetically. "The things that child should have had that her mother simply denied her. Sometimes I think Polly must have been crazy."

Lenore Van Arsdale shot Eleanor a disapproving look. "It was Berkeley that did that," she pronounced. "If she'd gone to college at a decent school, she'd have been fine. She was my best friend for years, and I can tell you that there was nothing wrong with her until she went to California. But when she came back, she was never the same."

"Well," Kay Fielding said brightly, "at least we're getting Teri back while there's still time for her to get off to a good start in life."

The conversation went on, but Phyllis was no longer listening. Instead, her mind was working furiously. Until a few moments ago, though she'd not said a word of it to anyone, she'd wondered what on earth she was going to do with Teri MacIver in the house. It was bad enough having to cope with one teenage girl, especially one as difficult as Melissa. But two? The prospect had been almost more than she could cope with. And yet, she saw now, there was another side to the coin. These women—these women who never let her forget for a minute that she was not really one of them—were obviously ready to accept Teri MacIver back into the fold, despite the fact that they hadn't seen her for more than thirteen years. Teri, she was certain, would be invited to all the little parties from which Melissa had been excluded. And there would be parties at Maplecrest now, too, for it would be up to her to reciprocate the hospitality that certainly would be showered on Teri. Yes, perhaps Teri would finally provide the key to acceptance in Secret Cove that Phyllis knew had always been withheld from her.

And it wasn't fair.

Just as it wasn't fair that she'd always had to live with the knowledge that if Polly herself had come back, these women would have accepted her back into their circle just as if she'd never left at all.

Just as if Polly Porter had been as good a wife to Charles as she herself was.

But at least in her heart she knew it wasn't true. Polly hadn't been nearly the eccentric paragon all these women remembered. Indeed, sometimes Phyllis wanted to tell them what had *really* gone on at Maplecrest before Polly had finally left. Even now the memories still burned brightly.

One night, in particular.

There was a party scheduled at Maplecrest, and though it hadn't been Phyllis's job, she'd done all the planning for it, working out the details of the menu with Cora, ordering the flowers from the shop in the village, making certain every aspect of the party would be perfect.

And all that day Polly, clad in frayed jeans and a sweatshirt, had sat curled up on the sofa in the library, reading poetry.

Poetry, for God's sake!

An hour before the party was to begin, when Charles had suggested she might want to start dressing, she'd only glanced indifferently up from her book. "Maybe I'll skip it," she'd said. "It's just the same old dull crowd, going on and on about nothing."

Phyllis, who had happened to be in the library at the time, had seen the hurt in Charles's eyes. He'd even glanced at her, but it hadn't been a glance of embarrassment because she was overhearing his wife's words.

It had been a plea for understanding.

And she *had* understood.

Understood that Charles needed a wife who would willingly throw herself into the only life he'd ever lived.

He'd needed a hostess who could entertain his business associates without her eyes glazing over from boredom.

He'd needed a partner who understood that the Holloway fortune was something to be appreciated and nurtured, not sneered at.

He'd needed her, not Polly.

But none of them—not one of the women who had been Polly's childhood friends, had ever understood that. Polly would forever be Polly, whom they'd known all their lives, and she would forever be Phyllis, the outsider.

But now, with Teri MacIver coming back, all that might possibly—finally—change.

As the lunch wore on and the women began discussing the final plans for the costume party that traditionally marked the middle of the Secret Cove season, Phyllis managed to pay attention, if not actually participate in the discussion. But most of her mind was occupied with planning for Teri's arrival. Perhaps she was wrong, after all, about the small room next to Melissa's. Maybe Teri should have something larger. It wouldn't do, not to welcome this second, unexpected child properly into their lives. She made a mental note to talk to Cora again when she got home. No, better to call her now—perhaps she'd stay after lunch and enjoy a martini or two out by the pool. Excusing herself, she left the table and went in search of a phone.

As soon as she was gone, Lenore Van Arsdale leaned forward again, her voice low. "My God," she said. "Can you imagine what Polly must be thinking now? Not only did Phyllis manage to get hold of her husband, but now she's got her daughter, too!"

"What I don't understand," Kay Fielding put in, "is why Charles stays with that woman at all. The way she treats him—"

"It's Melissa," Eleanor Stevens replied. "Charles has always been a decent man, and I simply can't imagine him abandoning Melissa to Phyllis."

"But he wouldn't have to," Kay protested. "There isn't a court in the world that wouldn't give him custody."

"Of course not," Eleanor agreed. "But that's not really the point. The point is that Phyllis would put up a terrible fight, and Melissa would be right in the middle of it. And knowing Phyllis, she'd drag it on for years, even if she knew she'd lose. Charles won't put Melissa through that, and I don't blame him."

"But to stay with Phyllis." Kay sighed. "It just seems so unfair. And it's not as if it's helping Melissa. Living with Phyllis would drive anyone crazy, and poor Melissa just keeps getting stranger and stranger. It'll be a wonder if—" She fell silent as she felt Kay Fielding kick her under the table, and turned her head just in time to see Phyllis herself standing frozen behind her chair.

Five minutes later, behind the wheel of her Mercedes, Phyllis vented her cold anger as she slammed the accelerator to the floorboard and heard the rear wheels screech as they lost their traction. She shot out of the parking lot and started down the coast road, rolling the window down to let the wind blow in her face.

The words she'd heard Kay Fielding utter as she came back to the table still burned in her mind: ". . . poor Melissa just keeps getting stranger and stranger." No wonder she'd had so much trouble breaking into the world of Secret Cove. Everyone in town thought there was something wrong with her daughter! And why shouldn't they? Ever since the day she was born, Melissa had been different from the rest of the kids in Secret Cove. She hadn't been like Teri at all.

Teri, in the few months during which Phyllis had been her nurse, had been a perfect baby. Blond and blue-eyed, she'd never fussed at all, instead smiling happily up at anyone who happened to be there. She'd seemed to watch whatever was going on around her, smiling and laughing, reaching out for everything and everybody.

Not like Melissa, who seemed to spend most of her time crying, except when her father picked her up. And while Teri, even as a baby, had been so outgoing, Melissa had been painfully shy, refusing to play with the other babies on the beach, always preferring to be by herself. Always shutting herself away. Behaving strangely. Making her mother a laughingstock.

Since the day she was born, Phyllis thought, Melissa had kept her from being part of the Secret Cove Crowd.

It wasn't fair. It wasn't how she'd planned it at all. She'd taken Polly's place as Charles's wife and as the mother of his child. It was only right that she should also have had Polly's place in the Crowd. But it had never happened.

Except that now Teri was coming, and Phyllis would have one more chance, if Melissa didn't ruin it for her. Silently, she prayed that Teri hadn't changed, that she was still as perfect as she remembered her.

Charles Holloway switched off the television set in his room at the Red Lion Inn and rolled over, checking the alarm clock on the nightstand. It was eleven-thirty, and the alarm was set for six. He punched at the too-hard pillow that modern hotels seem to specialize in, then picked up the murder mystery he'd been putting himself to sleep with for the last month. So far he'd only managed to get through a hundred pages, which meant he'd been sleeping pretty well. But tonight he suspected he'd read at least twenty-five more. Well, just a few more days and he'd be back home.

He read a couple of paragraphs, then found himself distracted by a muffled sound from the next room. He listened for a moment, put the book aside and went to the door that separated his room from Teri's. A moment later he heard the sound again. This time he recognized it.

Teri was crying.

Pulling his bathrobe on and tying the belt around his waist, he opened the door and slipped into the other room. The lights were out, but in the glow of his own table lamp he could see Teri, curled up tightly in her bed, her arms clutching at the pillow. He moved to the bedside, eased himself down onto the bed itself and laid his hand on his eldest daughter's shoulder. "Teri? Honey? Are you all right?"

Teri rolled over onto her back and stared up at him through moist eyes. "I—I'm sorry," she said. "I was just feeling sort of lonely. I didn't mean to wake you up."

"You didn't," Charles assured her. "You should have come in."

"I didn't want to bother you," Teri breathed. "I mean, you already had to come all the way out here, and—" Her voice broke and she choked back a sob.

Charles gathered her into his arms, rocking her gently. "It's not a bother at all, and I don't ever want you to think that. I'm your father, and I love you." He felt Teri stiffen slightly in his arms, and then she pulled away enough to look searchingly up into his face.

"You do?" she said, her voice tinged with uncertainty.

"Of course I do," Charles said.

"Th-That's not what Mom said."

Charles frowned in the half darkness of the room. "What do you mean, that's not what your mother said."

Teri choked back another sob. "Sh-She said you only loved Melissa now. She said that's why you never sent me letters, or presents for Christmas or my birthday."

Charles froze. Was it possible? Could Polly really have said something like that? But it wasn't true. "Honey, what are you talking about?" he asked. "I've always sent you letters, and I never forgot your birthday or Christmas at all. Every year I've sent you a package. Didn't you get them?"

Teri shook her head. "I—I wasn't even sure you'd come today."

"Oh, Lord," Charles groaned, pulling her close once again. "No wonder you were crying. You must have been terrified."

"Y-You don't have to take me home if you don't want to," Teri said. "I can stay here—I have friends, and I can get a job. . . ."

Charles gently pressed a hand over her mouth to stop the flow of words. "I don't even want to hear anything like that," he said, feeling a sudden flash of anger toward his ex-wife. It was one thing to cut herself off from her past, but to try to alienate Teri from him was unforgivable. No wonder he'd never gotten a letter from Teri—she thought he didn't want to hear from her. "Now listen to me," he said, doing his best to keep the anger out of his voice. "I don't know why your mother would tell you something like that, but it isn't true. I never stopped loving you, and I never stopped thinking about you. And there was certainly never a question about my coming for you. You're my daughter, and you always have been. I've missed you every day you've been gone, and I've hated never seeing you. As for the letters and the presents, I can't imagine why your mother kept them from you. Why, just last Christmas I sent you a pearl necklace. It was beautiful— pink pearls, perfectly matched. And there were others, too. Toys when you were little—clothes—all kinds of things. So you mustn't think you're alone. You still have a father, and now you have a stepmother, and a sister, too."

Teri sat up now, propping herself up against the headboard. Nervously, she peered at Charles. "A sister," she whispered. "What's she like?"

Charles smiled in the darkness. "You'll love her. Yesterday was her thirteenth birthday, and she's the nicest girl you'll ever meet. In fact, she wanted me to tell you how sorry she is about what happened, but that the one thing she's always wanted is a sister. Now she has one."

Teri shifted uneasily in the bed. "But—But what if she doesn't like me?"

Charles reached out and took her hand, squeezing it gently. "Of course she'll like you," he said. "She'll love you just as much as I do."

They talked for a few more minutes, and slowly Teri calmed down, her sobs dying away. At last Charles tucked her in and kissed her good night. "And remember," he said, "if you get lonely again, you come in and wake me up."

Teri nodded. When Charles left the room, closing the door behind him, she lay still in the darkness for a few minutes, thinking.

Thinking about her mother.

Her mother, and her stepfather.

And her real father.

In a way, tonight was no different from all the other nights when she'd lain awake in her bed, trying to figure out why her mother had left her real father. It seemed to her that everything had been perfect back when they had all lived together in the huge house by the sea. Of course, she couldn't remember it now—she had been so young when the divorce had come. But even though she'd been away from Secret Cove for most of her life, deep inside she still thought of it as her real home, the place where she truly belonged.

And now she was going home again.

If only her mother could be going with her. Then everything would be the way it had been when she was a baby. Everything would be perfect. . . .

She determinedly put the thought out of her mind, refusing to dwell on the impossible.

She rolled over and tried to go to sleep, but sleep would not come. Finally, she reached out and turned on the lamp on the nightstand. Leaving the bed, she padded over to the closet and reached into the pocket of her bathrobe. When she went back to bed, she was carrying the only thing she had taken with her when she'd fled the blazing house.

She held it in her hand, studying it carefully.

It was a string of perfectly matched pink pearls.

She stared at them for a long time, fingering their smooth surfaces, rubbing them gently against her face. When she finally went to sleep an hour later, the pearl necklace was still in her hand.

CHAPTER

5

"Teri? We'll be landing in twenty minutes."

Teri blinked, then opened her eyes and stretched awkwardly in the first-class seat of the DC-9. Her mouth felt dry, and though she knew she'd fallen asleep for a while after they'd changed planes in Chicago, she felt as if she'd been awake all night. Her eyes stung and every joint in her body seemed to be aching. Her father smiled at her as if he knew exactly how she felt. "I hate night flights," Charles Holloway said ruefully. "Especially going east in summer. You get on when it's still light, and then it's morning when you arrive, but you don't feel as if there was any night. Why don't you go up and wash your face? You'll feel better."

Still not trusting her voice, Teri nodded and stepped across her father to the aisle, then went forward to the tiny lavatory, carrying the purse her father had bought her two days ago. She splashed cold water on her face and tried to comb her hair. She winced as she looked at her image in the mirror—her eyes looked puffy, and it seemed as if she'd somehow lost her tan overnight.

The person who gazed back at her had a sallow look, as if she'd been sick for a long time. She fumbled with the clasp on the leather bag and groped inside for her lipstick. Washing her face once more, she applied some color to her lips, then looked at her image once again.

A little of the puffiness had disappeared, and she didn't look quite as bad as she had a few minutes ago. Deciding she'd done the best she could, she returned to her seat and gratefully took a sip of the orange juice her father had ordered while she was gone. Then she raised the blind on the plane's window and looked out.

They were descending rapidly. As the plane banked for its final approach, Teri had a startling view of the Maine coastline, a series of rugged cliffs broken here and there with coves cut into the mainland, and an occasional strip of beach. She searched her memory, trying to recall any feeling at all of having been here before.

But there was nothing—it was all totally unfamiliar to her. "I keep thinking I should remember it," she said, turning back to her father.

Charles offered her a wry smile. "It would be pretty surprising if you did," he observed. "When you left, you weren't even three years old, and you went in a car."

Teri shook her head. "But there are things I remember. Not much, but a couple. I remember a big lawn, and a beach."

Charles chuckled. "Well, there's plenty of big lawns in Secret Cove, and we certainly have a beach." Then, as he saw Teri nervously take a small mirror out of her purse to study her face one more time, he was certain he knew what was on her mind. "Stop worrying—no one looks her best after flying all night."

"B-But what if Phyllis and Melissa don't like me?"

Charles took her hand in his and squeezed it affectionately. "How many times do I have to tell you that you aren't going to have a problem? I talked to Phyllis yesterday, and they've been getting a room ready for you. In fact, they've gotten a couple of rooms ready, so you can choose. And apparently Melissa hasn't talked about a single thing except her sister for the last two days."

Teri heard the words but wasn't certain whether to believe them or not. For the last two days she'd been trying to convince herself that it was going to be all right, that her father really did want her, that he wasn't going to send her away somewhere.

But he'd let her go once, a long time ago, when she was almost too small to remember.

What if he decided he didn't want her again?

What would she do?

Melissa watched the plane touch down and taxi toward the terminal. Unconsciously, her fingers went to the sleeve of the white sweater tied around her neck and began kneading nervously at the knitted material.

"For heaven's sake, Melissa," Phyllis said sharply. "Don't fidget. And can't you leave that poor sweater alone? It was perfectly clean when we left the house this morning, and now look at it."

Instantly, Melissa's hands dropped away from the sleeve. She shoved them in the pockets of her shorts, then changed her mind. "What if she doesn't like me?" she asked.

Phyllis's lips tightened as she gazed down at her daughter. "Well, I don't suppose there's any reason why she shouldn't," she replied. "If you'd just make an effort, everyone would like you. But if you won't try, you can't expect to have a lot of friends."

Melissa bit her lip, wishing she hadn't asked the question in the first place. Nervously, she reached up to run her fingers through her hair, then stopped herself as her mother's oft-spoken words rose up in her mind. "How can you expect to have nice hair if you treat it like that?"

And then, finally, the plane was at the jet way, and a moment later she saw her father coming toward her, his leather garment bag slung over his shoulder. She darted forward, throwing her arms around him as he let the bag slide to the floor, and a second later she felt his lips press against her cheeks.

"Miss me?" she heard him ask, and she nodded vigorously. Then he gently freed himself from her hug and turned toward the girl who now stood next to him. "This is your sister, sweetheart."

Melissa's breath caught in her throat as she looked at Teri for the first time. It seemed to her that Teri was even more beautiful than her picture. Her eyes were a deep blue, and her hair, combed back from her face, looked like she'd just washed it. She was wearing a white blouse and a pair of khaki shorts very much like the ones Melissa herself had on, but on Teri the clothes seemed to hang just like they did on the models in the magazines. "H-Hi," Melissa stammered uncertainly, feeling even gawkier than usual in front of her half sister.

"The least you can do is kiss your sister, Melissa," Phyllis said, prodding her forward. Melissa felt herself flush, and took a step toward Teri, but then Teri, apparently sensing her self-consciousness, grinned at her.

"Maybe you'd better not," she said. "I feel all grungy."

"Well, you certainly don't *look* grungy," Phyllis declared, stepping past Melissa to put her arms around Teri. "Do you remember me at all? I used to take care of you when you were just a baby." She hugged Teri close and her voice dropped. "We're all so terribly sorry about what's happened," she went on. "How dreadfully awful for you."

Teri gave her stepmother a hug but said nothing. There was an awkward moment, broken finally by Charles.

"Why don't we get out of here?" he asked, picking up the garment bag with one hand. "Where's the car?"

"In the lot," Phyllis replied. "Why don't you and Melissa bring it around while I help Teri find her baggage."

"I—I don't have any," Teri said softly. "I only have a few things Father bought me. The rest . . ." Her voice trailed off, and instantly Phyllis put a sympathetic arm around her.

"Now, don't worry about a thing. We have lots of wonderful shops in Secret Cove, and tomorrow we'll start working on putting your wardrobe back together again."

Melissa fell in next to her father, slipping her hand into his, but she found herself glancing back at Teri every few seconds.

Finally her father winked down at her. "What do you think?"

Melissa shrugged. "She—She's so beautiful," she whispered.

Charles squeezed her hand. "Not as beautiful as you, baby," he told her, then pulled her close.

Melissa, pressed close against her father's solid strength, felt some of the tension of the last few days with her mother begin to drain away. Her father was back, and for a while, at least, she was safe. And now, with Teri here, maybe her mother wouldn't be as hard on her anymore. Maybe Teri would offer the same kind of protection her father did.

*   *   *

Teri stared out the back window of the Mercedes as they turned off the main highway and dropped down toward Secret Cove, searching the road for anything that looked in the least bit familiar. As they wound through the little village, with its perfectly kept shops, all of them either built during the last century or carefully constructed to look as though they'd been, she saw nothing that stirred any sort of memory at all. But what she saw was fascinating.

Unlike the streets of the San Fernando Valley, which ran on for miles through a borderless morass of fast-food outlets and 7-Eleven stores, the main road into Secret Cove emerged from a patch of forest, then twisted through what looked to Teri almost like some kind of park. Every shop had flower boxes at its windows and gardens in front, and many of them had apparently once been private homes, their yards perfectly tended behind black wrought-iron fences.

"It's beautiful," Teri breathed, finally looking over at Melissa. "Has it always been this way?"

Melissa nodded. "Nobody lives in the village anymore. All the houses where the year-round people live are on the west side. But there's all kinds of rules about what they can do in the village. There's a historical society that makes sure no one changes anything." She giggled softly. "Cora—that's our housekeeper—says they're trying to turn the whole town into a museum, but Tag says it doesn't matter, since most of the people who live here are fossils anyway."

Teri cocked her head. "Who's Tag?"

"Cora's grandson. He lives with her. His folks ran off and just dumped him with her. Can you imagine?"

Teri shook her head. "What's he like?" she asked. "Is he cute?"

Phyllis's voice cut into the conversation from the front seat. "He's a very ordinary boy," she said. "He does some work around the place, and I suppose when he grows up he'll marry one of the local girls."

"No, he's not," Melissa put in. "He's going to go to college and be an architect."

Phyllis turned and shot her daughter a dark look. "Is he?" she said. "And how does he expect to pay for all of that?"

Melissa shrugged. "I—I guess he'll work, or get a scholarship or something. And everybody doesn't go to Harvard or Yale or one of those places."

"The people who *count* do," Phyllis replied. "What about you, Teri? Have you thought about college yet?"

Teri shook her head. "I was going to go to Cal State, I guess. But now . . ." Her voice trailed off again as everyone in the car realized that any plans she might have made had burned to ashes only a few days ago.

"Well, there's plenty of time to think about it," Phyllis said quickly. "We can have such fun, looking at schools for you. Eleanor Stevens is taking Ellen to Vassar over Labor Day weekend, just to look around. Perhaps we should tag along."

Charles cast a sidelong glance at his wife. "Come on, Phyllis— give her a break. She's got two more years of high school."

"Well, you can't start planning too early," Phyllis replied. "The really good schools are so difficult to get into, and it doesn't hurt to begin making connections now."

Teri turned to Melissa. "Where do you go to school?"

"Prissy Preston," Melissa replied, then grinned at the puzzled look on her half sister's face. "Actually, it's the Priscilla Preston Academy for Young Ladies," she explained. "I hate it, but Mom says I have to go there because it's where everyone goes. It's really old, and kind of creepy, and they're real strict. That's why all the kids call it Prissy Preston—because all the teachers are really stuffy."

"It's an excellent school, Melissa, and you should be grateful you're there."

Melissa rolled her eyes, and Teri grinned at her, and suddenly Melissa decided that everything was going to be all right after all. Then the car turned through the gates of Maplecrest and began winding down the long drive that led from Cove Road to the house. Teri's eyes once again fixed on the landscape beyond the car's windows.

They emerged from the woods, and Teri gasped.

And finally something clicked in her mind.

She wasn't certain if it was the size of the house, or its shape, or only the vastness of the lawn in front of it. But there was something about it she remembered.

It loomed ahead of them, an enormous shingled structure, a wide veranda fronting it, with French doors opening onto the veranda from most of the first-floor rooms. There was a large front door in the center of the house, and as she looked at it, Teri suddenly remembered what was inside those doors.

An enormous foyer—or at least what had seemed to her like an enormous foyer when she was tiny—with a staircase that went straight up toward the back of the house, then split off in both directions to a huge landing on the second floor. And then . . .

And then there was nothing, for the staircase was all she remembered.

Charles pulled the car to a stop on the gravel drive that circled around in front of the house, and Teri almost hesitantly left the car to stand staring up at Maplecrest.

"It's so big," she breathed, her words barely audible. "I never realized. It—It's a mansion!"

"Well, it's comfortable," Phyllis told her, using the slightly deprecating tone she always used when showing the house to strangers for the first time. "But it's hardly a mansion. Absolutely *no one* can afford those anymore. They've all been turned into institutes, or religious centers."

The door opened, and Cora, a fresh apron tied around her waist, bustled out. Brushing past the housekeeper with barely a nod, Phyllis marched briskly inside while Tag, who had followed his grandmother, waited on the front porch.

Cora hurried down the steps.

"Teri? Is it really you? Oh, my goodness, just look at you!" She wrapped her arms around the girl, pulling her to her ample bosom, then held her away at arm's length. "Look at you—all grown up, and the spitting image of your mother!" Then, as she heard her own words, her smile faded away. "Oh, dear," she murmured. "It's all so terrible, and here I am, acting like you've just come to visit." Her eyes flooded with tears and she dabbed at them with a corner of her apron. "I just—well, I just don't know what to say, and you must think I'm a terrible old fool. You probably don't even remember me, do you?"

Teri shook her head. "I—I don't really remember much of anything. It's been so long. But it all seems sort of familiar, somehow."

"But your mother must have shown you pictures of the place," Charles suggested.

Teri nodded. "But it's different. It's almost like I've dreamed about it."

"Well, of course you have," Cora told her. "After all, you were born here, weren't you? There's some things you never forget. Now, come and meet my grandson." She turned. "Tag? Come down and meet Teri."

Tag slowly came down the steps and offered Teri his hand. "Hi," he said.

"Hello," Teri replied, smiling at Tag as she took his hand. There was a loud barking, and she turned to see a big Labrador lumbering across the lawn, his tail wagging furiously.

"Come on, Blackie!" she heard Melissa shout. "Come on, boy!"

The big dog raced up to Melissa and rose up on his hind legs, planting his forepaws on Melissa's chest and lapping eagerly at her face. Laughing, Melissa scratched the dog's ears, then pushed him off. "This is Teri," she said, turning to her half sister. "Can you shake hands, Blackie?"

But instead of raising up a paw and holding it out toward Teri, Blackie shrank back against Melissa's legs. A low growl rumbled up from his throat. "Blackie!" Melissa exclaimed. "Is that any way to treat a new friend?" She grinned eagerly at Teri. "Come on, Teri. Let him sniff your hand. He's scared."

Teri hesitantly took a step forward and reluctantly held out her hand for the big dog to sniff.

But Blackie bolted away, charging back across the lawn to disappear over the crest of the low rise that separated the grassy expanse from the beach beyond. "Blackie!" Melissa called after him. "Blackie, you come back here!"

"It's all right," Teri told her. "Let him go."

Melissa glanced once more toward the beach and shrugged. "Come on," she said. "Let me show you your room."

She led Teri into the house, and as soon as Teri stepped into the foyer, she stopped.

It was exactly as she'd expected. The room was paneled in wood, all of it painted white, and there were French doors on either side of the broad staircase, leading to the terrace at the back of the house. Above the stairs, set into the high ceiling more than two floors above, was a domed skylight, its stained glass sending a rainbow of colors cascading down the stairs to splash across the white marble floor.

"I remember this," she whispered. "I remember the stairs from when I was a baby. They looked so big." She giggled. "They *are* big, aren't they?"

Melissa nodded. "I used to like to slide down the banister. Cora always used to say I'd kill myself, and Mama said it wasn't ladylike, but I did it anyway. Want to try?"

Teri gazed up at the polished walnut balustrade that curved down from the floor above and shook her head. "I think Cora's right. I'd probably fall off and break my neck."

"No you wouldn't," Melissa protested. "It's fun. We'll try it tomorrow."

They climbed up the stairs, turning to the right, where the flight split in two, and finally came to the big second-floor landing. A mezzanine encircled the staircase, with broad halls leading to the wings of the house.

"You get your choice of rooms," Melissa told Teri. "One of them's supposed to be a guest room, but Mama says you can have it if you want it. It's over this way."

She led Teri toward the eastern corner of the house and opened a door to reveal a large and airy room with windows in three of its walls. From two of the windows the cove and the ocean beyond were spread out in a broad panorama, while the third window looked out over the terrace cradled between the two rear wings of the house. "My room's the one straight across the terrace," Melissa told her. "It's not as big as this one, and this one has its own bathroom."

"Where's the other room?" Teri asked.

Melissa's smile faded slightly. "It's not as big as this one," she said. "And the view isn't as good."

"Well, can't we go look at it?"

Melissa led the way to the other side of the house, then paused outside the door to the room her mother had first chosen for Teri. "It—Well, it's hardly even a room at all," Melissa said. She pushed the door open and let Teri go in first.

The little room had been cleaned—Melissa herself had helped Cora scrub every surface until it sparkled, and they'd found some better furniture in the attic. The little chest of drawers had been replaced with an ornately carved highboy that Tag had discovered in a far corner of the attic, and they'd found an antique bedstead that Cora remembered from decades earlier. The rocker still stood where it had been, but the cushions on its seat and back had been covered with fresh chintz in a bright flowered pattern.

"I bet we could put wallpaper up if you decide you like this room," Melissa said.

Caught by the plaintive note in her half sister's voice, Teri turned and cocked her head slightly. "What's special about this room?" she asked. "I mean, it's not nearly as big as the other one, or as nice, either."

"I know," Melissa sighed. "And if it were me, I'd probably take the other room in a minute. But look." She crossed the room and opened the door to the small bathroom that separated the nurse's room from the bedroom beyond. "If you go through the other door, you can get into my room without ever going out into the hall. So if you take the little room, we can sneak back and forth without Mom and Dad ever knowing."

Teri glanced around the bathroom. Though it wasn't big by comparison to the rooms in Maplecrest, it was still larger than the bathroom she had shared with her parents in California. And the room Melissa had just apologized for was still larger than her room at home.

No, she silently corrected herself. *This* is my home now.

She moved toward the second door of the bathroom, the one that led to Melissa's own room, and suddenly she had another of those strange flashes of recognition.

"Go on in," she heard Melissa say.

Slowly, she pushed the door open.

As soon as she stepped into the room, she knew.

This had been hers.

All of it felt familiar, despite the fact she hadn't been in it since she was less than three years old.

Even the smell of it seemed to bring back old feelings, feelings of warmth, security, and of arms cradling her, and images of faces smiling down at her.

Yes, this had been her room; this had been where she lived when she was a baby.

She hesitated, her emotions churning.

The other room—the room on the other side of the house—was much larger, much brighter than the little room next to Melissa's.

But that was the side of the house where guests stayed.

Guests, who would come for a few days, or maybe a couple of weeks, and then leave.

But Teri wasn't leaving. This was her home again, and she didn't want to feel like a guest.

And, of course, there was Melissa.

Melissa, the half sister she'd had for so many years but had never known, was watching her now, anxiously waiting to see what she was going to do.

She smiled. "I think you're right," she said. "I think I'll take the little room. The other one's too big, and I'd always be looking over here across the terrace, wondering what you're doing and wishing I could talk to you. If I'm over here with you, it'll be a lot more fun."

Melissa gazed at the beautiful girl who was smiling at her, and suddenly threw her arms around Teri.

"I know what happened is really terrible," she whispered. "But I'm so glad you're here. I've just been so lonely, and now I'm not going to be anymore."

Teri hesitated, then let her own arms go around Melissa.

But though her lips smiled warmly as she accepted the embrace, her eyes—had anyone noticed—betrayed an emotionless chill.

CHAPTER

6

Brett Van Arsdale watched the volleyball arc upward and waited until the very last second before launching himself into the air, his right arm stretching above his head, his hand clenched into a fist. At exactly the right moment he swung his arm downward, spiking the ball back over the net and into the sand between Kent Fielding and Cyndi Miller, who glared accusingly at each other. Both spoke at the same instant.

"Why didn't you get it?" "It was coming right at you!"

"Game!" Jeff Barnstable yelled gleefully from Brett's side of the net. "Anybody want to play girls against the boys?"

"Give me a break," Ellen Stevens groaned. "You never wanted to play that two years ago, when we were all bigger than you guys!"

"So?" Jeff countered, grinning impudently. "Things change. Got to keep up, Ellen."

Ellen abandoned the court and flopped down on her beach towel. "I'll tell you what," she offered, stretching languidly as she applied another coat of sunscreen to her arms and felt Jeff's eyes admiring her. "After lunch we'll get a tennis court, and Cyndi and I will take you and Kent on at doubles."

Jeff groaned, dropping down beside her. "You think I'm nuts? I'm not gonna let everyone at the club watch you whip me."

Ellen's brows rose. "But it's okay if everyone watches you guys beat us at volleyball?" she teased. "You're such a sexist creep sometimes."

Jeff picked up a handful of sand, and Ellen rolled away from him, giggling. A second later Jeff let the sand trickle through his fingers. "Hey," he said to no one in particular. "Has anyone seen Teri yet?"

Cyndi Miller shook her head. "It's weird—she's been here two whole days. Wouldn't you think she'd be on the beach?"

"Maybe she's as nutty as Melissa," Marshall Bradford said, the corners of his eyes wrinkling with a grin. "And she's a couple of years older—maybe they have to keep her locked up in the attic."

Ellen Stevens snickered. "My mom keeps telling me I ought to call her, but what am I supposed to do? Invite her over and not ask Melissa?"

"Why not?" Cyndi countered. "I mean, it's not as if Melissa likes us. She actually kicked us out of her birthday party the other day."

"Some party," Brett groaned. "A game of water polo and some of Cora Peterson's Ritz crackers with peanut butter. Big deal. We could have—" And then he fell silent, frowning slightly as he gazed up the beach to the north.

Jeff Barnstable followed his friend's gaze, then nudged Ellen Stevens, who was stretched out on her back, one arm shielding her eyes from the sun. "Guess who's coming down the beach? Melissa and someone who has to be Teri MacIver."

Ellen uttered an exaggerated groan. "Can't they do something about the pollution around here?"

Jeff snickered, but as the two girls drew closer, with Blackie frolicking at Melissa's heels, he nudged Ellen again. "If you ask me, Teri doesn't exactly look like a lump of tar."

"I didn't ask you," Ellen replied, but nevertheless sat up and blinked as the sun struck her eyes. A moment later her pupils adjusted to the glare and she saw the familiar figure of Melissa, a little too plump, with her brownish hair hanging limply around her shoulders, walking along the beach just above the waterline.

But next to her was another girl, and the contrast between the two made Ellen's eyes widen slightly, for Teri, her perfect figure clad in a slightly too tight bathing suit that exposed most of her skin to the sun, was the exact opposite of Melissa. Her blond hair, brushed back from her face, had the kind of natural highlighting that Ellen herself had been struggling for a month to coax out of a bottle from the local drugstore. Her tan, a deep glowing bronze that was set off perfectly by her black bathing suit, was absolutely even, and Ellen found herself automatically glancing down at the pale patches on the insides of her own thighs.

"California girl," she commented, knowing even as she spoke that the words sounded like sour grapes. She glanced around at her friends, all of whom—even Cyndi Miller—were staring at Teri. "Come on, you guys—she's not *that* gorgeous."

"Oh, yes she is," Brett Van Arsdale said. "Face it, Ellen," he added, never taking his eyes off Teri, "she makes you look like dog meat."

"That is so gross!" Ellen snapped. "You're the one who looks like a dog, Brett. Your tongue's hanging out and you're practically drooling. And just because she's wearing a bathing suit a couple of sizes too small! Why don't you grow up?"

"I think I just did," Brett sighed. "How am I going to meet her?"

"Have you thought of just walking up to her and saying hello?" Ellen asked, her voice acid.

"I could have, if you hadn't been so crappy to Melissa the other day."

"Me?!" Ellen shrieked. "What did I do?"

Brett's eyes shifted over to fix on Ellen. "Oh, get off it—I heard what you and Cyndi were saying about her, and she did, too."

"Well, if you're so crazy about Melissa all of a sudden," Ellen complained, "then why don't you go ask her to introduce you to her sister?"

"Maybe I will," Brett said, but made no move to leave the blanket he was sharing with Kent Fielding.

"Well, go on," Kent goaded, giving Brett a shove. "Why don't you go talk to Melissa? First you can tell her how sorry we all are about her crappy birthday party, and then you can tell her you have the hots for her sister."

"Aw, Jeez," Brett groaned. "Give me a break, will you?"

"Well, how else are you going to meet her?" Jeff asked.

Brett shrugged. "Well, I'm sure not going to try with you guys around. Anyway, she's bound to show up at the club."

Cyndi Miller snickered. "Right. Along with Mrs. Holloway and Melissa. Forget it, Brett—you're not going to get to Teri without getting stuck with Melissa, too." She rolled over, turning her back on the two girls, who had now stopped fifty yards down the beach and were busy whispering to each other. "And who cares anyway? I'll bet she's just as weird as Melissa."

"But don't you know them?" Teri asked, her head tilting toward the group of teenagers clustered on the beach next to the volleyball net.

Melissa chewed at her lip. She knew Teri wanted to meet them, but the painful memory of her birthday was still fresh in her mind. "Yes, I know them," she finally admitted. "But that doesn't mean I like them. They're just a bunch of snobby Cove Club kids."

Teri frowned. "But we're members of the club, aren't we?"

"Yes, but . . ."

"But what?" Teri pressed. "I mean, you've been here every summer of your life. Aren't they your friends?"

Melissa took a deep breath, then shook her head. "No, they're not," she finally admitted. "They—They don't like me." Her eyes fixed on the ground as she spoke the words, unable to meet Teri's stare.

"What do you mean, they don't like you?" Teri asked. "Why wouldn't they?"

Melissa shrugged, wishing they hadn't come to the beach today. But for the last two days she and Teri had lain around the swimming pool, and this morning, when Teri had suggested they take a walk up the beach, she hadn't been able to admit she didn't want to because she was afraid of running into the kids from the club. And yet, when she finally managed to look up at Teri, her half sister wasn't looking at her in that awful superior way the other kids always did.

"They just don't, that's all."

Teri glanced once more at the group of kids sprawled on their blankets and instantly understood. Even from here she could see that all of them were alike—they all had blond hair, the girls were all slim, and the boys were all broad-shouldered with deep chests and well-developed muscles.

They were the kind of kids she'd seen back home sometimes, when she and her friends took the bus into Beverly Hills to look around, not doing anything, but just hanging out. She'd always been able to spot the kids who lived there—they all looked alike, and they all did their shopping along Rodeo Drive, and spent their days during the summer lying around their pools and playing tennis on their own courts.

And when they glanced at Teri and her friends at all, which they practically never did, Teri thought she knew what they were thinking:

You don't belong here—why don't you go home?

And yet as she stole another glance at the group of kids on the beach, she was certain at least one of them was giving her a look she'd seen before, a look that said he, at least, wanted to get to know her. Unless he was just staring at the skimpy bathing suit she'd found in the pool house yesterday.

He was the tallest one of the group—a little over six feet, and when he grinned at one of his friends, she could see deep dimples in his cheeks. "Who's that?" she asked Melissa.

Melissa didn't even have to look at the group of kids to know whom Teri was talking about. It had to be the boy on whom she'd had a secret crush for the last two summers. "Jeff Barnstable," she said out loud. "Isn't he adorable? I love his curly hair, and his eyes are just incredible."

Teri eyed her half sister speculatively. "You like him, don't you?"

Though Melissa shook her head in denial, her flush of embarrassment belied the gesture. "Well, maybe I've got kind of a crush on him," she finally admitted, then sighed heavily. "But he doesn't even know I'm alive."

Teri squeezed Melissa's hand sympathetically. "Well, don't worry about it," she said. "I bet if we can just get his attention, he'll notice you. Besides," she added, "it wasn't him I was talking about. Who's the tall one?"

Melissa covertly let her eyes scan the group of teenagers, and then understood who Teri was talking about. "Brett Van Arsdale," she said.

"What's he like?"

Melissa, relieved that it wasn't Jeff who interested Teri, shrugged indifferently. "I don't know—he's okay, I guess." She started walking once more. "Come on—just ignore them, and they'll probably leave us alone."

Side by side they walked along the waterline, the foam from the gently breaking waves lapping at their feet. Teri could feel the eyes of the teenagers on the beach watching them as they passed, but she didn't look up. When they were about a hundred yards farther along, she glanced at Melissa. "Let's go for a swim," she suggested. "I'm all hot and sticky." Without waiting for an answer, she turned and dashed into the water, running out until she was knee deep, then diving into a small wave. The chill of the water hit her skin with a shock, but she swam underwater for a few yards, then surfaced, rolling over onto her back. "Come on in," she called to Melissa.

Melissa hesitated, then waded into the water, stopping when it reached her knees. "It's cold!" she called.

Teri laughed and started swimming toward her half sister. "It isn't cold—it's freezing! But come on in. If I can do it, you can do it! And once you get numb, it's not bad at all!"

As she heard Teri's laughter, Melissa felt a pang of hurt stab through her. But then, as she listened to what Teri was saying, she realized Teri wasn't laughing *at* her at all—she was laughing *with* her! Taking a deep breath, she held her nose, then dropped down into the water, only to jump up again, screeching with the shock of the sudden cold. "It's the only way I can do it," she told Teri a moment later, finally stretching out into the water and slowly dog-paddling toward the other girl, with Blackie, who'd plunged happily into the water the moment she'd started wading in, swimming along beside her. When she came close to Teri, she rolled over on her back, too, and they floated for a while, side by side, the warmth of the air on their faces barely compensating for the ocean chill.

They drifted for a few minutes, enjoying the gentle rise and fall of the swells, and finally Melissa let her feet drop down and began treading water. Though they hadn't been floating more than five minutes, they were already thirty yards from the beach. "Teri?" Melissa called. "We'd better go back—the tide's taking us out!"

Teri rolled over and glanced around. "We're fine. You go back if you want to—I'm going to swim for a while."

Melissa hesitated. Did Teri think she was chicken? But then Teri said, "Really—go on back to the beach. I'll be fine."

Still Melissa hesitated. "Okay," she said. "But come in closer, all right? If the tide pulls you out of the cove—"

"Then I'll drown," Teri finished for her. With a couple of strong strokes, she swam over to Melissa, passed her, then slowed down to let her half sister catch up. When they were in water shallow enough for them to stand up in, Teri paused. "Okay?"

Melissa nodded, then swam on in to the beach, where she dropped down onto the hot sand, shivering from the freezing water. A moment later Blackie trotted out of the water, bounded over to her and violently shook himself, covering Melissa with an icy spray. Teri, floating on her back again, was bobbing once more on the gentle swells. Melissa watched her for a few minutes, then a flock of sandpipers, skittering along the waterline a few yards up the beach caught her attention. When Blackie dashed off to chase them, Melissa's concentration shifted from her sister to the frolicking dog. The birds fanned out in front of the lumbering animal, letting him get within a few inches of them before spreading their wings and leaping into the air, wheeling out over the water, only to settle back on the sand an enticing few yards away from the dog. Melissa watched the game for a few minutes before her attention was jerked away by a terrified yell.

"Help! Someone help me!"

Melissa leaped to her feet, her eyes scanning the bay. A moment later she saw Teri, fifty yards out now, frantically waving her arms in the air. Melissa gasped, and instinctively ran down to the water, but to the north she saw Brett Van Arsdale already sprinting across the beach. He dived into the water, and launched himself into a powerful crawl that took him out to Teri within less than a minute. Meanwhile Melissa raced down to the beach to join the group that had gathered at the water's edge, her feelings about the other kids forgotten. Jeff Barnstable was in the water now, too, swimming strongly, but not fast enough to catch up with Brett before he'd reached Teri.

Almost before it had begun, it was over. Brett, one arm curved around Teri's chest, was using the other arm in a clumsy backstroke, but after a few moments Teri said something and Brett let her go. Side by side, with Jeff escorting them the last twenty yards, they came back to the beach. Teri, shivering with cold, pulled herself out of the water and dropped onto the sand. Instantly, the small crowd of teenagers surrounded her.

"Are you all right?" Ellen Stevens asked.

Teri, gasping, nodded, then spat some saltwater out onto the sand. "Dumb," she finally managed to say. "I feel so dumb."

Kent Fielding knelt down next to her. "What happened?"

Teri shrugged. "I went out too far. Melissa warned me what would happen, but I guess I didn't listen. The tide caught me, and I panicked. I thought I was going right out to sea." She looked up at Brett Van Arsdale, standing a couple of feet away. "Thanks," she said. "I was so scared—I don't know what I would have done if you hadn't been there."

Brett grinned. "Nothing to it," he said, holding out his hand. "I'm Brett Van Arsdale."

Teri scrambled to her feet. "I'm Teri MacIver—Melissa's half sister."

The rest of the kids began introducing themselves to Teri, and soon she was in the midst of the crowd, telling them what had happened. "I was just floating with my eyes closed, almost asleep. And then I decided to look around and see where I was, and I'd gotten so far out, I just panicked. It was really stupid to start screaming like that. I mean, it's not like I was drowning or anything."

"Well, you might not have been then," Brett told her. "But if you'd drifted out of the cove, you could have been in real trouble. The rips get really bad out there, and if you drift south, there's nothing but rocks. Last summer a guy was surfing out there, and a wave took him right in. Tore all the skin right off his chest and stomach. He was lucky he wasn't killed."

"Oh, come on," Teri protested. "I wasn't anywhere near the

point. I just got scared. I—I'm really sorry I made you swim all
the way out there."

Brett's face reddened. "I didn't mind—really!"

"He's not lying, either," Kent Fielding crowed. "The way he's
been talking about you, we all thought he was going to try to
drown you himself, just so he could save you."

Brett groaned. "Will you shut up," he said, his blush deepening. "Jesus, she's going to think I'm some kind of nerd!"

"Well, aren't you?" Cyndi Miller teased, ducking away as Brett
kicked sand at her.

Melissa watched for a few minutes, and noticed that Teri
seemed instantly to meld into the group, chattering along with
them, falling immediately into their idle banter. Finally, as the
group seemed to close around Teri, Melissa wandered away,
Blackie trailing along after her.

Ten minutes later Teri, now sitting on a huge beach towel with
Brett Van Arsdale and Ellen Stevens, glanced around. "Where's
Melissa?" she asked. "She was here a minute ago."

"Who cares?" one of the kids replied.

Teri frowned, and turned to Brett Van Arsdale. "What's wrong
with Melissa?" she asked. "How come no one likes her?"

Brett's face flushed and his eyes shifted away from her. It was
Ellen Stevens who answered her question, her voice dark with
scorn.

"Oh, come on—just take a look at her. She's got to be at least
twenty pounds overweight, and she always looks terrible. I mean,
that hair of hers is so gross—does she ever even wash it? And
she's such a klutz. She can barely swim, and she can't play tennis
at all. She never even has anything to say. Everyone thinks she's
crazy."

"And her mother!" Cyndi Miller groaned.

Instantly, a tiny alarm sounded in the back of Teri's mind.
"Her mother?" she asked. "What's wrong with Phyllis?"

Cyndi's brows arched in an expression that was older than her
years. "Well, I suppose there's nothing wrong with her," she said
in an almost perfect imitation of her own mother's inflections. "I
mean, if you like that kind of person. But she's not one of us, and
she never will be."

"You mean because she didn't grow up here?" Teri asked, certain she already understood exactly what was meant.

"She didn't grow up *anywhere*," Ellen Stevens replied. "My mother says no one knows where she came from or who her family is." Her voice dropping just the way her mother's did when she was about to say something cutting, she went on, "And she's always trying to push her way in, just like she was one of us!"

Teri got to her feet, her mind furiously at work, sorting out everything she'd heard in the last few minutes. "I—I better be going," she said. She started up the beach toward the Holloway house, but turned back when she heard Brett calling to her.

"Why don't you come over to the club this afternoon? Maybe we'll play some tennis."

Teri hesitated, then shrugged. "I'll see," she said. Then turning away from the group of kids once more, she hurried on up the beach.

A few minutes later she found Melissa sitting on the sand, staring out to sea, with Blackie at her side. As Teri approached, the big dog growled softly and Melissa glanced up. But she said nothing, her eyes quickly returning to the water.

"Are you mad at me?" Teri asked.

Melissa shook her head.

"You are," Teri insisted. "You're mad because I was talking to those kids, aren't you?"

Melissa shrugged but didn't deny it.

Teri plopped down onto the sand next to her. "They're not such bad kids," she said. "They're a little bit snobby, but look how they live. They're all rich." There was a hint of envy in Teri's voice that made Melissa look at her.

"They'll probably like you," she said, her voice reflecting her pain. "I mean, you're so pretty, and you look like them. You'll fit right in."

Now it was Teri who shrugged. "I don't know," she sighed. "I sort of got the feeling that the thing that really counts with them is where you're from and who your parents are. And I'm from California."

Melissa finally managed a grin. "No you're not," she said. "You were born right here, and so were your parents. So you're one of them."

Teri frowned. "But you are, too, aren't you?"

Melissa shook her head, then took a deep breath, as if trying to make up her mind to say something she really didn't want to say.

"What is it?" Teri pressed.

"It's Mom," Melissa said. "Nobody likes her. She keeps trying to make them, but they won't. They talk about her behind her back, and laugh at her just like they laugh at me."

Teri shrugged. "I bet they'd stop if you didn't let them know it hurts you. Just pretend you don't hear. Like I pretended to be drowning this morning."

Melissa gaped at her half sister. "You mean you weren't?"

A sly smile curled the corners of Teri's mouth. "Of course not," she said. "I can swim like a fish. But there's no better way to meet boys on a beach than to let them save you. So I let Brett Van Arsdale save me."

Melissa's mouth dropped open. "But—But that's like lying, isn't it?"

"So what?" Teri asked. "I wanted to meet him, and I did. If it works, do it."

Melissa made no reply, but as she lay back on the sand, feeling the warmth of the sun on her face, she was thinking about what Teri had said.

"If it works, do it."

It sounded so easy, and apparently for Teri it was. After all, it hadn't taken her more than a few minutes to make friends with all the kids Melissa herself had grown up with but never fit in with.

So if Teri could do it, why couldn't she?

But she already knew the answer: even if she knew what it was she was supposed to do, she still wouldn't be able to do it.

No matter how hard she tried, she'd still mess it up, and once again people would laugh. But not *with* her, like Teri had earlier. No, like all the other times, they would laugh *at* her.

Better not to try at all.

That evening, as dusk was gathering, Teri was in the library with the rest of the family. The television was on, but only Phyllis was watching it. Teri herself was leafing through an old copy of *Town & Country*, while Melissa was playing a game of chess with her father. Teri watched for a moment, both of them intent on the board, apparently oblivious to everything around them.

She looked around the walnut-paneled room, and suddenly the walls seemed to close in around her—she'd been here two days already, and hardly been away from the house at all, except for a few minutes at the beach today.

And then she remembered Brett Van Arsdale's words that afternoon, when he'd invited her down to the club. She hadn't gone, of course. Though Melissa had told her to go by herself if she wanted to, Phyllis had told her she shouldn't—she was still in mourning for her parents, and what would people think?

Well, what were they supposed to think? And how long was she supposed to wait before she started living again? Did they want her to spend her whole life thinking about the past?

And if Melissa had wanted to go to the club, she'd bet it would have been fine with Phyllis.

Suddenly, she thought if she didn't get out of the house for a while, she'd go crazy. "I think I'll go for a walk on the beach," she said, putting the magazine aside and standing up.

Phyllis's eyes flicked away from the television screen for a moment. "Don't go swimming—it can be very dangerous at night."

"Want me to go with you?" Melissa asked, looking up from the chessboard she'd been studying.

Teri shook her head. "I just want to be by myself for a little while," she said. "I won't be gone long."

A few minutes later, as she walked along the beach listening to the gently breaking surf, she saw the lights of the Cove Club glowing in the distance. Faintly, she could hear music—a hard rock beat she hadn't heard since she'd left California. Her pace picking up, she started toward the club, drawn by the music and the lights.

She hesitated as she came to the grounds of the club itself. There was an outdoor shower at the top of the beach, with a sign saying FOR THE USE OF MEMBERS AND GUESTS ONLY, and from the shower an intricately patterned brick walkway wound through perfectly tended gardens to a terrace and swimming pool. From there a series of steps led up the cliff to the clubhouse itself, which was perched at the very end of the point. Even at this distance, Teri could see people inside the clubhouse, dancing to the compelling beat of the rock music.

She started up the path, ignoring the discreet but definite NO TRESPASSING sign. After all, her father was a member of the club, and even if he hadn't been, she'd been invited by Brett Van Arsdale. But as she came to the pool terrace, she suddenly realized that it wasn't empty. Three people were sitting on chaise longues, quietly talking.

Suddenly feeling like an outsider, Teri stepped off the path and ducked into the deep shadows of a small grove of pine trees. As she was about to slip back toward the beach, she heard a snatch of conversation.

"I still say she won't go."

Teri stopped, recognizing Jeff Barnstable's voice.

"Why not?" Brett Van Arsdale replied.

"Because of Mrs. Holloway," Ellen Stevens's voice chimed in. "If you invite Teri to the bonfire, you can just bet Mrs. Holloway's going to make her bring Melissa with her."

Teri froze. Were they talking about her? They had to be! Moving carefully, she crept through the trees.

"Well, so what if Melissa comes?" Brett asked. "I mean, she doesn't do anything."

"But that's the whole point," Ellen replied. "She just sits there and stares at you. Besides, she's such a little pig—she'd eat all the food before any of the rest of us had a chance."

"Oh, come on," Jeff objected. "So she's not perfect. So what?"

"I don't care if she's perfect or not," Ellen sneered. "But she's just not one of us. Not like Teri, at all."

The conversation went on, but Teri had heard enough. She slipped back through the trees, not returning to the beach until she was far enough from the club that she wouldn't be seen.

She started home, going over and over the conversation she'd just heard.

So now she wasn't going to be invited to a bonfire, just because the kids didn't like Melissa.

It wasn't fair. Why should she be left out just because Melissa didn't fit in? After all, Melissa already had everything she could possibly want.

And most of it had once been hers.

Melissa had her house. She even had her old room.

And her father, too.

An image flashed into Teri's mind of Melissa and her father, bent over the chessboard, concentrating only on each other and their game.

A game Teri hadn't been part of.

And now Melissa was going to keep her from making friends with all the kids she should have grown up with herself.

No, she decided as she approached the big house above the beach once again, it wasn't fair.

It wasn't fair, and it wasn't how things were supposed to be at all.

And it certainly wasn't how she'd planned them.

CHAPTER

7

The large clock in the library began to chime the hour. Phyllis glanced over at the chess game that had been going on for more than two hours. Her lips tightened in disapproval—how could her husband and daughter just *sit* there, hour after hour, staring at nothing but a bunch of figures on a checkerboard? Never speaking, never doing anything. She got up from her chair and moved to the table, casting a shadow over the board as she blocked the light from the floor lamp a few feet away. "Ten o'clock," she announced. "Time for you to go to bed."

Melissa's eyes flicked up from the board, resting first on her father, then moving on to her mother. "Just a few more minutes? Please? I've almost got him."

Phyllis shook her head. "You know the rules, dear. You need your rest."

"But it's just three more moves," Melissa pleaded. "Look, all I have to do is back Daddy's king over to the side of the board . . ." Her words trailed off as her father laid his king down on the board.

"It's all right, honey," he said. "I resign. When there's no hope, why prolong the agony?" He straightened up in his chair, stretched, then grinned crookedly at his daughter. "I'm starting to wonder if it was such a good idea teaching you this game in the first place. How long has it been since I've beaten you?"

Melissa began setting the pieces up on the board, placing each man in the exact center of its starting square. "You almost beat me tonight," she said. "You could have trapped my queen an hour ago."

"How?" Charles asked.

Melissa began moving the men around the board, re-creating from memory the position that had existed sixteen moves into the game. Then her mother's voice stopped her.

"Now we'll have none of that," she commanded. "You're not going to replay the whole thing—you'll both be up all night."

Melissa's hand, holding her father's queen, hovered in the air for a moment as she looked hopefully at him once again, but when Charles shook his head, she set the piece back on the board, sighing.

Ten minutes later she was in her nightgown, propped up against the headboard, a book resting against her knees. A cool breeze blew through the open windows, and the night air was filled with the sounds of crickets chirping against the background of the cove's gentle surf washing up the beach. Melissa snuggled comfortably into the pillows and found her place in the book. A few minutes later, though, as her door opened, she started to slip the book guiltily under the covers. She relaxed as her father came in. He settled on the edge of the bed, then glanced at the book on his daughter's lap.

"*Anne of Green Gables?*" he asked. "How many times have you read it now?"

Melissa shrugged. "I don't know—ten, I suppose. I love it—I'm in the part now where Anne accidentally dyes her hair green."

Charles grinned, remembering Melissa's rapt attention when he'd first read the book to her four years ago. "Is she as mortified as ever?"

Melissa's head bobbed eagerly. "She doesn't think she'll ever leave her room again." She giggled, but then her giggle died away. "It's just the kind of thing that would happen to me," she said, averting her eyes. "Every time she gets in trouble, and it's not really her fault, I feel like I'm reading about myself. Maybe that's why I love her so much."

Charles leaned over and kissed his daughter. "It seems to me," he observed, "that there's a difference between you and Anne. For one thing, you're not an orphan, and for another, you never had to take care of twins."

Melissa's giggle bubbled up again. "But I feel like her anyway," she said. "You know—how she was always trying to do the right thing but messed it up? That's what I do." She sighed once more. "I wish I were more like Teri," she said, her voice taking on a wistfulness. "She's so pretty, and she gets along with everyone. Like today—she didn't even know all those kids, but she could talk to them like she's known them all her life. And I *have* known them all my life, but I never know what to say, and I always feel like they're laughing at me."

"Like Anne thought Gilbert Blythe was laughing at her?" her father teased.

Melissa shook her head. "I don't have a Gilbert Blythe. And besides, at least Anne had a bosom friend. I—"

But before she could say anything else, her father silenced her with a gentle finger to her lips. "You have Teri now," he reminded her. "And it seems like she's going to be as good a friend as you could want."

Melissa suddenly felt foolish. "I'm sorry," she said. "I guess I was feeling sorry for myself."

"Well, just stop," her father told her. "You're a very, very lucky little girl, and you should count your blessings. And," he added, winking at her, "if you count them right, they just might help you beat me at tennis tomorrow morning." He kissed her again, then stood up and went to the door. "Do you want me to leave the light on?" he asked.

Melissa shook her head, putting the book on her night table as her father turned off the light. He closed the door, plunging the room into darkness. Then her eyes began to adjust to the silvery glow of the rising moon that shone through the window. She snuggled deeper into the pillows and watched the shadows of the immense maple outside her window dance against the ceiling. When she'd been much smaller, the shadows had sometimes frightened her, but now she enjoyed them, trying to imagine them as small creatures that enjoyed playing in her room while she slept. Finally, she closed her eyes and was about to drift off into sleep when she heard footsteps in the hall outside her door.

Her mother's footsteps.

She stopped breathing, silently praying that the footsteps would move on, that tonight her mother wouldn't come into her room. When the door opened, she knew her prayers were not to be answered.

She lay still, spacing out her breaths in the slow and steady pace of sleep, but a moment later she felt her mother's hand on her shoulder.

"Melissa, I know you're not asleep yet."

Melissa rolled over and opened her eyes.

Above her, her mother's silhouette loomed against the window.

"You were a bad girl today," her mother said. Melissa's mind raced as she tried to remember what she'd done to make her mother angry at her.

And in her mind she silently spoke to D'Arcy. *What did I do? What did I do to make her mad at me?*

"You were rude to your friends again," Phyllis said, almost as if she'd heard the unspoken question. "They saved Teri from drowning, and all you did was walk away."

Melissa felt a knot of fear form in her stomach. That wasn't how it had been! It wasn't how it had been at all! The kids weren't even talking to her—they were only talking to Teri! But it was like her birthday all over again—it wouldn't matter what she told her mother. Her mother had already made up her mind what had happened. She said nothing, only staring up at her mother, waiting for whatever was to come. And then, in her mother's hands, she saw the straps.

"N-No," she stammered. "P-Please, Mama, don't make me wear the straps."

Her mother stared down at her. Her voice rose and fell in a strange singsong, as if she were speaking to an infant. "But you have to wear them. You've been a bad girl, and when you're bad, you walk in your sleep. Give me your hand."

Melissa, fighting back the scream of protest that rose in her throat, tried to raise her hand in fulfillment of her mother's command, but her muscles refused to obey.

"Your hand!" Phyllis demanded, grabbing at Melissa's arm and jerking it so hard that a wrenching pain slashed through the child's shoulder. "How can you be such an *idiot?*"

As the pain stabbed through her, Melissa cried out for help once again, and this time she heard D'Arcy's silent answer, whispered to her from somewhere in the shadows of the night.

Sleep, Melissa—I'm here now, and you can go to sleep.

Even as she heard the words, Melissa relinquished herself to the darkness that began closing in around her, and left D'Arcy to accept whatever punishment her mother meted out.

Phyllis, poised above the bed, drew back her hand, ready to strike her disobedient child once again, but suddenly Melissa relaxed on the mattress and her arms came up as she held out her wrists to accept the thick leather straps.

One at a time Phyllis fastened the bands around Melissa's wrists, then moved to the foot of the bed to attach the restraints to her ankles. Finally she connected the free ends of the straps to the bed frame, then covered Melissa with a thin sheet.

"It's warm tonight," she said, her voice gentle now as Melissa lay bound to the bed. "You won't need a blanket at all. Sleep well."

She leaned down and let her lips brush against Melissa's forehead, then silently slipped out of the room, closing the door behind her.

In the bed, Melissa slept, though her eyes remained open as D'Arcy watched the shadows play silently on the walls.

Teri avoided the beach as she walked back to Maplecrest, instead moving slowly along a path that wound through the patches of woods separating the estates fronting on the cove. As she came to each house, she paused, gazing up at the silhouettes that seemed to loom even larger in the moonlight. Most of them were dotted with brightly lit windows, and Teri crept across wide expanses of well-trimmed lawn to peer curiously in at the paneled walls and glowing chandeliers that seemed to fill every mansion.

Nowhere did she see anything to remind her of San Fernando and the tiny frame house in which she'd grown up.

All of it, though, had an odd familiarity about it, as if she'd come back from a long visit to a foreign land.

Here, she knew, was where she belonged.

At last she came to Maplecrest and skirted the tennis court, moving toward the large swimming pool. Suddenly, out of the darkness, she heard a low growl.

She froze for a second, her eyes searching the night around her. At last she saw a shadow that was even darker than the rest.

As she stared at it, another growl rose up from the blackness and the spot moved slightly, edging toward her.

"Blackie," she whispered to herself, feeling a twinge of annoyance at the pang of fear she'd fallen victim to a few seconds earlier. As the dog crept closer, she lashed out at it with her left foot, then felt a twinge of satisfaction as the Labrador yelped in pain and leaped away from her.

A second later, though, she heard a voice call out from a few yards away. "Blackie? Blackie!"

The dog, crouched suspiciously on the ground just far enough away to be safe from another kick, turned slightly toward the sound of the voice and uttered a sharp bark. A moment later Tag stepped out of the shadows of the pool house and strode down the path, stopping short when he recognized Teri.

Blackie, his hackles raised, pressed against Tag's legs, and once more a low growl rose from his throat. Tag reached down to soothe the dog, and Blackie yelped softly as his master's fingers touched the spot where Teri had kicked him.

"What the hell's going on?" Tag demanded, his eyes fixing on Teri. "Did you kick him?"

"Why would I do that?" Teri countered.

"Well, something happened to him. He's got a sore spot. I can feel it swelling."

Teri shrugged impatiently. "Well, what if I did? He was growling at me."

"Jeez, that's what he's supposed to do," Tag protested. "He's just protecting the property."

"Well, he could have bitten me," Teri complained. "And you

should have him locked up at night anyway—we could get sued if
he went after someone."

Tag's eyes narrowed angrily. "He's not going after anyone. All
he ever does is bark—he's never bitten anyone in his life."

"Well, he sure acted like he was going to bite me," Teri shot
back. "And if you don't do something about him, I'll tell Phyllis!"

Tag said nothing. He took Blackie's collar and led him away
toward his grandmother's house. But his mind was seething. Ever
since the minute he'd seen Teri, Blackie hadn't liked her. That
first day he'd even run away from her. And to Tag that meant
something—he'd long ago learned that if dogs didn't like someone,
there was a reason.

He paused and glanced back down the path toward the spot
where Teri had been standing, but she was gone. "Okay, boy," he
said to the dog, releasing his grip on its collar. "Go on and finish
your business. But stay away from Teri, huh? We don't want her
telling Mrs. Holloway on you, do we?" The dog bounded away
into the woods, and once more Tag turned back toward the main
house. Teri was just disappearing through the back door.

Satisfied that Blackie would get in no more trouble that night,
he headed home.

Teri glanced at the back stairs that led directly from the kitchen
to the upper floors of the house, but then walked the other way,
moving through the butler's pantry and dining room into the large
entry hall, to go up the grand staircase to the second floor. The
upstairs hallways were almost pitch-black, lit only at the head of
the stairs by a dim lamp that stood on a sideboard on the landing.
Teri paused for a moment, listening, but the house was silent—
everyone had already gone to bed. She felt a twinge of anger—
couldn't her father have waited up for her? Apparently not. But if
it had been Melissa out walking on the beach . . . she cut the
thought short and switched off the single lamp that had been left
for her, then went to her room, not turning on the light until she
was inside and the door was closed. She began taking off her
clothes, but paused as she heard a sound.

A soft, sobbing sound, which almost seemed to come from the
attic above her head.

She hesitated, then went on undressing.

The sound came again, muffled, but clearly audible.

Frowning, Teri pulled on the bathrobe Phyllis had given her and slipped out into the hall. She hesitated there, blinded by the darkness, but then her eyes adjusted to the moonlight that streamed through the enormous fanlight above the stairs' landing, and she started down the hall toward the door that led to the attic.

She paused once more at the attic door, then made up her mind. Turning the knob, she pulled the door open.

Above her the attic was nothing but a yawning black chasm. Unconsciously holding her breath, she started up the stairs, not breathing again until she had reached the top.

Her fingers groped in the darkness for the light switch she knew was there. Finding it, she snapped on the bare bulb that hung suspended from the rafters a few yards away.

She choked back a scream as she saw a ghostly white form hovering in the darkness at the far end of the big chamber beneath the house's eaves.

A moment later she began breathing again as she realized what it was—an old-fashioned dressmaker's mannequin, draped in an equally old-fashioned white dress.

She hesitated, getting her bearings, then started through the attic toward the area above her room.

There, carved out of the main part of the attic, she found a small room with a single daybed and a chest of drawers.

The room was illuminated only by the pale moonlight, but as Teri looked around it, she had a strange feeling that although no one lived here anymore, the room was not completely abandoned. Frowning in the darkness, she went to the chest and began opening its drawers.

There was an old sewing box, still containing its needles and thread, scissors and thimbles.

Other than that, the chest was empty.

And then, once again, Teri heard the soft sobbing sound.

Only this time it seemed to come from beneath her feet.

She waited where she was, and the sob came again.

As she left the little room and made her way back to the head of the attic stairs, she carefully counted her steps. Finally, glancing once more at the old mannequin with its antiquated dress, she turned off the light and returned to the second floor.

Once again she counted her steps as she walked down the long corridor. Before she had reached the area beneath the little room in the attic, her progress was blocked by a door.

Melissa's door.

Teri gazed at the door for a moment, then tentatively touched the knob. Her hand closed on it and she twisted it.

The door was locked.

She returned to her own room, closing her door behind her once more, then went to the bathroom that separated her own small room from Melissa's much larger one.

She pressed her ear against the door separating the bathroom from her half sister's room, and a moment later thought she heard the sound again.

A sob, as if a child were crying but trying not to be heard.

Teri tried the door and found it unlocked. She pulled it open an inch, and whispered through the crack.

"Melissa?"

There was no response.

She pushed the door farther open and stepped into Melissa's room. Moonlight flooding through the open windows cast a silver sheen across the bed. From the doorway Teri could see her half sister lying on her back, her eyes open.

"Melissa? Are you all right?"

Again there was no answer. Her brows knit into a slight frown, Teri crept into the room and slowly approached the bed. At last she stood next to it and gazed down at her half sister's face.

In the moonlight Melissa's skin took on a deathly pallor, her features were expressionless as her eyes gazed steadily up at the ceiling. A chill passed through Teri. For a moment she had the feeling that Melissa had died.

Then she saw the steady movement of Melissa's chest as it rose and fell with her gentle but steady breathing.

Teri reached out and touched Melissa, prodding her shoulder.

"Melissa, wake up," she whispered.

Her half sister didn't move.

Teri took a step backward, wondering if she should go and get her father. But then, as her eyes scanned the bed once more, she saw something.

It looked like a strap, emerging from beneath the sheet that covered Melissa, its end securely fastened to the bed frame.

Teri stared at the strap for a moment. Then, her hands shaking slightly, she reached out and drew the sheet away from Melissa's body.

She gasped slightly as she saw the cuffs that were bound around Melissa's wrists and her ankles.

For a moment she felt an urge to undo the straps, to release her half sister from the bonds that held her to the bed, but she changed her mind as the words of the kids on the beach that afternoon echoed in her mind. "Everyone thinks she's crazy . . ."

Was that it? Was that why Melissa was tied to her bed?

Was she crazy?

Carefully pulling the sheet back up so it covered Melissa's shoulders again, Teri backed away from the bed, then turned and hurried into the little bathroom, closing Melissa's door behind her.

And when she returned to her own room, she made sure she locked her own door to the bathroom behind her.

She lay awake in bed for a long time that night, thinking about what she'd seen.

And as she thought, an idea began to form in her mind.

Teri's dream had the perfect crystalline clarity of an autumn afternoon. In it she awoke just before dawn, far from Maplecrest. Indeed, she was back in the small house in San Fernando, the house in which she'd spent all but the first few years of her life.

The soft chime of her never-before-used travel alarm barely disturbed the quiet of the night, but she turned it off quickly, then listened for a few minutes.

The house was silent, her stepfather's soft snoring the only disturbance to the predawn silence. She got out of bed, slipped into her bathrobe, and glanced around the little bedroom. At last, slipping her hand into the pocket of her robe to make sure the strand of pearls her father had sent her last Christmas was still there, she left the room and made her way silently down the stairs, carefully stepping over the fourth one from the bottom, the one that always creaked, no matter how careful you were.

At the foot of the stairs she paused again, listening, but the silence of the house was still undisturbed. From here, indeed, she couldn't even hear Tom MacIver's snoring.

She turned through the dining room, then into the kitchen and out onto the service porch, where the washer and dryer stood side by side above the stairs to the basement. Moving quickly even in the darkness, she went down the cellar stairs, into her stepfather's workshop. There was wood everywhere—some of it ready to be put together into a bookcase he was building, other pieces just scraps, piled here and there against the concrete walls of the subterranean chamber.

At last she came to the furnace, and, groping in the darkness, found what she was looking for.

A pile of rags, rags she'd made sure were well-soaked with linseed oil only that afternoon. She placed the rags on the floor next to a pile of wood.

Then she took a match from the box that always sat on her stepfather's workbench and struck it.

She held the match to the rags. A second later the oil that had been absorbed in the cotton fibers ignited, bursting into flames with a speed that made Teri lurch backward. She stared at the fire for a moment, as if fascinated by it, then shook the match out, tossing it away.

As the flames grew and spread to the wood around them, Teri moved to the foot of the stairs. After one more look at the spreading fire, she hurried up the stairs, back into the service porch. But instead of moving on, going out the back door into the yard, she went into the kitchen instead, then the dining room.

Then she waited at the foot of the main stairs, waited for the fire to take hold, waited for the flames to begin engulfing the house.

It seemed to take forever, but finally she could hear a faint crackling in the basement, and then she began to sniff the first faint wisps of smoke creeping through the floor beneath her feet.

Still she lingered.

At last the floor of the dining room itself began to glow, and then the fire burst through, spreading quickly. The crackling grew to a roar, and then, as more flames began to eat through the living room floor, Teri bolted to the front door. A moment later she was in the front yard, her bathrobe clutched tightly around her neck. She turned to watch as the flames rampaged through the first floor and began to creep upward.

Around her, lights started to come on in the neighbors' houses, but Teri was barely aware of them as she watched the flames advance through her home.

At last she heard her mother scream, the sound instantly lost in the roar of the blaze. She moved across the lawn to the driveway, where she looked up to see her parents' window.

Her mother was there, sitting on the ledge, swinging her legs over the windowsill.

Then she jumped, and the spread she'd wrapped herself in caught on something.

She was falling, her head striking the pavement.

Teri ran, screaming, to her mother, and knelt beside her, to take her mother's bleeding head in her arms.

Only this time her mother wasn't dead.

This time her mother was staring up at her, her eyes accusing her, her lips forming the terrible words.

"Why? Why did you do this?"

Rage rose in Teri. This wasn't the way it was supposed to be! Her mother wasn't supposed to survive at all!

Her mother was supposed to be dead!

Her fury rising inside her like a monster, she raised her fist and smashed it down into her mother's face.

And woke up, her clenched fist smashing into the pillow where only a split second earlier her mother's head had been.

She lay still for a few moments, willing the dream to release her from its grip, the pounding of her heart slowly returning to its normal pace. Slowly, reality began to creep back into her mind.

She wasn't on the driveway in San Fernando; she was in her bed at Maplecrest, and the sun outside was shining brightly, and she could hear the lapping of the surf on the beach.

Her mother was dead, and no one had found out what she had done.

She was safe.

An hour later she awoke once more, this time not from a recurrence of the dream, but because of a shout from somewhere outside the house. She got out of bed and went to the window. On the tennis court, just beyond the pool, she could see her father playing tennis.

Playing tennis with Melissa.

A brief spasm of the anger she'd felt in the dream seized her for a moment. Her father should be playing tennis with *her*, not with Melissa. That was the way it was supposed to be, the way she'd planned it.

She'd dreamed about coming home for so many years; dreamed about the immense house facing the sea, and the big room she would have, and all the other things her mother had walked away from.

And she certainly hadn't planned on sharing any of it with a half sister, especially not one who had taken her home and her father and everything else she should have had.

Her mind went back to the strange scene she'd witnessed in Melissa's room last night, and the idea that had begun to form in her head just before she'd gone to sleep.

Turning away from the window, she unlocked the bathroom door and went through to Melissa's room. She glanced around, uncertain of what she was looking for, but knowing with a deep certainty that somewhere in here there was something she could use.

She went to the little vanity that stood against the wall between two of the windows and began opening its drawers.

In the middle one she found a slim black box, and knew even before she opened it what was inside. Still, she opened the box to stare at the single strand of pearls that lay on its satin bed.

A single strand of pearls that was identical to her own.

Another wave of anger washed over her. Melissa even had the pearls, even though she was almost two years younger than she was. Closing the box, she put it back where she'd found it, then went through the rest of the vanity.

Nothing.

At last she went to the big chest on the opposite wall and began going through its drawers.

In the second drawer, hidden beneath a pile of socks, she found what she was looking for.

It was a small diary, bound in black leather, with Melissa's initials embossed in gold on its cover. Teri opened the book and quickly began scanning its pages.

All the entries in the diary seemed to be written as if they were letters to someone named D'Arcy. But if they were letters to some friend of Melissa's, why were they in a diary?

Had she given the diary itself a name?

But then as she began to read, she also began to understand.

D'Arcy, she was almost certain, didn't actually exist at all, nor was it a name she'd assigned to the diary.

Rather, it seemed as if D'Arcy was someone Melissa had made up.

An imaginary friend.

Teri scanned some of the pages quickly, turning several of them at a time. Much of what she found was almost illegible, scrawled in an awkward script that looked as if a five-year-old might have done it. But from what she could decipher, it became clear that to Melissa, at least, her friend had become real:

> . . . I wanted to thank you for coming to help me last night. Mom was real mad at me, and I don't know what I'd have done without you . . .

> . . . I hope Mama didn't hurt you too much last night. I don't know why she was so mad, but I guess you know how she is. Did she hit you? I hate it when she does that. If she ever did it to me, I think I'd die . . .

Teri was still reading, trying to figure out what it all meant, when she heard the door to the hall open. She dropped the book back into the drawer and was about to shut it when she heard Cora Peterson's apologetic voice.

"Oh, I'm sorry, I thought—" And then her tone shifted as she saw it wasn't Melissa in the room at all. "Teri? Why, what are you doing in here?"

Teri's mind raced, then her fingers closed on a pair of Melissa's socks.

Turning, she smiled at the old housekeeper. "I ran out of socks," she explained, leaning on the drawer to close it. "I just came in to borrow a pair of Melissa's." She composed her features into an anxious expression. "She won't mind, will she?"

Cora's eyes, which had been fixed suspiciously on Teri, cleared. "Well, of course not," she said, clucking her tongue. "And I'll just speak to your father—it seems to me you ought to be doing some shopping. You can't keep wearing the same clothes over and over again, can you, now?"

Teri suppressed a sigh of relief and smiled gratefully at the housekeeper. "Would you?" she asked. "I just hate asking for anything. I mean, everyone's been so nice to me . . ."

Cora gently silenced her. "Now, you mustn't think that," she admonished. "Why, you belong here just as much as anyone else does, and you should have everything you need." The housekeeper began making up Melissa's bed, chattering along as she worked.

But Teri had stopped listening, for she was still reflecting on Cora's earlier words.

"You should have everything you need . . ."

And I will have, Teri thought to herself a few minutes later as she left Melissa's room and returned to her own.

I'll have everything I need, and everything I want.

CHAPTER

8

"Look at that! Isn't it the most gorgeous skirt you've ever seen?"

Melissa gazed through the shop window at the white cotton skirt splashed with a flowered pattern in a blue that exactly matched the shade of Teri's eyes. It was at least the sixth skirt they'd seen so far that would look perfect on her half sister, and so far they hadn't even gone into any of the shops.

They'd been in the village for almost an hour, wandering from store to store, enjoying the cool shade of the huge maple trees that formed a broad canopy over the streets and sidewalks. In almost every window they'd seen something—a skirt like the one they were looking at now, or a blouse or sweater, maybe only a pair of shoes—that seemed to cry out for Teri to try it on. But Teri had so far resisted going into any of the shops.

"I can't stand to think about how much they must cost," she'd explained. "Out in California, I used to spend whole days wandering around in the mall, pretending I could afford anything I saw."

"Well, now you can," Melissa replied, grasping her half sister's hand and pulling her toward the door. "Didn't you hear what

Mama said? You're supposed to be buying clothes, not just drooling over them. Now come on."

She pushed through the door to the shop. A moment later the
owner, a chic-looking woman in her thirties, stood up from her
chair behind a small desk toward the back of the store and strode
toward them.

"Melissa!" she said. "I've been wondering when you'd come in.
Your mother called and told me to let you charge whatever you
want today." She winked conspiratorially. "Stretching out your
birthday?"

Melissa flushed and shook her head. "It's not for me," she
explained. "It's for my sister. Well, she's not really my sister.
We're half sisters. This is Teri MacIver." She turned to Teri.
"This is Polly Corcoran, but everyone calls her Corky."

Teri smiled and held out her hand. "I'm very pleased to meet you."

Corky Corcoran's eyes sparkled as she shook Teri's proffered
hand. "Well, there certainly isn't any mistaking whose daughter
you are, is there?" she asked. Her smile faded away as a sad frown
creased her forehead. "I always loved your mother so much—I
used to pretend I was named after her, even though it wasn't true.
I—I'm so sorry about what happened."

Teri's own smile ebbed away as she cast her eyes toward the
floor and managed a slight nod. "Th-Thank you," she murmured.
"I still can hardly believe it. Without Daddy . . ." Her voice
trailed off and there was an awkward moment before Corky
suddenly clapped her hands together and forced her expression
back into a cordial smile.

"Well, we're not here to dwell on our sorrows, are we?" she
asked, wincing at the false brightness that had come into her
voice, but determined not to make Teri any more uncomfortable
than she already had. "Did you see something in the window you
liked?"

Teri nodded. "The white skirt? The one with the blue flowers?"

Corky's smile broadened. "Perfect," she declared. "In fact I was
just thinking about the very same skirt for you myself." Her eyes
expertly scanned Teri's figure. "A size four?" Teri nodded, and
Corky disappeared into a back room.

While Corky was gone, Teri glanced around the shop. It was
set up more like a living room than a store, with only a few

garments on display, and those laid casually over the backs of chairs or hanging from mannequins discreetly posed in the corners.

It was exactly the kind of shop Teri had seen before, except today she was not on the outside looking in. She felt a shiver of anticipation as she waited for Corky to reappear with the skirt.

Five minutes later the shop's proprietor returned from the back room, her arms laden with half a dozen items. "I thought you might like to try a blouse or two with the skirt, and perhaps a sweater," she said, spreading the garments on a mahogany library table for Teri's inspection. Teri's eyes immediately went to a silk blouse whose color perfectly matched the blue flowers on the skirt, and as she picked it up, Corky nodded approvingly. "I thought you might like that." She nodded toward a changing room concealed behind a three-paneled oriental screen, and when Teri had disappeared with the skirt and blouse, turned her attention to Melissa. "What about you?" she asked. "I have some beautiful things for fall that are just your colors."

Melissa hesitated, recalling her mother's words just before they'd left the house. "Now remember, Melissa, you're *not* shopping for yourself. You have all the things you need—Lord knows your father's bought you more than you ever wear anyway—and today you're shopping for Teri. And for heaven's sake," she'd added, "try not to talk Teri into all the drab things you like so much. With her coloring, she can wear all the wonderful colors that only make you look like you have the flu." Now, the words still stinging, even though she tried to tell herself her mother hadn't meant them to sound mean, she shook her head. "I—I don't think so," she murmured.

Before Corky could urge her any further, Teri emerged from the dressing room. "Well?" she asked Melissa. "What do you think? Is it just perfect, or what?"

Melissa gazed at her half sister, doing her best to put down the feelings of envy that rose unbidden from somewhere in the deep recesses of her mind. But when she saw the eager look in Teri's eyes, the feeling died away. It wasn't Teri's fault that clothes seemed to fit her as if they'd been made just for her. The blouse, a soft blue that seemed to turn Teri's blond hair almost flaxen, had full sleeves that were caught at the wrists with tight cuffs, and its bodice clung to Teri's bosom with just the right draping to set off her figure yet not appear too revealing. The skirt flowed down from her waist in a gentle line to a point just below her knees. Altogether it was, indeed, perfect.

"It's beautiful," Melissa murmured.

"How much is it?" Teri asked.

Corky smiled. "The skirt's only one hundred and sixty, but the blouse is a bit more."

Teri's eyes widened and she glanced nervously at Melissa. "How much more?" she asked, her voice quavering.

"Two fifty," Corky replied. "It *is* silk, after all."

Teri's eyes, already reflecting disappointment, shifted back to Melissa. "It's too much, isn't it?" she asked, and Melissa was sure she heard a pleading note in her voice.

Melissa turned to Corky. "Can I call Mom and ask her if it's okay?"

"The phone's on my desk," she said. "But I already talked to your mother, and she said anything you wanted was fine. And if anyone knows what clothes cost these days," she added, her brows arching slightly and her voice dropping as if she were taking the girls into her confidence, "it's your mother."

"Then we'll take them," Teri declared, her expression clearing as she went back to the table and began inspecting another blouse.

Half an hour later they left the shop with two more skirts, five blouses, and a sweater neatly packed in cardboard boxes, each of them with Corky's champagne-bottle logo emblazoned on its top in gold foil.

"Let's go back to that other place," Teri suggested as they started down the street once again. "The one with the sports clothes. This stuff's all wonderful, but I still need tennis clothes and things to wear at the club during the day."

"You mean PlayThings?" Melissa asked.

Teri nodded. "They had some great bathing suits in the window."

They walked a block down the street, and soon Teri was busy in the changing room, trying on bathing suits and shorts, knit shirts and cotton slacks. When she was finally done, a stack of garments lay on the counter. They had all looked perfect on her, and they all were exactly the kinds of clothes the other kids in Secret Cove were wearing. The clerk finished writing up the bill, then looked up at Teri. "Will that be all?" she asked.

Teri was about to nod, then changed her mind as she saw
Melissa look longingly at a magenta jogging suit with black stripes
running diagonally across the top and repeated in a vertical stripe
down the legs of the pants. "Why don't you try it on?" she asked.

Melissa reddened and shook her head. "It wouldn't look right
on me."

"How do you know?" Teri argued. "You can't tell anything
unless you put it on." Without waiting for Melissa to reply, she
turned to the clerk. "Do you have that in her size?"

The clerk surveyed Melissa doubtfully. "Well, I don't know.
She's sort of an off-size. But let me take a look." A few minutes
later the clerk returned from a storeroom and handed a hanger to
Melissa. "Why don't you give this a try?" she suggested.

Two minutes later Melissa came out of the dressing room and
stared at herself dolefully in the mirror. To her own eye the pants
seemed a little too tight and the top a size too large.

And the color—the color that had looked so wonderful until
she'd put it on, now seemed to give her complexion an odd,
almost yellowish hue. "Oh, God," she groaned, turning away
from the mirror to gaze at Teri. "Why do I even try?"

"But it looks great," Teri told her. "If we can just get the top a
size smaller, it will be perfect."

"But it won't," Melissa protested. "Look at me—it makes me
look like I've got some kind of disease."

"Oh, it doesn't, either," Teri declared. "Besides, remember
what your mom said? You're not supposed to get anything drab."

"I'm not supposed to get anything at all," Melissa reminded
her. "I already have enough clothes."

"Well, maybe you do, but they don't look right." Melissa's eyes
clouded with hurt, and Teri instantly apologized. "I don't mean
they look bad," she said. "But they aren't very stylish. I mean,
look at the way the other kids dress—they always wear white
shorts, and polo shirts, and that kind of stuff." She moved over to
a table stacked high with knit shirts and began riffling through
them, pulling out one in a bright lime green and another in
mustard yellow. "You could wear these," she said, holding the
green one up against Melissa's chest.

Melissa gazed at the shirts wistfully, comparing them in her
mind with the browns and dark greens she always picked for

herself. But try as she would, she simply couldn't see herself in any of the bright colors. "Try on this one," Teri told her, pushing the shirt into her hands and handing her a pair of white shorts. "And while you're changing, I'll see if they have the jogging top in a smaller size."

A few minutes later Melissa emerged from the dressing room and once again stared at herself in the mirror.

The shirt seemed baggy on her, while the shorts stretched too tightly over her hips, making her look even plumper than she already was. Teri, reading her eyes, turned to the clerk.

"Don't you have something with pleats?" she asked.

Twenty minutes later, over Melissa's objections, Teri added a pair of white shorts, two of the polo shirts, a bright red bathing suit, and the jogging outfit to the pile of clothes already on the counter.

"Can I charge it?" she asked. "I'm Teri MacIver—Mr. Holloway is my father."

The clerk smiled. "Of course," she said. "Mrs. Holloway called this morning—she said you're to have anything you want."

Teri stared at the pile of clothes, then her eyes wandered to a tennis outfit she'd looked at earlier. Finally, seeing Melissa's eyes bulge as she read the total on the cash register, she shook her head. "I guess that's all," she said. The clerk wrote up a charge slip for the clothes and handed it to Teri along with a pen.

Teri gazed at the figure at the bottom of the slip. Together with what she'd bought at Corky's, the total came to more than three thousand dollars. For just a fraction of a second she thought of the two hundred dollars she'd had to spend on school clothes the year before.

But that was a long time ago, she told herself, putting the thought out of her mind.

With a feeling of intense pleasure, she took the pen from the clerk and scrawled her signature across the bottom of the charge slip.

Phyllis Holloway glared at her husband, her eyes glittering with anger. "But isn't that what we have lawyers for?" she demanded.

Charles removed his reading glasses and pressed the thumb and forefinger of his right hand against the bridge of his nose, partly in an effort to relieve the headache that was growing along with the argument with his wife, and partly to give himself a moment's respite from that same argument. Finally he sighed, put his glasses back on, and picked up a stack of papers from his desk. "I've already told you—it's a simple matter, and I can take care of it myself. I suppose I *could* call a firm in L.A. to handle it, but why bother? I am, after all, a lawyer myself—"

"Oh, come on," Phyllis sniffed. "You haven't practiced a day in your life, and you know it."

Charles's jaw tightened, and, not for the first time, he wondered why he stayed with Phyllis. He couldn't remember the last time she'd spoken an affectionate word to him—at least when they were alone. Of course, in public, she was the image of the loving wife. She never failed to stay close to him when they were out together, never let an evening go by without telling whomever they were with about her wonderful husband.

But it was all an act, for when they were alone together, she rarely spoke to him at all, except to complain about one thing or another—if it wasn't one of Cora's shortcomings, or Melissa's, it was usually one of his own.

Had she always been like this?

He didn't know, for when he'd first met her, when his relationship with Polly was already breaking up, she'd seemed perfect.

Bright and vivacious, she'd been like none of the girls he'd grown up with, certainly nothing at all like Polly. Where Polly had had a natural sense of reserve, Phyllis had seemed a free spirit, doting on his daughter but always ready to take time to chat with him. And after Polly had left, it seemed the most natural thing in the world for them to come together, both of them mourning the loss of Teri.

When Phyllis had become pregnant, he'd been more than pleased to marry her. And for the first six months, until Melissa was born, everything had been fine. Then everything changed. Indeed, it had changed from the first moment Phyllis had seen her daughter. She'd looked down into Melissa's tiny face, framed by wisps of brown hair, and her eyes had filled with tears.

"She was supposed to be blond," Phyllis had said, looking up at Charles. "I wanted her to be just like Teri."

Charles had picked up the baby, snuggling her close to his chest and kissing her forehead. "But she can't be just like Teri," he'd protested. "Teri was Polly's daughter. Missy is ours."

Phyllis had said nothing more, at least not directly. But over the years, Charles had always known that for her, Melissa never measured up to the standards set by Teri.

Nor, apparently, had he met her expectations as a husband.

On the other hand, almost from the moment he'd married her, Phyllis had changed.

Her effervescence had vanished, and now Charles sometimes wondered if it had ever been there in the first place, or if he'd simply imagined it, the desire acting as father to the thought.

Within a year Phyllis had transformed herself from the pretty, if not quite beautiful, young nurse from Philadelphia, into her own version of a woman born into the Crowd.

The Secret Cove Crowd.

She shopped at all the right stores and wore all the right clothes.

In New York, where they spent most of the year, she went to all the right restaurants and served on all the right committees.

When, that is, she was invited to serve on the committees, which, though he'd never told her and never would, was only after he himself had a few words with the other women's husbands in the privacy of one of their clubs.

But although she wore the right clothes and went to the right places, she somehow had never quite fit in.

Charles, of course, understood it perfectly—with the Secret Cove Crowd, you didn't simply fit in.

You were born in.

And Phyllis hadn't been.

But she'd never stopped trying to find herself a place in the Crowd, never stopped trying to become the woman his first wife had been.

Nor had she understood that one of the reasons he'd married her was that she *wasn't* Polly.

Still, the marriage had endured, for Charles had long ago decided that he could tolerate any amount of unhappiness in his marriage, as long as it meant he had Melissa with him.

For Melissa, to Charles, was perfect.

If she had any shortcomings, he didn't see them, or chose to overlook them. He found his daughter's almost painful shyness to be an endearing quality, and if she didn't fit in well with the other kids in the Crowd, that was all right with him.

Despite what his wife thought, his private opinion was that Melissa wasn't missing much. He was sure she would learn a lot more from the books she devoured than from listening to the idle chatter of a lot of kids with nothing to do except feel snobbish about their families.

So he tolerated the marriage, rather than risk losing Melissa as he'd lost Teri. But sometimes—times like today—it was not easy.

"But it's so *thoughtless* of you," he heard Phyllis complaining. "We've been invited to dinner at the Stevenses' day after tomorrow, and now you want me to cancel at the last minute, just so you can fly out to California."

"You hardly have to cancel," Charles observed. "It's not formal, and you know as well as I do that Eleanor always has extra men around. I don't know where she finds them, but they're always there."

Phyllis's eyes blazed with anger. "So now you don't care who I go out with?"

A movement outside the window caught Charles's eye, and he saw Teri and Melissa walking up the driveway, their arms filled with boxes. "Look," he said, "can't we deal with this some other time? The girls are coming in, and—"

"No, we can't!" Phyllis shouted. "How dare you? Do you know how hard I've had to work to get that invitation from Eleanor Stevens? Do you know who's going to be there? The governor, that's who! And I do not intend to go either by myself or on the arm of one of Eleanor's prissy decorators! If I'd known how much trouble all this was going to be—"

Suddenly Charles had enough. His fist slammed down on the table and his eyes fixed darkly on his wife. "That's it!" he exclaimed. "Look! All this isn't my fault—I didn't plan on Teri coming to live with us any more than you did! But she's here, and the least we can both do is make the best of it. And I'm not just her father, in case you didn't know. I'm also the trustee of her estate."

"Estate!" Phyllis fairly spat. "My God, everyone knows Polly gave away every cent she had. There isn't any estate!"

"There's actually more than you might think. Tom had some insurance, and the house itself was worth a quarter of a million."

Phyllis's lips curled into a sneer. "In California that only buys a slum, doesn't it?"

Exhausted by the argument, Charles shook his head. "All right," he said. "Do what you want. Go to the party alone or go with someone else. Or don't go at all. But I have an obligation to Teri, and I intend to carry it out. So just drop it, all right? It doesn't matter what you think—I'm flying to Los Angeles tomorrow."

Phyllis opened her mouth as if to carry on the argument, but changed her mind when she saw the look in her husband's eyes. She knew there was a point beyond which she shouldn't push him. But still, the idea of having to show up at the Stevenses' alone, feeling everyone watching her, and wondering if Charles was really away on business or had simply not wanted to come . . .

They might even think he'd found another woman and was getting ready to leave her.

No, better not to go at all than risk what the gossip might be.

Silently, she turned her back on her husband and walked out of the room, not noticing the look of relief that came over his face as she left.

At the foot of the stairs Teri heard the last few words of the argument between her father and her stepmother, and a flash of anger burned in her mind.

An obligation?

Was that all she was to her father? Just someone he had to deal with because she was his daughter?

Then she felt Melissa's eyes on her and heard her half sister's voice, soft and sympathetic. "He didn't mean that," Melissa was saying. "It was just a fight with Mom. It—It happens all the time."

Teri carefully took control of the anger within her, and when she turned to face Melissa, her eyes were damp and her chin quivered slightly. "It's all right," she breathed. "I—I just hope someday he'll learn to love me as much as he loves you, that's all."

Melissa impulsively dropped the boxes she was holding and threw her arms around Teri. "He will," she promised. "I know he will. He'll love you just as much as I do."

Teri accepted the embrace in silence.

"I don't see why we don't use the club on days like this,"

Phyllis said. It was the middle of the afternoon, and she sat in the shade of an umbrella next to the pool. A few feet away Charles was sprawled on his back on a chaise longue, reading yesterday's *Wall Street Journal*. Teri was stretched out in the sun, while Melissa swam up and down the pool in a vain attempt to exercise off enough pounds to make her new bathing suit fit her properly.

She hadn't wanted to wear it at all, but Teri had insisted that it looked fine, and when she'd finally worked up her courage to leave the pool house, her mother had agreed with Teri. "It's so nice to see you wearing some color for a change. And if you could just lose five pounds—"

"She looks fine just the way she is," Charles had interrupted, but the remark had already sunk in, and ever since then Melissa had been in the pool, valiantly attempting to achieve at least fifty laps.

"Did you hear me, Charles?" Phyllis asked.

Charles nodded absently. "What's the point? Our own pool's almost as big as theirs, and not nearly as crowded."

"But all our friends are there," Phyllis went on. "It seems as though we never see anyone."

Charles put the paper down. "If you want to go, you're certainly welcome to. I just can't see putting up with that mob."

The phone in the pool house rang, and he stood up, but Phyllis stopped him. "Let Cora get it," she said. "Lord knows, it's not as if she does much anymore. I think we're going to have to start thinking about getting someone else, Charles. I know how—"

This time it was her own words that were interrupted as Cora herself stepped out the back door and called across the lawn.

"For you, ma'am. Mrs. Van Arsdale."

Instantly, Phyllis left her chair and hurried into the pool house, where she picked up the phone. "Yes, Lenore?"

"Hello, Phyllis." Lenore Van Arsdale's voice came over the line with a cool tone of confidence that Phyllis had never been able to master. "The most awful thing has happened, and I do hope you'll forgive me."

Phyllis held her breath, certain she was about to be told she would be replaced on the Social Committee.

"I suppose you know Brett's having some of his friends for a bonfire on the beach tomorrow night?"

Phyllis's jaw tightened. No, she certainly didn't know any such thing. "Why, yes," she said, as casually as she could. "I think I heard one of the girls mention it."

"Well, I've just discovered that somehow Melissa's name got left off the invitation list. I know it's short notice, but is it too late to invite her? And, of course, Brett would love to have Teri come, too."

Suddenly Phyllis understood. It wasn't Melissa who was being invited at all.

It was Teri.

She'd barely met the kids, but already they were taking her in, including her in their group.

Almost involuntarily her eyes went to the window. Teri was sitting up now, listening to Melissa, who was squatting on the terrace at her half sister's feet, like an overgrown puppy dog, her hair, still soaking wet, hanging limply down her back. Dear God, Phyllis thought, why can't she even learn to sit like a normal person? Does she have to squat down like a peasant? No wonder the Cove kids didn't want her around.

"I'm sure they'd both be delighted to come tomorrow night," she said into the phone. "And it's so kind of you to include Teri."

"I'm looking forward to seeing her again," Lenore replied. "I understand she's just like Polly."

They chatted on for a few more minutes, until Lenore finally pleaded other calls to make and hung up. But before she went back out to the pool, Phyllis found herself gazing once more through the window.

They were still together, side by side.

The daughter she'd always wanted, and the daughter she'd actually had.

But now, miraculously, Teri had come home to her, and perhaps things were finally going to work out the way she'd always hoped they would.

Unless Melissa ruined things for Teri, Phyllis thought, the same way she'd ruined things for her.

She stepped out into the bright sunlight, and as the two girls glanced up at her, she smiled. "You two," she announced, "have just been invited out tomorrow night."

Now Charles put his paper aside once more. "What's going on?"

"Brett's having a bonfire on the beach tomorrow night, and Lenore wants both our girls to go."

Teri's face lit up, but then her smile faltered as she heard her father's next words.

"Isn't it a little soon for her to start going to parties?" he asked worriedly.

Teri searched her mind for something to say, some way to argue with him, but then her stepmother came to her aid. "Apparently, Lenore Van Arsdale doesn't think so," she said. "And I can't say I do, either. It's not going to do Teri any good to sit around here with us. She has to start making her own friends."

Teri's eyes fixed on her father, who seemed to consider the matter forever before he finally nodded. "Well, I don't suppose it can do any harm." Then he turned to Melissa. "What do you think, Missy? Does it sound like fun?"

Melissa bit her lower lip, remembering her birthday party. The same kids who had been there would be at the bonfire tomorrow night.

The same kids who had all but ignored her on the beach yesterday.

"I—I don't know," she said finally, unwilling to tell her parents what she was thinking. "I—Well—"

Charles, sensing his daughter's nervousness, smiled at her encouragingly. "If you don't want to go, just say so," he told her. "Just because someone invites you, it doesn't mean you have to go."

"I—I'd really rather stay home," Melissa stammered.

"Then that's what you'll do," Charles declared. He went back to his paper, not noticing the look of annoyance that crossed his wife's face.

"Perhaps she'll change her mind," Phyllis said, her eyes fixing on Melissa.

Though Charles, engrossed in his paper, failed to see his youngest daughter flinch as his wife spoke the words, Teri did not.

CHAPTER

9

Melissa sat silently at the table that evening, staring at the food on her plate, willing herself to eat it. But she kept feeling her mother's eyes on her, and even though nothing had been said, her mother's anger still hung over her like a dark cloud, making it impossible for her to eat. But she knew she had to finish her dinner—if she didn't, her mother would make her sit at the table for at least an hour, listening to a lecture about her bad manners and how she was hurting Cora's feelings by not eating the meal the housekeeper had worked so hard to prepare.

She sank her fork into the steak which appeared to have somehow grown even larger as it sat on her plate, carefully cut a small piece off, and put it in her mouth.

Her throat seemed to close even as she chewed the meat, and for a moment she was afraid she wouldn't be able to swallow it at all. But finally it went down, and she started on the next piece. Surreptitiously, she glanced around the table; everyone else had already finished, and her father was laying his knife and fork in the center of the plate and wiping his lips with his napkin. Smiling at her, he pushed his chair back a few inches.

"What does everyone think about going to a movie tonight?" he asked.

Instinctively, Melissa's eyes flicked to her mother, and for a moment she thought perhaps everything was going to be all right after all. But then Phyllis's eyes met hers, and she saw that she had not yet been forgiven for saying she didn't want to go to the bonfire tomorrow night. But what was the big deal? They didn't even really want her to come—it was Teri they wanted. So why couldn't Teri go alone?

Her thoughts were interrupted by her mother's voice. As she heard the words, she felt an icy knot of fear forming in her stomach.

"Why don't you and Teri go?" Phyllis said to Charles. "The two of you haven't been able to spend much time together alone, and I think it would be nice if Melissa and I had an evening to ourselves. Just the two of us."

Melissa's eyes darted to her father. "Can't I go, too?" she pleaded. "Please?"

Before Charles could say anything, Phyllis spoke again, this time addressing her daughter. "Melissa, you're being very, very selfish. You've been absolutely monopolizing your father. You mustn't forget that he's Teri's father, too. And," she added, the hard look in her eyes belying both her words and her smile, "the two of us will have such fun together."

Melissa wanted to argue with her mother, plead with her father, but she knew it would only make things worse than they already were. Because once her father and Teri were gone . . .

She forced the thought out of her mind, concentrating instead on making herself finish the food on her plate. "Besides," she heard her mother go on, repeating the words she'd heard so often before, "you haven't finished your dinner yet, and you know the rules. We eat what's put before us, whether we like it or not. You can't expect to be invited to nice places if you're going to be rude to your hostess."

Doing her best to shut the words out of her mind, Melissa attacked her steak once again, cutting the pieces as small as she could, forcing them down one by one. When her father leaned over to kiss her good-bye before he and Teri left for the movie, she wanted to cry, but held back her tears as she heard his murmured words.

"Your mother's right, sweetheart. I know it's hard to eat when you're not hungry, but it's impolite not to finish what's on your plate." He gave her an encouraging hug, and she wanted to throw her arms around him and beg him to take her with him, but knew it would do no good.

Her mother had decided she would stay home, and there was no point in arguing.

Arguing would only make it worse.

Twenty minutes later, under her mother's watchful eyes, she finally finished her dinner. Around her the other empty plates still sat on the table. She was expected to clear them and then help Cora with the dishes. Silently, afraid that whatever she might say would only make her mother angrier, she rose to her feet.

"What do we say?" Phyllis instantly demanded.

Melissa froze, then remembered. "M-May I be excused?"

Phyllis nodded curtly, and Melissa gratefully began stacking the dishes. A moment later she backed through the door separating the butler's pantry from the kitchen. Cora, who'd already finished all the dishes except those that had been left on the table for Melissa to clear, took the stack of plates from Melissa's hands. "I guess dinner wasn't very good tonight, was it?" she said.

"It was fine, Cora. I just wasn't very hungry."

"Well, I know how that goes." Cora sighed, putting the plates into the sink. "Sometimes I have days when the very thought of food just makes me sick to my stomach. And it seems to me a body shouldn't be forced to eat food it doesn't want."

Melissa picked up a dish towel and began drying the silverware as Cora placed it in the rack on the sink. Melissa cast a longing eye on the dishwasher under the counter, but knew better than to suggest they use it. On evenings like this, when she was being punished, the use of the dishwasher was strictly forbidden, even for Cora.

"She has to learn to work," her mother had said more than once. "I won't have a spoiled child in the house."

Melissa had just picked up the last plate from the drainer when the door from the butler's pantry flew open, crashing loudly against the kitchen wall. Melissa jumped, then froze as she felt the plate slip out of her grip and shatter on the floor.

There was a slight gasp from Cora, whose eyes instantly went to the door where Phyllis now stood, staring coldly at her daughter. "It's all right, honey," the housekeeper said, stooping down to pick up the shards of china. "Those things happen to us all."

"Don't, Cora." Phyllis's words, though spoken quietly, held a note of authority that made the housekeeper straighten up before she'd touched the broken plate. "The only way Melissa is going to learn not to be clumsy is to take responsibility for her own messes." Cora hesitated for a moment, as if she weren't sure what to do, and Phyllis spoke again. "That will be all for tonight, Cora. Melissa will take care of the rest. You may go."

Wordlessly, knowing better than to argue with her employer, Cora took off her apron and hung it on a peg by the back door. A moment later Melissa, her heart thumping with fear, was alone with her mother.

Phyllis continued to regard her daughter coldly. "I'm afraid we'll have to have one of our little talks, Melissa," she said after a silence that seemed to Melissa to have gone on forever. "Clean up this mess, then wait for me in your room."

Her eyes blurring with tears, Melissa began picking up the pieces of shattered plate. She worked as slowly as she dared, but finally the floor was clean, as were the sink and counter top.

She could put it off no longer.

She went up to her room, and waited for her mother.

As the door opened and Phyllis stepped into the room, Melissa's eyes went first to her mother's hands.

They were empty. But then she remembered. If her mother was going to bind her to the bed, she wouldn't do it now. She'd wait until later, after her father had already gone to bed.

Phyllis closed the door, leaning against it for a moment as she regarded her daughter, who was cowering on the bed. She hated using the word, even to herself. And yet she knew that that was exactly what Melissa did.

She cowered.

If the child only had some spirit!

She discarded the thought. Melissa had never had any spirit

and never would. But the least she could do was learn to behave properly and stop embarrassing her mother.

"Stand up, Melissa," Phyllis commanded.

Obediently, Melissa scrambled off the bed and stood up straight.

Phyllis eyed Melissa's clothes with distaste. Teri had appeared for dinner that evening in one of the new outfits she'd bought that day, but Melissa was still wearing the same worn pair of jeans she'd put on after her swim that afternoon, together with a T-shirt that had long ago lost whatever color it might have started with.

"Where are the new clothes Teri picked out for you?" Phyllis asked, her voice deceptively even as she tried to control the same anger that welled up inside her whenever she laid eyes on her daughter.

"I—In my dresser," Melissa whispered.

"What?" Phyllis asked. "Talk so people can hear you, Melissa!"

"I said they're in my dresser," Melissa repeated, her throat threatening to close with each word she spoke.

"Why didn't you wear them tonight?"

Melissa's tongue ran nervously over her lips, and her eyes scanned the room as if she were looking for some sort of refuge.

"I—They don't look right on me," she finally said. "They don't fit me very well."

Phyllis's nostrils flared and her lips tightened. "Nothing fits you very well, Melissa. Why do you think that is?"

Melissa quailed from the words, but knew she had to answer.

"I—I'm too fat," she said, her eyes blurring with tears once again.

"And?" Phyllis pressed.

Melissa swallowed the lump that was rising in her throat. "And I don't stand up as straight as I should," she said, forcing herself to repeat the horrid catechism her mother had drilled into her for as long as she could remember.

Phyllis's eyes bored into the trembling child. "And whose fault is that?" Melissa stared at the floor, but said nothing. Phyllis took a step forward, and Melissa pressed closer to the bed. "Whose?" Phyllis demanded once again.

"Mine." The word issued from Melissa's throat like the dying gasp of a tiny bird, but finally she looked up at her mother. "It's my fault, Mama," she went on, the words suddenly tumbling from her mouth in a babbling stream. "I eat too much, and I eat the wrong things, and I spend too much time reading. I should play with the other kids more, and spend more time at the club."

"And why don't you?" Phyllis demanded. "Why don't you do all the things the other children do? Why do you want to make me ashamed of you?"

"I—I don't know," Melissa wailed. She felt her tears threatening to overwhelm her now, and wanted nothing more than to throw herself on the bed, curl up, and close the world out. But she couldn't do that.

Not now.

Not yet.

She had to stay where she was, and keep facing her mother, and try not to let the words hurt her.

Help me, she cried out in her mind. *Help me, D'Arcy. Don't leave me by myself. Please . . .*

"Get your new clothes out of the dresser, Melissa," Phyllis told her.

Silently calling out to D'Arcy once more, Melissa moved to the dresser and took out the stack of new clothes that Teri had chosen for her. As her mother directed, she placed them on the bed.

"The white shorts," Phyllis finally said. "Put on the white shorts and the green top."

Her heart fluttering, Melissa stripped off her jeans and T-shirt, then pulled the shorts on and struggled to get the knit shirt over her head, finally managing to pull it down over her chest.

"Now look at yourself in the mirror."

Melissa hesitated. She already knew what the clothes looked like on her. She'd already tried them on twice, first in the store and then again when she came home.

And no matter what anyone told her, she knew they didn't fit her.

The bright colors made her look funny, and the cut of them made her look fat.

"Look!" Phyllis commanded.

She moved across to her daughter, her hands closing on Melissa's shoulders. Jerking her around, she propelled her toward the mirror. "Look at yourself!" she commanded once more.

As Melissa felt her mother's fingers dig into her flesh, and winced with the pain of it, she suddenly heard D'Arcy's voice whispering to her.

It's all right, Melissa. I'm here. You can go to sleep now.

She felt her mother jerk her toward the mirror, and then she was looking into the glass itself.

But instead of her own image reflected there, she saw D'Arcy, her eyes gentle, smiling at her. The image in the mirror moved toward her, reaching out to her. She felt D'Arcy's gentle fingers on her cheek, and closed her eyes as her friend's cool touch brushed away her tears.

The familiar darkness closed around her, and the last words she heard before she drifted away into the blackness were D'Arcy's. *I'm here now, and you can go to sleep. I'll take care of you. I'll take care of everything.*

Phyllis felt Melissa's body relax slightly, and eased her grip on her daughter's shoulders. "Well?" she demanded. "Tell me what you see."

Melissa said nothing, and Phyllis's anger rose again. "Look at yourself!" she screeched. Her grip tightened on Melissa's shoulders again and she began shaking the girl violently.

Melissa's head jerked back and forth, but no matter how hard her mother shook her, she uttered no sound.

"You look terrible!" Phyllis hissed. "You're fat, and you're ugly, and you don't even care! Dear God, how can you be my daughter?"

Phyllis propelled Melissa away from the mirror, slamming her into the chair in front of the small vanity. "You could be as pretty as Teri, if you'd just try! But just look at you. Look at your hair! It's a disgrace!"

She reached out and pulled open the top drawer of the vanity, snatching up the scissors that lay there. A moment later she began cutting off Melissa's hair, hacking at it with the scissors. Slowly, as Melissa watched in the mirror with a strange detachment, her hair fell away until all that remained was a ragged bob.

"There!" Phyllis snapped when she'd finished her work. "Look! Isn't that better? Isn't it?"

Melissa said nothing, and Phyllis, her whole body trembling with rage and frustration now, abruptly leaned forward. "Answer me!" she screamed. "Why won't you answer me!"

Melissa remained silent, sitting quietly on the chair in front of the vanity, her eyes fixed on the image in the mirror.

"Fine," Phyllis said, her hands again clamping down on Melissa's shoulders. "If you don't want to talk to me, then you don't have to. But I suggest you listen to me very carefully, young lady. If you want to spend your entire life all by yourself, I don't really care. But I will no longer tolerate you being rude to my friends or their children. Do you understand?"

Melissa said nothing at all, nor did she acknowledge her mother's words with so much as a nod of her head.

Phyllis's fingers dug deeper into the flesh of her daughter's shoulders. "I know you can hear me, Melissa. You're not deaf. So keep listening. I am not going to let you spoil Teri's life the way you've spoiled your own and tried to spoil mine. So tomorrow night, whether you want to or not, you are going to the bonfire. It was very kind of Mrs. Van Arsdale to invite you, and you are not going to insult her by refusing to go. And you are going to be friendly, and polite, and you will not do anything to embarrass me. Now, tell me if you heard what I just said."

Melissa remained silent and impassive, staring into the mirror.

"All right, Melissa!" Phyllis hissed. "If you want it to be difficult, so be it." She jerked Melissa to her feet once more and propelled her across the room to the closet. Opening the door, she shoved Melissa inside, then closed the closet again, locking it. "I suggest you think about it," she said through the door. "I'll come back in an hour. Perhaps by then you'll have decided to start behaving the way I raised you to behave."

She started out of the room, but then her eyes fell on the jeans and T-shirt that were still lying on the floor where Melissa had left them. Picking up the scissors once more, she cut the offending clothes into pieces, then flung them on the bed.

At last, her frustration with her daughter finally vented, she left the room.

It was nearly ten o'clock when Teri and Charles got back from the movie. Only the light in the foyer was on downstairs, and upstairs they found Phyllis lying in bed, reading. She put her book aside as they came into the bedroom and smiled up at Teri. "How was the movie?"

"Great," Teri replied. "It was a horror thing, and I've never been so scared in my life. But at least I sat through it—Daddy had to go out to the lobby."

Charles smiled wryly. "I'm afraid cutting people up with machetes just isn't my cup of tea. But Teri loved every minute of it."

"Well, I'm certainly glad I didn't let Melissa go," Phyllis observed. "She'd have had nightmares for a month."

"Is she in bed already?" Charles asked, glancing at his watch.

Phyllis nodded. "We had a nice little talk, and then both of us decided to turn in early," she said. "I think she went to sleep an hour ago."

The three of them chatted for a few more minutes, and finally Teri kissed her father and stepmother good night and went to her room. She paused in front of the mirror on her closet door, admiring her new clothes once more, then took them off and carefully hung them up. Pulling on her robe, she went into the bathroom to brush her teeth. And then, just as she was about to turn the water on, she heard Melissa's voice.

"What am I going to do, D'Arcy? What's Mama going to say? Now she's going to be mad at me again."

Going to the door, Teri pressed her ear against it, listening. She could still hear Melissa's voice, but the words had become indistinct, and it sounded as if Melissa was crying.

Teri paused, thinking. Perhaps she should just pretend she hadn't heard anything at all and go to bed.

And yet she'd distinctly heard the name D'Arcy, the same name she'd seen in Melissa's diary early that morning. Was it possible that Melissa actually thought she was talking to someone? Making up her mind, she grasped the doorknob, turned it, and let herself into Melissa's room.

Melissa was sitting at the vanity in the near darkness of her room, staring into the mirror. But as the stream of light from the bathroom door struck her, she turned, her eyes widening as she saw Teri.

"What are you doing home already?" she asked. "Didn't you go to the movies?"

Teri frowned. "It's after ten. The movie's over."

Melissa's brows knit in puzzlement. "But it seems like you just left. I mean, it seems like it's only been an hour, maybe."

Teri moved over to the vanity. Her eyes widening as she looked at her half sister's face, she reached over and switched on the small lamp that sat on top of the vanity.

She gasped as she saw the ruins of Melissa's hair. "What happened?" she breathed. "What did you do to your hair?"

Her eyes brimming with tears, Melissa peered up at Teri. "I—I don't know. I think D'Arcy must have cut it."

"D'Arcy?" Teri asked. "Who's D'Arcy?"

Melissa tensed, and her eyes flicked apprehensively toward the hall door. When she saw that it was safely closed, she seemed to relax slightly. "P-Promise you won't tell?" she asked.

Teri nodded quickly, her mind suddenly tingling with anticipation.

"She—She's a friend of mine," Melissa said. "Sometimes she comes to help me."

Teri's brow furrowed. What on earth was Melissa talking about? "What do you mean? Where does she come from? Does she live around here?"

Melissa shook her head. "N-Not exactly," she said. "She— Well, she's sort of like an imaginary friend. You know, like the one Anne of Green Gables had, who lived in the mirror?"

Suddenly Teri smiled. "I know what you mean—I had one when I was a little girl. Her name was Caroline, and I used to pretend she was my maid. She'd do anything I wanted her to. Clean my room for me, pick up my things. All the things I hated to do. I'd pretend I was her, and she'd do all the work."

Melissa nodded eagerly. "That's the kind of friend D'Arcy is. When I get afraid of something, D'Arcy comes and helps me." Her eyes shifted back to the mirror. "Only look what she did tonight," she said, her voice quavering. "She cut off all my hair. Mama will be so angry."

Teri's thoughts raced as a series of images began to come into her mind.

The swimming pool that afternoon, when Phyllis had said that she and Melissa would talk about the bonfire "later."

Melissa, just for a moment, had looked terrified.

And then again, at the dinner table, when Phyllis had suggested that she and Melissa would have an evening at home together.

Once again Melissa's eyes had filled with panic.

It was her mother who had frightened her tonight.

Jesus, is that what she does? Teri wondered. When her mother starts yelling at her, she just pretends she's someone else?

But then she remembered something else.

The other night, when she'd found Melissa tied to the bed, with her eyes open. She'd been sure Melissa was awake, but when she had spoken to her, Melissa hadn't answered.

And tonight she'd thought Teri hadn't gone to the movies.

She doesn't remember, Teri thought. She doesn't remember what happened at all.

Now, as she gazed at Melissa's reflected image in the mirror, she smiled gently. "I'll tell you what," she said. "Let's get a comb and some scissors, and I'll see if I can fix your hair. And tomorrow, if Phyllis gets mad, we'll just tell her I cut it. We'll tell her it was all my idea, and then she can't get mad at you, can she?"

In the mirror, Melissa's eyes met Teri's. "Would you really do that?" she asked. "Would you do that for me?"

Teri slipped her arms around Melissa. "Of course I would," she said. "I'm your sister, aren't I? Isn't that what sisters are for?" She took the comb and scissors Melissa found in the top drawer of the vanity and began snipping carefully at her half sister's hair, evening it out as best she could. As she worked, Melissa watched in the mirror, her eyes fixed adoringly on Teri. But then, as Teri was finishing up the trimming, her smile faded.

"What are the kids going to say tomorrow night?" she asked. "With my hair like this, they'll all laugh at me."

Teri cocked her head. "I thought you weren't going to the bonfire," she said.

Melissa was silent for several seconds, but finally shook her head. "I changed my mind," she said. "I had to. D'Arcy's afraid of the dark, and Mama wouldn't let her out of the closet until I said I'd go."

By the time she went to bed twenty minutes later, Teri was certain she understood exactly who D'Arcy was.

What she didn't yet know was exactly how she could use D'Arcy. But she knew she'd find a way.

After all, when they'd left the movie earlier that evening, the first thing her father had said was, "I wish we'd brought Melissa— she loves movies like this. They scare her half to death, but she loves them."

Melissa.

Even when he was alone with her, her father still only thought about Melissa.

As Teri went to sleep, she knew she was starting to hate Melissa almost as much as she'd hated her mother and stepfather.

It hadn't been hard getting rid of them.

It would be even easier getting rid of Melissa.

After all, "D'Arcy" would help her, now that Teri knew who she was and where she'd come from.

She was nobody, and she lived nowhere.

Nowhere, except in Melissa's own mind.

But that would be enough. As long as Melissa believed she was real, that would be quite enough.

CHAPTER

10

"Daddy?"

It was the following afternoon, and Charles Holloway, about to leave for the airport in Portland, glanced up the stairs to see Melissa standing uncertainly on the landing, looking down at him. "D-Do you really have to go?" she asked, her voice trembling. Charles held out his arms, smiling at her, and she ran down the stairs to fling her arms around her father's neck. "I don't want you to go," she whispered into his ear. "Please, can't you get someone else to do whatever it is?"

Charles gently disengaged himself from his younger daughter's hug. "I wish I could," he told her. "But I really have to do it myself. It all has to do with Teri, and there's just so many things that have to be signed. If I don't go, it'll drag out forever, and in the end I'll have to go anyway. And you wouldn't like that, would you?"

Melissa sighed and shook her head, then pulled away from her father as he reached out and ran his fingers through her newly short hair.

"Hey!" he protested. "Where are you going?"

"You're laughing at me," Melissa accused.

"No, I'm not," Charles told her, pulling her close once again. "In fact, I like you with short hair. It makes you look even cuter."

Melissa gazed up at him, wondering if he was telling her the truth. She searched his eyes, but saw nothing except the same warm twinkle that was always there when he looked at her. "Do you really like it?" she asked wistfully. "You're not just saying that to make me feel better, are you?"

"You know I wouldn't do that," Charles replied. "If it looked like straw, I'd tell you." He cocked his head, his eyes squinting critically. "Actually," he went on, his voice taking on a gently teasing tone, "if you bleached it out, it *might* look kind of like straw." He ducked away as Melissa swung at him, then hugged her once more. "Tell you what—I'll bring you a surprise. Okay?"

"What?" Melissa asked.

"If I told you, it wouldn't be a surprise."

Suddenly, from the top of the stairs, another voice spoke. "What about me?" Teri asked. "Will you bring me a surprise, too?"

Charles, his arm still around Melissa's shoulders, smiled up at Teri. "Absolutely," he told her. "Aren't you going to come down and give your father a hug?"

Teri, moving almost shyly, came down the stairs. "I—I didn't want to get in the way," she murmured.

Charles slipped his free arm around Teri. "You couldn't," he said. "Two daughters, two arms. Seems like it works out perfectly." Then his voice took on a more serious tone. "Look out for Melissa while I'm gone, okay?"

Teri smiled at him. "Sure," she said. "We'll have so much fun, she won't even know you're gone."

"Great," Charles replied, giving Teri a quick squeeze, then letting her go to hug Melissa once more. "You'll be fine," he assured her once more. "And I'll only be gone a couple of days. Okay?"

Melissa nodded but said nothing. *And maybe he's right*, she thought a few minutes later as her father disappeared around the curve in the long driveway. *Maybe with Teri here, it will be okay.*

*   *   *

Darkness fell, and as Melissa sat on the quickly cooling sand, her back propped up against one of the large logs that surrounded the fire pit on the beach below the Cove Club, she decided she was glad she'd changed her mind about coming. It hadn't been nearly as bad as she'd imagined it would be—in fact, she'd actually been having fun. The first few minutes, of course, had been terrible. As she and Teri had approached the crowd already gathered on the beach, she'd had an almost irresistible urge to turn around and go back to Maplecrest. But, as if sensing her sudden panic, Teri had taken her hand. "Come on—it's going to be fine. Just stop worrying."

It turned out that Teri had been right. If anyone had noticed that her clothes didn't quite fit right, no one said anything about it. Jeff Barnstable had even told her that her hair looked nice.

"You should have done it a long time ago," he'd said. "You always looked like you were trying to hide or something."

Slowly, as the evening went on, she'd let her guard come down, and even joined in a game of volleyball. When they began to choose up sides, she was sure she'd be the last to be chosen, but then Teri had suggested they just split up into two teams and let everyone play on whatever side they wanted to. Except that every time one of the teams scored a point, the person who scored it had to drop out.

Melissa found herself giggling as she remembered the result, for after an hour in which all the best players did their best not to score, only she and Jerry Chalmers were left on the court. The rest of the kids had all gathered around, cheering for their last remaining teammate, and for nearly ten minutes she and Jerry had struggled just to complete a serve. In the end, when Melissa finally managed to get the ball over the net, and Jerry—who it turned out was even clumsier than she was—missed it entirely, everyone, including she and Jerry, were laughing so hard that no one cared who had won.

When she'd asked Teri where she learned those rules for volleyball, Teri had winked at her. "I just made them up. But it was kind of fun watching everyone trying to do badly, wasn't it?"

Now, as darkness gathered around them and Jeff Barnstable threw another log onto the fire, Teri dropped down onto the sand beside her. "Isn't this fun?" she asked. "And we have the whole beach to ourselves. Back in California the beach would have been jammed."

From the other side of the fire Brett Van Arsdale grinned at Teri. "What makes you think we have the beach to ourselves?" he asked.

Teri stared at him. "But we do—there's no one on it but us."

Brett's eyes widened strangely in the flickering firelight. "Isn't there?" he asked, his voice dropping low as he drew the words out. "Maybe," he suggested, "there is. Maybe there's someone out there, watching us."

Despite herself, Teri shivered and scanned the darkness that surrounded the fire. "Oh, come on," she said. "You're just trying to scare me. And if you're going to tell the story about the man with the hook, don't bother—I already heard it about a million times."

"Sure," Brett said. "But I'll bet you haven't heard the one about the ghost of Secret Cove."

Teri cocked her head suspiciously. "Oh, come on . . ."

"Tell her," Ellen Stevens said. She turned to Teri. "It's really weird, and no one tells it as well as Brett. Come on, Brett—tell it for us."

A silence fell over the group, and then, his voice barely audible, so that Teri had to strain to hear him, he began. "It was the night of the August Moon Ball. They'd just built the clubhouse, and everyone was there. Everyone, anyway, except the servants. And one of them was planning to go, too."

Around the fire the teenagers snuggled closer together as Brett, in a low voice filled with portent, went on with the story . . .

It was almost eight o'clock, and the girl peered at her reflection in the flickering light of the oil lamp that stood on the small table by her cot. She looked beautiful tonight—the white dress she'd been working on for two months fit her perfectly, and with its long sleeves ending in lacy cuffs, and the fifteen rows of tiny ruffles that covered its bodice, it looked almost like a wedding dress.

Perhaps, indeed, it might be her wedding dress, except that she was sure it would be bad luck to wear the same dress at her wedding that she'd worn at her first big party.

But she could never afford another dress like this one—

She stopped herself. Of course she could. After she married Joshua, she'd be able to afford anything she wanted. Surely he would buy her the material so she could make herself a wedding dress even more beautiful than this one.

Her eyes wandered to the third finger of her left hand and the small gold ring set with a single perfect diamond that he'd secretly given her three months ago.

"We won't tell anyone," he'd said. "We'll keep it secret until the ball. By then I'll tell my parents, and everything will be all right."

And tonight, the night of the ball, they were going to make the announcement. She would stand beside him as he told all his friends that he'd fallen in love with her and was going to marry her.

They'd be surprised—she knew that. But when they saw how happy Joshua was with her, they'd all gather around her, and suddenly she'd be a part of them.

She checked her dress one last time, then blew out the lantern and left her room under the eaves of the mansion, making her way quickly down the back stairs. She was about to slip out the door when she heard the cook's voice speaking sharply to her.

"And where do you think you're going?"

The words made the girl freeze, but finally she turned to face the woman she'd worked for since she was fourteen. "To the ball," she said.

The cook glared scornfully at her. "And what makes you think they'll let the likes of you into a place like that?"

The girl smiled serenely. "They'll let me in," she said. "I've been invited."

"Have you, then?" the cook asked, her skepticism clear in her voice. "Well, if I were you, I wouldn't pay any mind to what the boys around here tell you. They'll say whatever they have to to get into a girl's—"

"Not Joshua!" the girl exclaimed, her face burning with embarrassment at the cook's insinuation. "He's not like that!"

She scurried out the back door before the cook could say anything else, and hurried across the lawn to the beach, carrying her dancing shoes— the shoes she'd spent nearly a week's salary on—in her hands. She hiked up the skirt of the dress, determined not to let anything stain its hem, and started down the beach toward the bright yellow gaslights that glowed from the windows of the new clubhouse perched on the southern point of the cove.

She came at last to the foot of the path leading up from the beach to the clubhouse, and stopped to put on her shoes. She waited for a few minutes, for it was here that Joshua had promised to meet her. Together they would walk up the path and enter the clubhouse, and people would know what had happened before Joshua even told them. In her mind she'd rehearsed the scene over and over again: Joshua, tall and handsome in his cutaway jacket, his arm protectively around her shoulders, his handsome features set determinedly as he announced to his friends that he'd decided to marry her. She had even imagined the disapproval she would see in their eyes for a moment, before they realized how much in love she and Joshua were. But when they saw, their disapproval would vanish and they would welcome her with open arms.

A slight breeze came up, and the girl shivered, then looked around once more for her fiancé. She looked at the watch tucked into her tiny beaded bag and saw that it was almost eight-thirty.

She was late.

He must have already been here, and was waiting for her up above, in front of the clubhouse itself.

She climbed the path, carefully holding her skirts well above the dusty trail. At last she reached the top and stopped to catch her breath. Now, through the windows, she could see everyone dancing. All the women in their beautiful dresses, their throats covered with beautiful necklaces, jewels dangling from their ears, sparkling in the gaslight with an almost unnatural beauty.

And then, spinning out of the crowd, his arms around a beautifully pale girl in a dress the color of an emerald, she saw Joshua.

He was smiling down at the girl, and she seemed to be laughing at something he was saying. Then he looked up and saw her.

Instantly, she saw him recognize her and stop dancing, and she turned away from the window, hurrying toward the door, knowing he would be waiting for her just inside.

She pushed the door open and stepped into the clubhouse, then crossed the foyer to stand in the immense double doors that opened into the huge dining room where the ball was being held.

Joshua, still standing with the pale girl in the green dress, was staring at her.

Then, slowly, the other couples on the floor stopped dancing and began to turn toward her as well.

She paused, puzzled. Why wasn't Joshua coming over to her? Why was he just standing there, looking at her, his eyes looking . . .

And then she knew.

His eyes looked frightened.

As if he hadn't expected to see her.

He hadn't told his parents at all.

She could hear the people around her murmuring among themselves now, and here and there a soft titter of laughter. Instinctively, her eyes locked on Joshua's, she started toward her fiancé.

And then, miraculously, he came to life and started toward her. A moment later he was there and his hand was on her arm.

And then he spoke.

"I have to talk to you," he said, his voice low. "In the kitchen."

His fingers closing on her arm like a vise, he steered her across the room, weaving through the crowd, which seemed to draw back to let them pass. Then they were through the door, standing in the kitchen.

The cooks and waiters, all of them in their uniforms, stared curiously at her.

"Wh-What is it?" the girl murmured. "What's wrong?"

Joshua licked nervously at his lips, and his eyes refused to meet hers. "I can't marry you," he said. "I talked to my father, and he said if I marry you he'll disown me."

The girl gasped. This couldn't be happening—it was impossible.

"I have to have the ring back," Joshua told her. He was holding her hand now, his fingers on the ring.

It wouldn't come off.

Jerking her hand away, the girl tugged at the ring, struggling to pull it off her finger. "Is that all it's about?" she demanded. "Just money? You told me you loved me. You told me—" She choked on her own words, her eyes flooding with tears. She pulled harder at the ring, but it seemed to have become a part of her finger.

Joshua, his eyes suddenly cold, was already turning away from her. "It's all right," he said, as if talking to a child. "Why don't you just leave? I'll get the ring tomorrow."

And then he was gone, disappearing through the doors to the dining room, not even looking back at her.

She stood stunned, staring at the door through which her lover had gone. It had been so easy for him—he'd never cared about her, never!

She struggled with the ring again, but still it refused to budge. But she had to get it off her finger—it felt like it was burning her!

She had to get it away from her.

Her eyes darted around the kitchen, and then she saw it.

On a large chopping table only a foot away, there was a meat cleaver.

A strangled cry coming from her throat, she seized the cleaver in her right hand, at the same time laying her left arm on the chopping block.

The cleaver rose above her head, hovered for a split second, and then she brought it down.

The razor-sharp blade slashed through her left wrist, and she froze for a moment, her hand lying severed on the wooden table, blood spurting from the stump where the hand had been only a second before.

As one of the kitchen girls screamed, she dropped the cleaver to the floor and picked up the severed hand.

A moment later she pushed through the door into the ballroom. The dancing had started again, but she shoved her way through the whirling couples, her eyes scanning the crowd until she finally found Joshua.

She stopped, waiting for him to turn.

And then, at last, he saw her.

His eyes widened slightly as he gazed at her blood-drenched dress. And then, as she hurled her left hand at him, the hateful ring still on its third finger, he stepped backward.

The hand struck his chest, then fell to the floor, leaving his white shirt stained with crimson.

As screams began to fill the ballroom, the girl fled, plunging out into the night.

For her, the ball was over. . . .

Brett's voice trailed off. For several seconds no one said anything at all. And then, at last, Teri spoke. "But what happened to her?"

Brett shrugged. "No one knows," he said. "No one ever saw her again. Or the hand, either. After the panic died down at the dance, the hand was gone, and so was she. She just disappeared. But they say she's still around. They say that sometimes she walks on the beach, or in the woods, hunting for her hand. And this year, she's supposed to come back."

Teri smiled. "Come back?" she asked. "But you just said she never left."

"But this year is different," Brett said slyly. "The Cove Club opened exactly one hundred years ago. This year's August Moon Ball is the centennial."

"So?" Teri smirked. "What's supposed to happen?"

Brett leaned forward and once more his voice dropped. "She's supposed to come back," he said. "She's supposed to come back and get her revenge."

Teri glanced around at the rest of the kids, trying to decide if any of them believed it. "What's she supposed to do?" she asked. "And who was she? What was her name?"

"D'Arcy," Brett told her. "D'Arcy Malloy. She was a maid in your house."

"D'Arcy?" Teri repeated. She turned to Melissa, who was sitting very still, staring into the fire. "But that's the name of your friend, isn't it?" she asked.

Melissa's head turned, and her eyes, large and hurt, met Teri's. "You weren't supposed to tell," she said, her voice trembling. Then, before Teri could say anything else, Melissa jumped up and darted off down the beach, instantly disappearing into the darkness.

When she was gone, Ellen Stevens looked over at Teri. "What do you mean, her friend?" she asked.

Teri was silent for a moment, but then her lips curved into a faint smile. "Melissa has an imaginary friend," she said. "She told me about her last night. Her name is D'Arcy."

CHAPTER

11

Melissa stumbled along the beach, determined not to give in to the sob that lurked in her throat. At last, when the bonfire was only a spot of orange light in the distance, she came to a stop and sat down on the sand, staring out to sea.

It's no big deal, she told herself. So what if Teri told them about her friend? It was she herself who had behaved stupidly. If she'd just taken a second to think about it, she could have laughed it off—even made the story Brett had told better by admitting that her friend *was* the ghost. After all, in a way it was true—ever since she'd first heard the story of D'Arcy Malloy when she was only six or seven years old, she'd thought about D'Arcy, even gone up to the attic to the little room where she was certain D'Arcy must have lived.

And then, as she'd gotten older and found it harder and harder to make friends with the rest of the kids, she'd started talking to D'Arcy, and imagined that D'Arcy was talking back to her.

Except her friend wasn't the real D'Arcy, of course. Her friend was just someone she'd made up, someone the same age as she was.

Someone she could talk to about all the things she couldn't talk to anyone else about.

But now, after she'd been dumb enough to run away, everyone was going to think she was nuts. Why had she done it? Why hadn't she just made a joke of it? After all, when she'd been the last one on the volleyball court, fighting it out with Jerry Chalmers, she'd thought the whole thing was as funny as everyone else had. It hadn't been a joke on *her*. It had just been a *joke*, and for once she'd been a part of it.

But now she'd wrecked it by being stupid again.

All she'd had to do was go along with it. There were all kinds of stories she could have made up.

She could have told them she knew who D'Arcy was going to come for at the August Moon Ball.

Then she thought of something even better—maybe she should have told them that D'Arcy had found her hand and was going to leave it on the bed of her victim the night before the ball.

The sob that had threatened to overwhelm her only a few minutes earlier suddenly gave way to a giggle and then a sigh.

If the kids were going to laugh at her again, it was her own fault, not Teri's. And there wasn't anything she could do about it tonight.

As she got up and started home, she almost wished that D'Arcy *were* real. And if she were . . .

She tried to put the thought out of her mind, but as she neared the house she found herself giggling again. What would the kids do if they actually *saw* D'Arcy? she wondered.

But they wouldn't, of course, for there was no D'Arcy, except for the friend who existed only in her own mind.

She paused as she neared the house. In the library all the lights were on, and she could see her mother sitting in front of the television set. If she went in the front door, Phyllis would surely hear her, and then the questions would start.

"Why are you home so early?"

"Why didn't Teri come with you?"

"Is the bonfire over?"

She glanced back. In the distance the fire was burning brighter now. Someone must have thrown more wood on it, and even from here she could see the silhouettes of the rest of the kids, some of them sitting on logs, some of them standing near the fire, toasting marshmallows.

Her mother would see them, too, and the questions would get worse.

"What did you do?"

"Were you rude to your friends again?"

"Did you do something stupid?"

"Did you?"

She backed away from the front of the house, then skirted around it, losing herself in the deep shadows. From the back the house was dark, and as she approached the kitchen door she began to relax. If she could just slip inside without her mother hearing her.

And then, out of the darkness, a great shadow leaped at her, and a moment later Blackie, his tail wagging furiously, rose up to put his big forepaws on her chest as his tongue licked eagerly at her face.

"Blackie!" Melissa said, doing her best to keep her voice as soft as possible. "Will you get *down*?"

Obediently, the dog dropped back to the ground, and Melissa knelt next to him for a moment, scratching his ears and rubbing his back. Wriggling with pleasure, the big Labrador pressed against her, his tongue lapping affectionately at her arms.

"All right," she whispered, rising once more to her feet and glancing nervously toward the house to be sure no new lights had come on. "Now go home. Do you hear me? Go home!"

She moved up the steps to the back door. The dog, after hesitating only a moment, scrambled after her.

"No!" she hissed. "You can't come in!"

She felt around for the key that Cora always kept hidden in the large terra-cotta planter to the right of the door, found it and slipped it into the lock.

There was a loud click as the bolt slid free, and Melissa froze for a moment. But then, hearing nothing, she returned the key to its hiding place and slipped through the door.

As soon as she closed it behind her. Blackie began anxiously scratching at it, a disappointed whine issuing from his throat.

As the whine grew louder, Melissa uttered a silent prayer that he wouldn't actually bark.

As she held her breath, Blackie uttered a single sharp yelp.

Instantly, Melissa opened the door again, grasping the dog's collar as he slipped eagerly through the gap. "All *right*," Melissa whispered. "You can come in, but you have to be quiet, and you can't stay all night."

The big dog cocked his head and peered up at her exactly as if he'd understood every word she'd said.

Her hand still clamped onto Blackie's thick leather collar, Melissa scuttled across the kitchen to the seldom-used servants' stairs. Opening the door to the stairwell slowly, praying that there would be no creak, she led the dog through.

A minute later she was finally safe in her room. She'd paused at the top of the stairs, peeping down into the foyer beneath, half expecting to see her mother's accusing eyes glaring back at her, but the foyer had been empty, and she could only dimly hear the sound of the television drifting up from the library. Closing the door to her room, she released Blackie, who promptly bounded onto the bed and curled up on her pillows. She glared at the dog. "Isn't it bad enough that you managed to get in here?" she asked. "If you mess up my bed, Mama will kill us both."

Blackie's tail thumped happily against the headboard, and he made no movement to get off the bed. Instead he rolled over, his legs in the air, then stared at her, his huge brown eyes pleading to have his belly rubbed.

Feigning a lot more exasperation with the dog than she really felt, Melissa flopped onto the bed herself and began scratching Blackie's belly. Then, from the open window, she heard Tag's voice.

"Blackie! Blackie, come!"

Instantly, the big dog rolled over, scrambled off the bed and ran to the window. As Tag called out again, Blackie reared up, placed his forepaws on the windowsill and began barking loudly.

Melissa rolled off the bed and scuttled over to the dog. "No!" she said sharply, trying to clamp her hands around the dog's mouth. Blackie wriggled free of her hands and once more began baying loudly as Tag called to him yet again.

"Tag!" Melissa called out the window as loudly as she dared. "He's up here! Stop calling him!"

And then, behind her, Melissa heard her mother's voice, and the lights in her room suddenly went on.

"Melissa? What on earth?" Phyllis fell silent when she saw Blackie, who had spun around and was now crouched at Melissa's feet, a warning growl rumbling up from his throat. Instinctively, Phyllis took a step backward, but her eyes flashed with anger. "What is that dog doing in here?" she demanded.

"I—I'm sorry, Mama," Melissa stammered. "I—He—When I opened the back door, he just sort of came in."

Phyllis's eyes narrowed. "Came in?" she repeated. "Dogs do not simply come into houses. People let them in."

Melissa nodded. "I'll put him out," she said quickly. "Right now."

Grasping Blackie's collar again, she attempted to slip past her mother, but Phyllis's hand closed around her arm.

"And why are you home?" she demanded. "Why aren't you still at the bonfire with your friends?"

"I—I didn't feel very good," Melissa lied.

"But you felt good enough to bring that dog up here so you could play with it, didn't you?"

Melissa, trapped, nodded glumly. "Y-Yes."

Her eyes still blazing with anger, Phyllis marched Melissa down the back stairs and watched in silence as her daughter opened the kitchen door and sent Blackie out into the night. But as Melissa started back toward the stairs, Phyllis stopped her.

"Look," she commanded.

Melissa stared at the floor at which her mother was pointing, and her heart sank.

Across the linoleum, leading from the kitchen door to the foot of the servants' stairs, were Blackie's muddy pawprints. Gasping, Melissa looked at her shirt.

It, too, was covered with brown smudges. Fearfully, she looked once more at her mother.

"Scrub the floor," Phyllis said, her tone of voice leaving no room for argument. "And while you scrub it, think about why you left the party early. And don't tell me you felt sick—I can see perfectly well that you aren't. I'll want you to tell me the truth, and then I'll decide what needs to be done."

Phyllis turned and walked out of the kitchen. This time, as Melissa filled a bucket with soapy water and fished the mop out of the depths of the broom closet, she didn't fight the sob that rose in her throat. As she began scrubbing the kitchen floor clean of every trace of dirt that Blackie had tracked in, she knew that this was the best part of what was likely to happen tonight.

The worst would be upstairs, where her mother would be waiting for her in her room.

A cool breeze wafted in from the sea, and the dying flames of the bonfire leaped back to life, orange fingers reaching upward into the darkness as if seeking something to feed on. Teri, sitting next to Brett Van Arsdale now, his arm resting gently across her shoulders, gazed into the blaze. An image of another fire briefly rose out of her memory, and for a few seconds she could hear once more the crackling roar and the screams of her mother.

She shivered slightly and put the memory out of her mind, snuggling closer to Brett. Then, as the moon began to drop below the horizon, she glanced at the watch on her wrist.

It was nearly midnight.

"I guess maybe I'd better be going home," she said, reluctantly getting to her feet.

"Want me to walk you?" Brett asked, scrambling up from the sand.

Teri shrugged. "You don't need to."

"Oh, I don't know—you wouldn't want D'Arcy to catch you out alone at night, would you?"

Teri said nothing until they'd started down the beach, when she slipped her hand into his. "No one really believes that story, do they?"

"Which part?" Brett countered.

Teri glanced sideways at him in the dark. "Well, all of it."

"I don't know if anyone really believes D'Arcy's still around," he replied, then snickered softly. "Except maybe Melissa." Then his voice turned serious. "But most of the story's true. My great-grandparents were at the dance when it happened. Half the people around here used to keep diaries. And they all wrote the same thing. There must have been fifty people who saw what happened."

"Maybe they made it up," Teri suggested.

Brett peered at her in the darkness. "What do you mean?"

"Well, I don't know, but it just seems like maybe they all got together and decided it would be fun to start a ghost story."

Brett chuckled. "You'd better come over to my house sometime and take a look at the portraits. One look at my great-grandfather and you know he never made up a story in his life. I mean, he was a lawyer, and some kind of big deal in the church we go to in New York. And my grandma says she can't remember either of her parents ever laughing. Besides, I'll bet if you ask your dad, he'll tell you all about it."

Teri shrugged. "Well, even if it's true, I can't believe anyone really thinks she's still around. I mean, it's just an old story, isn't it? And I'll bet it's always someone *else* who saw her." She turned to face Brett. "I mean, did you ever see D'Arcy? Or did anyone you know?"

Brett shrugged. "No. But so what? There's lots of people who've seen her."

"Name one," Teri challenged.

Brett stared at her for a moment, then started laughing. "I can't believe it," he moaned. "Are we actually arguing about a ghost? It was only a story."

They were approaching Maplecrest now, and the house was dark except for a light in the master suite on the second floor. "Want to come in for a Coke or something?"

Brett nodded, grinning. "Sure. And then you can walk me home, so D'Arcy doesn't get me, and then I can walk you home, and we can go back and forth all night."

"Forget it," Teri said. "You get a Coke, and then you walk home by yourself. If a ghost gets you, tough."

They started across the lawn, then froze as a low growl drifted out of the darkness. "What the hell?" Brett said.

"It's just Blackie," Teri told him. "He's so stupid . . . Blackie! Go home!"

She reached down and picked up a stick, then threw it in the direction from which the growl had come.

There was a yelp, and then Blackie began barking, shattering

the quiet of the night. A moment later, from upstairs, they heard
Phyllis Holloway's voice.

"Tag! You get that dog inside! I will *not* have him disturbing
the neighbors all night!"

Brett glanced uneasily at Teri. "I think I'll skip the Coke," he
said. "She sounds pretty pissed off."

"It's okay," Teri protested. "She really likes you."

But Brett shook his head. "I think I'll just skip it. It's pretty
late."

Phyllis yelled at Blackie once more, and then Tag, too, shouted
at the dog. After one last bark at Teri and Brett, Blackie trotted
off around the corner of the house. A moment later, on the front
porch, Brett gave Teri a quick kiss before starting toward the path
that would eventually take him home.

Teri let herself in the front door and went through the dining
room and butler's pantry into the kitchen to find a Coke for
herself. But as she opened the kitchen door, the acrid smell of
Lysol filled her nostrils, and when she turned on the light, she
saw that the floor was still damp, as if someone had washed it that
night.

Cora?

It couldn't have been—Cora always left right after supper.

Besides, Cora wouldn't have left it wet.

She fished a Coke out of the refrigerator, opened it, then went
back the way she'd come, mounting the main stairs to the second
floor. When she got to the landing, she heard Phyllis calling out to
her.

"Teri? Is that you, dear?"

She went to the master suite, whose door was ajar, and tapped
softly.

"Come in," Phyllis said. Teri pushed the door open, and saw
her stepmother propped up in bed, a magazine resting on her lap.
Phyllis patted the wide expanse of the bed. "Come sit down and
tell me all about it."

Fifteen minutes later Phyllis smiled happily. "I'm so glad you
had a good time," she said, reaching out to take Teri's hand. "And
though I suppose it's really rather unkind of me, given what
happened, I want you to know how happy I am to have you back
here again. I've always thought you belonged here. You're—Well,

I guess sometimes I used to feel like you should have been my own daughter. Is that terrible of me?"

Teri smiled gently at her stepmother. "I don't think so," she said. "But you already have Melissa."

Phyllis's smile faded. "Yes," she said, "I do, don't I? But Melissa isn't like you. Oh, I don't mean I love her any the less for it, but she just doesn't have your—well, your ability to get along. I do my best, of course, but sometimes I'm not sure she really cares about the things that count. I mean, like tonight," she went on, her voice taking on a rough edge of annoyance. "What must the other children have thought of her, leaving the party just because she 'didn't feel good'? *Every*one has times when they don't feel good, but you don't simply leave a party because—" Her words trailed off as she saw an oddly uncertain look come into her stepdaughter's eyes. "That *was* why she left the bonfire, wasn't it?"

Teri, her body tingling as she sensed an opportunity, ran her tongue nervously over her lower lip as if she were reluctant to say anything, but finally shook her head. "It—It was the ghost story," she said at last. "Brett was telling us the story of D'Arcy, and it scared Melissa."

Phyllis groaned out loud. "Are you telling me she ran away over a silly ghost story?"

Teri shrugged helplessly. "Well, it *was* pretty scary. And nobody really minded." She cast her eyes carefully downward. "But I suppose I should have gone with her, just to make sure she was all right."

"Don't be silly," Phyllis retorted, her anger at Melissa's childishness still burning within her. "The only way Melissa is going to learn anything is by having an example." She smiled fondly at Teri. "And I can't think of a better one than you. Besides, there's no reason in the world why your good time should have been spoiled by her childishness."

"Then you're not mad at me?" Teri asked, looking shyly at Phyllis once more.

"Mad at you? Don't be ridiculous. I don't think I could ever be mad at you." She squeezed Teri's hand, then offered her cheek. "Now give me a kiss, and run along."

A few minutes later, in the bathroom between their bedrooms,

Teri pressed her ear against Melissa's door. She heard nothing, and finally opened the door to slip into Melissa's room.

As before, Melissa was lying on her back, her eyes open, staring fixedly at the ceiling. Teri stood by the bed for a few minutes, gazing down at her half sister. Finally, her voice all but inaudible, she spoke.

"Melissa?"

No response.

"Melissa, are you awake?"

Once again, no response.

Teri pulled the sheet back. There, fastened securely to Melissa's wrists and ankles, were the restraints that held her to the bed.

Teri hesitated, and then an idea came to her. "D'Arcy?"

Melissa's eyes shifted away from the ceiling and came to rest on Teri.

"D'Arcy, can you hear me?"

There was a moment of silence, and then Melissa's lips moved. "Yes, I can hear you." A slight chill coursed through Teri as she heard the voice issuing from Melissa's lips, for though it was recognizable, it had changed somehow. There was a flatness to it, a toneless quality.

Almost, Teri found herself thinking, as if a dead person had spoken.

"Do you know who I am?"

Melissa's head moved, and then D'Arcy's odd voice spoke again. "You're Teri. Melissa told me about you."

"Did she?" Teri asked, suddenly tense. "What did she say?"

Melissa smiled slightly. "That she loves you very much."

Teri relaxed. "Will you tell me who you are?"

A moment of silence, then: "Melissa's friend."

"Where do you live?"

"Upstairs."

Teri glanced upward, her heart beating faster. "Then why are you here?"

"Because Melissa needed me."

"Needed you for what?"

"To protect her from her mother. When her mother's mad at her, I come and take care of her."

Teri turned the words over in her mind, then spoke again. "But what happens to Melissa? Where does she go?"

"She goes to sleep," D'Arcy replied.

"What about you?" Teri asked. "Don't you want to go to sleep, too?"

D'Arcy was silent for a moment, then shook her head. "I can't sleep," she said. "When Melissa's tied up, I have to watch out for her."

Once again Teri thought for a while. And then, working carefully, she began to unfasten the restraints from Melissa's ankles.

A moment later she'd freed her half sister's wrists as well. "There," she said. "Now you can go back upstairs."

But Melissa's eyes had already closed, and now her breathing had taken on the deep rhythms of sleep.

Her lips curving in a dark smile, Teri pulled the sheet back over Melissa. Silently, she slipped away, leaving Melissa alone in the darkness.

Alone, and released from her bonds. . . .

CHAPTER

12

The bonfire had burned down to no more than a pile of glowing embers, and the breeze from the sea had taken on a dank chill. Wisps of fog were swirling over the beach, and as she glanced around, Ellen Stevens shivered slightly. "Let's go home," she said to Cyndi Miller. From the other side of the fire pit, his face barely visible in the reddish light of the coals, Kent Fielding grinned evilly.

"Scared?" he asked.

Cyndi Miller shook her head. Yet as the breeze died away and the fog began to thicken, she felt her nervousness increase.

But it was stupid—she'd grown up here, and never felt scared on the beach at all. And all her life she'd run back and forth between her friends' houses and her own, threading her way through the patches of woods with never a second thought.

But tonight, somehow, it was different.

It was the ghost story.

And it was stupid, because it certainly wasn't the first time she'd heard it. In fact, she and Ellen had been talking about it only the other day.

Except that when they'd been talking about the ghost of D'Arcy then, the sun had been shining brightly and they'd been lying around the pool at the club, surrounded by their friends.

Now it was night, and the fog was closing in around her, and suddenly everything looked different.

Telling herself she was being stupid, she resolutely got to her feet and zipped up the light jacket she'd put on an hour ago. "Why should I be scared?" she asked, more to hear the sound of her own voice than anything else.

"Because of D'Arcy," Kent told her, his grin broadening. "Look around—it's just the kind of night she likes. She can sneak through the fog, searching for her bloody hand, and no one can see her." His voice dropped, growing more menacing. "In fact, she could sneak up behind you, and reach out . . ."

Cyndi felt the skin on the back of her neck begin to crawl, as if there were someone behind her, reaching toward her, but she refused to give Kent the satisfaction of turning around to look.

". . . she could grab you by the neck . . ." Kent went on.

And suddenly Cyndi felt fingers closing around her throat.

She screamed, jerked away, then spun around just as Jeff Barnstable burst out laughing.

"Gotcha!"

Her face flushing hotly, Cyndi glared at Ellen Stevens. "Did you know what he was doing?" she demanded.

Ellen, unable to suppress her own giggles, nodded. "I'm sorry," she finally said. "It was just too good to pass up. The way you were staring at Kent. And he kept talking while Jeff sneaked up on you—"

Suddenly, Cyndi, too, was giggling. "Well, if D'Arcy really is out there, it won't be us she comes after," she said, shifting her glare to Jeff and Kent. "After all, it's boys she's mad at, isn't it?" She turned to Ellen. "Are you ready?"

Ellen nodded, shoving the last of her things into her beach bag.

"Sure you don't want us to walk you home?" Kent asked.

Cyndi eyed him archly. "I think I'd rather have D'Arcy chase me than have to fight you off," she said.

Leaving Jeff and Kent to shovel sand onto the last embers of the fire, the two girls started along the beach. A few seconds later, when Cyndi turned around, the boys, and the fire pit as well, had disappeared into the thickening fog.

Once again Cyndi shivered and moved closer to Ellen. "I—I'm not sure I like this," she admitted, keeping her voice low to make sure Kent and Jeff couldn't hear her.

"Oh, come on," Ellen replied. "It was only a ghost story, and there's no such thing as ghosts."

And yet as she, too, peered into the dense gray mist that covered the beach now, she felt a tiny flash of doubt. But that's stupid, she told herself. There *aren't* any such things as ghosts.

But what else might be out there, concealed in the fog, waiting for them?

"L-Let's get off the beach," she said out loud, her own voice dropping to the same level as Cyndi's. "The fog's never so bad in the woods."

They turned to the left and walked a few paces, and suddenly Cyndi felt water swirling around her feet. "What—" she began, then shook her head as she realized what had happened. "We got turned around," she said, reaching out and taking Ellen's hand. "Come on."

They turned their backs to the water and started across the beach once more.

Even the soft lapping of the surf was oddly muffled by the thick, nearly black mist that had settled around them. Cyndi found herself straining to pierce the fog with her eyes, but no matter how she tried, she could see nothing. Her foot struck something, and she tripped, nearly losing her balance.

"Are you okay?" Ellen whispered.

Cyndi nodded. "I think these are the steps that go between the Fieldings' and the Chalmerses'. How come you didn't bring a flashlight?"

"Who thought we'd need one?" Ellen countered. "I mean, there wasn't any fog last night."

They moved up the wooden steps that led from the beach to the path that formed the only boundary between the Fielding property and the ten acres next door that the Chalmerses owned. They came to a stand of pine trees, and a few yards farther on, as Cyndi had hoped, the fog began to thin. Now they could see the trunks of trees around them, though when they looked up, the treetops seemed to fade away into nothingness.

"It's weird, isn't it?" Ellen whispered. "I mean, it's like everything just ends all around us."

They moved quickly along the path, and after a few moments, off to the right, they could see the Chalmers house looming out of the fog. Then, as they watched, the fog grew thicker and the house slowly disappeared, as if it had been swallowed up by the mists. A tiny gasp caught in Cyndi's throat. "Come on," she whispered, her voice taking on a new sense of urgency. "Let's get to your house."

They scurried along the path for a few more yards, but although they were moving inland, the fog seemed only to thicken. And then, like the cold breath of the living dead, the breeze began again.

It was nearly pitch-black now. Something slapped against Ellen's cheek. She yelped with shock more than pain, and as she stopped short on the trail, Cyndi collided with her from behind.

"What's wrong? How come you stopped?"

"S-Something hit me in the face," Ellen replied. She reached out, her fingers timidly exploring the damp air around her. And then, a moment later, she felt the familiar soft prickliness of a pine branch. "It was just a branch," she whispered. She started forward again, then froze in her tracks.

Ahead of her, somewhere in the mist, she saw something.

Indistinct, almost formless, it was barely visible.

But it was there.

"L-Look!" she whispered, reaching back to grab Cyndi's hand and pull her forward.

A second later Cyndi was beside her. "What?" she hissed. "What did you see?"

Ellen strained her eyes, peering into the black fog.

Where a second ago there had been something, now there seemed to be nothing. Her heart, which had been racing in her chest, calmed slightly. "I—I don't know. I thought . . ."

She felt Cyndi's hand tighten on her own as the fog ahead dissipated.

In the path ahead of them a strange form seemed to be hovering a few inches above the path.

A white form, almost shapeless.

"Oh, God," Cyndi whispered. "What is it, Ellen?"

"I—I don't know," Ellen replied, her voice trembling now with the fear building inside her.

A moment later, as the fog closed in once more, the strange apparition disappeared.

Cyndi, her hand clinging to Ellen's so hard it hurt, trembled in the pathway. "Wh-What are we going to do? Should we go back to the beach?"

Ellen started to nod, then remembered the fog that already shrouded the beach, blinding them completely.

"No," she whispered. "L-Let's keep going. Maybe it's nothing."

But even as she started forward once more through the dank chill of the night, she didn't believe her own words.

They moved onward, and suddenly the invisible woods around them came alive with unseen menace. Everywhere, they could hear tiny twigs cracking and the heavy breathing of invisible creatures. They kept going, uncertain of where they were, but too terrified to stop.

And then, from behind them, they heard a sound, louder than the rest, and different.

A moan, low and anguished, that made them freeze in their tracks.

"Wh-What is it?" Ellen breathed.

"I don't know," Cyndi wailed, her words choking as a terrified sob rose in her throat.

Slowly, Ellen turned around and forced herself to peer once more into the darkness of the forest.

The wind picked up, and once again a rent appeared in the fabric of the mist.

Standing in the path, behind them now, was the distinct form of a girl, her face veiled, in a white ball gown.

The figure didn't move, but simply stood still in the path, staring at them.

Then, slowly, its right arm came up and a finger pointed at them.

Ellen stared at the figure for a moment. Panic welled up in her and a scream emerged from her throat as she turned and fled down the path, ignoring the pine branches that whipped at her face, the tendrils of vines that threatened to entangle her feet.

Only a few feet behind her, struggling to keep up, Cyndi Miller also fled from the terrifying specter that emerged from the fog.

*   *   *

Jeff Barnstable and Kent Fielding were making their way across the broad lawn in front of the Fieldings' rambling shingle-style house when they heard Ellen's scream.

For a moment neither of them was sure where the cry had come from, but then Kent broke into a run. "It was from behind the house," he yelled to Jeff. A second later both boys were racing through the fog, Kent leading the way, his feet so familiar with the landscaping around his home that he had no need to see where he was going. At the back of the house the blackness of the fog was brightened to a pale gray as the floodlights on the terrace came on. His father, clad in a flannel bathrobe, stepped through the French doors from the living room.

"Kent?" Owen Fielding called. "Is that you?"

"I'm over here, Dad," Kent called back as Jeff caught up with him. "Someone screamed."

Just then, both of them crying, Ellen Stevens and Cyndi Miller staggered up the terrace steps and ran to Mr. Fielding.

"Ellen?" Owen asked, as both girls clung to him. "Cyndi? What's wrong? Was that you screaming?"

Cyndi, regaining her breath barely enough to talk, nodded. "We—We saw something out there," she gasped. "In the woods."

Jeff and Kent, moving closer to the girls, eyed them suspiciously. "What?" Kent asked, exchanging a knowing glance with Jeff, a scornful grin already playing around the corners of his mouth.

Cyndi stared at him. A glimmer of doubt entered her mind as she saw the white running suit Jeff was wearing. Instead of answering Kent's question, she asked one of her own. "Was that you in the woods?"

Kent's grin faded slightly. "We were just coming up from the beach," he said. "We had to put the fire out, remember?"

Her breathing finally settling back to normal, Ellen looked up at Owen Fielding. "We—We saw something in the woods," she said. Her eyes shifted to Cyndi, as if pleading for help. "It—It looked like a ghost," she went on, her words sounding hollow now that she was safe on the Fieldings' terrace, the terrifying darkness and fog held at bay by the glowing halogen floodlights. "At least, it looked like—"

"It looked like D'Arcy!" Cyndi Miller said. Her voice, much stronger now, had taken on a defiant note as she met Kent's mocking eyes.

"Oh, sure," Kent drawled. "We sit on the beach and tell ghost stories all night, and then the fog comes in and the moon goes down. The two of you were already so scared you'd have thought a bush was a ghost."

"That's not true!" Cyndi shot back, turning to Ellen. "Tell them, Ellen. Tell them what we saw."

"It—It looked like a girl," Ellen said. "The first time we saw her, she was in front of us, and we weren't really sure what it was. It kept disappearing in the fog. So we kept going, and then we heard something behind us."

"It was like a moan, or something," Cyndi interrupted. "Really scary."

Now Ellen's eyes shifted from Kent and Jeff to Owen Fielding. "And when we turned around, there she was. It was a girl, wearing a white dress, with a veil over her face."

"She was staring at us," Cyndi added, shivering at the memory. "And then—And then she pointed at us."

She turned away from Kent's skeptical smirk and looked instead at his father. "It's true, Mr. Fielding," she said. "That's what we saw. You believe us, don't you?"

Owen Fielding, one arm still around Ellen Stevens's shoulders, reached out to give Cyndi's arm an encouraging squeeze. "Well, I certainly believe *you* believe that's what you saw," he said. "But before we all scare ourselves to death, why don't we go inside and make some cocoa. And then I'll drive you home." He waited for a moment, and as he'd expected, the girls did not object to his offer of a ride, although neither of their homes was more than a few hundred yards away. "You guys coming in?" he asked as he steered the girls toward the French doors.

Kent hesitated, glancing at Jeff, then shook his head. "I—I think maybe we'll take a look around," he said.

Owen Fielding chuckled appreciatively. "Have a good time," he said, "and don't stay out all night. And be careful," he added with a mischievous leer before he closed the doors. "The girls might be right. D'Arcy might be out there, and she might be looking for you."

Half an hour later, with the fog so thick they could barely see their hands in front of their faces, the boys were back.

They had seen nothing.

They had heard nothing.

And yet, as they hurried back toward the glow of the floodlights on the terrace, both of them had the eerie sense that someone— someone they could neither see nor hear—had been watching them.

Phyllis Holloway woke up at six-thirty the next morning, rolled away from the bright shaft of sunlight pouring through the window, and opened her eyes. She'd been dreaming, a wonderful dream in which she'd been at the August Moon Ball, proudly watching her daughter—the most beautiful girl in the room— dancing with Brett Van Arsdale. All the women she'd known for years, the women who had made her life miserable with their deliberate slights and their snubs made only more hurtful by their subtlety, were gathered around her, complimenting her on her daughter's beauty and hanging on every word she had to say.

In the dream, Teri MacIver had been her daughter.

She lingered in bed, clinging to the warm comfort of the dream, then remembering once again the conversation she and Teri had when her stepdaughter had come home last night.

It had been the kind of talk every mother dreams of having with her daughter.

And the kind that had been denied her with Melissa, she reflected bitterly.

Sighing, she threw back the silk sheet and got out of bed, pulling on a robe before leaving her room to go down the corridor toward her daughter's room.

She paused outside Teri's door, then tapped softly in the vain hope that Teri might call her in and she could put off going in to Melissa for a few more minutes. But when there was no answer, she went on to the room next door, giving the mahogany panel only a perfunctory tap before turning the knob and letting herself in.

She stopped just inside the door, frowning.

Melissa was sound asleep, lying on her side, her right arm curled up under her pillow.

Her frown deepening, Phyllis strode across the room and pulled back the sheet that covered her daughter.

The restraints—the leather straps and nylon mesh belts that she'd carefully secured to her daughter's limbs the night before—were lying haphazardly across the mattress.

"Melissa?" Phyllis said. "Melissa!"

Her daughter stirred on the bed, then rolled over, pulling the pillow with her to cover her head.

Phyllis reached down and jerked the pillow away, then grasped Melissa's shoulder and shook her sharply.

Startled, Melissa sat up, her eyes snapping open. As she recognized her mother, she automatically drew back against the headboard.

"Look!" Phyllis commanded, pointing at the straps that snaked across the mattress.

Melissa's eyes widened as she stared at the restraints, then her gaze shifted to her mother.

"I didn't take them off, Mama," she began "I can't. I—"

"Then who did?" Phyllis demanded, her voice rising dangerously.

Melissa cowered back, drawing her legs up so her knees pressed against her chest.

"I asked you a question, Melissa. I expect an answer!"

Melissa's eyes darted about the room as if searching for a means of escape, but there was none. "D-D'Arcy—" she stammered, then instantly wished she could retrieve the forbidden name. But it was too late.

"D'Arcy?" her mother repeated, flinging the word back at Melissa like a missile. "I thought we were through with that nonsense."

Melissa swallowed hard, trying to free herself of the lump that had suddenly formed in her throat. "Y-Yes, Mama," she whispered.

"Then who did it?" she demanded. "Who took the restraints off you?"

Melissa, her whole body trembling now, shook her head helplessly.

Phyllis moved closer to the bed, leaning forward so she loomed above her daughter. Her hand rose up as if she were about to strike the girl. From the door, Cora's voice stopped her.

"Oh, I'm sorry, ma'am," the elderly woman murmured. "I didn't know you were up yet."

Phyllis spun around. "Really?" she asked. "Is that what you've been doing, Cora? Releasing Melissa's restraints, then sneaking in early in the morning to put them back?"

Cora lurched back a half step, the accusation striking her like a physical blow. "Oh, no, ma'am," she breathed. "I wouldn't do that. I—"

"Wouldn't you?" Phyllis cut in, her voice edged with heavy sarcasm. "Well, if you wouldn't, it would certainly be the first time you'd obeyed my orders. I swear, I don't know why Charles insists on keeping you here." She strode across the room, and Cora scuttled out of her way. "We'll talk about this later, Cora," she said as she passed the housekeeper.

A minute later, as she poured herself a cup of coffee from the urn in the breakfast room, she was startled by the sound of Teri's voice.

"Is something wrong, Phyllis?"

She turned, then smiled as she saw her stepdaughter, already dressed in a pair of khaki pants and a white blouse, looking worriedly at her. Just looking at Teri seemed to ease some of her anger.

"Oh, it's just Cora," she said. "She went into Melissa's room last night and—" She cut herself off abruptly.

Teri's eyes widened and her right hand rose to cover her mouth. "Oh, dear," she breathed. "You're talking about those straps, aren't you?"

Phyllis stared at the girl for a moment, confused. "Why—Why, yes," she said at last.

"But it wasn't Cora who undid them," Teri said. "It was me."

Phyllis slowly sank into one of the six wicker chairs that surrounded the breakfast table. "You?" she asked. "I'm afraid I don't understand."

Coloring slightly, Teri's eyes dropped to the floor. "I—Well, I went in to say good night to Melissa. And she looked so uncomfortable, all tied down like that. Well, I just felt sorry for her, so I undid the straps."

Phyllis's frown deepened for a moment, but then her expression cleared and the sharp words that had been on the tip of her tongue died away. "I see," she breathed.

"I'm sorry if I did something wrong," Teri said, her voice soft

and her eyes still fixed on the floor. "I didn't mean to—I just—
well, she just looked so miserable."

The last of her anger draining away in the face of Teri's
apparent unhappiness, Phyllis held out her arms to the girl. "Of
course you didn't do anything wrong," she said. "You didn't
know what the restraints were for, and you were just trying to
help."

Teri brightened. "You're not mad at me?"

"Of course not," Phyllis assured her. She sighed, picked up her
cup of coffee and took a sip before going on. "It's just that—well,
Melissa has had some problems. She—She sleepwalks sometimes,
especially when she's upset, and I'm afraid she was very upset last
night. So sometimes, to keep her safe, I have to put the restraints
on her."

Teri gasped. "But I could have hurt her!" she exclaimed. "If I'd
known, I never would have done it."

Phyllis reached out and patted Teri's hand affectionately. "Well,
don't worry about it," she said. "Apparently she stayed in bed last
night, so no damage was done." Her smile faded and she stood
up. "I suppose I'd better go talk to Cora. I accused her of doing it,
and if I don't make some show of apologizing, she'll probably ruin
dinner."

Taking her coffee with her, Phyllis started toward the kitchen.

Alone in the breakfast room, Teri poured herself a cup of coffee
and looked happily out through the glass at the perfect morning
outside.

The sun was shining out of a cloudless sky, and there was no
longer even a trace of the fog that had come in so late last night.

Teri smiled to herself, and wondered if it was too early to call
Cyndi Miller or Ellen Stevens. She could hardly wait to hear
what had happened after she'd left the bonfire last night.

CHAPTER

13

Thwack!

Melissa's tennis racket connected with the ball, and for the first time that morning she heard the nice solid sound that meant she'd finally hit the sweet spot. The ball arced over the net, and she held her breath as her father backed away from the net, swung at it . . .

. . . and missed!

The ball sailed over his head, and suddenly Melissa was afraid it was going to go too far, but then it started falling, dropping onto the court just an inch inside the baseline.

"Good shot," Charles called to her.

Flushing with pleasure, Melissa trotted back to her own baseline, took a bead on her father's forecourt, and tossed a ball into the air. Her swing was a fraction of a second too late, and the ball drove into the net. She saw her father move forward, preparing himself for the easy lob she always used for her second serve. She waited for him to get into position, already knowing what she was going to do.

She was ahead 40–15, and even though she was certain her father was deliberately missing a lot of easy shots, he did it so well that so far this morning she hadn't been able to catch him at it. But this time, if she were lucky, she'd get a point by really earning it.

She tossed the second ball into the air, but instead of lobbing it slowly—and reasonably accurately—across the net to drop right into the middle of his court, she put all the force she could muster into her swing.

Thwack!

Once again she hit the sweet spot, and the ball shot over the net, straight and low, speeding past her father to strike the forecourt just inside the line. He stared at her in surprise for a moment, then a grin spread across his face. "I figured you'd take that risk sooner or later," he called. "I just wasn't expecting it right now."

Flushed with her victory, Melissa moved to her backcourt, spread her legs and waited for her father's first serve. A moment later the ball came over the net, but too late she realized he'd pulled the same trick on her she'd just worked on him. Instead of his usual fast and low first serve, the ball was arcing high, and Melissa started running forward. But she misjudged the distance, and when she finally got close enough to the ball to swing at it, she missed completely.

"For heaven's sake, Melissa," her mother's voice called from the next court. "How could you miss a simple shot like that?"

Melissa froze, flushing scarlet with embarrassment. Why couldn't they have stayed home like they usually did, she wondered, and played on their own court? Then at least everyone wouldn't have to hear her mother criticizing her.

But of course she knew the answer—her mother had decided she wanted to play today, too, and had insisted the whole family come to the club. "But you can't get courts on Sunday," Melissa had protested.

Phyllis had shaken her head. "I called early in the week and reserved two for us this morning. You and your father can play, and Teri and I can play. Then we can switch. It'll be fun."

So far, to Melissa's surprise, it hadn't been nearly as bad as she'd anticipated. At first she'd felt self-consciously certain that everyone was staring at her. But when she hadn't heard any laughter as she muffed her first four serves, she finally looked around.

No one was even watching her.

In fact, the few people who were watching the activity on the tennis courts at all had their eyes on Teri, and after sneaking a few glances at the next court herself, Melissa knew why.

Teri, looking gorgeous in her whites, had obviously played tennis before.

And Melissa had had a sneaking suspicion that Teri was giving her mother almost as many points as their father was giving her.

But now, the match with Teri over, her mother was watching her.

All her insecurities flooding back, Melissa took up her position for her father's second serve.

And missed again.

Six serves later, the game, and the set, were over. Though Melissa had at least managed to connect with two of her father's serves, her mother's scrutiny had made her so nervous that she'd blown both the shots, firing one of them into the net and the other one right over the fence, where it went bounding around among the breakfast tables that were set up on the wide terrace between the tennis courts and the swimming pool.

"What happened?" her father asked as he came around the end of the net. "You were doing so well."

Melissa shrugged. "I just fell apart," she said, unwilling to admit that it had been her mother's critical gaze that had made what few skills she had crumble.

Her father smiled at her. "It's harder when people are watching," he said, his voice dropping. "But don't worry about it—nobody plays tennis well all the time."

Melissa grinned. "I bet Teri does," she said. "In fact, I bet she could beat you in straight sets."

Charles glared at his daughter with exaggerated outrage. "You'd bet against your own father? That's treason!"

Melissa giggled. "Then go on," she urged. "Try to beat her."

"And you," Phyllis chimed in, "can try to beat *me*!"

Melissa's breath caught in her throat. Though her first instinct was to plead that she was too tired, she instantly changed her mind. For the last week—ever since the bonfire, in fact—things had been going better. Her mother hadn't seemed as angry at her as usual, and Melissa was certain she knew why.

Teri had been protecting her.

The day after the bonfire had been the worst, for early that morning Cyndi Miller had called Teri to tell her about seeing the ghost the night before. And when Teri had told her about it, Melissa had had a horrible moment of panic, certain that she'd been sleepwalking again.

But Teri had insisted she didn't have anything to worry about. "Even if it *was* you, nobody believes Cyndi and Ellen really saw anything. And we'll tell Phyllis it happened before I got home, so she'll think you were still tied to the bed."

Melissa had impulsively thrown her arms around Teri. "Would you do that for me?" she asked. "Really?"

"Of course," Teri replied. "I'm your sister, aren't I? You'd do the same for me, wouldn't you?"

Melissa had nodded, but still hadn't been certain it would work. But when her mother finally heard the story, Teri had been as good as her word.

"But it *couldn't* have been Melissa," she'd insisted. "Cyndi and Ellen left at the same time I did, so it must have happened while you and I were talking. Besides, I was reading for at least an hour after I went to bed, and if Melissa had gone out, I'd have heard her. She'd have had to go right past my door, and there's a squeaky board."

To Melissa's relief, her mother had accepted the story. Since then, with her mother convinced that she hadn't walked in her sleep, she'd even been allowed to sleep without her restraints. But if her mother got mad at her now, with her father going back to the city tonight . . .

She came out of her reverie and forced herself to smile. "Okay," she said. "Do you want to serve?"

"Don't be silly," Phyllis replied. "We'll volley."

Her mother lobbed the ball directly to her, and she managed to return it. It came back right in front of her, and once more she hit it back over the net. But when she'd returned it a third time, her mother suddenly stepped to one side, chopped hard at the ball, and it shot past Melissa almost before she realized it was coming.

"My serve," Phyllis announced.

Twenty minutes later, with the first set over and the second set at 3–0, Melissa felt tears of frustration welling up in her eyes. So far she hadn't scored a single point against her mother, and the longer the torture went on, the worse things got.

On the second court, Teri and her father were hard at it, and her father, completely occupied with trying to keep up with Teri's game, hadn't even noticed what was happening to Melissa.

Now, as her mother prepared to serve, Melissa's eyes wandered once more to the second court. Teri, playing close to the net, was firing the ball back at her father, whose shirt was showing splotches of sweat as he darted back and forth across the court, doing his best to return his elder daughter's shots. Suddenly Melissa heard the sharp snap of her mother's racket hitting the ball, and jerked her eyes away from the other court. But it was too late, for just as she turned, the ball ricocheted off the court a couple of feet in front of her, smashing into her chest with enough force to make her yelp with pain. Before she could say anything, her mother's voice, harsh and grating, followed the ball toward her.

"Really, Melissa! If you're not going to concentrate on the game, I don't see why you want to play it at all. It hardly makes it any fun for your opponent, you know!"

Melissa's emotions, held in check for so long, suddenly boiled over. "You knew I wasn't ready," she cried. Tears, caused more by outrage than by pain, streamed down her cheeks. "And it's not any fun for me, either! All I'm doing is chasing balls for you!"

On the other court, Charles let Teri's last shot slip past him, turning toward the sound of his younger daughter's voice just in time to see her drop her racket on a bench by the gate and rush off the court, her head down, her shoulders hunched over.

"Melissa?" he called, starting after her.

"Oh, for heaven's sake, Charles!" Phyllis snapped, her voice cutting sharply through the morning air. "Just let her go! The only way she's going to learn to be a good sport is by taking her losses with good grace. And she can't learn to do that as long as you throw every game to her and make up to her every time she bursts into tears."

Charles's jaw set, he started off the court, ignoring his wife's words. But then Teri spoke.

"Daddy? Aren't we going to finish our game?"

He hesitated, turning to look back at Teri, who was standing on the other side of the net, disappointment in her eyes. He vacillated for a moment, then stifled a sigh, knowing that if he abandoned the game with Teri to go after Melissa, it would only mean a fight with Phyllis later.

For once Melissa would have to take care of herself.

His hand tightening on his racket, he went back to his game, while Phyllis settled down on one of the benches to watch.

Tag grasped the machete with both hands, raised it over his right shoulder like a baseball bat, then swung. The blade flashed brightly in the sunlight, then struck the main trunk of the ivy that clung to the east face of the house, slicing almost through it before it lost its momentum and stuck fast. He grunted, twisted at the blade, then pulled it loose, letting it drop to the ground as he paused for a moment to catch his breath. He'd been working steadily for nearly two hours, but it seemed as if there was still almost as much ivy on the wall as when he'd started. Still, when his eyes shifted to the pile of vines that already lay on the lawn at the base of the wall, he knew he must be making *some* progress. But was it really possible for the ivy to double its mass as he pulled it off the house? He wiped the sweat and grime from his forehead with the right sleeve of his shirt, then picked up the machete once more. A moment later, with another swipe of the big blade, he finished cutting through the vine's thick stem. Then began the fun part.

Grasping the stem with both hands, he began pulling it away from the face of the wall, feeling the tendrils reluctantly give up their grip on the stones with which this side of the house was faced. The game he played with himself was simple—the whole idea was to see how much of the plant he could work loose before the main stem itself broke and the whole thing collapsed down on him.

Half an hour ago, working carefully, he'd managed to get everything loose except a few tendrils that had stubbornly clung to the crevices around the attic dormer, and when the mass of vine had finally fallen, it completely covered him. Blackie, surprised at his master's sudden disappearance, began barking madly, then started digging at the tangle, burrowing in as if trying to save Tag. In the end he had spent more time freeing the wriggling dog from the snarl than in getting himself loose.

He gave the main stem another exploratory pull. Near the second floor the stem split, the larger half of it snaking off to the right. If he could work that part free, the weight of the vine itself would pull the rest of it loose. Just as he was about to start working at it, Blackie began barking, then dashed off across the lawn, his tail wagging furiously. Cocking his head, Tag abandoned the ivy for a moment, turning to watch the dog.

A moment later Melissa, her head down, her hands stuffed in the pockets of her shorts, appeared at the head of the path that wound through the woods toward the club. As Blackie bounded up to her, her hands came out of her pockets to fend off his leap. "Stop that!" Tag heard her say, her voice trembling.

"Melissa?" he called out. "Hey, Melissa!" She glanced over at him, then turned away. Frowning, Tag trotted across the lawn, catching up to her as she was about to duck around a curve in the trail. "Hey! What's wrong?"

Melissa was still for a moment, but finally turned around. Tag could see she'd been crying—her cheeks were still stained with tears and her eyes were circled in red.

"You okay?"

Melissa snuffled, then reached down to pet Blackie, who was pressed against her legs. "I guess," she sighed.

Tag's head tilted slightly and he placed his hands on his hips. Melissa had been like a sister to him almost since the day she was born, and she'd never been very good at hiding her feelings from him. "So if you're okay, how come you're crying?"

"I'm not crying," Melissa replied.

Tag shrugged. "Big deal—you were a minute ago. What happened?" When Melissa still hesitated, he moved toward her. "You might as well tell me," he said. "I'll just keep pestering you till you do."

Almost against her will, a tiny smile crept into the corners of Melissa's mouth. "You can't. You have to get the ivy off the wall, and if you don't do it, I might tell Mother on you."

"Sure," Tag agreed. "And I might jump over the moon."

A giggle escaped Melissa's lips, and she fell in next to Tag as they started walking toward the house. By the time they came to the tangle of ivy that was heaped on the ground next to the east wall, Melissa had told him what happened at the club. "I know I can't beat her," she said, sighing heavily. "But how come she has to make a fool of me?"

'Cause she's mean as shit, Tag thought, but decided he'd better keep the words to himself. Then, his eyes falling on the machete, he had an idea. "You want to beat up on her?" he asked. Melissa frowned in puzzlement.

"What do you mean?"

"Maybe you should try doing what I do," he said. "Sometimes, when I get real pissed off at someone, I start hacking away with the machete, and pretend whatever I'm hacking at is the person I'm mad at." He handed the machete to Melissa, and nodded toward the heap of ivy. "I've got to chop all that up to get it out of here anyway," he went on. "Try it."

Melissa gazed at Tag for a few seconds, trying to decide if he was serious. At last she reached out and took the machete from him. She grasped it with her right hand, but when Tag released it, she almost lost her grip.

"Careful," Tag cautioned. "If you drop it on your foot, you can kiss your toes good-bye."

Melissa grasped the handle of the huge blade with both hands, eyeing the pile of ivy. "What am I supposed to do?" she asked. "I feel stupid."

"Who are you mad at?" Tag countered.

"My . . . my mom."

Tag tilted his head toward the pile of vines. "Then pretend that's her," he said.

Melissa stared at the pile of ivy, trying to figure out how she could pretend that it was her mother. Then she had an idea.

She pictured the ivy as hair.

Human hair.

Her mother's hair.

And suddenly her rage of a few moments ago, the rage she had carefully gotten under control as she walked home from the club, welled up inside her.

"I hate you!" The words erupted from her, and as she spoke them she raised the machete over her head. A second later it arced downward, and as the blade slashed through the tangle of vines, she imagined it was her mother she was hitting.

She slashed at the ivy again, and inside her she could feel the dam she'd built around her anger begin to crumble. Her pent-up fury raged like a torrent, down into her arms and out the slashing, hacking blade of the heavy machete. She kept at it, moving forward a step at a time as the pile of vines disintegrated under her attack.

She pushed on, chopping away at the vines, and as her arms rose and fell, she kept seeing and hearing her mother over and over again.

Ridiculing her clothes, criticizing her figure, correcting her manners.

Standing over her bed, the dreaded restraints held in her hands.

The machete kept moving, rising and falling, as Melissa slashed away at the hateful images.

Then, as suddenly as the rage had built up inside her, it was gone.

She dropped the machete to the ground and stood panting for a moment as she stared at the destruction she'd caused. And then she heard Tag's voice behind her.

"Feel better?"

She blinked, and turned around to face him. Her arms were sore from swinging the blade and she was sweating all over.

But she felt better.

The anger—the simmering fury that had threatened to over-whelm her only a few minutes before—was gone. A crooked grin spread across her face. "That's weird," she breathed. She was silent for a moment. "But it felt good. Really good."

An hour later, his match with Teri over and Teri herself already involved in another—this time with Brett Van Arsdale—Charles sank down at a table on the terrace and gratefully took a sip of the drink Phyllis had ordered for him. "I guess I'm not as young as I used to be," he said, finally catching his breath. "Whoever taught her how to play did a good job."

Phyllis, watching Teri volley with Brett, smiled happily. "She's wonderful, isn't she? And isn't this nice, finally being able to spend a Sunday morning at the club while our daughter plays tennis with her friends?"

Charles's eyes narrowed. His voice took on a hard edge. "In case you've forgotten," he said, dropping his voice so only Phyllis could hear it, "*our* daughter went home in tears, thanks to you. Just once in a while you could give her a break."

Phyllis's smile froze on her lips. "I'm just trying to do what's right for her," she countered. "You're not helping her by constantly letting her win." She paused for a moment, waving to Kay Fielding, who nodded back at her, then returned her attention to her husband. "She's not stupid, you know—she knows exactly what you're doing, and all it does is undermine her self-confidence even more."

Charles took another sip of his drink while he considered his wife's words. Was she right? *Was* he spoiling Melissa? Probably he was—after all, during the summers, he only got to see her on weekends, and even when they were in the city he was often so busy he only had an hour or so a day for her.

And he still remembered what Burt Andrews had told him two years ago, when Melissa's sleepwalking had first manifested itself. The morning that Cora had found her in the little room in the attic, sound asleep, with no memory of how she'd gotten there, neither he nor Phyllis had had any idea of what to do. But at last he'd called their family doctor in the city, who had immediately recommended a psychiatrist in Portland. And Andrews, if nothing else, had at least eased their worries.

Sleepwalking, he'd told them, was not in and of itself a terribly serious problem. He'd suggested a light restraint—just something strong enough to wake Melissa up when she started to leave her bed at night.

But most of Andrews's advice had been directed at Charles himself: "You have to be careful, Mr. Holloway. All fathers have a tendency to spoil their daughters, and since you gave Teri up to her mother, you're going to have a very strong tendency to over-indulge Melissa. It's simply a matter of guilt."

"But I don't feel guilty," Charles had replied. "I gave up Teri because it was best for her. It was either that or drag her through the courts for God-only-knows how long."

"I'm not arguing that," the doctor had interrupted. "I'm sure you did exactly the right thing. But I'm afraid guilt isn't rational, and no matter how logical your actions were, you're going to have to guard against spoiling Melissa to compensate for your subconscious feelings that you abandoned Teri. It puts both Melissa and your wife in a difficult position. Phyllis becomes cast as the disciplinarian, and Melissa gets mixed messages from her parents, and becomes confused. And out of the confusion . . ." His voice had trailed off, leaving the thought hanging, but Charles had understood it perfectly well.

Whatever Melissa's problems were, the root of them lay within himself.

And Andrews, he supposed now, was probably right. But still . . .

"I guess I just don't see how humiliating her in public is going to help," he began. Before he could go on, Phyllis cut him off.

"And *I* don't see how airing our dirty laundry at the club is going to help anything at all," she said, her voice brittle.

Charles's eyes fixed coldly on his wife, and when he spoke, his voice had a note to it that told her she had pushed him far enough. "Then don't do it," he said. "If you can't bring yourself to let Melissa have some fun at tennis—no matter how poorly she plays—then don't play with her at all."

Phyllis's jaw set angrily, but she said nothing, and for the next half hour the two of them sat at their table, nodding to the people who passed by, talking briefly with Marty and Paula Barnstable when they paused on their way to brunch.

To each other, they spoke not another word.

"Ready to go home?" Charles asked Teri after she'd finally lost her match with Brett and joined them at the table.

Teri's brows rose questioningly. "I thought we were staying for brunch."

Charles smiled sympathetically. "I know, but don't you think we ought to go see how Melissa's doing?"

Phyllis stirred in her chair, her head turning almost imperceptibly toward her husband. "Why don't you go?" she suggested. "Teri and I can stay here, and perhaps Melissa might feel like coming back with you."

"No," Charles said, his tone once more conveying that he would stand for no argument. "I can't imagine she'd want to come back here today, and I don't blame her. So if you're finished with your drink . . ." He let his voice trail off, signed the check, and rose to his feet.

Phyllis, on the verge of arguing, suddenly changed her mind, but did her best to smile at Teri. "When your father makes up his mind," she said, not quite bringing off her attempt to make light of their quarrel, "it just doesn't do any good to argue with him."

Ignoring his wife's comment, Charles strode across the terrace, Teri hurrying after him. Phyllis, seething silently, followed more slowly, deliberately taking her time.

Ten minutes later, as they climbed up the gentle rise from the beach to the edge of the lawn, Phyllis came to a sudden halt. On the lawn in front of the house, Melissa and Tag were engaged in a playful wrestling match, with Blackie doing his best to join in.

"Melissa!" Phyllis called, the sharpness in her voice instantly bringing her daughter to her feet. "How many times have I told you you're too old for that sort of thing? You're a teenager now, and I expect you to act like one." She strode across the lawn, but as she approached Melissa, Blackie put himself between the two of them, a low growl rumbling in his throat.

Phyllis stopped short, glaring at the dog, then turned her anger toward Tag. "This is the last time I'm going to tell you, Tag. If you can't keep that dog under control, I'm going to get rid of it. And as for you, young lady," she went on, refocusing on Melissa, her eyes raking the grass stains on her daughter's white shorts and blouse, "I want you to get upstairs right now and get yourself cleaned up. Those clothes you're wearing are brand new, and I'll be surprised if they're not ruined."

Her happiness while playing with Tag having evaporated like dew in the morning sun, Melissa turned and fled into the house.

"Very good, Phyllis," Charles said tightly before he hurried after his younger daughter. "At this rate, we should have her back to Dr. Andrews before the end of the summer."

CHAPTER

14

Teri lay restlessly on her bed. A book was propped on her lap, but she was no longer even trying to concentrate on its pages. Instead, her mind kept replaying the scene after dinner, when her father had left to go back to the city for the week.

Once again she'd stood silently to one side while he gathered Melissa into his arms, whispering into her ear, making plans with her for the next weekend. Finally, glancing at his watch, he'd turned to Teri, giving her a quick hug.

"Take care of Melissa for me?" he'd asked.

Take care of Melissa! What was she? A baby-sitter? Wasn't it bad enough that Melissa had thrown one of her tantrums at the club and ruined brunch for everyone? But she'd given her father her sweetest smile and promised to take care of her half sister. "We'll have a great time," she'd said. "Maybe I'll even give her some tennis lessons."

That, she reflected now, would be a real thrill. She could picture herself, standing in the center of the private court behind the swimming pool, lobbing one easy shot after another to Melissa and keeping up a steady stream of encouragement, no matter how clumsy her half sister might be.

"Good, Melissa! That's a lot better!"

"Great shot, Melissa! Right past me."

The whole idea of it made her want to throw up, but she could do it—she *would* do it, if she had to.

Just as long as Melissa kept thinking of her as her best friend.

And by the time Melissa caught on, if she ever did, it would be too late.

Far too late.

She shifted on the narrow bed, her hips aching slightly from the too-hard mattress, and an image of Melissa flashed into her mind, lying in her own oversized bed in the huge room next door.

My room, Teri thought. My room, in my house, with my father.

But not for long.

She got out of bed, pulling on her bathrobe as she moved restlessly to the open window. Outside, a thin layer of fog was drifting in from the sea—no more than a gentle swirl of mist that eddied around the treetops, blurring their forms just enough to give them an eerie, ghostly look.

D'Arcy weather, Teri thought to herself. Just the kind of night when a ghost would be wandering around the beach.

Her thoughts were interrupted by a nearly inaudible whining sound, followed by a faint scratching noise.

Blackie.

It had to be the dog, sniffing around the back door, trying to sneak into the house again.

Maybe she should let him in. She could bring him upstairs and slip him into Melissa's room.

And in the morning . . .

Her mind shifted gears as another idea came to her. She thought about it for a few seconds, playing it out.

It would work.

She went to the highboy next to her closet door and opened the top drawer, feeling around until her hands closed on the string of pearls her father had sent her for Christmas last year, the string of pearls identical to the ones in Melissa's own drawer. Slipping them into the pocket of her robe, she went into the bathroom, listening for a few seconds at the closed door to Melissa's room.

She opened the door a crack, peering inside.

Yes.

It was going to be all right.

Once again Phyllis had left Melissa's bed restraints off, and Melissa was curled up on her side, her head sunk deep into her pillow. Teri could even hear the steady rhythms of her breath as she slept. Satisfied, she closed the door again, then moved silently back into her own room, locking the bathroom door behind her. She switched off the lamp on her nightstand before going to the door, opening it a crack, and pausing to listen once more.

The house was silent.

Teri opened her door wider, slipped out into the hall and pulled the door closed. Carefully, she inserted the old-fashioned key into the lock, wincing at the distinct click the bolt made as it slid in. The hall was lit only by the small night-light at the head of the stairs, but Teri made her way easily through the gloom and a few seconds later was at the foot of the main staircase. She crossed the foyer and went through the dining room and the butler's pantry to the kitchen.

Blackie's snuffling and whining at the door was louder now, and when he scratched at the door, the rasping of his claws seemed oddly amplified.

Teri moved toward the door, and for a moment Blackie's whining grew eager as he heard the approaching footsteps. But when Teri opened the door, the whine turned into a low growl.

"It's me, Blackie," Teri whispered, holding the door wide open. "Don't you want to come inside?"

Blackie, his tail dropped low to the ground, backed away a couple of feet, and once more a growl rumbled softly in his throat.

Teri stepped outside onto the back porch and stooped down, holding her hand out to the big dog. Blackie hesitated, as if confused by the gesture, but then stretched his neck out to sniff suspiciously at Teri's fingers.

"Good dog," Teri whispered. "See? It's only me. You don't have to be frightened." She rose up from her crouch and moved closer to the dog, but Blackie backed warily away from her.

For a moment Teri considered trying to grab his collar, but then changed her mind. If the dog got frightened and ran off into the woods or down to the beach, she'd never find him.

An idea came to her. "Stay," she whispered. "Stay there!"

Blackie hesitated a moment, his eyes riveted to her, then sank down onto his haunches. Leaving the kitchen door open an inch or two, Teri went back inside and searched in the cupboards until she found a box of Milk Bones. Taking one of them, she went back to the door.

Blackie was exactly as she'd left him.

"Here," she whispered. "Do you want this?"

Blackie's head stretched forward and he whined pleadingly, but when Teri reached out to him, he shied away once more, slinking down the steps and a few yards out onto the lawn. But as Teri spoke to him again, he turned back.

"Come on, don't you want a cookie? Don't you see what Teri has for the nice doggie?"

Once again the whine rose in Blackie's throat, and this time, as Teri moved closer to him, he held his ground. His head came up and he stretched his neck out to take the treat.

As she gave Blackie the Milk Bone with her left hand, the fingers of her right hand slipped through his collar. "Good," she said. "That's a very good dog."

Blackie, munching happily on the Milk Bone, wagged his tail.

While he chewed, Teri used her left hand to untie the thick terry-cloth belt of her robe and pull it free from its loops.

As Blackie finished the Milk Bone, licking the last crumbs from the closely-cropped lawn, she slipped the belt around his neck.

"That's right," she crooned softly. "That's such a good dog."

The belt was all the way around Blackie's neck now, and finally Teri released her grip on his collar to take the other end of the belt.

Blackie looked up expectantly, hoping for another treat.

And Teri, with a sudden jerk, pulled the terry-cloth belt tight around his neck.

The big dog's eyes jerked wide open as his breath was suddenly cut off. He tried to twist free from the noose, but Teri stood straight up, lifting the Labrador half off the ground, his forequarters suspended helplessly from the knotted belt. His legs lashed out, kicking wildly as he searched for something to brace himself against, and then his lips curled back as he bared his fangs. His hind legs, still touching the ground, clawed helplessly at the lawn as he tried to free himself from his tormentor, but as Teri began jerking on the belt, yanking it first one way and then the other, he lost what little traction he had.

The struggle went on, eerily silent in the darkness of the foggy night, and for a moment Teri thought she might lose her grip on the belt.

But then, with a sharp snap, the battle came to an abrupt end.

Blackie's body, sixty pounds of violently thrashing bone and muscle, suddenly went limp as his neck broke, severing his spinal cord.

Teri held onto the belt for a few more seconds, until she was certain the dog was dead. Then, half carrying Blackie's corpse and half dragging it, she went back into the house and started up the servants' stairs.

At first Melissa didn't know what the sounds were; didn't even know when she'd first become aware of them. She was sitting alone in the featureless white room, a room that sometimes seemed so immense she could barely see the walls that surrounded her. But at other times those same walls seemed to press in on her with a terrifying closeness that made her feel as if she were suffocating.

She didn't know why she was in the white room or how long she'd been there.

But she knew it was some kind of punishment, some kind of penance she was required to suffer for some crime she couldn't even remember having committed.

But the room had been silent, so silent that the only sound she'd been able to hear at all was the quiet rasping of her own breath and the rhythmic beating of her own heart.

It seemed as though she'd been sitting in the silence forever, but at some point the sounds had begun.

She knew what they were now.

They were footsteps.

They had an ominous sound to them, and Melissa knew that whoever was approaching the room was coming for her.

The footsteps would not pass her by and fade away again. Instead they would stop, and then she would have to wait.

Wait for the door to open.

The hollow thumping grew louder, and suddenly the walls began to close in, moving toward her, threatening to crush her. She looked around, searching for a door or a window, but there was nothing.

And even if there were a way to escape the room, all that waited beyond was the terrifying being whose ominous tread came ever closer. The walls pressed in yet closer, and suddenly Melissa lashed out at them, shoving back at them with all the strength she could muster.

She jerked awake, and for a moment didn't know where she was. Then, as the remnants of the dream slipped away from her consciousness, the room began to take shape around her.

Her room.

She was home, and in bed, and . . .

Tied up.

Her heart sank. Had her mother come back tonight, after she'd gone to sleep, and put the restraints on?

The familiar panic she always felt at the sight of the hateful straps boiled up inside her, and in her mind she started to call out for D'Arcy. But even as she summoned her friend, her muscles automatically contracted against the bonds.

And her legs moved.

She wasn't strapped down at all.

Instead, she was tangled up in her sheet, one of her arms pinned to her side. She rolled over, squirming, and the sheet released its hold on her. Working her arm loose, she began tugging the folds of material away from her body, and finally kicked the sheet away entirely. She sat up, reaching for the sheet to straighten it out.

And heard the footsteps again.

Clear and distinct, they echoed in the silence of the night.

Melissa froze, listening.

The footsteps came again, and for a moment Melissa was certain that it was her mother after all. She must have cried out as she woke up from the dream, and wakened her mother.

There was a thump, and then the footsteps sounded once more.

But not from outside her room, not from beyond the door to the hallway.

From above.

From the attic.

Melissa's breath caught and she unconsciously held it, waiting for the sound to come again.

It came. Once, twice, three times. Then silence.

A moment later it happened again. Three distinct steps, and then silence.

D'Arcy.

Melissa released her breath as the name came once more into her mind. But it couldn't be D'Arcy—D'Arcy wasn't real. She'd made D'Arcy up herself.

Or had she?

The footsteps echoed from the ceiling once more, and at last Melissa got up and put on her robe, then found her flashlight in the second drawer of her desk. She opened her door a crack and peered out into the hallway.

All along its empty length closed doors seemed to gaze blankly at each other. Pulling the robe close around her and tying its belt, Melissa crept out into the hall, leaving her door open.

She moved slowly toward the far end of the corridor, coming at last to the door behind which lay the stairs to the attic. She hesitated.

What if her mother woke up and heard the footsteps, too?

What if her mother found her in the attic in the middle of the night?

But it wouldn't be like the other times. This time she was awake and knew what she was doing.

At last she turned the knob and pulled the door open. The stairs, the familiar flight she'd been up and down hundreds and hundreds of times, now appeared steeper.

Steeper, and darker, rising upward into what seemed nothing more than a black void.

She switched on the flashlight, but its beam barely penetrated the darkness.

And yet, despite the darkness, the ominous shadows above seemed to be reaching out to her, beckoning her. Taking a deep breath, Melissa started up the stairs.

She came to the top and stepped through the second door, into the attic itself. She paused, listening, but the seconds ticked by and she heard nothing.

She reached for the light switch, and the single bare bulb that was the attic's only light came on.

Suddenly Melissa stood in the center of a pool of light, and the darkness in the far reaches of the attic grew even deeper. Then, as if from far away, she heard a faint sound, almost like a soft chuckle of laughter.

A twinge of panic grasped at her. Could there really be someone up here?

And then she understood.

Teri.

It had to be Teri, playing a trick on her.

The fear drained away from her and she giggled out loud, but cut the laughter short as it echoed loudly around her. "Teri?" she whispered as loudly as she dared. "Come on, I know it's you."

There was silence for a moment, and then the strange chuckle came again. Melissa listened, trying to determine from which direction it came.

"Teri? Where are you?"

She began playing the light around the attic, certain that at any moment she would catch her half sister in its beam.

A moment later, as she aimed it toward the far end of the musty chamber, the end above her own room, a figure loomed up in the darkness.

A figure clad in white, its face veiled.

And next to it, suspended from the rafters by a white rope, was Blackie's corpse.

Even from here she could see the dog's grotesquely twisted head and bulging eyes, see its swollen tongue hanging over its sagging jaw.

And around the dog's neck she saw something else, something that made her blood run cold.

It was a string of pearls.

The pearls her father had given her for Christmas last year.

She stood spellbound, her eyes fixed on the softly glistening beads as her mind tried to accept what it meant.

She began moving forward, her vision narrowing until the

string of pearls blotted out all else around it. She reached out, her fingers touching the pearls, and then clutched at them, pulling them over the dog's head.

A split second later a scream erupted from her throat, shattering the silence in the attic. Panic welled up inside her, overwhelming her, and she bolted toward the door, leaving the light on as she pounded down the stairs. She reached the second-floor hall, turned the corner and hurled herself through the door of the master suite. An instant later a light came on and her mother sat up in bed, staring at her in bewilderment.

"Melissa? What on earth?"

"It's Blackie," Melissa wailed. "I saw him, Mama. I *saw* him!"

The last vestiges of sleep dropping away from her, Phyllis reached for her robe. "What on earth are you talking about, Melissa? If you've brought that dog into the house—"

"But I didn't," Melissa cried. She was crying now, tears streaming down her cheeks as she instinctively ran to her mother.

But instead of taking her into an embrace, Phyllis grasped Melissa's arms and sat her firmly on the edge of the bed. "Melissa, I haven't the slightest idea what you're talking about. Now stop crying and tell me what's wrong!"

With an effort of pure will, Melissa caught the sob that was rising in her throat. "U-Upstairs," she stammered. "He's upstairs. He—He's dead, Mama."

Phyllis stared at her daughter, exasperated. "Melissa, I haven't the vaguest idea what you're talking about."

"Blackie," Melissa wailed. "I keep telling you, Mama. He's up in the attic. He—He's dead!"

Slowly, the story coming out in fragments, Melissa tried to tell her mother what had happened, but even as she repeated what she had seen, she could tell her mother didn't believe her. Finally, when Melissa was done, Phyllis shook her head. "Melissa, you know how I feel about the things you make up."

"But I'm not making it up, Mama," Melissa pleaded, offering her mother the string of pearls. "I found these up there."

Phyllis eyed the necklace. "Your pearls, Melissa? Why would they have been in the attic?"

"Th-They were around Blackie's neck," Melissa stammered,

her voice quavering as her sobs threatened to overwhelm her. "If you don't believe me, go up and look!"

Phyllis abruptly stood up. "I will," she said, taking Melissa's hand and pulling her off the bed. "We'll both go. And," she added, her voice ominous, "I hope for your sake you haven't made all this up."

Phyllis marched her daughter out of the bedroom and down the hall. They came to the turn at the main stairs, and Melissa stopped abruptly as she saw Teri, clad in her pajamas and bathrobe, standing at her door.

"Melissa?" Teri asked, cocking her head as a worried frown creased her brows. "What's wrong? I thought I heard someone scream a few minutes ago."

Melissa wiped at the tears that still flooded her eyes, and nodded.

"I-It's Blackie—" she began, but her mother didn't let her finish.

"She seems to think she saw that stupid dog up there, along with some kind of ghost. It's nonsense, of course, but she insists I go see."

Teri's eyes widened. "Can I go, too?" she asked.

Phyllis hesitated, then smiled grimly. "Why not?"

A few seconds later, with Teri right behind her, Phyllis mounted the stairs to the attic. Melissa, still too terrified by what she'd seen to go back up to the shadowy chamber beneath the roof, hovered in the hall on the second floor. A few seconds later, though, Melissa heard her mother's voice speaking to Teri. "Well, there's the ghost, anyway!" Her voice rose as she called down the stairs. "Melissa, come up here." Melissa hesitated, and Phyllis spoke again, her voice sharp. "Did you hear me? I told you to come up here!"

Melissa crept up the stairs, already certain that something had happened, that whatever she'd seen, her mother and Teri had not.

"Look," her mother said as she reached the top of the stairs. "Is that what you saw?"

Melissa's eyes followed her mother's pointing finger, and she felt an icy finger of apprehension as she saw the old dressmaker's mannequin.

The mannequin she and Teri had seen only a few days earlier.

The mannequin that still wore an old white ball gown.

The mannequin that, only a few minutes ago, must have looked like a ghostly figure looming in the shadows. Her chest tightening, Melissa's eyes searched the attic for any trace of Blackie.

"Look around carefully," she heard her mother's voice instructing her. "Where, exactly, did you see the dog?"

A lump rose in Melissa's throat, and she tried to swallow it. "O-Over there," she breathed. "Right by the mannequin."

Grasping her daughter by the hand, Phyllis threaded her way across the cluttered floor until they stood only a foot from the mannequin. "Well?" she demanded. "Do you see him?"

Melissa shook her head.

"But you said he was right here."

Melissa nodded.

"And now he's not." When Melissa made no answer, Phyllis jerked at her arm. "He's not here, is he?"

"N-No, Mother."

"And there's no ghost wearing a veil, is there?" Phyllis demanded. "N-No."

"Then what happened?" Phyllis asked, her voice taking on a patronizing tone, as if she were talking to a five-year-old.

"I—I don't know," Melissa whispered, her eyes darting around the attic, searching for something, anything, that might prove what she'd seen.

"Well, then, since you don't seem to know what happened," Phyllis went on, starting back toward the stairs, "why don't I tell you. You had a bad dream, that's all."

"But it wasn't a dream," Melissa insisted, her eyes instinctively going to Teri for support. "I heard footsteps up here and came to see what they were. I—I thought it was you. I thought you were playing a trick on me."

Teri shrugged, shaking her head. "It wasn't me," she said. "I was asleep. I only woke up when you screamed."

"But—"

"But nothing," Phyllis declared. "You've been up here—you've seen that there's nothing here. If you were up here before and really saw what you say you saw, then you must have been walking in your sleep again."

The words battered at Melissa's mind. Was it possible her

mother was right? Could she have been sleepwalking again, and only dreamed the sounds she'd heard and the things she'd seen?

It didn't seem possible.

She stared once more at the pearls still clutched in her hand. "But I found these—" she began.

Her mother cut her off. "You brought those in hoping to convince me you were telling the truth. But it won't work. You're going back to bed, and this time you'll stay there."

Melissa felt a chill as she heard the words, for she was certain she knew exactly what her mother was talking about. And when they got back to the second floor, her mother's next words confirmed her fears.

"Why don't you go on down to the kitchen, Teri?" she suggested. "Put on some milk for cocoa, and I'll be down in a minute." She paused, her eyes fixing on her daughter. "As soon as I get Melissa settled into her bed," she finished. But instead of going with Melissa to the room at the end of the hall, she sent her daughter ahead.

When she came into Melissa's room a minute or so later, the girl flinched as she saw the straps in her mother's hands.

"I don't like these any more than you do," Phyllis said as she began fastening the leather cuffs around Melissa's arms and legs. "But I just don't know what else to do. You can't just wander around the house at night, can you?"

Melissa made no answer, for the moment she had seen the dreaded straps in her mother's hands, she had called out to D'Arcy to come and help her.

And D'Arcy had responded, sending Melissa instantly to sleep while she herself stayed awake to endure the terror of the bondage.

Half an hour later Teri came back upstairs with Phyllis, kissed her stepmother good night, and returned to her room. She waited until she heard the door to the master suite close, then crossed to the bathroom door, unlocked it, and moved through the bathroom itself to Melissa's door. She paused, listening, and heard nothing.

Finally, she opened the door and slipped through it into the darkness of Melissa's room. Her bare feet padding silently across the floor, she went to the bed and looked down into her half sister's face.

Melissa lay on her back, her eyes open, staring at the ceiling.

"Melissa?" Teri whispered. "Are you awake?"

There was no answer.

Teri smiled in the darkness, her lips curving upward in an expression of hard cruelty. "They're going to think you're crazy," she whispered. "They're all going to think you're crazy, and they're going to lock you up."

Laughing silently to herself, she returned to her room and quickly drifted into a deep and dreamless sleep.

CHAPTER

15

Teri awoke a second or two before the alarm on her nightstand went off, her hand clamping over the little clock before its soft buzzing reached full volume. She peered at the clock's dimly glowing hands; it was four-thirty, and outside her window the sky was still black. She lay in bed for a few minutes, listening to the night sounds, but there was nothing out of the ordinary; only the chirping of crickets and frogs against the backdrop of gentle surf lapping at the beach.

The house itself was silent.

She slipped out of bed, pulled her robe on, and went to the window. Beyond the pool, Cora Peterson's house was no more than a shadow against the dark mass of the woods at whose edge it sat.

Next she crept into the bathroom, where she listened at Melissa's door for a moment. But Melissa wasn't a problem, for Teri knew that she had at least a couple of hours before Phyllis would come in to take the restraints off her half sister.

And all she needed was a few minutes.

Going back into her own room, she dressed as quickly as she could, fumbling only a little bit in the darkness. At last she found her sneakers, exactly where she'd placed them last night, right next to the night table. She slipped her bare feet into them, pulled the laces tight and tied them.

She crept to her door, listening once more before she opened it, but the house was still as silent as a tomb. A tiny smile of satisfaction curving the corners of her mouth, she pulled her door open, slipped through it and shut it silently behind her.

She crossed the broad landing around the head of the staircase, brushed past her stepmother's door, then turned right into the guest wing.

At the end of the hallway she came to the closed door of the servants' stairs.

She opened the door, stepped through it into the pitch-black shaft and pulled it shut behind her. Now, blinded by the total darkness, she was operating only by her memory of her earlier climb up these stairs, when she had been carrying Blackie's corpse up to the attic. The moon had still been up then, and there had been enough light coming in the skylight at the top of the stairwell to see the turns in the stairs. Now, though, she had to feel her way along, carefully counting the steps as she went.

If she stumbled on the way down . . .

She put the thought out of her mind. So far, almost everything had worked perfectly.

The only bad moment had been when Melissa, instead of running screaming from the attic the moment she saw Blackie, had taken the pearls from his neck first. She hadn't counted on that happening. She'd assumed that the sight of the dead dog would be enough to send her half sister into hysterics. But Melissa had crossed the attic, almost as if she didn't believe what she was seeing.

And then she'd taken the pearls.

Teri, hidden behind a trunk a few feet away, had almost panicked when that happened. But even as Melissa had run screaming back to the stairs, she'd figured out what to do. Untying Blackie's body, she'd stuffed it into one of the trunks, then hurried back down the servants' stairs to the second floor. By then Melissa was already in her mother's room, blubbering out her story, and Teri had slipped by unnoticed in the darkness of the hallway.

She'd unlocked her room and gone through the bathroom into Melissa's room. Melissa's pearls were exactly where Teri had found them a few days before, and she'd been back in her own room, the pearls hidden away in her own chest, long before Phyllis and Melissa had started up to the attic.

The whole thing had worked perfectly.

She came to the top of the stairs and pushed the door open. Its unoiled hinges squealed in protest, and Teri froze, but then reminded herself that she was at the other side of the house. No one could possibly have heard the faint squeaking noise.

She began threading her way through the attic, groping in the darkness, until finally she came to the trunk in which Blackie's body lay. She opened it, lifted the dog's dead weight out onto the floor, then eased the lid back down.

Five minutes later, the corpse heavy in her arms, Teri emerged into the kitchen. She went out the back door, making her way across the lawn to the shelter of the pool house. A faint glimmer of light was showing on the eastern horizon now, and above her the night sky was losing its inky blackness.

Taking a deep breath, her arms already beginning to ache from the weight of Blackie's corpse, she started across the patio around the pool.

And froze.

From somewhere in the darkness, eyes were watching her.

But it was impossible—the house was dark; everyone was asleep.

She turned, scanning the house once more. The windows were all dark and everything seemed peaceful. But then, as she turned away once more, a flicker of movement—barely visible—caught her eye.

The attic.

Had someone been at the small dormer window in the attic, looking out at her?

She paused for a moment, thinking, her eyes fixed to the window. But as the sky began to brighten further, she decided she'd been mistaken. There was nothing there; no eyes were watching her.

She was safe.

She skirted the pool house, then paused once again, gazing intently at Cora's house before crossing the lawn toward the old pottingshed behind the garage.

"But what's it for?" she'd asked Melissa only a few days ago, when they'd come across the crumbling lean-to while her half sister was giving her a tour of the grounds.

"It's where the gardeners used to grow flowers. They'd plant the seeds in pots in here, so when they went into the garden they were already blooming. But nobody's used it for years."

"Why don't they tear it down?" Teri had asked, gazing at the sagging walls. "It looks like it's about to collapse."

Melissa giggled. "It is. But every time Daddy says he's going to have someone pull it down, Mom tells him she's going to use it for something. Once it was going to be an art studio, and another time she was going to do ceramics. But she never does. She never even comes near it."

Which was why Teri had thought of it tonight.

Dropping Blackie's corpse to the ground she pulled the door open. Inside, just as she remembered when she'd peered into the shed before, were the loose floorboards. It only took her a moment to lift three of them free.

She went back outside, picked Blackie up for the last time, and carried him up the steps.

Less than a minute later it was over. The floorboards were back in place and the crumbling shack was exactly as she'd found it.

Except that now it concealed Blackie's body in the space beneath its floor.

It's all right, D'Arcy's voice whispered. *I'm going away now, and it's all right for you to wake up.*

Melissa came awake slowly, her eyes fluttering for a moment, finally opening as Phyllis loosened the last of the straps that held her to the bed. She felt a flash of panic as she saw the restraints, but a moment later her mind cleared and she realized the night was over. It was morning, and a stream of bright sunlight was pouring through the window. "What time is it?" she asked.

Phyllis's brows rose slightly. "Oh, so you've finally decided to speak to me?" Melissa gazed blankly up at her. "Oh, please, Melissa. Why do you always do that?"

"D-Do what, Mama?" Melissa asked, her voice wary. Was it possible she'd already done something wrong this morning? But she'd just awakened a second ago!

And then the memory of the scene in the attic last night came flooding back to her. Was her mother still angry about that? But it wasn't fair.

She *had* seen Blackie up there, and—

Phyllis's sharp voice broke into her thoughts. "Do you think I don't notice?" her mother demanded. "You don't fool me, young lady. I know you're always awake when I come in."

Awake? What was her mother talking about? "But I wasn't," she began.

Her mother silenced her with an angry look. "Don't lie to me, Melissa. I know you hate the restraints, but they're for your own good. How do you think it makes me feel when I come in in the morning and you just stare at the ceiling, then pretend to be asleep when I start taking them off? If you don't want to say good morning to me, fine. But don't insult my intelligence by pretending to be asleep."

Suddenly Melissa understood.

It wasn't she who had been awake when her mother came in.

It had been D'Arcy, watching over her, letting her sleep through the night. She shuddered slightly, wondering how D'Arcy could stand it, remembering the panic she herself always felt when her mother came in with the horrible straps. But D'Arcy didn't seem to mind them at all.

"I—I'm sorry, Mama," Melissa murmured. "I just—I guess maybe I wasn't quite awake yet."

Phyllis, slightly mollified by her daughter's apology, nodded. "All right," she said. "It's almost eight. Teri and I have already had breakfast, and we're going to the club."

Melissa nodded automatically, and a moment later her mother was gone. Melissa went into the bathroom, stripped off her pajamas, and took a shower. As she was pulling on her favorite pair of faded jeans a few minutes later, she heard Tag's voice drifting in through the open window.

"Blackie! Here boy! Come on, Blackie!"

Melissa's heart leaped. She must have been wrong last night after all. If Tag was calling Blackie—

But then she remembered the pearls. Instantly, her eyes went to her nightstand, where she'd put them last night.

They were still lying there, exactly as she'd left them.

She pulled a T-shirt on over her head and ran to the window. Tag was moving along the edge of the lawn that bordered on the woods, calling out to the dog every few yards. She watched him for a moment, her throat constricting as she realized what she had to do.

She shoved her feet into a pair of sandals and hurried downstairs. Cora, alone in the kitchen, smiled at her, tilting her head toward a glass of orange juice on the counter. "Your mama and Teri are already gone," she said. "I saved you some juice, and I've got some bacon in the oven. And I could fix some eggs."

Melissa shook her head at the offer, and Cora looked sharply at her. "Is something wrong, honey? You look—"

"Blackie's gone, isn't he?" Melissa asked.

Cora caught her breath. "Well, now, I'm not sure you could say that, but—"

"But he is, isn't he?" Melissa insisted, reading the truth in Cora's expression.

"Well, he didn't come in last night," she admitted. "But like I told Tag this morning, that's right normal for a dog. I mean, all it'd take is one female in heat, and you have to expect him . . ." Her words trailed off as Melissa dashed out the back door, running across the lawn toward Tag, already calling out to him.

"Tag? Tag!"

He was just about to go into the woods when Melissa's words stopped him. He turned around to see her trotting toward him. A few seconds later she was beside him.

"He's gone, isn't he?" she asked, her breath coming in quick pants.

Tag's brow furrowed slightly. "How'd you know?"

Melissa hesitated, remembering once more the look on her mother's face last night when she'd told her about seeing Blackie's body hanging from a rafter in the attic. Would Tag look at her that way, too? "I—I saw him last night," she said. "Anyway, I think I did."

Tag cocked his head uncertainly. "What do you mean, you *think* you saw him?"

"Well, I don't *know*," Melissa went on. "Mama said I had a nightmare, or made the whole thing up. But I didn't." Slowly, she told him the whole story, starting from when she'd awakened and heard the footsteps in the attic. When she was finished, Tag's frown deepened.

"And there wasn't anything there at all when your mom took you back up?"

Melissa shook her head. "Nothing but a dumb old mannequin with a dress on it," she told him.

"Well, mannequins don't make footsteps," Tag replied. "Maybe we should go up there and see what we can find."

Melissa's eyes widened slightly. "Do you think we should?"

"Why not?" Tag asked. "I mean, it's your attic, isn't it? Did your mom tell you not to go up there?"

Melissa shook her head, and the two of them started back toward the house.

Twenty minutes later their search was over.

The mannequin still stood in the attic, but there was no sign of Blackie.

"But it still could have been a dream," Tag insisted as they went back downstairs.

"It wasn't!" Melissa insisted. "I wasn't dreaming, and I wasn't sleepwalking. I know what I saw! Besides, what about the pearls? They were around Blackie's neck!"

"Hey, take it easy," Tag protested. "I wasn't accusing you of lying. I just meant—Well, you *do* walk in your sleep sometimes. Maybe—Well, maybe you took the necklace up there yourself."

Melissa's eyes darkened. "I didn't! I wasn't sleepwalking, and I know what happened."

Tag backed away a step or two. "All right," he said, his voice rising in the face of Melissa's anger. "Then you tell me what happened! What did you do? Kill him yourself?"

Melissa's mouth dropped open. "I—I—"

But she could say nothing more, for suddenly she realized that what Tag had just said was exactly the same thought that had been lurking in the back of her own mind.

It had been *her* necklace around Blackie's throat.

If she hadn't put it there, then who had? Nobody else even knew where she kept it.

Was it possible that she *had* been sleepwalking?

Could she have done it and not remembered?

The footsteps.

What about the footsteps?

What if she hadn't heard them at all? What if they had only been part of the dream she'd had?

Suddenly she felt as if her head were stuffed with cotton. Nothing made sense anymore—she couldn't figure out what was real and what had only happened in her own mind.

She felt as though she were going crazy. Her eyes welled with tears and a sob rose in her throat, threatening to choke her. "Y-You really think I could have killed him?" she finally asked, her voice trembling in spite of her efforts to control it.

Tag groaned. "Aw, come on. Why would I think that? I just said it because you were acting like you were mad at me. Of course you didn't kill him. Why would you have?"

"But if I didn't, where is he?" Melissa countered, her voice bleak as the tears in her eyes finally began running down her cheeks. "Where is he, Tag?" she repeated. "What if I killed him and don't even remember it?"

Without waiting for an answer, she fled into her room, slamming her door behind her.

Teri lay stretched out on a chaise longue, her eyes closed against the brilliance of the morning sun. She felt good—she'd played a set of tennis with Phyllis, which she'd managed to let Phyllis win, then beaten Ellen Stevens in straight sets. After that, she and Ellen had gone for a swim, and ever since then she'd been lying by the pool, enjoying the warmth of the sun and the babble of voices around her.

A shadow fell on her face, and she opened her eyes to see a dark silhouette looming above her. She squinted, trying to make out who it might be, and was just about to sit up when a splash of icy water hit her legs. Gasping at the shock, she jumped off the chaise, then spun around to see Brett Van Arsdale standing at the edge of the pool, grinning at her. "You looked like you might be burning, so I decided to baste you," he said.

"Oh, really?" Teri replied. "Well, how's this for a basting?" With a quick shove she pushed him into the pool, then dived in after him, hitting the water just as he broke the surface. Grabbing his shoulders, she shoved him under again and pushed away, twisting out of his grip as he reached for her. He caught up with her halfway across the pool, and she barely managed to snatch a breath of air before he pulled her below the surface. She struggled for a moment, freed herself, then shot away, finally slithering out of the pool a fraction of a second before he caught up with her. By the time he'd scrambled out of the water, she was already drying herself off with the towel one of the pool boys had brought her the minute she'd appeared on the terrace. Finished with it, she tossed it to Brett, then stretched out on the chaise again. A moment later Brett dropped down on the one next to her.

"You going to the dance next weekend?" he asked.

Teri cocked her head. "What dance?" she asked.

"The costume party," Brett replied. "It's next Saturday, and if you're not going with anybody . . ." His voice trailed off, and Teri grinned mischievously at him.

"You mean you want me to go with you?" she asked.

Brett flushed, nodding. "If you want to."

Teri was about to accept his invitation, then hesitated. What about Melissa? Would she be allowed to go if no one asked her half sister? She glanced over to the table where her stepmother was sitting talking to Brett's mother. After this morning, she suspected that Phyllis wouldn't care whether Melissa went to the dance or not.

But what about her father? In her mind she heard his words once again. "Take care of Melissa for me, okay?"

And then, once more, an idea began to take shape in her mind.

"It sounds like fun," she said, smiling at Brett. But then she let her brows form into a frown. "But—Well, what about Melissa?"

The grin that had spread across Brett's face wavered. "Melissa?" he repeated. "What about her?"

Teri's eyes shifted demurely to her lap. "Well, it would be kind of mean of me to go without her, wouldn't it? I mean, I just got here, and hardly know anyone. How would she feel if I went with you, and no one asked her?"

Brett's tongue ran nervously across his lower lip. "What am I supposed to do?" he asked. "Find a date for her, too?"

Teri looked up at him, her expression a perfect mask of surprise. "Could you?" she asked. "Could you really?"

Brett swallowed. Now what had he gotten himself into? Who did he know who would be willing to go anywhere with Melissa Holloway? "I—I don't know," he hedged.

Teri's smile faded away. "Well, then I don't see how I can go, either. I just don't think it would be right for me to leave her sitting at home by herself." Then, as if she'd just thought of it, she brightened. "What about Jeff Barnstable?"

Brett stared at her. "Jeff? What made you think of him?"

Teri hesitated, then lowered her voice. "If I tell you a secret, will you promise not to tell anyone else?" Brett nodded. "Melissa has a crush on him," Teri went on. "If you can get him to ask her, then I'll go with you."

"What if I can't?" Brett asked.

Teri shrugged. "You can," she said. "You'll find a way."

An hour later Brett found Jeff Barnstable sprawled out on a towel on the beach in front of Kent Fielding's house, a pair of earphones on his head and a magazine in his lap. Kent himself was stretched out on his stomach, apparently asleep. Dropping down on the sand next to his friend, Brett turned the volume on the Walkman all the way up, then snapped it off. Jeff jumped at the sudden blast of sound in his ear, then glared up at Brett.

"Hey, man, what the hell'd you do that for?"

"I've gotta talk to you. I've got a problem."

"Melissa?" Jeff howled after Brett explained what he wanted him to do. "Gimme a break, man. You think I'm going to ask Melissa Holloway for a date? Do I look crazy?"

"Aw, come on," Brett replied. "What's the big deal? What about that cousin of yours I went out with last year?"

Jeff rolled his eyes. "It's not the same thing. My cousin is at least human."

"Barely," Brett shot back. "Besides, what's so terrible about Melissa? She wasn't so bad at the bonfire the other night—"

"Riiight," Jeff drawled. "Until she got all upset and went running home to her mommy. Of course," he added, his voice taking on a sly note, "if you want to make a deal . . ."

He let the words hang in the air. "What kind of deal?" Brett asked suspiciously.

"The Porsche. Let me drive the Porsche Saturday night and all day Sunday, and I'll think about it."

Brett hesitated. He'd only had the car six months, and so far he hadn't let anyone else drive it at all. And then, unbidden, an image of Teri came into his mind.

She was smiling at him, and in her eyes . . .

"All right," he said, agreeing to the deal before Jeff had a chance to change his mind. "We'll call them this afternoon. Okay?"

Jeff, who'd been almost certain Brett would turn the deal down, hesitated. But then he saw himself behind the wheel of the black sports car, speeding along the road that wound in a series of hairpin curves along the coast. Surely he could put up with Melissa for a couple of hours, he decided. And maybe he could even figure out a way to bribe some of the other guys into taking her off his hands every now and then. "Okay," he agreed. "I'll ask her."

Kent Fielding rolled over and sat up, blinking in the sun. "And you might get lucky," he suggested, grinning at Jeff. "I mean, you could always get sick on Saturday night, couldn't you?"

Jeff and Kent stared at each other for a moment, and then both of them burst out laughing as they imagined the look on Melissa's face if Jeff were to stand her up.

CHAPTER

16

"It's perfect," Teri declared, her eyes reflecting her excitement as she examined the dress she'd just found on the rack at the back of the Historical Society thrift shop. "Don't you just love it?"

Melissa's brow furrowed as she tried to see the dress through Teri's eyes, but to her it looked like exactly what it was—an old prom dress, maybe from the fifties, with a princess waistline and puffed sleeves. The skirt, made of satin, had a stain on it, and its hem was partially ripped out. Over the satin was a layer of tulle that might once have appeared to float like a cloud around the dress but now hung limply, its netting badly snagged. It might once have been pink, but its color had faded badly, and was now a sort of uneven peach.

Melissa's eyes shifted from the dress to her half sister. "It's horrible," she said.

"It isn't, either," Teri protested. "Let me try it on." Without waiting for an answer, she disappeared behind a curtain that was hung across the door of a makeshift dressing room, and Melissa went back to picking through the racks of discarded clothes in search of something that might pass for a costume.

She still wasn't sure she really wanted to go to the dance on Saturday night. In fact, when Jeff Barnstable had called on Monday afternoon, she'd been certain he was playing some kind of joke on her, and told him she'd call him back. But when she'd asked Teri about it, Teri had insisted that the invitation was real. "We're going to double date," she explained. "You and Jeff, and Brett and I."

Melissa had looked at Teri suspiciously. "Whose idea was it?"

"Well, I don't know," Teri had hedged. "We were just talking about it at the club this morning, and we all sort of decided it together."

Melissa had still hesitated, but then Phyllis came out to the terrace where they were sunning themselves. "Decided what?" she'd asked, and before Melissa could stop her, Teri had told her mother about the invitation. "Well, of course you'll go," she said. "It's just perfect for your first date."

"But I don't—"

"Not another word," Phyllis told her, and though she'd kept smiling, her voice had taken on a hard edge that warned Melissa that she would tolerate no argument. "After all, I *am* on the Social Committee this year. How would it look if my own daughter didn't go? And Teri can help you find a costume. Besides," she'd added, "it will give you something to think about other than that dog."

Melissa had said nothing, certain that whatever she might say about Blackie would only make her mother angry. Besides, what could she say? She and Tag had searched everywhere they could think of, walking through the woods, calling out to Blackie, but there had been no sign of him. And Melissa had only become more confused as they searched. If she'd really seen the dog in the attic, then why hadn't they been able to find his body?

Was it possible that the whole thing really had been a nightmare, that she had, after all, been walking in her sleep? Could she have seen the whole thing only in her mind and only awakened when she screamed?

She hadn't dared talk to anyone about it except Teri, and even Teri hadn't been able to think of an answer. "He probably just ran away," she'd said. Then she'd grinned mischievously. "Or maybe D'Arcy got him."

D'Arcy.

Melissa had been thinking about it ever since, trying to figure it out. Was it possible that D'Arcy had done something to Blackie? But how could she? D'Arcy didn't exist, except in her own mind.

Did she?

What if she did?

What if she were real?

A slight shudder ran through her, and then she jumped as a hand touched her shoulder. She spun around to see Teri, clad in the old pink formal, gazing at her curiously. "Hey, what's wrong?"

"N-Nothing," Melissa stammered.

"Well, didn't you hear me talking to you just now?" Teri said, turning around. "I can't get the stupid zipper up."

Her fingers trembling, Melissa pulled the zipper up, and Teri turned around once more. "I can fix the hem and we can put a whole lot of sequins and rhinestones on the overskirt. Then we can make a wand and I can go as a fairy godmother. It'll be perfect."

Melissa frowned, perplexed. "But what about the stains?"

"Who cares about them?" Teri asked. "It's a costume party, right? Everybody will be digging around looking for old clothes." She giggled. "I bet half the people there wind up looking like their own grandparents. Now let's see what we can find for you." She disappeared into the dressing room, coming back out a few moments later with the dress over her arm. Together they began searching through the old clothes for something that might be converted into a costume for Melissa, but every time Melissa found something, Teri had an objection:

"It won't fit you right. See? We'd have to let out all the seams."

"It's falling apart! We don't want your clothes to fall off you in the middle of the dance, do we?"

"It's miles too big—we could never take it in in time."

Finally, Melissa found an old-fashioned tuxedo, complete with a top hat, that seemed to be in a boy's size. "How about this?" she asked hopefully. "I could be a magician, or Charlie Chaplin, or something." But once again Teri shook her head.

"It's just not *right*. We need something really spectacular." She glanced around the shop, looking for a corner they hadn't yet searched. But they'd been through everything. "Why don't we go get a Coke?" she suggested. "Maybe if we stop hunting, we'll come up with an idea."

Melissa took a last longing look at the tuxedo. She was certain it would fit, and if they could make a cape . . .

"No," Teri decreed, as if she'd read Melissa's mind. "It's just not right for you. Anyway, if we can't think of anything better, we can always come back for it."

Melissa hung the tux back on the rod and followed Teri to the front of the store. She was passing a case full of antique costume jewelry when a bright sparkle caught her eye. Lying on the top shelf of the case was an old tiara, topped with a fleur-de-lis, all of it thickly encrusted with rhinestones. "Look!" she cried out. "It's your crown!"

Teri gazed at the tiara, then shook her head. "It's perfect," she agreed. "But how much is it going to cost?"

"Mrs. Bennett?" Melissa called to the manager, who came over and went behind the cabinet to take the tiara out. "How much is it?"

Freda Bennett peered at the price tag. "Seventy-five dollars," she said. "It's an antique." She placed the tiara on Teri's head, and Teri turned to look at herself in a gilt-framed mirror that hung on the opposite wall. Sighing, she took it off and handed it back to Mrs. Bennett. "It's perfect, but I can't afford it."

"We'll take it," Melissa said just as the shop manager was about to return the tiara to the case.

Teri turned to look uncertainly at her half sister. "But we can't," she protested. "I don't have the money."

"But I do," Melissa replied, grinning as she groped in her purse for her wallet.

Teri stared at the wad of bills stuffed into the wallet. "Where'd you get all that?" she breathed.

Melissa shrugged. "It's from my allowance. All I ever buy are paperback books, and Daddy gives me money practically every weekend, but I never spend it. So you pay for the dress, and I'll buy the tiara for you."

"But—"

Melissa shook her head. "I *want* to buy it for you. It'll make your costume perfect. Please?"

Teri smiled, and let Mrs. Bennett wrap up the tiara.

* * *

Half an hour later, as they were about to leave the drugstore, the door opened and Brett Van Arsdale, followed by Kent Fielding, came in. A grin spread across his face as he saw Teri. "Hey, there you are. Just the person I've been looking for."

Teri cocked her head. "Me?"

Brett nodded. "Kent's dad is going to let us take their boat out this afternoon. I just thought you might want to go along."

Teri glanced quickly at Melissa, who seemed suddenly to have become fascinated with a display of magazines just inside the door. "Who all's going?" she asked.

"Everybody," Brett replied. "Us, and Jeff, and Ellen. Maybe Cyndi and a couple of others. You want to come?"

Teri turned to Melissa. "What do you think?" she asked. "Should we go?"

Melissa turned around, her cheeks flushing, certain that Brett hadn't meant to include her in the invitation. "I—I don't know—" she floundered. "If you want to go—"

Teri nodded eagerly. "Of course I want to go! What kind of boat is it?" she asked, turning back to Brett. "Is it a sailboat?"

Brett nodded. "It's not much—just a thirty-two-foot Lord Nelson." His eyes involuntarily flicked toward Melissa. "If Melissa doesn't want to come—" he began.

But Teri cut him off. "Why wouldn't she want to?" she said. "What time shall we meet you?"

Brett glanced at Kent, then shrugged. "I don't know—two o'clock?"

The time agreed to, Teri and Melissa left the drugstore and started back toward Maplecrest. As soon as they were gone, Kent glared at Brett. "Smooth move, Van Arsdale. Now we're going to be stuck with Melissa all afternoon."

"Well, what was I supposed to do? She was standing right there. Besides, what's the big deal? It's not like she's your date or anything." Then, as a thought occurred to him, he snickered. "Jesus, it'll be worth it just to see the look on Jeff's face when she shows up. He'll think we did it on purpose."

Kent rolled his eyes. "You really got it bad for Teri, haven't you? I mean, so far you've asked her out twice, and both times she's dragged Melissa along. What are they, Siamese twins?"

"Well, what's she going to do?" Brett countered. "She barely got here, and she's already got more friends than Melissa. She's just trying to be nice to her sister, that's all."

"So all the rest of us have to put up with her, too?" Kent groused. "Shit, next thing, you'll be trying to get *me* to take her out."

Brett gave his friend a punch on the arm. "Who knows?" he teased. "You might fall for her." He ducked away quickly as Kent took a swing at him, then darted out the door.

But as Kent fell in beside him again, he wondered what was really going on. *Was* Teri ever going to go out with him without insisting that Melissa go along?

Well, he'd wait until after the dance Saturday night and see what happened. After all, she couldn't insist on him finding dates for Melissa if no one would go out with her.

Still, that was one of the things he really liked about Teri—she always seemed to care about what other people were feeling.

Even people no one else cared about, like Melissa Holloway.

He turned to Kent, grinning. "She's really nice, isn't she?" he asked.

Kent cocked his head. "Who?"

"Teri," Brett replied. "You know what? I think she's about the nicest girl I've ever met."

Melissa's step slowed as they approached the small marina tucked in behind the leeward side of the point that formed the south boundary of the cove. "M-Maybe I'll just stay here," she suggested to Teri, her eyes nervously scanning the whitecaps that were scattered across the surface of the sea beyond the protection of the cove. "What if I get seasick?"

"Why would you do that?" Teri asked, though she remembered perfectly well the conversation they'd had one day last week, when they'd been sprawled out on the beach watching a regatta of small boats wheeling around the cove.

"How come we don't have a boat?" she'd asked. Melissa had giggled. "Because Daddy and I both get seasick. He took me fishing for my tenth birthday, and we both barfed our brains out. It was really gross. I don't care if I never get on a boat again."

Now, her eyes widening as if she'd just recalled the conversa-

tion, Teri looked at Melissa apologetically. "Oh, God. I forgot."
But then she brightened. "But that was a long time ago," she said.
"You'll be fine. Besides, look at the water. The cove's perfectly
flat—why would you get sick?"

Melissa rolled her eyes. "I'm getting sick just thinking about it."
They were on the dock now, and Melissa came to a complete
stop. "Would you be real mad if I didn't go?" she asked, her voice
anxious.

"Of course not," Teri assured her. "If I'd remembered, I wouldn't
have told them we'd go at all. But what are we going to tell your
mom?"

"M-Maybe we don't have to tell her," Melissa suggested. "I
could just wait here till you get back, and she wouldn't know I
didn't go."

Teri shook her head. "She'd find out. She's coming to the club
this afternoon, and you know how she is. She'll be talking about
how we're both out on the Fieldings' yacht and acting like it's a
big deal. And if anyone spills the beans that you didn't go . . ."

Melissa groaned, knowing Teri was right. She could already
hear her mother, furiously telling her how rude she'd been to
accept an invitation and then not go. And then later tonight, after
she'd gone to bed . . .

And besides, she thought, Teri's right. If I concentrate real
hard and stay up in the fresh air, I'll be fine. And if I don't go, I'll
just look like I chickened out. "You're right," she said, making her
voice sound a lot more confident than she felt. "Why should the
kids like me if I won't ever do what they like to do?"

Teri gave her arm a reassuring squeeze. "Good for you," she
said. "And it'll be all right—you'll see. It'll be fun."

They walked down the dock and found the boat, *Zargon*, its
varnished teak gleaming in the sun, the rest of the kids already on
board. Teri and Melissa stepped onto the deck and down into the
cockpit as Jeff and Brett loosened the dock lines and Kent started
the engine.

Teri looked at him uncertainly. "I thought we were sailing."

"We are," Kent replied. "But the wind's all wrong to try to sail
away from the dock. We'll go out into the cove and put the sails
up there."

Jeff and Brett cast the lines off, then jumped aboard as Kent pulled the boat away from the dock. "I'm opening Cokes," Ellen Stevens called from below. "Anyone want one?"

"I'll come down and help," Teri replied, ducking her head as she made her way down the narrow companionway into the cabin. A moment later she emerged, holding three cans of soda. She passed them out, giving the last one to Melissa, who shook her head.

"You better drink it," Teri urged her. "It'll help keep your stomach settled."

Kent's eyes shifted over to Melissa. "Oh, no," he moaned. "You don't get seasick, do you?"

"Once," Teri told him, as Melissa's face turned crimson. "She only got sick once, and that was years ago. She'll be fine."

"Well, she better be," Kent shot back. "Dad'll kill me if she pukes all over the boat."

Melissa bit her lip as her eyes welled with tears, but then she forced herself to stay calm. All she had to do was sit still and keep her eyes on the shoreline and she'd be fine. But still, she took the Coke from Teri, who gave her an encouraging grin.

Kent took the boat out into the middle of the cove, cut the engine, and signaled to Brett to raise the main sail. Brett began hauling on the sheet and the canvas lifted upward, snapping loudly as it caught the breeze. A minute later Jeff Barnstable began hoisting the jib, while Ellen and Cyndi manned the lines. With the sails set, Kent brought the boat around, and suddenly the sails filled and the boat heeled over. Melissa, caught by surprise by the sudden shifting of the hull, almost dropped her Coke, but grabbed it just before it spilled onto the deck.

"This is great!" Teri sighed as the boat began to pick up speed. "Don't you love it?"

Melissa, sitting rigidly in the cockpit, hanging onto the gunwale so hard her fingers ached, forced herself to look away from the beach a couple of hundred yards away and face her half sister. Teri was stretched out on the opposite side of the boat, her hair blowing in the breeze, her face tipped up to catch the sun.

"Relax," Teri told her. "Just stretch out and enjoy it."

The boat cruised smoothly northward, the only noise the gentle swishing of the water as the hull cut through the cove. Ellen Stevens and Cyndi Miller came up from the cabin, moved forward, and stretched out on the foredeck, while Brett came back to the cockpit to drop down next to Teri. "What do you think?" he asked. "Like it?"

"I love it," Teri replied, shifting her legs to make room for him. "Where are we going?"

Brett shrugged. "I don't know. Where do you want to go?"

Teri glanced out to the open sea. "Can we go out there?"

"Sure," Brett replied. "Hey, Kent. Can I take the helm?"

Kent slid out from behind the wheel at the stern, and Brett took over. "Ready about," he called out, and Jeff quickly released the jib sheet on the port side and handed it to Melissa.

"Do you know what to do?" Jeff asked, and Melissa shook her head. Jeff rolled his eyes impatiently. "Just hang onto it, and let go when Brett calls out 'coming about,' okay?" Without waiting for an answer, he crossed to the starboard side and took the other sheet.

"Coming about," Brett called out, spinning the wheel. Melissa dropped her line and the jib flapped in the wind. A second later Jeff hauled in on the sheet, and then, as the main swung over, the jib filled again and the boat heeled over the other way, its bow pointing out to the open sea.

Five minutes later they passed through the opening to the cove, and almost immediately the swell increased and the bow of the boat began rising and falling. A moment later, steadying themselves with the boat's lifelines, Ellen and Cyndi came back from the bow and settled into the cockpit.

Melissa felt the first faint beginnings of queasiness stir in her stomach, and reached for her can of Coke. She drank deeply, but the sweet liquid didn't seem to help.

No, she told herself. I'm not going to get sick. I'm going to be all right.

Brett adjusted the tack and trimmed the main sail, and the boat gained a little speed. The wind picked up, and more whitecaps appeared. They were in a heavy swell now, and Melissa glanced nervously at Teri. But her half sister, sitting up on the gunwale, seemed oblivious to the pitching of the boat.

The queasiness in Melissa's stomach got worse, and finally she turned to Brett. "M-Maybe we better go back," she said. "I don't think I feel very good."

"Go below," Brett told her. "Just lie down for a few minutes. You'll be fine."

Melissa hesitated. The last time she'd gotten sick, when she and her father had been out on the fishing boat, the captain had told her to stay up on deck. "It's a lot better," he'd said. "The dizziness isn't so bad if you can see where you're going." She hesitated, and then Brett spoke again: "Will you go down below? If you're going to start throwing up, at least there's a head down there."

Melissa stood up, almost lost her balance as the boat pitched once more, and grabbed at one of the bars next to the hatch. She made her way down the steps into the cabin and sank down on the sofa, the queasiness in her stomach growing into a sharp pain.

Two minutes later she knew she was going to be sick. She got up, lurched toward the head in the bow, but lost her balance as the boat rolled to port.

Staggering, she dropped down to her knees, and then the seasickness hit her with full force.

The vomit rose in her throat. She tried to fight against it, but it was too late. As she began gagging and choking, her mouth opened and a stream of bilious liquid spewed out onto the floor.

"Oh, Jesus," she heard someone groan a few feet away. She looked up, vomit dribbling off her chin, to see Jeff Barnstable staring at her with an expression of total disgust. Her heart sank. Of all the people who had to see her this way, why did it have to be Jeff? He'd never take her to the costume party now—never! He'd probably never even want to *see* her again! And then, from behind Jeff, she heard Kent Fielding's angry voice.

"What the hell did you have to do it down there for?" he demanded, then turned away. "Let's go back," she heard him telling Brett. "The little creep's puking her brains out, and she didn't even go into the head."

The nausea subsiding slightly, Melissa struggled to her feet and looked for something with which to clean up the mess on the floor. She found a roll of paper towels on the galley counter and pulled off a handful, then got down on her hands and knees once more. But the smell of her own vomit filled her nostrils, overwhelming her, and suddenly she was retching again.

This time the mess spilled down her shirt and onto the white pants she'd put on especially for the sail.

Sobbing with humiliation, she forced herself to keep working at the mess on the floor, doing her best to sop it up with the paper towels.

Half an hour later they were back at the dock.

Melissa stayed below as long as she dared, but at last she could wait no longer. Her legs weak, she made her way up the companionway and emerged from the hatch.

They were all standing on the dock, staring at her.

There was a long silence, finally broken by Kent Fielding. "Why the hell did you come at all?" he asked. "If you were going to get sick, why didn't you just stay home? No one even wanted to ask you in the first place."

Melissa's eyes flooded with tears, but anger suddenly flared up inside her. She hadn't wanted to come—she'd even tried to get out of it. And did they really think she'd gotten sick on purpose? She climbed off the boat and started up the dock, but then whirled around.

"I hate you," she screamed at the six kids who were watching her. "I hate all of you, and I hope you all die!"

Then, her tears overwhelming her, she ran up the dock and began stumbling along the beach toward home. For a moment, just a moment, she wanted to turn back, to tell Jeff, at least, that she hadn't really meant what she'd just said. But she couldn't, for her humiliation was still scorching inside her.

If she had turned back, she might have seen the smile on Teri's face.

The smile that would have told her she'd done exactly what Teri had hoped she would.

CHAPTER

17

Phyllis Holloway glanced at the clock on her husband's desk. It was a little after three, and she had a committee meeting at the club at half past, which meant she just had time to brush her hair and touch up her makeup. She glanced down at Cora's account book, her lips tightening as she regarded the housekeeper's nearly illegible scrawl. The least the old woman could do was make her entries in the book clear enough so a person could read them. It was bad enough that she had to spend half the day going over them once a week—the fact that she had to translate each and every entry from Cora's scribble into English made the job nearly intolerable.

And, of course, she got no help from anyone else. She couldn't even count how many times she'd talked to Charles about Cora's sloppy records, but his response was always the same: "Why bother with it at all? Cora's been doing the shopping for the family since before I was born. Father always said he trusted her more than he did his own lawyer."

"Did he?" Phyllis had replied archly the first time she'd talked to him about auditing Cora's expenses. "Well, I can't say I'm surprised. I've always been amazed at the people who let their help steal them blind. When I was working at—" She had cut herself off abruptly, for even with Charles she did her best never to discuss her life before she'd married him. "It's the principle of the thing," she'd insisted. "If the staff knows you're not watching them, they'll take advantage. Not that they don't anyway—I hate to think how much of our food disappears into Cora's house every week."

Charles had merely shrugged. "Who cares? Even if she stole everything they eat—which she doesn't—it wouldn't be enough to get upset about. But if it makes you feel better, go ahead and ask her to keep an account book. Just don't ask me to go over it—I'd feel like I was asking my own mother to account for her expenses."

Phyllis had seen the resentment in the housekeeper's eyes when she'd first given her the ledger more than a decade ago and explained what it was for, but the woman had known better than to complain about it. Instead she dutifully filled it in every day, presenting it to Phyllis every Wednesday morning for the weekly audit.

And then Phyllis had to spend most of the day going over it, matching receipts against the scribbles in the book, even spot-checking to be sure that what Cora had bought was actually in the house. She'd rarely found any discrepancies—and those she had discovered had been minor—but in her own mind she was certain that only her Wednesday labors were keeping Cora honest.

Sighing, she closed the ledger and glanced out the window. Far across the lawn, past the tennis court, Tag was emerging from the woods. Phyllis frowned and her eyes swept the hedge on the north edge of the lawn, which she had specifically told Cora to have Tag trim that very morning. Even from here she could see the uneven growth along the top of the row of hawthorn that separated the property from the estate next door.

Irritated, she picked up the phone and pressed the button that would allow her to page the entire house. "Cora, come to Mr. Holloway's study, right away."

She dropped the phone back on its cradle, her fingers drumming impatiently on the desk until Cora bustled in half a minute later.

"Yes'm?" the housekeeper asked, gazing uneasily at her employer. She was certain the accounts had balanced perfectly this week—she'd stayed up until midnight last night going over them herself.

"What is Tag doing?" Phyllis demanded, her eyes going once more to the window where the boy was still visible, moving slowly along the perimeter of the tennis court.

Cora's fingers twisted nervously at the hem of her apron. "He's looking for Blackie, ma'am," she admitted.

Phyllis swung around to fix her eyes coldly on the servant. "And what about the hedge?" she asked. "Are we expected to simply let the property go wild while Tag chases after a runaway dog?"

Cora's jaw tightened and she looked up, meeting Phyllis's eyes squarely. "He doesn't think the dog ran away, ma'am. He thinks something's happened to it."

"Happened to it?" Phyllis echoed. "And just what is it he thinks might have happened?"

Cora hesitated. "I—I don't like to say, ma'am."

"You don't like to say?" Phyllis echoed, her voice shrill. "Well, I think you'd better decide you *do* 'like to say.' " Her lips curled into a mocking smile. "What does he think happened? Has he decided he believes Melissa's story of a ghost in the attic?"

"No, ma'am," Cora muttered. "He thinks—well, he thinks Teri might have done something to the dog."

Phyllis's jaw dropped. "Teri? What on earth—"

"He saw Teri kick the dog one night. She was coming home and—"

Phyllis's expression hardened. "That's enough, Cora. I don't know what could have made Tag suggest such a thing. Teri MacIver is one of the nicest young ladies I've ever met, and I won't stand for Tag suggesting that she—"

Her words were interrupted by the slam of the front door and the pounding of feet running across the foyer. Stepping out of the study with Cora following her, she saw Melissa starting up the stairs. "Melissa!" she snapped, her voice sharp. Her daughter froze on the stairs but didn't turn around. "How many times have I told you not to . . ." Her words trailed off as she saw a dark stain on Melissa's white pants. "Melissa, turn around." Melissa didn't move for a moment, but then took another tentative step up the staircase. "Did you hear me?" Phyllis demanded. "I asked you to turn around, and I expect you to obey me!"

Melissa, doing her best to stifle a sob, turned around to face her mother. Phyllis stared at the smears of vomit that covered Melissa's blouse and pants. "What in the world—" she began, but Melissa burst into tears.

"I got seasick," she wailed. "I didn't want to go at all, but everyone wanted me to, so I went. And I threw up all over the Fieldings' boat, and . . ." The humiliation of what had happened flooding over her once again, Melissa fled up the stairs.

"The poor child," Cora murmured, starting after Melissa. "I'd better go up with her."

"You'll do no such thing," Phyllis snapped, stopping Cora in her tracks. "I'm quite capable of taking care of my daughter myself. The last thing she needs right now is coddling from you." She was about to go on, but the front door opened again and Teri came in.

"Did Melissa come through here?" she began. "I've been trying to catch up with her, but—"

"She's upstairs," Phyllis told her. Then, as Teri started toward the stairs, Phyllis spoke again. "Teri, darling, Cora has something to tell you."

Teri paused at the bottom of the stairs and turned to the housekeeper, whose already ruddy complexion had turned beet red. "Please, ma'am," she said, her fingers once again working at the hem of her apron. "I didn't mean for you to—"

Phyllis silenced her with a look. "Cora tells me that Tag thinks you might have done something to his dog."

Teri's eyes flashed toward Cora for the tiniest fraction of a second, but then she recovered herself. "He thinks what?" she asked, as if unable to believe she could have heard her stepmother's words correctly. Phyllis, her expression a hard mask of anger, turned to Cora.

"Tell her," she commanded. "Tell her what you told me."

Cora took a deep breath and faced Teri. And suddenly she remembered the day a couple of weeks ago, right after Teri had arrived at Maplecrest, when she'd found her in Melissa's room, claiming she was hunting for socks. There'd been a look about her then—nothing Cora had been quite able to put her finger on, just a sort of furtiveness—that was reflected in her expression now. "He thinks you might have done something to Blackie," she said, her voice gaining strength. "He says he saw you kick the dog one night."

"And you *believe* him?" Teri asked, her tone freighted with an incredulity that Cora almost found herself accepting. Teri turned to Phyllis, her eyes glistening with sudden tears. "Phyllis, you don't believe that, do you? I couldn't— I *liked* Blackie! I—"

Phyllis held out her arms to the suddenly crying girl, and Teri buried her head against her stepmother's breast. "It's all right, darling," Phyllis crooned. "Of course I don't believe it, and no one else will, either." Her voice hardened again as her eyes shifted back to Cora. "I don't want to hear another word about this, Cora. I think you'd better tell Tag that it's time for him to get back to work and accept the fact that dogs sometimes just run away. And if you can't do that," she added, "perhaps you'd better think about whether you and Tag want to stay on here. I don't see how we can tolerate keeping you if Tag is going to start spreading rumors about my stepdaughter."

The color drained out of Cora's cheeks, and for a moment she thought her legs might buckle beneath her. But then she took another deep breath and nodded quickly. "Yes, ma'am," she said, almost inaudibly. "I'll talk to Tag." Turning away, she hurried out through the French doors, leaving Phyllis and Teri alone together.

Teri, wiping her tears away, looked beseechingly at her stepmother. "Y-You don't believe him, do you?" she pleaded.

Phyllis gave her one more reassuring squeeze. "Don't be silly. I'd hardly take the word of a servant over yours, would I? Besides, I think I know you a lot better than Tag, and I can't imagine you harming anything." Her tone changed slightly and her eyes moved toward the stairs, up which Melissa had fled a few moments ago. "Now, what happened on the boat?" she went on.

Teri shook her head sadly. "It was awful. It's all my fault, really. She didn't want to go, and—"

Phyllis held up a hand. "That's very generous of you, dear, but there's no need to make excuses for Melissa. Just tell me what happened."

Slowly, almost reluctantly, Teri told the story. "I don't know why she went down into the cabin," she finished. "If she'd stayed up on deck, she probably would have felt better."

But Phyllis had already turned away, quivering with anger. Now, because of her daughter's weak stomach, she was going to have to miss her committee meeting. She could already see the patronizing look in Kay Fielding's eyes when she tried to apologize for the mess Melissa had made on the boat. Well, this was the last time Melissa would make a fool of herself in public. Her anger growing steadily, she stormed up the stairs.

Teri, feeling a tingle of excitement run through her body, let her voice trail off, and silently followed her stepmother.

Melissa sat on the toilet in the little bathroom she shared with Teri, her head bent down almost to her knees. The sour smell of her own vomit filled her nostrils, and sobs racked her body.

Why had she gone on the boat? She'd known what was going to happen, known it right from the very beginning. And it had happened, just the way she'd known it would.

Just the memory of it seemed to trigger the nausea again, and she slid off the toilet, crouching on the floor, her head above the toilet bowl as the retching started again. As the water in the bowl turned brown with the last of the Coke she'd drunk, she reached up and groped for the handle, then felt a cool draft on her face as fresh water surged into the bowl from the tank above.

Another spasm struck her, and she retched once more, but this time only a thin dribble of foul-tasting spittle ran down her chin. And then she heard her mother's voice as the doorknob rattled loudly.

"Melissa? Melissa, unlock this door and let me in!"

Melissa coughed, spat into the toilet, then raised her head slightly. "Leave me alone," she wailed.

Outside, Phyllis's lips tightened and she rapped loudly on the door. "Didn't you hear me?" she demanded. "I told you to open this door!" She grasped the handle once more, jerking on the door so hard it rattled on its hinges.

"I'm all right," Melissa called, her voice muffled by the heavy door. "Just go away and leave me alone."

Her anger inflamed into fury by her daughter's words, Phyllis turned to Teri. "You have a key to this door, haven't you?" she demanded.

Teri hesitated. Why didn't Phyllis just go around to the other door? But even as she asked herself the question, she knew the answer—Phyllis's fury had robbed her of reason. Teri shrank away from her stepmother's anger and hurried to her room. A moment later she was back. Wordlessly, she handed Phyllis the key.

Phyllis, hands trembling with anger, fumbled for a moment, then got the key into the lock and twisted it. Turning the knob once more, she jerked the door open to find her daughter curled up on the floor, her hands clutching her stomach, staring up at her.

"Get up!" she demanded. Reaching down, she grasped Melissa's arm and yanked her to her feet. "My God, just look at you!" Phyllis hissed. Melissa shrank away from her mother, but Phyllis twisted her arm, spinning her around to face the mirror.

Melissa stared at herself, her eyes red and puffy, her blouse stained with vomit, her hair damp with the perspiration that had accompanied the nausea, plastered to her scalp.

"How could you do such a thing?" Phyllis hissed. "If you knew you were going to get sick, why did you get on that boat?"

Melissa's eyes widened with fear. "I didn't want to—" she began.

But her mother squeezed her arm so hard her words dissolved into an incoherent squeal of pain. "Didn't want to?" Phyllis repeated, her voice harsh and mocking. "Didn't want to? If you didn't want to, then why *did* you?"

"I—Teri said—"

"Stop it!" Phyllis screeched. "Stop trying to blame Teri! I won't have it! Do you hear? I won't have you blaming anyone else for your own failings!"

Melissa gasped as her mother's hand clamped down on her arm once again, then felt a wrenching pain in her back as Phyllis spun her around. Suddenly, her mother's hand released her arm and reached for her blouse.

"Look at your clothes," Phyllis hissed. "They're ruined! Take them off!"

Grasping the front of Melissa's blouse with both hands, Phyllis jerked at the material and the buttons ripped loose, scattering over the floor. With another jerk, Phyllis spun Melissa around again and stripped the blouse off, hurling it into the far corner of the bathroom. "Now take off those pants," she ordered, suddenly letting go of Melissa to turn the water on in the shower. "Do you hear me?" she shouted when Melissa, apparently rooted to the floor, didn't move.

Teri, who had been standing in the open doorway, watching the scene in silence, took a step toward Melissa, but Phyllis shook her head. "Don't help her," she snapped. "She has to learn to take responsibility for the things she does." Her hands dropping to her sides, Teri stepped back again.

The bathroom began to fill with steam as the stream of water pouring from the shower head turned hot. Phyllis glared angrily at her recalcitrant daughter. "Take off those pants," she repeated, her voice quivering with anger.

Numbly, Melissa fumbled with the button at the waistband of her pants, and a moment later they dropped to the floor. She kicked her feet loose from them, then stripped off her underwear.

"Get in the shower," her mother commanded.

Melissa stared at the billowing cloud of steam filling up the bathroom. "I-It's too hot," she whimpered.

Phyllis ignored her words, grabbing her daughter's arm again, then twisting it around her back into a clumsy hammerlock. "I said, get in the shower!" Tightening her grip on Melissa's arm, Phyllis pushed the girl forward. Melissa reached out to brace herself against the wall, but Phyllis knocked her arm aside and grabbed her hair, yanking her head back.

"No!" Melissa cried out. "Please, Mama, no—"

But it was as if her mother didn't even hear her words, and Melissa stared at the steam, wide-eyed, as her mother forced her into the shower. The first drops of the scalding water struck her skin and she gasped.

Then, in her mind, she screamed out one more time.

D'Arcy! D'Arcy, help me!

And out of the mists of steam she saw a face coming toward her, smiling at her. Then she felt the presence of her friend and heard her voice. *It's all right, Melissa. I'm here, and it's all right. Just go to sleep.*

She let the comforting blackness close around her, and listened only to D'Arcy's gentle voice. *That's right . . . go to sleep . . . just go to sleep . . .*

As Phyllis forced Melissa's head under the shower a moment later and the scalding water struck her daughter's face, she felt her child relax in her grip. "Stay there," she said. She reached for a rough washcloth and a bar of soap, and a moment later began scrubbing furiously at Melissa's skin.

Melissa stood still, oblivious to it all, lost in the strange sleep to which she had retreated.

Teri, still watching the macabre spectacle from the bathroom door, saw the change come over Melissa's face, saw her features suddenly relax, saw her eyes go oddly blank.

At last, as Phyllis continued to scour Melissa's skin, Teri turned away.

She smiled to herself as she started down the stairs to spend the rest of the afternoon lying in the sun by the pool. It had been fun watching Phyllis torture Melissa.

Almost as much fun as it was torturing Melissa herself.

CHAPTER

18

"What do you think?" Teri asked. It was Saturday afternoon, and she was in Melissa's room, staring critically at her reflected image in the mirror on the closet door. The two of them had spent most of the morning attaching rhinestones to the tulle netting on the pink dress—hundreds of them, it seemed, which their father had brought with him when he'd flown up from New York the night before—and now, as the sun streamed through the window, the whole dress sparkled with myriad colors as the tiny prisms refracted the light.

"It's fabulous," Melissa breathed. "Put on the tiara, too."

Teri picked up the tiara from Melissa's vanity and carefully placed it on her head. Finally she picked up the "magic wand," a piece of wood cut from an old broom Cora had found in her cleaning closet, which they'd wound with pink ribbon and capped with a tinsel-covered Christmas tree finial that had been Phyllis's contribution to the costume.

"Well?" Teri asked, pirouetting in front of the mirror, then touching Melissa's shoulder with the "wand."

"It's perfect," Melissa breathed, smiling at her half sister. "You're going to be the most beautiful girl there."

"Who is?" her father asked from the door to the hall.

Melissa turned. "Look," she said proudly. "Isn't she gorgeous?"

Charles uttered a soft whistle of approval. "That's some tiara," he said. "Where'd it come from?"

"The thrift shop," Teri replied. "Melissa bought it for me. I told her not to, but—"

"But it's perfect," Melissa broke in. "Without the tiara, it's just an old dress. Nobody'd know what you were supposed to be."

Charles cocked his head at his younger daughter. "So we know Teri's going as a fairy godmother. What about you?"

Melissa's grin faded. "I—I don't think I'm going to go," she said.

Charles frowned. "What do you mean, not go? Why not?"

What could she tell him? That she was sure Jeff Barnstable wouldn't show up tonight? But why would he, after what had happened on the Fieldings' boat Wednesday afternoon?

Even now she could still feel the embarrassment of it. She'd stayed home yesterday and the day before, unwilling to risk the stares she was sure she'd get from anyone she might run into. She could picture the kids playing volleyball on the beach. They'd start laughing at her, bending over with their fingers down their throats, making gagging sounds and pretending to throw up on the sand.

"No they won't," Teri had insisted when Melissa had told her why she wouldn't go to the club, or even the beach. "It wasn't your fault you got sick. Why would anyone laugh at you?"

Melissa hadn't been able to answer her. How could she explain it to Teri? Teri was beautiful, and everyone liked her, and no one ever laughed at her. How could she explain what it felt like to know people were talking about you behind your back, and making fun of you? If it had never happened to you, you *couldn't* know how it felt.

"I—I just don't want to go," she said now. "Can't I stay home? Please?"

Charles's shoulders rose in a small shrug. "Well, I think you'd better see what your mother has to say," he suggested. "After all, you *did* tell Jeff Barnstable you'd go with him."

"And she most certainly *will* go," Phyllis declared, appearing in the doorway, frowning at Melissa. "There isn't a problem, is there?" she asked.

Melissa felt suddenly weak under her mother's icy gaze. "But I don't have anything to wear," she pleaded.

Phyllis brushed the objection aside. "I'm sure Teri can figure out something for you," she said.

Teri nodded, taking off the tiara and reaching up to pull the zipper of the dress down her back. "Help me get out of this," she told Melissa. "Then we'll go up to the attic. There's got to be all kinds of neat things up there."

But in her own mind, she'd long ago chosen the costume Melissa would wear that night.

A few minutes later, as Teri led the way up the stairs to the attic, Melissa found herself hanging back. In her mind's eye she still had a vivid image of coming up these stairs when she'd seen Blackie, a rope around his neck, hanging from one of the rafters.

But it hadn't been real—it had only been a dream.

All week she'd been repeating the words, trying to convince herself that what she'd seen hadn't been real. But the image was so vivid . . .

And Blackie was still gone. Even Tag had finally given up looking for him yesterday. "I don't know what happened to him," he'd said. "I guess maybe your mom's right. He must have just run away."

Her reverie was broken by Teri's voice. "Come on," her half sister was urging her. Then, smiling as if she understood what was going through Melissa's mind, she reached out and took the other girl's hand in her own. "It's okay," she said. "Remember when we were up here the other day? There's nothing here but a bunch of old junk."

Melissa took a deep breath, then determinedly put her fears aside. Teri was right—it was just an attic. There was nothing in it she needed to be afraid of.

Teri opened the door and stepped inside, and a second later Melissa followed her. She looked around and felt herself relaxing a little. Now, with sunlight coming through the small dormers, the attic didn't look nearly as scary as it did at night, when the single bulb left most of it lost in seemingly endless shadows. Now only a few corners were still dark, and even they didn't have that horrible, threatening blackness to them. She giggled self-consciously, looking around, but her laughter died abruptly on her lips as she spotted the dress on the mannequin. Yet now, in the muted daylight, the dress seemed only to be exactly what it was—a long-discarded garment, put on the mannequin for some planned alteration and then forgotten.

"Where shall we start?" she asked Teri.

Teri looked perplexed. "Do you know what's in the trunks?"

"All kinds of stuff," Melissa replied. "A lot of it's stuff for winter, in case we come out here for Christmas. You know—quilts and blankets and things." She started moving across the attic, stepping around some of the larger pieces of discarded furniture, pausing here and there to show Teri something. "Daddy keeps threatening to get rid of all this junk," she said, staring at an old sofa whose rotted upholstery had finally given way, letting a spring pop through. "He says if we keep bringing more stuff up, the whole house is going to collapse. This one was my grandmother's." She pointed to a tattered wing chair. "Daddy says she put it up here when he was our age, and every time Grandfather wanted to get rid of it, she'd say she had plans for it." She chuckled again, poking experimentally at the fabric, which crumbled under her touch. "Daddy says she had plans for it right up until she died, and after that Grandfather wouldn't get rid of it because he was afraid of what Grandmother would say when he met her after *he* died."

Teri shook her head. "But there's so much of it," she said. "I bet it's worth a lot of money."

Melissa shrugged, her eyes shifting over to the corner near the mannequin. "Let's look over there," she suggested. "I think there's some old stuff in those trunks."

They crossed to three large steamer trunks lined up in one of the dormers, and Melissa fumbled with the catch of the first one for a few seconds, then swung its door open. There was a scuffling noise, and a second later a mouse darted out, disappearing into a crack between two of the planks on the floor. Melissa jumped back, recovered from the shock of the sudden movement, then reached out and thumped the trunk. Finally she shook it a couple of times, and when nothing else scampered out of its depths, began pulling open its drawers.

Except for some old shoes—their leather so dried out it had begun to crack and peel—the trunk was empty.

The second trunk yielded another mouse, and a collection of linen tablecloths and napkins that were yellowed and riddled with holes.

The third trunk, though, turned out to be full, and when they opened it, both girls simply stared silently at its contents for a moment.

"It's weird," Teri finally breathed. "It looks like someone came back from a trip and never bothered to unpack it."

Melissa gasped and her eyes widened. "Great-Aunt Dahlia," she said. "I bet it was Great-Aunt Dahlia's."

Teri glanced at her half sister out of the corner of her eye. "Who was she?"

"Grandmother's sister, I think. Daddy says she was really strange. And I bet this stuff is hers." Melissa's eyes left the trunk and met Teri's. "She went on a cruise somewhere, and she just disappeared. Nobody ever found out what happened to her."

Teri's lips twisted into a crooked grin. "Come on," she said. "Nobody just disappears."

"Great-Aunt Dahlia did," Melissa insisted. "Everybody thinks she probably jumped overboard. Anyway, I bet this is her stuff. I bet they sent it back, but nobody ever unpacked it."

The two girls began to sort through the clothes. There were several dresses, all of them in the style of the 1930s, along with silk blouses, several jackets, a coat, and several pairs of lounging pants. In the small drawers that filled half the trunk, they found a collection of underwear, stockings, lingerie, and half a dozen pairs of shoes.

Melissa pulled one of the dresses out and held it up. Teri giggled. "No wonder she killed herself," she said, gazing at the folds of material trailing on the floor at Melissa's feet. "She must have been six feet tall."

Melissa sighed with disappointment, knowing there was no way the dress would fit her. And then she saw Teri staring speculatively at something behind her.

Turning, she once more saw the old white dress, covered with ruffles and bows, hanging from the mannequin. A moment later she understood what Teri was thinking.

"That?" she breathed.

Teri nodded. "Why not?" she said, grinning. "You could go as D'Arcy."

Melissa stared at her, trying to decide if she was kidding. "But I couldn't," she started to protest.

"Why not?" Teri asked. Moving around Melissa, she began carefully to unbutton the back of the dress, and a moment later pulled it off the mannequin. "It'll be fun. And after what happened at the bonfire, you can prove to the rest of the kids that you're not afraid of D'Arcy. And we won't tell any—"

She suddenly fell silent as Melissa, eyes wide, stared at the bare floorboard, now exposed, that the skirt of the dress had covered only a moment before. Frowning, Teri let her own gaze follow her half sister's.

On the floor near the base of the mannequin lay a worn leather strap. Fastened onto a metal ring near the buckle at one end was a small plastic tag. A single word was etched in white on its dark blue surface.

BLACKIE.

Trembling, Melissa reached down and picked up the dog's collar, then her eyes went to Teri. "I was right," she breathed. "I *did* see him up here."

Teri stared at the collar silently for a moment, finally shifting her eyes to her terrified half sister. "But what did you do with him?" she asked.

Melissa felt a wave of dizziness come over her. "D-Do with him?" she repeated.

Teri nodded. "Don't you see?" she asked. "If he really was up here and you really did see him, you must have done something to him."

Melissa's head slowly swung back and forth. "N-No," she stammered. "I didn't . . ."

Teri reached out and took the collar from Melissa's hand. "I didn't say you did it on purpose," she said. Then, as if she'd just thought of it, she spoke again, seeming to formulate the idea while she talked. "Maybe—Maybe it wasn't you at all," she suggested. "Maybe it was D'Arcy."

Melissa gasped. "D-D'Arcy?"

"But it has to be. You know how she comes to you at night, to help you when your mom straps you down?"

Melissa tried to swallow the lump of fear rising in her throat, and managed a slight nod.

"Well, maybe she came that night, too. Maybe she came and let you go to sleep, and then did something to Blackie. And when you woke up, you remembered parts of it and went upstairs to see."

"But I saw—" Melissa protested.

"Maybe you didn't see," Teri suggested. "Maybe you just remembered what D'Arcy did."

Melissa had begun to tremble, her mind spinning as she tried to cope with Teri's words. Was it possible? Could D'Arcy have done something like that? She didn't know.

"Wh-What am I going to do?" she breathed, her terrified eyes fixing on Teri. "If Mama finds out—"

Teri reached out and took Melissa's hand. "She's not going to," she said. "If D'Arcy did it, it's not your fault, is it? So we'll just act like nothing happened. We'll get rid of the collar and not tell anyone."

Melissa blinked back the tears that threatened to overwhelm her. "You'll do that for me?" she whispered. "You won't tell Mama?"

Teri smiled. "Of course not," she said. "Why would I want to do that?"

Taking the dress with her, she led Melissa out of the attic.

Charles glanced at his watch. It was almost seven, which meant they were going to be at least thirty minutes late for the predance buffet dinner at the Barnstables'. Not that it mattered, really. During the summer no one really cared if you were late for a buffet. He glanced in the mirror, adjusting the black cummerbund of the tuxedo that he'd finally agreed to wear. "I'm not putting on a costume," he'd told Phyllis when she tried to convince him to go as George Washington. "I'll put on my tux and go as a waiter, but that's the limit."

Phyllis, knowing better than to push him, had mentally shifted gears, deciding on a flapper costume from the twenties. It wouldn't be as elaborate as the gown she'd originally planned, but at least it wouldn't look out of place next to Charles's tuxedo. Now, hearing his impatient sigh and seeing him glancing at his watch yet again, she checked her makeup for the last time and stood up from her vanity. "Ready," she announced. "And we won't be more than forty minutes late, which is fine." She smiled happily. "Shall we check on the girls?"

Together they walked down the hall to Melissa's room, but just as they were about to go in, Teri stepped out, pulling the door closed behind her. "You can't see Melissa," she said. "We're planning a surprise, and we don't want anyone to see her before the party."

Charles arched his brow. "Well, that'll make it interesting," he observed. "What are you going to do? Throw a blanket over her when Brett and Jeff arrive?"

"Well, of course, *they'll* see her," Teri retorted, then spun around so her father and stepmother could see her dress. "Well?"

"You look lovely, dear," Phyllis told her, bending over to give Teri's cheek a kiss. "You'll be the belle of the ball."

Charles smiled proudly at his eldest daughter. "And I think the fairy godmother idea's perfect," he added. "You've certainly been one to Melissa. Without you . . . well," he finished, feeling suddenly self-conscious, "let's just say I suspect she wouldn't be going to the party at all." His eyes shifted nervously to the closed door. "How's she doing?"

"She'll be fine," Teri told him. "Now go on to the Barnstables' so we can finish getting her ready."

Kissing her good-bye, Charles and Phyllis started down the stairs, but Charles abruptly turned back. "I'm leaving a camera on the table in the foyer," he said. "Don't forget to take pictures. This is Melissa's first date, and—"

"I know," Teri replied. "You already told me three times. I won't forget." Waving one last time, she turned and went back into Melissa's room.

Melissa, clad only in her underwear and a slip, was looking doubtfully at the dress, which now lay across her bed. "What if it doesn't fit?" she asked.

"We'll make it fit," Teri told her. "And look what I found at the thrift shop," she said, opening a bag she'd refused to let Melissa peek into since she'd brought it home from the village late that afternoon. Reaching inside, she pulled out a long blond wig. "And I found all the right makeup, too," she said. "Now let's get the dress on you. The guys will be here in an hour."

Melissa stood up, and Teri slid the dress over her head, holding the sleeves while Melissa worked her arms into them. Finally she pulled the dress down and began buttoning it up the back.

It was a little too large, but not nearly as bad as the dress Melissa had found in the old steamer trunk, and Teri started to drop to her knees, but changed her mind as the yards of pink material that formed her own dress began to crumple beneath her.

"Stand on the stool," she told Melissa. "I can't get down on the floor, and I have to pin the hem."

Melissa gathered the skirt up and climbed onto the stool in front of her small vanity. "What if it comes loose?" she asked.

"It won't. I got safety pins, and the skirt's got so many ruffles they won't even show. Just hold still."

She began working, folding the hem up a few inches and securing it with a neat row of safety pins. After fifteen minutes she straightened up and stood back, eyeing her work carefully. "Turn around," she told Melissa. She made a few adjustments, then told Melissa she could get off the stool.

The hemline, almost perfectly even, hung only an inch off the floor.

"Now let's do the back." Teri began folding the material over on itself, carefully pinning the temporary pleat as flat as she could. "Well, it's good enough," she said. "Now let's see what you look like."

Hesitantly, Melissa moved over to stare at herself in the mirror.

The dress was the right length, but the bodice was way too loose and the left sleeve kept falling off her shoulder. "Oh, God," she sighed. "I look awful, don't I?"

Teri snickered. "Well, it's not great yet, but give me a chance. Let's get some socks to put in your bra."

Melissa stared at her. "We can't—" she protested.

"Sure we can," Teri replied. "Why can't we? What's the big deal? I mean, D'Arcy must have been at least eighteen, and you're only thirteen." She went to Melissa's bureau and pulled out two pairs of white socks, handing them to Melissa. "Go on. Try it!"

Feeling foolish, Melissa stuffed the socks into her bra, then looked into the mirror again. To her surprise, her chest seemed to have filled out, and even when she looked closely, the ruffles along the bodice of the dress concealed the socks completely.

And there was something else, something she couldn't quite put her finger on.

She *felt* different.

She grinned crookedly at Teri. "Did you ever do this?" she asked. "I mean, before you—"

"Of course," Teri replied. "I started doing it when I was twelve. All the boys thought I had the biggest ones in the world. Except they were only there once in a while. Boys are so dumb— they never figure anything out. Now come on. Let's get the makeup on."

Melissa sat at the vanity, staring at her image in the mirror. "Wh-What are you going to do?" she asked.

Teri smiled at her. "I'm going to make you pretty," she said. "I'm going to make you just as pretty as D'Arcy must have been."

She began working, applying a base of light makeup to Melissa's skin, then adding color. First she worked on Melissa's cheekbones, highlighting them carefully so they appeared to stand out slightly. Then she began shadowing Melissa's eyes, finally using a pencil to line the lids and draw the corners out slightly, so they appeared to be set wider than they actually were.

As Melissa watched, a new face slowly began to emerge. It was still her face, but somehow it had changed. Her features seemed to have taken on a new definition.

And inside she felt different, too. As she watched her face develop, she began to feel a strange sense of confidence grow inside her. And then she knew what was happening.

I'm not me anymore, she thought. I'm turning into someone else. Someone . . . pretty!

She held perfectly still, hardly daring to move while Teri worked. Finally, after what seemed to Melissa to be an eternity, she stood back. "There. How's that?"

Melissa stared at her image in the mirror, hardly daring to breath. "It—It's weird," she whispered at last. "I mean, I don't even feel like myself anymore. I feel like—like somebody else."

"That's the way you're supposed to feel," Teri told her. "That's the neat thing about costumes and makeup. When you put them on, you can be anybody you want. I mean—" The doorbell rang, and Teri glanced at the clock on Melissa's bed table. "Oh, God," she said. "It's already after eight. They're here." She handed Melissa the wig. "Put this on while I go let them in, and I'll come back to comb it for you."

She hurried out of the room, and Melissa fingered the wig for a moment, her eyes still fixed on the image in the mirror.

The image that wasn't her but was still familiar.

She started to put the wig on, then hesitated as a strange thought drifted into her head. Once the wig was on, once her own hair was covered, the transformation would be complete.

The last vestige of her real self would be gone and she would become someone else.

Who?

D'Arcy?

But D'Arcy wasn't real, she told herself once more. D'Arcy was only a story, and a friend she'd made up.

Taking a deep breath, she put the wig on her head and let the long blond hair cascade down over her shoulders to frame her face.

And now, in the mirror, she was looking at a stranger.

But it was a stranger who was familiar to her, a stranger whom she had met before.

She picked up the brush on her vanity and began stroking it gently through the mass of blond hair.

And with every stroke, she felt the personality in the mirror, the personality that was not her own, gaining strength inside her . . .

Teri pulled the front door open, smiling at Brett Van Arsdale, who was wearing a black matador's costume trimmed in a pink that matched her dress almost perfectly. She grinned at him and pulled the door wider. "How did you know?" she asked. "Did someone tell you what I was wearing?"

Brett cocked his head. "Maybe I'm psychic."

Teri rolled her eyes, but then as she looked outside at the empty black Porsche sitting in the driveway, her grin faded. "Where's Jeff?"

For a split second she thought a guilty look flashed through Brett's eyes, but then he shrugged. "He got sick," he said. "He called me half an hour ago and said he was barfing all over the place."

Teri's eyes narrowed. "If you're making this up—" she began.

Brett held up both his hands in a protesting gesture. "Hey, is it my fault if Jeff got sick? I got him to ask Melissa, didn't I? And that was the deal—if I got him to ask her, you go with me. But if he got sick, what am I supposed to do? I mean, I can't make him go, can I?"

Teri thought quickly. How was she going to get Melissa to go to the dance if Jeff was standing her up? She could already see the tears streaming down Melissa's stupid cheeks. She'd probably throw herself on the bed and have a tantrum or something. But then, as she thought about it, the answer came to her.

It would be just like the story.

She grinned at Brett. "Do me a favor, okay? I'm going to tell her that something happened and that Jeff's going to meet us at the club. If I don't, she won't come."

Brett snickered. "So what if she doesn't come?" he asked. "Nobody'll care."

"Oh, yeah?" Teri asked, her grin turning into a sly smile. "The way she looks tonight, nobody at the club's going to want to miss her. Just wait here."

She hurried up the stairs to Melissa's room, already working out the details of the story she would tell her half sister.

But when she got there, Melissa's room was empty.

Quickly, she searched the second floor, then went up and looked in the attic. But Melissa seemed to have disappeared off the face of the earth. At last she went back downstairs where Brett was waiting by the door.

"She's gone," she said. "She must have heard us talking and taken off."

"Taken off?" Brett repeated. "Where would she go?"

Teri rolled her eyes once more. "Who knows?" she said. "But you know Melissa—when something gets to her, she runs away."

"Yeah," Brett agreed, his grin widening again as he opened the door and led Teri down the steps to the Porsche. "And maybe this time we'll get lucky. Maybe this time she won't come back."

Teri said nothing, but as the Porsche sped down the driveway, she glanced back at the house.

And, as she had on the night she'd taken Blackie's body out to the pottingshed, thought she saw a flicker of movement in one of the attic windows.

But she'd looked in the attic and Melissa hadn't been there.

Or had she?

CHAPTER

19

Jeff Barnstable lay on his back staring at the ceiling. The television on his desk was on but he was oblivious to it, concentrating instead on the rock music blaring directly into his ears from the headset of his Walkman. His right foot moved in a steady rhythm, keeping time to the beat, and every now and then his arms swung wildly as he smashed at an imaginary percussion set.

The tape came to an end, the last chord fading away, and Jeff reached for another one, glanced at the label, then tossed it back on the night table. Getting up, he wandered over to the window and gazed out into the gathering dusk. In the distance the lights of the Cove Club were beginning to glow brightly on the tip of South Point. A small frown furrowed his brow as he imagined his friends all dancing to the music of a live band.

Still, when he'd awakened this morning and thought of actually taking Melissa Holloway to the dance, just the idea of it had almost made him sick to his stomach, and by the time he'd made up his mind to follow through on Kent Fielding's idea of pretending to be sick, he wasn't even sure it was a lie anymore. Now, though, an hour after the time he was supposed to have picked up Melissa, he felt fine.

In fact, maybe he'd change his clothes and go to the dance after all. By then it would be too late to go get Melissa—knowing her, she'd be in the middle of a crying fit anyway and wouldn't want to go even if he showed up at her house.

He grinned as he imagined himself showing up at her door, all dressed up, maybe even with a bunch of flowers from his mother's garden. And there she'd be, her eyes all red and swollen, staring at him. She'd probably slam the door in his face, and then he'd get credit for actually *trying* to take her to the dance. But what if she were just sitting there, waiting for him? Then he wouldn't have any excuse at all for getting out of it.

The soft buzzing of his parents' party, still going strong downstairs, suddenly increased as his bedroom door opened. He turned around to see his mother, standing with her back against the jamb, her face set in an expression of disapproval that always meant she'd caught him doing something wrong.

"Feeling better?" Paula Barnstable asked, her voice neutral but her eyes betraying her anger at her son.

Jeff started back toward the bed, doing his best to look sick again. "I—I just needed some fresh air," he stammered.

"It seems to me," Paula said slowly, "that perhaps you need some fresh manners, as well."

Jeff dropped down onto the bed. "I'm not feeling so good—" he began.

But his mother didn't let him finish. "I suppose I should have known you were up to something when you said you didn't feel well this afternoon. It isn't really like you to skip a party, is it?" Jeff glanced uneasily at his mother but said nothing. "How do you think I felt when Phyllis Holloway told me how nice it was of you to have asked Melissa out tonight?" Paula went on. "Aside from the fact that I knew nothing about it, I also knew you were up here, 'sick.' " The last word flicked from her lips like a whip, and Jeff cringed, knowing he was indeed in trouble.

"But I *was* sick," Jeff began again.

"I don't want to hear it, Jeff," she told him. "I don't want to know what led up to this, and I don't want to hear any excuses. What I want to know is if it's true. *Did* you invite Melissa to the dance tonight?"

"Y-Yes, but—"

"Then you'll go," Paula informed her son. "I can't imagine *why* you invited Melissa, but I can tell you right now that since you did, you will take her. Aside from the fact that there's nothing wrong with Melissa that getting out from under her mother's thumb wouldn't cure, there's the matter of simple good manners." Her voice dropped, a sure sign that she was angry. "You don't make a date with no intention of keeping it, Jeff. It's not only rude, but it's cruel, and no matter what you or anyone else thinks of Melissa or her mother, you have no right to be cruel to her."

"But—"

Paula shook her head. "No buts," she said. "If I'd known you had a date tonight, I'd have called the doctor this afternoon. And if you'd been sick enough to warrant it, I'd have called Phyllis and Melissa myself and explained the situation. But now," she went on, her voice dropping further, "if you're really sick, I'm sorry for you. Because you're going to get off that bed, get dressed, and go get Melissa. You're going to take her to that dance, and you're never going to leave her side. And if you don't, believe me, you're going to have a very lonely summer, because there will be no more parties, no more days at the club, no more days on the beach. You'll sit here and think about what it means to go back on your word." Without waiting for her son to reply, Paula turned and left his room, silently closing the door behind her.

Jeff sat on his bed for a moment as if paralyzed, his mother's words echoing in his head. He should have known he'd get caught—he'd been stupid even to think he could get away with it. Sighing, he pulled himself off the bed and went to his closet. It was too late to figure out a costume now. He'd just have to wear a sports jacket and make the best of it.

But he could already hear Kent Fielding laughing at him when he showed up with Melissa on his arm. As he finished dressing a few minutes later, though, another thought occurred to him. He'd made a deal with Brett Van Arsdale, and if he had to make good on his part of it, then Brett had to make good on the rest of it.

Pausing as he went out the front door to drain a nearly full drink that someone had left on the table in the entry hall, he headed along the trail toward the club to get the Porsche from Brett Van Arsdale.

*   *   *

Cora lifted the heavy tray of hors d'oeuvres, still covered with a layer of Saran Wrap, then backed through the kitchen door into the butler's pantry. She nearly dropped the tray as she turned around in the cramped space, but recovered herself and went on into the dining room where she added the tray to the three others already on the big oaken table that Tag had lengthened to its full twenty-four feet earlier in the evening. She paused for a moment to catch her breath, then began arranging the silverware in the difficult crescent pattern her mistress always insisted upon—and always inspected to be certain it was perfect. Momentarily, she wished she'd taken Tag up on his offer to help her this evening, but quickly decided she'd made the right decision—her grandson worked hard enough during the week without having to spend his Saturday night setting up a party he couldn't even go to.

She glanced at the French doors to the terrace, reminding herself to turn on the lights before she went back to the kitchen, and was about to begin arranging the napkins, when she thought she heard a sound from upstairs. She paused in her work, her eyes automatically gazing upward as if she could see through the floor.

The sound came again, barely audible, and a frown creased the old woman's brow. The house was empty—she'd seen the mister and missus leave long ago, and heard the roar of Brett Van Arsdale's Porsche as it sped up the drive just before she'd come in to start setting up the after-dance party the Holloways were hosting.

So the house should be empty.

Her frown deepening as the faint sound came again, she abandoned the napkins and walked into the foyer, mounting the stairs a moment later. Coming to the second-floor landing, she paused, listening, and then heard the sound again.

It was still coming from above, in the attic.

A moment later she was certain she knew the answer. It had to be Tag, taking advantage of the fact that Mrs. Holloway was gone to search the attic for the missing dog once again. "I just think he must be up there," he'd told her only that afternoon. "If Melissa says she saw him, I believe her."

Cora had done her best to talk him out of it, explaining once more about Melissa's tendency to sleepwalk. "I'm not saying she was lying," she'd finished. "But sometimes she has dreams that are so vivid she thinks they're real."

But apparently she hadn't convinced the boy, and now, as the sound she'd heard before—a sound that was now clearly that of footsteps—echoed from above, she started toward the attic stairs.

At the top of the flight she found the door standing ajar, but the lights were off. What was Tag doing? Hunting through the attic in the dark? But it was almost nighttime now, and even the windows in the dormers were all but indistinguishable in the darkness of the attic.

"Tag?" she called. She reached for the light switch, but as her eyes adjusted to the darkness in the chamber beneath the roof, she saw a faint glow of yellowish light coming from the far end. Her lips compressing into a thin line of annoyance, she flipped the switch and started through the attic.

The pool of light from the single bulb faded quickly as she moved away from it, but she could still make out the flickering light ahead of her. It seemed to be coming from the little room where she'd found Melissa a couple of times, sound asleep on the cot which was almost its only furnishing. At last she was in front of the room's door. Like the door to the attic itself, it was standing slightly ajar. She reached out and pushed it open, fully expecting to see Tag, looking guilty, turn to face her.

Instead she saw a figure in a long white dress standing at the window, staring out into the quickly gathering darkness. She gasped, her hand automatically going to her breast as her heart fluttered at the strange vision in the room.

The figure turned, and for a moment Cora felt as if her legs would give way beneath her.

In the flickering glow of an oil lamp, a face appeared—a face as pale as death—framed by long blond hair that dropped almost to the eerie figure's waist.

Instinctively, Cora reached out to steady herself against the doorjamb. And then, as the strange specter picked up the oil lamp and moved toward her, she recognized the face.

"Melissa?" she asked.

The figure stopped moving and its head tipped slightly.

"What on earth are you doing?"

"I'm going to the dance," Melissa replied.

Cora's eyes narrowed slightly, for there was something odd about Melissa's voice. It wasn't that it didn't sound like Melissa—just that it was different.

"The dance?" Cora repeated. "But didn't the boys come for you an hour ago? I heard the car—"

"I wasn't ready," Melissa said. "But now it's time."

Melissa moved toward her once more, and instinctively Cora drew back slightly, for again there had been that strange note in Melissa's voice.

Melissa brushed past her, but instead of turning toward the bright pool of light around the attic door, she went the other way, toward the long-disused servants' stairs.

Cora followed close behind her, and a moment later Melissa started down the steep flight that led eventually to the kitchen. "Melissa? Are you all right?" Cora asked when they were downstairs. Melissa was standing quite still, her eyes scanning the kitchen, her expression oddly puzzled. As Cora spoke, she turned once more, and this time she smiled. But it wasn't quite Melissa's smile, just as the voice with which she spoke wasn't quite Melissa's voice.

"I'm fine," she said. "Isn't it a perfect night?"

Cora took a step toward her. "Something's wrong," she said. "You don't sound right. And what are you got up as? My Lord, you're pale as a ghost—"

And suddenly she understood. It was the costume party! And Melissa was going as D'Arcy. The tension in Cora's body broke and she chuckled softly. "Well, aren't you a sight, though. All got up in that dress. When I first saw you, I almost fainted dead away. My goodness, I hope nobody sees you on the beach tonight. You'd scare the life right out of them." She moved closer to Melissa and held out her arms, but instead of accepting Cora's embrace, Melissa moved toward the door.

"Don't," she breathed. "It'll get wrinkles in my beautiful new dress." Setting the flickering oil lamp on the counter, she smiled once more at Cora, then stepped out the back door into the night.

Cora, nonplussed by Melissa's last words, hurried to the door. New dress? What was she talking about? The dress was ancient. And her voice!

It hadn't sounded like Melissa's voice at all. It had sounded older, somehow. And curiously toneless. She came to the back door and peered out into the darkness. Melissa, already halfway across the lawn, had all but disappeared from sight, and all Cora could see of her was an indistinct blur of white floating against the black background of the night. She hesitated for a moment, wondering what to do.

Should she call Mrs. Holloway at the Barnstables'?

She discarded the idea instantly, knowing what her mistress's reaction would be to being called away from a party simply because Melissa was acting strange.

She would be furious, and she'd take it out not only on her, but on Melissa, too.

Besides, maybe there wasn't anything wrong with Melissa at all.

Maybe she'd just been using her imagination, and was trying to act the way D'Arcy herself might have that night when she'd gone to a dance at the club. In her mind, Cora ran over the details of the legend she'd heard for the first time nearly fifty years ago, when she'd originally come to Secret Cove.

If it was true that D'Arcy Malloy had really lived in this house, then the room in the attic might well have been hers. And she was supposed to have been seventeen or eighteen that night almost a hundred years ago.

Cora smiled now as she remembered Melissa's face. With the pale makeup, the makeup that had given her face that strange ghostly cast, she might have passed for seventeen.

And her voice had taken on a more mature tone as well.

Yes, that was it.

Melissa, caught up in the spirit of the costume, was playing the role of D'Arcy as well as wearing the clothes.

And she's doing a pretty good job of it, too, Cora added to herself as she went back to her work. She sure fooled me—for a minute I'd have sworn she really *was* D'Arcy.

Jeff Barnstable twisted the key and listened to the Porsche's powerful engine leap into life. He gunned the motor a couple of times, dropped the transmission into low, and released the hand brake. Popping the clutch, he stamped down on the accelerator and the tires emitted a satisfying shriek as they lost their traction for a second. The car shot forward, accelerating rapidly as it roared up the drive toward the highway. He was doing nearly fifty when he came to the tight curve that would take him onto the road skirting the cove, and when he spun the wheel, all four wheels suddenly tore loose from the pavement. Instantly, he corrected his steering and the tires caught again. He slowed down as he came to the main highway, turned and headed down the road that led around the cove and eventually into the village. He came around another tight curve, then gunned the engine once more as he hit a long straightaway, the speedometer peaking at eighty-five before he began to slow for the turn into the Holloways' long driveway. Less than two minutes after he'd left the club, he stopped the car on the gravel drive in front of the house. Leaving the engine idling, he ran up the steps to the porch and rang the bell.

When nothing happened, he rang again, then heard Cora Peterson's muffled voice calling out from inside the house. "Hold your horses. I'm coming." The porch light came on and the door opened. Cora looked out at him, opened the door wider, but said nothing.

"Is Melissa here?" Jeff asked. "I came to pick her up."

Cora pursed her lips. "Pick her up?" she repeated. "Well, you're a little late, aren't you?"

Jeff felt a flush of heat in his face and hoped it didn't show in the light on the porch. "I-It took me longer to get ready than I thought," he said. "Then I had to get the car from Brett."

Cora's eyes moved to the Porsche. "Since when are you old enough to drive?" she asked.

"I have a learner's permit," Jeff told her. "Besides, all the kids drive around here. The cops don't care."

Cora's brows rose. "Maybe they don't, if they don't catch you," she retorted. "Anyway, I guess it don't matter, since Melissa's gone."

"Gone? What do you mean?"

"She left maybe five or ten minutes ago. All dressed up in her costume." She eyed Jeff suspiciously. "She didn't act like she was expecting to be picked up."

Jeff swallowed nervously, wondering if he should try to catch up with her. If she got to the club and he wasn't with her . . .

But it was all right. When he'd left his house, his mother's party had still been going, and people had just started leaving for the club. He still had time to get the car back and then go find Melissa.

"Which way did she go?" he asked.

Cora shrugged. "How should I know? I s'pose she was taking the trail. I don't think she'd want to go on the beach and risk getting her dress all dirty."

"Okay," Jeff said, starting back down the steps. "I'll find her."

Leaving the door open, Cora stepped out on the porch. "Well, you get rid of the car first. I don't want my girl running around in a car with anybody that doesn't know how to drive."

"I know how," Jeff called back, sliding once more behind the wheel of the Porsche. He put the little car in gear, let the clutch out, and slowly went on around the circular drive until he was back to the driveway itself. Then, just to show off, he hit the gas pedal hard, and a satisfying rain of gravel shot up from the car's rear. Laughing as Cora shook her fist at him, he raced up the driveway toward the main road.

Melissa, eyes wide and unblinking, moved along the trail, her skirt raised so she wouldn't get the hem of her dress dirty. The strange feelings that had begun to come over her when she'd first put on the dress—then grown stronger as Teri began to change her face with the makeup—held her firmly in their grasp now.

She wasn't Melissa at all anymore. She'd sent Melissa to sleep somewhere deep inside her, and it was D'Arcy who was now on her way to the dance.

Everything looked strange to her. She'd barely recognized Cora, and when she'd gone through the kitchen, it appeared different, too. It had looked older than she'd remembered it, and the icebox had disappeared. There was something new in its place—a big white box, made out of metal. And the lights in the kitchen had been brighter, too.

She'd been glad to get out of the house and into the more familiar darkness outside, and she'd started for the trail through the woods immediately. In the woods everything was the same as she remembered it. The path felt soft and spongy beneath her feet, and the twists and turns were the same as they'd always been.

But then, through the trees, she got a glimpse of the Cove Club. Like the kitchen in the house a few minutes ago, its lights were brighter than she remembered—almost as bright as day.

She moved on, and a few minutes later came to a bend in the trail she didn't recognize. The trail had a new fork, and above her was the road. She gazed uncertainly at the other fork for a moment, but had no idea where it might lead. But if she went up to the road, the club was no more than a three-minute walk away.

Jeff slowed the car down, steering into the last curve before the short straightaway leading to the coast road. Suddenly, in the glow of the headlights, a figure clad in white appeared along the side of the road. For a split second the memory of the story of D'Arcy leaped into his mind, but then he realized it had to be Melissa, on her way to the club.

He slowed the car, expecting her to turn around any second, but when she didn't, an idea came into his head. If he killed the lights and crept up on her, then blasted the horn . . .

He reached down and turned off the headlights, then slowed the car even further, until the idling engine was almost silent. Finally, when he was no more than ten feet behind the pale figure by the side of the road, he blasted the horn, and as the figure jumped and spun around to face him, switched the lights back on.

And gaped.

It wasn't Melissa at all.

Instead, he saw a ghostly face staring at him, a face framed with straight blond hair hanging almost to her waist.

The memory of the ghost story flooded back to him once again, and without thinking, Jeff jammed his foot to the floorboard and the powerful engine roared back to life. The car leaped forward, its wheels screaming against the pavement. Jeff's eyes left the road ahead to stare into the rearview mirror.

The grotesque figure in white still stood by the side of the road, staring at him.

His eyes flicked away from the image in the mirror and then widened in horror as he saw the safety rail of the coast road looming ahead of him, no more than twenty yards away.

A scream of terror building in his throat, his foot left the accelerator and smashed down on the brake pedal. The tires screamed once more as the wheels locked under the force of the brakes, and the car sloughed around, all its traction gone.

A moment later the Porsche slammed into the metal guardrail.

The force of the blow ripped the rail loose from the concrete pilings to which it was attached.

The car shot out over the edge of the cliff, seemed to Jeff to hover there for a single agonizing second, then dropped downward.

It turned as it fell, and for a moment Jeff stared straight down at the rocks that seemed to be rushing up at him. And then the car struck the rocks, and Jeff felt the windshield explode into his face. . . .

Melissa, snapped awake by the blare of the Porsche's horn, stared at the car as it shot through the barrier and disappeared over the cliff. For a moment she was stunned, uncertain of where she was or how she had gotten there.

The last thing she really remembered was being in her room, putting on the wig and staring at herself in the mirror.

Staring at the image that hadn't quite been her own.

But now, as she began to come fully awake once more, she knew whose image it was she'd seen.

It had been D'Arcy's image.

Tonight, as she put on the dress, the makeup, and the wig, D'Arcy had come to her, unbidden.

D'Arcy had come to her, and sent her to sleep.

She gazed numbly at the twisted wreckage of the barrier and tried to remember what had happened.

But there was nothing there. Only the memory of the noise that had awakened her, and the image of the car racing away from her.

A black car.

A black car like Brett Van Arsdale's.

Gasping, she pulled up her skirt and ran the forty or so yards to the coast road. She darted across, and stared down into the darkness below. On the rocks, just out of reach of the pounding surf, she could barely make out the wreckage of the car.

A scream welled up in her throat and she turned away, rushing toward the bright lights of the Cove Club.

CHAPTER

20

Phyllis paused by the swimming pool, gazing up at the brilliantly lit clubhouse on the promontory above. She'd hated leaving the Barnstables' party early, but in the end hadn't been able to resist her urge to get to the dance itself and make certain all her careful plans had worked out. Now, with the strains of music drifting out the open windows to fill the warm summer evening with a gentle melody, she began to relax. At least the orchestra had arrived, and she could see a few costumed figures already moving around the dance floor. "Look," she said to Charles, slipping her hand through his arm. "See the Japanese lanterns? I had them put on every single bulb on the chandeliers. And look at the light."

Charles's gaze followed his wife's and he smiled, partly at the rainbow of color that danced on the dining room's white ceiling, and partly at his wife's pleasure at the effect she had created. So far, at least, it appeared the party was going to be a success. "There's no point in just standing here," he said, taking a step forward. "Let's go inside." He led Phyllis up the steps from the terrace, but suddenly felt her fingers tighten on his arm. He glanced at her questioningly.

"I keep having a funny feeling," she said, hesitating once more on the front steps of the clubhouse itself. "I have this awful feeling that something is going to go wrong."

Charles chuckled. "Of course you do," he said. "But it's just nerves. And besides, even if something isn't perfect, there's not much you can do about it now. And whatever happens, it can't be as bad as the year Eleanor Stevens was chairman."

Phyllis groaned. "Don't remind me."

"Of course I'm going to remind you," Charles replied, his chuckle growing into a booming laugh. "What could be worse than having the whole refreshment table collapse? Especially when the whole staff had warned you it was going to happen? Eleanor didn't have anyone to blame but herself, and I have to say the look on her face was worth the mess it made."

Almost in spite of herself, Phyllis found herself laughing, too. She could still see Eleanor staring at the wreckage, then looking around for someone else to blame. But everywhere she looked, people seemed only to be gaping at each other's ruined costumes, and then, out of the silence that had fallen over the room, Eleanor's husband had finally spoken: "Is this your idea of crashing a party, dear?"

Eleanor, speechless for probably the first time in her life, had fled the room and not been seen for a week.

"You're right," Phyllis conceded. "Nothing could be worse than that." With Charles beside her, she walked up the steps and into the clubhouse, handing her wrap to the coat-check girl. At last, feeling a final thrill of anticipation, she stepped through the doors into the ballroom.

Her eyes swept the room quickly, checking the decorations. Around the perimeter a series of tables had been set up, each of which held a perfect centerpiece of roses nested in Queen Anne's lace surrounding three tall candles. Along the wall to her right were the tables of hors d'oeuvres, and even as she watched, a waiter expertly combined two half-filled plates of shrimp and replaced the empty one with a full one from the kitchen. Farther along was the bar, with another one serving only soft drinks opposite it. Outside on the terrace overlooking the sea there was another bar.

The room was already half filled, and Phyllis smiled as she watched the collection of costumed figures drift across the floor. There were angels and devils, three rabbits, several hoboes, and even a scarecrow, who, as Phyllis watched, lost a sheaf of straw from his left pant leg. In the center of the room, dancing with Brett Van Arsdale, she saw Teri, and once more her fingers tightened on Charles's arm. "There she is," she whispered. "I told you she'd be the most beautiful girl in the room."

And indeed, as Charles watched his eldest daughter move gracefully to the rhythm of the slow waltz the band was playing, Phyllis was right. The pink dress that only a few hours ago had looked tired and worn-out now glittered brilliantly, the rhinestones covering the tulle catching every ray of light the chandeliers emitted, refracting them into a rainbow that seemed to shimmer around Teri, dancing attendance on her as she spun across the room.

Suddenly spying her father and stepmother, Teri stopped dancing and hurried across the floor, her eyes sparkling almost as brightly as her dress. "Isn't it all beautiful, Daddy?" she asked. "Aren't you proud of Phyllis?"

Charles's smile broadened. "But none of it is as beautiful as you," he replied, his eyes scanning the room once more. "Where's your sister? I don't know how much longer I can wait for the big surprise."

Teri's eyes lost some of their sparkle. "Sh-She isn't here yet," she stammered.

Phyllis's smile faded away. "But didn't Jeff come to pick her up with Brett?"

Teri's mind raced. If Phyllis didn't know that Jeff had tried to stand Melissa up . . . "He did," she said, nothing in her voice betraying the lie. "But Melissa wasn't ready. So we came ahead, and Jeff took Brett's car back to get her."

"Jeff?" Charles said, frowning. "But he's not old enough to drive."

Teri composed her features into a mask of concern. "He isn't? I just—if I'd known—"

"But you didn't," Phyllis assured her. "And I'm sure it'll be all

right. It's not even a mile to the house, and Jeff will be careful."
She turned to her husband. "And if he's already gone, there isn't
much we can do about it now, is there? By now they're probably
on their way back."

Charles's frown deepened. "I think I'd better call—" he began.

But Phyllis took his hand and pulled him toward the dance
floor. "I think you'd better dance with your wife," she told him.
"If they aren't here within the next five or ten minutes, then we
can start worrying." She slipped herself into his arms, and after
only a moment's hesitation, Charles whirled her away into the
crowd.

Five minutes later, as the last chords of the music died away
and the babble of voices rose once more around her, Phyllis
smiled at her husband. "I've done it," she whispered softly enough
so that only he could hear her words. "Did you hear? Even
Eleanor Stevens said it's the most beautiful midsummer ball we've
ever had. And the August Moon Ball will be even better. I've
been thinking about it, and I think this year we'll forget all the fall
colors. They're such a cliché, and . . ." Her voice trailed off as
she realized that around her the murmuring voices had died away.
She glanced around, searching for whatever might have distracted
the partygoers from their conversations, and for a moment saw
nothing.

But then, realizing that everyone was facing the large double
doors to the foyer, she turned around.

And gasped.

Standing in the doorway was a strange figure clad in white.
Phyllis gazed blankly, her first impression being that it almost
appeared to be a ghost out of the past. It was a girl wearing an
old-fashioned white dress, with long blond hair dropping well
below her shoulders, partially covering her face. But what little of
the face showed was deathly pale and streaked with tears. And
then, her breath catching in her throat, Phyllis recognized the
dress.

She had seen it only a week ago, hanging on a mannequin in
her own attic.

And now it was on her daughter, who stood absolutely still in
the doorway, tears streaming down her face, staring at her.

Phyllis's heart sank. She'd been right—everything had been too perfect, everything had been going too well. And she should have known from the moment it began what the source of her misgivings was.

Melissa.

Once more her daughter was going to humiliate her, and this time on the one night she'd hoped would be her moment of glory. Her hand tightened on her husband's arm, and when she spoke, her voice was a barely audible hiss emerging from her clenched jaw. "Do something," she demanded. "Can't you—"

But it was too late. Melissa suddenly came alive, rushing through the mob of people who had been staring at her and who now drew back as she passed by as if they were afraid even of her touch. Ignoring her mother, Melissa threw herself into her father's arms.

"Missy?" Charles asked. "Honey, what is it? What's wrong?"

"A—A car," Melissa stammered. She looked beseechingly up into her father's face. "It went off the road, Papa," she went on, her voice trembling as she tried to choke back her sobs. "It wasn't my fault. I didn't do anything—"

Her words were suddenly drowned out by a rising tide of voices, and then the crowd in the room began to move, surging toward the doors.

"What car?" Charles asked.

Melissa swallowed. "A black one," she said. "Like Brett's."

Phyllis flinched at the words. "Brett's?" she repeated. "But weren't you—"

Charles cut her off. "Not now," he said, his voice carrying an urgency that silenced his wife. "Let's just find out what happened." Holding Melissa's hand tightly in his own, he turned away from Phyllis and pushed through the crowd toward the doors.

The scene above the rocky shore upon which Brett Van Arsdale's ruined car lay had a surreal quality to it. Cars lined the road, their headlights on, and a grotesque ballet of strangely clad beings seemed to be under way as the guests from the ball, still in their costumes, moved from one spot to another, whispering the latest news from the beach to each other before moving on, weaving in and out of the odd spotlights created by the automobiles' headlamps.

Melissa, her tears abated for the moment, pressed close to her father, holding onto his hand as his arm lay protectively around her shoulders. "Not Jeff," she breathed. "It can't be Jeff . . . It was *Brett's* car . . ." Her voice trailed off as she tried to accept what had happened. But it wasn't real—it couldn't be. Jeff was the last person she'd want to hurt. Choking back the sob that formed in her throat, she huddled even closer to her father.

A spotlight had been brought from the clubhouse, connected by a series of long extension cords that wound down the driveway to the nearest electrical outlet. Its brilliant halogen bulb cast a powerful flood of white light down onto the beach below, where seven people were working frantically to cut Jeff Barnstable loose from the wreckage of the black Porsche.

"I'm going down there," Charles said, withdrawing his hand from his daughter's grasp.

"No," Melissa protested. "Please? Don't leave me alone!"

"But you're not alone," Charles replied. "Your mother's here, and Teri. You'll be fine."

Before Melissa could say anything else, he hurried away and began working his way down the steep face of the cliff, following the same route the police and paramedics had taken only minutes before. At last he came to the rocky shelf at the base of the cliff and picked his way carefully through the maze of tide pools until he reached the wreckage. One of the policemen glanced up at him, nodding a greeting, and a moment later, when the light from above caught the man's face, he recognized him. Tom Mallory had grown up in Secret Cove, joining the police department right out of high school. "What's the situation?" Charles asked. "Is he going to make it?"

Mallory shook his head. "They're still working, Mr. Holloway, but it doesn't look good. His chest is pretty smashed up, and they think his back's probably broken, too."

Charles's eyes drifted away from the cop. A man with an acetylene torch was crouched by the driver's door, cutting away the crumpled metal as quickly as he could. The tide was rising, and as Charles watched, a wave broke offshore and a cascade of foaming water rushed toward him, churning around the rocks, momentarily engulfing the roof of the car in an inch or two of water.

His heart froze as he heard a muffled sound come from within the car itself. "Jesus," he muttered. "He's not conscious, is he?"

Mallory said, "We're not sure. If he is, it's just barely. He's moaned a few times, but we don't know if he's heard anything we've said to him." Then the cop's voice turned grim. "But if they can't get him out within the next few minutes, it'll be too late— the tide's coming in fast."

"What about moving the car?" Charles asked.

"It's already taken care of, Mr. Holloway. We've got a tow truck on the way, but we're not sure it'll do any good. What we need is a crane to lift the car straight up."

"Then get one," Charles said, unconsciously using a tone that told Mallory he expected his order to be obeyed instantly.

The police sergeant snorted impatiently. "You think we haven't tried? But the nearest one is fifty miles away. It's on its way, too, but by the time it gets here it'll be too late. Either they get him out in the next ten minutes or . . ." He shrugged eloquently as his head shook in hopelessness.

A moment later one of the paramedics spoke sharply. "Sarge? He's definitely awake now. I think he's trying to say something."

Mallory moved quickly to the side of the crumpled car, crouching low so his head was close to the window. Behind him, heedless of the water swirling around his feet, Charles Holloway hunkered down as well. "Jeff?" he said. "It's me . . . it's—"

Mallory silenced him with a look. "It's gonna be okay, son," he said, his voice low and calm, with no trace left of the tension that had been apparent only seconds ago when he'd been talking to Holloway. "We're gonna get you out, Jeff. You just take it easy and we'll have you out of here in just a few more minutes."

Jeff's eyes flickered, then opened, and even though the boy's face was in deep shadow, Charles had an instant and unshakable impression that the boy already knew he was going to die. Jeff's eyes moved, flicking toward him for a moment, returning immediately to the policeman.

Another wave crashed out to sea, and a moment later water once more flooded over the shelf of rocks. Charles felt a surge of helpless impotence as the water surged into the car, rising ominously, threatening to flood Jeff's nose and mouth before suddenly peaking and ebbing away again. When the water had receded once more, Tom Mallory reached out and gently wiped Jeff's face with a handkerchief.

As the boy's eyes opened once more, his mouth began to work, too, and both Mallory and Charles Holloway leaned forward.

For a second there was only silence.

And then, as yet another wave broke, a single word drifted from Jeff Barnstable's lips.

"D'Arcy . . ."

It came almost like a breath, and Charles thought—or imagined— that he saw Jeff shudder slightly.

The water suddenly rose around his feet once more, and this time it flooded into the car, rising quickly, submerging Jeff's face completely. Charles found himself holding his own breath in sympathy for the boy, and braced himself for the spasm of cough- ing that was bound to rack Jeff's broken body as soon as the water retreated.

But when it finally drained away, there was only silence in the car, and for several long seconds Charles found himself still hold- ing his breath as he stared into Jeff's empty eyes.

"He's dead," Tom Mallory said. He reached into the car and gently closed Jeff's eyes. Finally, he straightened up, drawing Charles erect along with him. Issuing orders to stop cutting the smashed door, Mallory started slowly toward the base of the cliff. Just before he began climbing, though, he turned back to face Charles.

"Did you hear what he said?" he asked.

Charles hesitated, then reluctantly nodded. "D'Arcy."

"D'Arcy," Mallory repeated. "Any idea what he could have meant by that?"

Charles said nothing for a moment, but at last nodded once again. "I think I do," he said. "I wish I didn't, but I think I do." Feeling numb, he followed the policeman back to the road where his family waited. His eyes went to Melissa, who stood where he had left her. "Come on, darling," he said, putting his arms around her and holding her for a moment. "I'll take you home."

As he led Melissa away from the suddenly silent crowd, a scream pierced the silence of the night.

Paula Barnstable had just learned that her only son had died, and heard what his last word had been.

"D'Arcy."

Teri MacIver, who had been silently watching and listening to everything that had happened since Melissa had appeared at the door to the ballroom less than an hour before, smiled softly to herself.

Jeff's last word, she was certain, would be enough. For already she had seen how people were beginning to look at Melissa.

After all, everyone knew there was no such person as D'Arcy.

There was only Melissa Holloway.

And it would be Melissa they would blame for Jeff Barnstable's death.

Teri's smile broadened in the darkness of the night, but no one saw it.

Except that, oddly, Teri once more had that peculiar sensation that she was being watched.

She turned, and peered into the darkness around her.

There was no one there.

But still, the feeling of unseen eyes watching her, looking right inside her, persisted. A slight shiver ran through her as she finally hurried away from the bluff over the sea.

CHAPTER

21

"He thinks she's crazy."

Phyllis's voice, crackling with a brittleness that clearly reflected the condition of her rapidly fraying nerves, broke the silence that had fallen over the Holloways' library in the moments after Tom Mallory had left. It was past eleven now; the sergeant had been there for nearly an hour, going over Melissa's fragmentary story again and again.

Phyllis had listened in silence, after objecting only a few minutes after Mallory had arrived that Melissa should say nothing until their lawyer could get there.

"I hardly think that's necessary," Charles had told her. "Aside from the fact that I happen to be a lawyer . . ."

"A *corporate* lawyer," Phyllis interjected, but Charles ignored her interruption.

". . . the fact of the matter is that Melissa wasn't in the car. All Sergeant Mallory wants is for her to tell him what she saw."

Melissa had done her best, but when she was done, no one knew much more than before. "All I remember is hearing a horn honking. I turned around, and then the car speeded up. It raced past me and went right through the rail."

"But what were you *doing* there?" Phyllis had demanded.

Melissa still wore the old ruffled dress, but her face had been wiped clean of the pale makeup that had given her a pallor of death. She squirmed uncomfortably in her chair, her eyes fixing on the floor. "I—I don't know," she'd breathed.

"You don't know?" Phyllis demanded.

Melissa shook her head unhappily. "I was in my room, getting ready for the party. I put the wig on, and then . . ." Her voice had trailed off and a tear trickled down her cheek. "It's like I went to sleep or something. I don't remember what happened until Jeff honked the horn at me."

Now, with Mallory gone and Cora sent home, Phyllis's eyes fixed angrily on her daughter. "You were sleepwalking again, weren't you?" When Melissa made no reply, Phyllis repeated the question. "*Weren't* you?"

Melissa shook her head and her eyes shifted to her father, pleading with him to help her.

"Why don't we just leave it alone for tonight, Phyllis," Charles said, glancing pointedly at his watch. "After what she's been through, you can't expect her to—"

"Been through?" Phyllis screeched, her voice rising. "What *she's* been through? What about Jeff Barnstable? My own daughter decides to get dressed up in that"—she floundered for a moment, her eyes fixing balefully on the dress—"that *rag*, and goes out and scares him to death! Why?" she demanded, suddenly turning on Melissa and bending down so her furious eyes were only a few inches from her daughter's face. "What possessed you? How could you do this to me?"

"I—I—" Melissa began, but the fear and confusion in her own mind suddenly overwhelmed her, and she buried her face in her hands.

"That's enough, Phyllis!" Charles snapped. "Stop badgering her. For God's sake, can't you think of someone besides yourself for once? What about Melissa? And what about Paula Barnstable? Her son is dead!"

Phyllis whirled around, her eyes glittering with fury. "Yes," she said. "He is! And our daughter may have killed him. Can't you understand the simplest thing? It doesn't matter what happened out there—it's what people *think* happened. And what happened is this!" Her voice suddenly dropped and she began enunciating her words with exaggerated clarity, as if speaking to a three-year-old child. "Jeff thought he saw D'Arcy, and it scared him so badly he ran off the road. And there is Melissa—our Melissa—dressed up like a ghost! Do you understand? Am I getting through to you? We'll be lucky if anyone in the cove ever speaks to us again!"

Charles, the veins of his forehead standing out starkly from his pale skin, raised his hand. "Stop it!" he roared. "Don't you think Melissa feels bad enough without you accusing her of—" He bit off his own words, falling silent for a moment as he regained control over his fury toward his wife. "We're going to bed," he announced. "There won't be another word said about any of this tonight." His eyes fixed on his wife. "Is that clear?"

Phyllis's mouth opened for a second, then closed again, her lips pressing together and her nostrils flaring with barely suppressed rage. Taking Melissa's hand, she pulled her out of the chair and led her from the room.

"Where are you going?" Charles demanded.

Her hand tightening on her daughter's, Phyllis turned back to face him. "I'm putting her to bed," she said, her voice cold. "That *is* what you wanted, isn't it?" Without waiting for an answer, she spoke to Teri, who had been sitting in a chair by the fireplace, silently listening to her father and stepmother. "I think I could use some help," she said. Instantly, Teri rose to her feet and followed her stepmother out of the room.

Ten minutes later, with her mother and half sister watching her, Melissa struggled to pull her arms out of the sleeves of the dress. Teri moved forward to help, but before she could touch the dress, Phyllis stopped her.

"Let her do it. She can't keep on expecting people to do everything for her the rest of her life. She's thirteen—the least she should be able to do is undress herself!"

Melissa fumbled with the tiny mother-of-pearl buttons at the cuffs of the dress and finally succeeded in undoing them. At last she pulled her arms free and the dress dropped to the floor. Phyllis glanced at it distastefully, then shifted her eyes to Teri. "Get rid of it, will you, dear?"

Teri picked up the dress. "What do you want me to do with it?"

"I'm sure I don't care, as long as none of us ever sees it again. Put it in the trash, I suppose. Cora can burn it in the morning."

Teri hesitated, seeming about to speak, then apparently changed her mind. Carrying the dress with her, she left the room. When they were alone together, Phyllis spoke once more to Melissa.

"Put on your pajamas and get into bed," she said. "I'll be back in a minute."

Melissa stared at her mother, her eyes widening slightly, a cold knot of fear already forming in her belly. "Wh-Where are you going?"

Phyllis smiled coldly. "To get the restraints, of course."

"But—"

"You *did* say you'd been sleepwalking earlier, didn't you?"

"No," Melissa protested. "I didn't go to sleep. I—" She fell silent. How could she explain to her mother what had happened? She could imagine the look that would come into her mother's eyes if she tried to tell her how she'd felt as she'd gotten ready for the party.

That she'd felt as though she were changing into someone else.

"Who?" her mother would demand.

And when she told her mother she'd had the feeling she was turning into D'Arcy . . .

She put the thought out of her mind. Her mother's fury would boil over, and the restraints might be the least of what would happen.

"Maybe I *did* walk in my sleep," she breathed, her words all but inaudible.

"What?" Phyllis demanded. "I couldn't hear you."

Melissa forced herself to look at her mother and speak the words again. "I said, maybe I did walk in my sleep."

"And how do we stop that?" Phyllis pressed, her voice as relentless as her eyes.

Melissa tried to swallow the lump rising in her throat, threatening to choke her. "The—The straps," she finally mumbled.

"Yes," Phyllis repeated. "The straps. And it would make it a lot easier for both of us if you'd simply accept that they're for your own good. Now get ready for bed. I'll be back in a moment."

She left the room, and Melissa slid out of her underclothes, then pulled on her pajamas. Then Phyllis returned, the dreaded leather and nylon restraints over her arm.

But as she was beginning to fasten them to the bed, Charles appeared in the doorway. "I just came in to say—" he began, but the words died on his lips when he saw his wife. "Jesus Christ, Phyllis, what are you doing?"

Phyllis glanced up at her husband. "I'm strapping her down, of course," she said. "We can't have her wandering around in her sleep, can we?"

"Well, we're certainly not going to indulge in that kind of barbarism," Charles replied, his voice harsh. "I told you we weren't going to use those things, and I meant it."

Phyllis froze. "It's just for tonight."

But Charles shook his head. "Not tonight, and not any other night, either. I won't have my daughter strapped down."

"But Dr. Andrews said—"

"We haven't talked to Burt Andrews in months. And we certainly didn't talk to him tonight." He moved to the bed and gently stroked his daughter's cheek. "It's all right, sweetheart," he soothed. "Don't be frightened. Nothing's going to happen." He gazed into Melissa's eyes and frowned, recognizing what he saw there. Terror. And something else.

There was an oddly blank look, almost as if she'd sunk so far into her fear of the restraints that she wasn't even aware of his presence. His eyes shifted over to Phyllis. "Have you been using these?" he asked.

Phyllis gasped. "Of course not," she said. "Not until tonight—why would I?"

Charles's eyes narrowed slightly. "I don't know," he said. "And I hope I don't find out that you have." His gaze went back to Melissa, who was now looking up at him eagerly, the fear and the peculiar blankness ebbing away. "Are you all right, Missy?"

Melissa nodded.

"Have you had to wear the restraints before?" he asked. "I mean, this summer?"

Melissa hesitated, but just before she was about to speak, she saw her mother glaring furiously at her over her father's shoulder. And tomorrow night her father would be leaving for the week.

Her heart pounding, she shook her head. "No, Daddy," she whispered. "I—I didn't even know we still had them."

Charles put his arms around his daughter and hugged her. "And after tonight," he assured her, "we won't. I promise you." He glanced up at Phyllis. "I want you to get rid of them," he told her, his tone conveying that he would brook no argument. "Right now. Say good night to Melissa and then get those things out of the house. Tonight."

Phyllis's jaw worked as she struggled to keep her fury in check. Finally, taking the restraints with her but saying nothing at all, she left Melissa's room. Within five minutes the restraints were buried deep inside a cedar chest filled with blankets that was kept in Charles's own dressing room.

It was, she knew, the last place he'd look.

Teri stood behind the door that separated Melissa's room from the small bathroom the two of them shared. Through the heavy wooden panels she could hear the soft murmur of her father's voice as he comforted her half sister, and once or twice she thought she heard Melissa laughing quietly. At last, when she finally heard Charles saying good night to Melissa, Teri hurried back into her own room, leaving the hall door slightly ajar, and slipped into bed to wait.

In a minute her father would come in to say good night to her, too.

The seconds ticked by, and finally she heard Melissa's door being closed and her father's footsteps as he came down the hall.

She waited for the door to open and her father's face to appear.

Instead, a shadow passed by her room, and her father's footsteps faded away as he crossed the broad mezzanine above the stairs and turned into the wing in the opposite corner of the house, where the master suite was located.

As the house fell silent, Teri lay staring at the ceiling, her anger growing steadily.

She'd been perfect tonight—everyone at the club had thought she was the prettiest girl there.

She'd even seen the pride in her father's eyes when he'd watched her dancing in the center of the ballroom with Brett Van Arsdale.

But then Melissa had shown up, tears streaming down her face, and Teri herself had been instantly forgotten.

And from that moment her father had barely left Melissa's side, fawning over her, hugging her, kissing her.

Loving her.

And ignoring Teri as if she didn't exist.

The longer she thought about it, the more her anger grew.

In her own room, Melissa lay wide awake, trying once more to understand what had happened that night.

She let her imagination run free, and after a while it all began to make sense to her.

It *had* been D'Arcy's dress she'd put on that night. Up until now she hadn't been sure, but as she thought about it, the certainty of it grew in her mind.

Perhaps it was even the dress she'd worn that night when her fiancé had thrown her over.

But no, that couldn't be right—that dress would have been all covered with bloodstains. And besides, after the ball at the club that night, D'Arcy had never been seen again.

And then it came to her.

The dress had been intended for her wedding.

After all, the dress she'd worn tonight had no stains on it. It had been dusty, and yellowed with age, but even as she'd put it on she had the feeling it had barely been worn at all.

And that was why D'Arcy had come to her, even though she was wide awake.

She'd known where Melissa was going, and had wanted to wear her beautiful dress—her wedding dress—just once.

She got out of bed and went to the window. It was a clear night, and the moon, half full, was high in the sky. The ocean glinted with a silvery light, and the foam of the gentle surf on the beach glowed with an eerie phosphorescence.

She almost imagined she could see D'Arcy out there even now, a pale figure almost lost against the ghostly light in the churning waters.

What had truly happened to her tonight?

Until tonight she'd never actually believed that D'Arcy really existed, except within her own imagination. She'd simply made her up, and used her to face the world when things became so painful that all she herself could do was run away.

And until tonight D'Arcy had only come when she had called her.

But tonight she hadn't called D'Arcy at all.

Tonight, as she'd put on the dress and the makeup, D'Arcy had simply emerged out of nowhere.

Creeping in.

Taking over.

She shuddered, although the night was warm. Could it be possible? Had D'Arcy actually come and possessed her?

And if she had, what did it mean?

The story she'd heard on the beach kept running through her head. Was it true? Was D'Arcy coming back this year, a hundred years after she'd disappeared into the night?

Her thoughts were interrupted by a sound.

A sound from above her.

The sound came again, and this time she was certain what it was.

It was a sob, and it was coming from D'Arcy's little room in the attic, directly above her own.

A chill ran through her, and she tried to decide what to do. But even as she thought about it, she knew she had no choice.

She had to go upstairs and see if D'Arcy were truly there.

Her heart already beginning to race, she pulled on her robe and, taking her flashlight, went to the door. She listened for a moment, but save for the muffled sobbing from above, the house was silent.

She moved quickly down the hall, not turning on the flashlight until she'd reached the door that opened into the attic stairs. Finally she grasped the doorknob, twisted it, and pulled the door open.

Its hinges squealed loudly, and Melissa froze for a moment. Then she cast the beam up into the dark gloom above.

A figure stood there, clothed in white, its face veiled, its arms concealed behind its back. A scream rose in Melissa's throat but was strangled into a terrified gasp as the specter's right arm rose.

And then, as a gale of maniacal laughter erupted from the specter's mouth, an object flew toward Melissa, bouncing on the stairs, landing a moment later at her feet.

She stared at it, her eyes wide, her heart pounding.

It was a hand, glistening redly with fresh blood.

Moaning as her gorge rose and nausea threatened to overwhelm her, Melissa turned and fled down the hall, her feet pounding the floor as she raced to her parents' room.

She burst through the door, hurling herself onto her father's bed, her sobs of terror rattling in her chest, cutting off her breath.

Charles, suddenly wide awake, snapped on the light and stared at his daughter's ashen face. "Missy! What is it? What's wrong?"

In the other bed Phyllis, too, stirred, then sat up. When she saw Melissa clinging to her father, her expression darkened. "Oh, really, Melissa," she began, but Charles silenced her with a look.

"What is it, sweetheart?" he asked again.

"D-D'Arcy," Melissa stammered, her voice quavering. "I—Daddy, I *saw* her. She—She threw her hand at me." Her sobs overcame her once more, and Charles held her close, cradling her against his chest.

"No, honey. It was just a nightmare. You just had a bad dream."

"But it wasn't a dream," Melissa insisted. "Daddy, I saw it!" Even as she uttered the words, she realized they were an almost perfect echo of the words she'd spoken to her mother the night Blackie had disappeared. Instinctively, her eyes shifted to her mother, and her heart sank.

Her mother's face was a mask of anger.

But then she heard her father's soothing voice. "Of course you saw it, honey," he told her. "The things we see in dreams always look real. But it doesn't mean they're really there." He reached over to his nightstand and pulled a Kleenex from the box that always sat there, then gently wiped the tears from her eyes. "Now let's get your face washed and get you a drink of water." While his wife looked on with open disapproval, he got out of bed and led Melissa into his bathroom. He ran cold water in the sink, then soaked a clean washcloth and mopped Melissa's face.

As the cold water touched her skin, Melissa began to feel the terror she'd experienced only a moment ago start to loosen its grip, and she let herself relax slightly. But as she wiped her face on the towel her father handed her, her eyes darted furtively toward the door. "Mama's mad at me," she whispered. "She—She thinks I made it up."

"Well, if she does, she's wrong," Charles assured her. "A nightmare can be more frightening than anything else, and if you're scared, you have every right to come in here." He handed her a glass of water, waited until she'd finished it, then spoke again. "Now, what do you say you and I go take a look at the attic stairs and see what we can find?"

Melissa nodded, and followed her father out of the room. A moment later the two of them stood at the foot of the stairs to the attic. The hall lights were on, and even the shadows at the top were all but washed away.

Melissa stared at the floor where only a few minutes ago the bloody hand had lain.

There was nothing there.

She frowned. Was it possible?

Had she truly imagined the whole thing?

But it had been so real—so horribly real.

She stooped down, running her fingers over the dark-stained wood of the floor, then looked at them closely, uncertain whether she hoped to find traces of blood or not.

But again there was nothing. Except for a little dust, her fingers were clean.

"Do you want to go up and look at the attic, too?" Charles asked.

Melissa shook her head. "I—I guess I must have been wrong," she breathed. "But it was so real, Daddy. I was so sure I didn't dream it."

Charles slipped his arm around her and walked her back to her room, then tucked her into bed. "Do you want me to leave a light on?" he asked after he'd kissed her good night.

Melissa shook her head. "It's all right. I'm not afraid of the dark."

"Okay. Sleep tight, and if you have another bad dream, don't be afraid to wake me up." He switched off the light, closed her door, and returned to the master suite.

Phyllis, still sitting straight up in bed, arms crossed, began talking the moment he walked into the room. "She was sleepwalking again. If you'd let me use the restraints—"

Charles glared at his wife. "Those goddamned things aren't a solution to the problem. She's so terrified of them, they've become part of the problem itself! I'm calling Dr. Andrews tomorrow. I want him to talk to her."

Phyllis's head came up. "Oh, perfect!" she spat. "Everybody in town already thinks she's crazy, and now you want to pack her off to that psychiatrist!"

"For God's sake, Phyllis," Charles shot back, his own voice rising to drown out his wife's words. "She's been through a lot the last couple of weeks. She's had to adjust to Teri's arrival, and tonight she watched a boy die! She's in shock, and she's got to be feeling confused and frightened. But tying her to the bed isn't an answer, and it won't hurt any of us to talk to Burt Andrews again—"

"And what about me?" Phyllis demanded, her voice rising to match her husband's. "Do you think any of this has been easy for me? The only good thing that's come out of this summer is Teri! She's been an absolute angel to me, and to Melissa, too. And what does Melissa do? Dresses up like a ghost—whom she apparently thinks is real—and goes out and scares one of our friend's children literally to death! She's not crazy—she knows exactly what she's doing, and she does it just to embarrass me! Well, I won't have it. I tell you I—"

Her tirade stopped abruptly and she stared at Charles in stunned shock.

For the first time in their marriage, he'd slapped her.

Burying her face in her hands, she began to cry. Charles, stunned for a moment by his own action, stood frozen, then turned away. "I don't suppose I should have done that," he observed with ominous mildness as he got back into his bed. "But quite frankly, you deserved it."

He reached over and switched off the light, then rolled onto his side, turning his back on his weeping wife.

Teri, who had been listening in the hall outside the master suite, crept away, then hurried back to her room, where she opened the bottom drawer of her chest and removed an object wrapped in a handkerchief. Carrying it to the bathroom, she made certain the door to Melissa's room was locked, then unwrapped the object and placed it in the sink.

It was the hand from the mannequin in the attic, and now, as she washed the catsup she'd used for "blood" off the plaster, she looked it over carefully.

One of the fingers was chipped and another had cracked when she'd thrown it down the stairs.

But the trick had worked perfectly. Melissa, as she had the night she'd found Blackie hanging from the rafter, had instantly run to her parents' room, and Teri had more than enough time to strip off the dress, stow it away in one of the trunks, then clean the few drops of catsup from the stairs before returning to her room, fully prepared to "wake up" if Melissa started screaming.

Instead, it had been her father and stepmother who started screaming, and she'd listened to every word of the fight.

A psychiatrist.

She smiled as she thought about what the psychiatrist would say when Melissa told him about D'Arcy. With any luck at all, they'd lock her up right away.

She dried the hand off, then left her room and went back to the attic, where she fitted it back onto the mannequin. At last, turning off the attic light, she returned to the second floor and her own room.

As she turned off the light and climbed into bed, she glanced out the window.

Across the terrace, beyond the pool, she could see Cora Peterson's little house.

And in one of the windows on the second floor, she saw a figure dimly lit by the moonlight.

It was Tag.

She frowned, wondering how long he'd been there.

And how much he'd seen.

CHAPTER

22

Burt Andrews leaned back in the chair behind his desk, his eyes wandering to the calendar, where his regular Tuesday-morning golf game had been scratched out and the name "Holloway" scribbled in its place. When Charles Holloway had called him on Sunday morning, Andrews had tried to put him off until the following week, when one of his regular clients had canceled. But Holloway had kept after him, and finally, reluctantly, Andrews had agreed to reschedule his golf game. Now, listening to Charles explaining what had happened, his eyes flicked toward Melissa, who was sitting quietly in a chair between her parents, her hands folded in her lap, her head down. So far she hadn't said much of anything at all, and Andrews was certain he knew why.

Phyllis.

Though she'd done her best to appear as if the only thing on her mind was her daughter's welfare, she hadn't been able to pull it off. What was really bothering her, Andrews was certain, was not what might be wrong with Melissa, but what her friends in Secret Cove might *think* was wrong with the child. "All right," he said, leaning forward once more. "I think I have a grasp of what happened. Now I think it's time I talked to Melissa alone."

Charles rose to his feet immediately, but Andrews didn't miss the flicker of wariness that came into Phyllis Holloway's eyes, and he made a mental note to try to find out from Melissa what was really happening between mother and daughter. Then, as quickly as the oddly furtive look had crossed Phyllis's face, it was gone, and she stood up, too. "We'll be in the waiting room, dear," she said, bending down to give Melissa a peck on the cheek.

Andrews's expression reflected nothing as he saw Melissa unconsciously shrink away from her mother's lips, nor did he speak until her parents had left the room. But as the door closed, he leaned back again and smiled encouragingly at the girl. "Sounds like it hasn't been the greatest summer in history," he said. "Are things pretty bad between you and your mother?"

Melissa hesitated, but finally nodded. "It—It seems like she's mad at me all the time. It doesn't matter what I do, it's always wrong." Her eyes glistened with tears, but she wiped them away, determined not to give in to them.

Andrews smiled sympathetically. "Don't you just wish you could disappear sometimes?"

Melissa sniffled and looked up. How did Dr. Andrews know that? But then she remembered the last time she'd seen him, almost two years ago. At first she hadn't liked him at all. His beard had hidden his face, and she'd always felt like she was talking to someone she couldn't see. But as she'd gotten to know him, and begun to understand that he wouldn't laugh at her no matter what she said, she'd started liking him. In fact, now that she was actually here, she realized she really *wanted* to talk to him. Except for D'Arcy, he was about the only person she wasn't afraid to talk to. She nodded. "I wish we didn't come here in the summer at all," she said. "I like the city a lot better."

"You have a lot of friends there?"

Melissa shrugged. "More than out here, anyway."

"What about D'Arcy?" Andrews asked.

Melissa shifted in her chair and her eyes clouded slightly. "Wh-What about her?" she asked.

Andrews cocked his head slightly. "Well, she's always been your best friend out here, hasn't she?"

Melissa hesitated, but finally nodded. "B-But she's not real. I made her up."

"What if you didn't?" Andrews suggested, his brows lifting slightly. "What if she's a real person?"

The cloud in Melissa's eyes darkened. "But she can't be. I mean, there's the ghost story, but . . ." Her voice trailed off as she remembered the vision she'd seen at the top of the attic stairs late on Saturday night.

"I'm not talking about the ghost story," Andrews told her, leaning forward once more to rest his forearms on his desk. "But it seems to me that D'Arcy might be something more than someone you just made up. Maybe she's someone who helps you out when things get so rough you just want to disappear."

Now it was Melissa who cocked her head, her brows furrowing deeply. "You mean like when my mom's really mad at me about something?"

Andrews felt a tingle of excitement, for there was something in Melissa's voice that told him he'd struck close to home. "What happens when your mother gets really mad at you?" he asked, deliberately echoing Melissa's exact words.

Melissa's tongue ran nervously over her lower lip. "Sometimes," she said hesitantly, "well, sometimes D'Arcy comes, and lets me go to sleep. And then when I wake up, it's all over."

Andrews nodded. "I see." He picked up a pencil from his desk, twirling it idly. "What about when your father's home, on the weekends? Does your mother get as mad at you then?"

Melissa glanced unconsciously toward the door, then shook her head. "It's better on the weekends," she admitted.

Andrews nodded almost absently, as if the words held little importance to him, then smiled. "How would you like to try an experiment?"

Melissa looked at him cautiously. "What kind of experiment?"

Andrews grinned at her. "How would you like to be hypnotized?" Melissa's eyes widened and she looked almost frightened. "It would be just like going to sleep," Andrews assured her. "Like when D'Arcy comes. Only this time I would be the one who puts you to sleep."

"Why?" Melissa asked, her eyes wary.

Andrews considered his next words carefully. He didn't want

to frighten Melissa, but he didn't want to lie to her, either. "Well," he said, "I'd like to find out what happens when you go to sleep, and the easiest way for me to do that would be to talk to D'Arcy."

For several seconds Melissa said nothing, and when she finally spoke, there was a slight tremor in her voice. "W-Will it hurt?"

Andrews laughed out loud. "Of course it won't hurt," he replied. "In fact, it might not even work. But if it does, you'll just feel as though you're going to sleep, but you won't really be asleep."

Melissa still seemed to hesitate. "If you talk to D'Arcy, will you tell me what she says?"

Andrews nodded. "Of course." He talked to her for a few minutes more, explaining to her what he was going to do, and finally she nodded.

"Do I have to watch a pendulum or something?"

"Nope. Just listen to what I'm telling you, and try to concentrate on nothing except the sound of my voice. I'm going to talk to you, and you're going to get sleepy. You're going to find your eyelids getting heavy, and you're going to want to close them. Now your arms and legs are going to get heavy, too. So heavy you won't be able to lift them. And you're going to get sleepier and sleepier, and now you're going to go to sleep . . ."

His voice droned on, and after a few moments Melissa's eyes finally closed.

"Melissa, can you hear me?" he asked.

"Yes."

"Open your eyes, Melissa."

The girl's eyes blinked open, and she sat still in the chair, staring at him.

"Raise your right arm, Melissa."

Melissa's arm rose up until it extended straight out from her shoulder, where it remained, held so steady it could have been suspended by wires from the ceiling. He kept talking to her, his voice still droning quietly, and finally, when he was certain she was deep in a hypnotic trance, he told her to lower her arm.

"Now I want you to close your eyes," he went on, "and then I want you to go to sleep so I can talk to D'Arcy."

As he watched, her arm settled back onto the arm of the chair and her eyes closed once more.

"D'Arcy?" he asked softly. "D'Arcy, can you hear me?"

There was no reaction from Melissa at all. She simply sat in the chair, her eyes closed, unmoving.

Andrews kept talking, urging the second personality he was almost certain resided within Melissa to come forth. "I need to talk to you," he said. "I need to talk to you about Melissa. Wouldn't you like to talk to me, too?"

There was no reaction from Melissa, not even a flicker of movement from her eyes. And yet, from what she'd told him, he was sure that somewhere within her subconscious, the "D'Arcy" personality was there, if he could only reach it.

In his mind he reviewed what he knew of the multiple personality disorder, in which a single individual literally divided the various aspects of his personality into separate entities, each of which reacted to the outside world in a specific manner. If he was right, then D'Arcy—the personality equipped to deal with Phyllis Holloway's unending criticism and anger toward her daughter— might see no reason to come forth now. Indeed, if she feared discovery might lead to something that could harm Melissa, it could be very difficult to reach her. Finally, he decided to try a different tactic. "Melissa," he said. "Can you hear me?"

"Yes."

"I want you to talk to D'Arcy for me. Can you do that?"

There was a momentary silence, then Melissa uttered a single word. "No."

Andrews frowned. He'd been so sure. "Why not?" he asked. "Why can't you talk to her?"

"Because she isn't here."

Andrews's frown deepened. "Where is she? Do you know?"

Melissa hesitated, but finally spoke again. "Yes," she breathed.

"Tell me where she is, Melissa."

There was a long silence, and then Melissa spoke once more. "She—She's at home," she breathed. "She's in the attic."

Andrews probed a little further but could find out nothing more. Apparently the D'Arcy personality was buried so deep that Melissa couldn't contact it unless she were under stress. But in time, Andrews was sure, that would change. Or perhaps he was completely wrong and D'Arcy didn't exist at all.

Five minutes later Melissa blinked, opened her eyes, then cocked her head. "When are we going to start?" she asked.

Andrews grinned at her. "We already started," he said. "In fact, we're all finished."

Melissa's eyes widened in surprise. "We are? How come I don't remember what happened?"

Andrews chuckled. "Well, for one thing, not much happened. I tried to talk to D'Arcy, but I don't think she trusts me yet. She wouldn't talk to me at all."

Melissa seemed to shrink into the chair slightly. "Did I do something wrong?" she asked, her voice anxious.

"No, of course not," Andrews hastily reassured her. "It will just take some time, that's all. But you could do me a favor." Melissa gazed at him questioningly. "When you talk to her, you could tell her it's all right for her to talk to me."

"But if she doesn't want to . . ." Melissa began.

Dr. Andrews shrugged. "If she doesn't want to, she doesn't have to," he said. He leaned back in his chair, then another thought occurred to him. "Do you ever talk to D'Arcy in the city?"

Now Melissa looked completely baffled. "How can I?" she said. "She lives out here."

Andrews nodded. And out here, he thought, your father isn't around all week. Out here, you're left alone with your mother, and that's when you need D'Arcy most. He reached out, pressed a button on his intercom, and a moment later Charles and Phyllis Holloway came in. "That's it for today," he told Melissa. "I'll just talk to your parents for a minute, and then you can go home."

Melissa's eyes once again flicked toward her mother, but she said nothing, scurrying quickly out of the office.

When he was alone with her parents, Andrews gave them an encouraging smile. "Well, I think we have a few problems, but nothing we can't handle. Melissa's been under considerable stress the last few weeks."

"We've *all* been under stress, Dr. Andrews—" Phyllis interrupted, but Andrews held up a hand.

"Of course you have," he agreed. "But at this point I'm not certain what's happening with Melissa. I have a couple of theories, and I'd like to talk to her again."

"Theories?" Phyllis demanded. "What kind of theories?"

Andrews sighed, and forced a smile. "I'm afraid that until I have a better grasp on things, I really can't go into it. I don't want you to worry when there may be nothing at all to worry about."

"But what are we supposed to do?" Phyllis pressed. "If she keeps walking in her sleep—"

"I'm not sure that's what's happening," Andrews broke in. "There are several possibilities I want to explore. For now, the best thing you can do is simply let her rest. She's been under a lot of strain, and it's affecting her." His eyes fixed on Phyllis. "Just let her be herself," he said. "Try not to pressure her."

Phyllis's eyes narrowed. "I don't," she said. "I give her guidance, which is my job, since I happen to be her mother. I just want her to fit in with all her friends. But the way she's been behaving, the things she thinks she sees . . ."

"Melissa and I will be discussing all that, too," Andrews said, rising to his feet and moving toward the door. "But the best thing you can do right now is simply be patient with her. She's going through a lot of changes. Her age—"

Phyllis's expression hardened. "That's easy for you to say, Dr. Andrews. But what about the rest of us? What about Teri and me? Perhaps—Well, perhaps we ought to send Melissa away for a while?"

Charles, stunned by the words, stared at his wife, but before he could say anything at all, Dr. Andrews spoke.

"That might be something to consider later on," he said. "But right now I don't see that it would accomplish anything except make her feel more insecure than she already does. The best thing you can do, Mrs. Holloway, is let her know that you love her and approve of her just the way she is. If she does things that annoy you, try not to show it. She's very frightened, particularly of you. She wants your approval, but doesn't know how to get it. So just show her that you love her. Do you think you can do that?"

Phyllis smiled tightly at the doctor. "She knows I love her," she said. "And she knows I want only the best for her. But I don't believe in letting children run wild. I believe they need to be trained. I shall do for Melissa what needs to be done." Without waiting for Andrews to reply, she stalked out of the office.

Charles hesitated by the door, then offered Andrews his hand. "I'll talk to her," he promised. "I know she tends to be overcritical of Melissa, but I can deal with that. If I have to, I'll take some extra time out here this summer."

Andrews nodded. "I think that would be a good idea," he said. "And the question isn't whether you can deal with your wife's attitude toward Melissa. The question is whether Melissa can."

Teri stepped back and surveyed herself in the mirror on her closet door. The dress she'd chosen for Jeff Barnstable's funeral was navy blue, with a wide red belt that wasn't quite bright enough that it could be criticized. She'd also found a pair of earrings in the exact same shade as the belt, but decided against wearing them. In a couple of months, though, when she had moved back to the city with her family, the earrings would set the outfit off perfectly. In fact, if she could find a string of beads in the same color . . .

Her thoughts were interrupted by the sound of muted voices, and after a last satisfied glance at her own image, she left her room. The voices were clearer now, and she knew where they were coming from.

The master suite, where her father and stepmother were also getting ready for the funeral that afternoon.

She glanced at Melissa's closed door, then moved quickly past the staircase, pausing to slip off her high-heeled shoes, since their tapping echoed loudly against the hardwood floor when the voices of her parents fell silent for a moment. Carrying the shoes, she padded down the hall to the door to the master suite. Though it was closed, she could hear the argument clearly enough.

Inside, Charles glared at his wife's image in the mirror as she sat making final adjustments to her makeup. "Is that what you want us to do?" he said, his voice heavy with anger. "Just lock her up somewhere?"

"Of course not!" Phyllis snapped back, leaning forward to apply a touch of mascara to her eyelashes. "It has nothing to do with 'locking her up,' as you put it. But if she needs a rest, I don't see any reason why we couldn't find her some nice place to go. Like a summer camp, or something."

"A summer camp!" Charles exploded. "What the hell are you talking about? If she's having a hard time coping with kids she already knows, how the hell do you think she's going to do suddenly being thrown in with a bunch of strangers!"

"Oh, really, Charles." Phyllis dropped the mascara brush onto a small tray and turned to face him. "It just seems to me that we have to think of Teri, too. How is it going to affect her if we have to spend all our time catering to Melissa's whims? Considering what she's been through—"

"So now it's Teri, is it?" Charles broke in. "Let's see—so far you've said we ought to send her away for her own good, and Teri's good. Now, what about you? It would make it a lot easier for you, wouldn't it? You could spend even more time than you already do lying around the pool at the club trying to impress all those bitches who won't give you the time of day!"

Phyllis, quivering with rage, rose to her feet. "How dare you?" she demanded. "How dare you talk that way about my friends? Lenore Van Arsdale is one of the finest people I've ever—"

"Lenore Van Arsdale is a crashing snob, which you should be the first to realize, since she won't even speak to you if she can find a way out of it. Christ, sometimes I think Polly was right. The only thing that seems to count around here is 'fitting in' with the 'right people.' Not that any of them do anything—most of them spend their lives bragging about what their grandparents did and spending the money they inherited. Half of them couldn't do a real job if they had to."

"And what about you?" Phyllis shot back. "What makes you think you're any different?"

Charles snorted derisively. "Who said I am? I'm not a real lawyer—I only went to law school because that's what Holloway men do. And what have I done? What's the biggest contribution I've ever made? I've figured out a few loopholes to keep myself and my friends from paying our fair share of taxes." A brittle laugh escaped his lips. "What a life, huh? And that's the life you're bound and determined that Melissa will lead, too? Frankly, I think she might be better off growing up and marrying Tag Peterson than one of the spoiled brats our friends have raised."

Phyllis's expression turned livid. "I don't want anything but the best for her," she hissed. "We've given her everything! And what thanks do I get? She humiliates me! She embarrasses me in front of our friends! And now she pulls a stunt that kills someone, and claims she doesn't even remember what happened. Maybe she *should* be locked up! Maybe she *is* crazy!"

For just a moment Charles was certain he was going to slap her again, as he'd slapped her on Saturday night. But then he regained control of himself. "That's what you want, isn't it?" he said, his voice suddenly devoid of emotion. "You want her to disappear, now that Teri's here."

Phyllis bridled. "Teri has nothing to do with—"

"Oh, don't bore me with that," Charles told her. "I'm not stupid, you know. All Melissa has ever been to you is a replacement for Teri. When Polly took her away, I think it hurt you even more than it did me. But when Melissa came along, I loved her for what she was. All you could ever do was try to turn her into another Teri."

"That's not true—"

"Of course it is. And now that Teri's back, you don't really have any further use for Melissa, do you? You got Polly's house, and her husband, and her friends. Now you've got her daughter, too. So what do you need your own for?" He turned and moved toward the door, then faced his wife again. "But I won't have it, Phyllis. I won't send Melissa away, and I won't have you making her life miserable anymore. Just let her be who she is. Because if you don't, I swear I'll send you away before I send her away."

By the time he opened the door and left the master suite, Teri was already halfway down the stairs. But she'd heard enough. Phyllis was already convinced.

Soon, her father would be, too.

"You're sure you can handle this?" Charles asked Melissa twenty minutes later. "If you don't want to go, you don't have to. I'm sure everyone will understand."

For a split second Melissa was tempted to seize the opportunity to stay home from Jeff's funeral, but even as she opened her mouth to speak, she remembered her mother's words an hour ago: "You will go to the funeral, and you will behave yourself. Not going would be as much as admitting you knew what you were doing Saturday night. It's bad enough that everyone already thinks you're crazy—if they think you did it deliberately, none of us will ever be able to hold up our heads here again!"

Now, as her mother glared darkly at her from her position a few feet behind her father, Melissa swallowed the words already on the tip of her tongue and managed a nod. "I want to go," she breathed. "I—I always liked Jeff."

But an hour later, as she sat in the small Episcopal church which was supported primarily by the Cove Club crowd, she wished she'd stayed home after all.

From the moment she'd walked into the church, her father beside her, she'd felt as if everyone there were watching her, staring at her, silently accusing her.

She'd tried to ignore it, sitting quietly in the pew between her father and Teri, her eyes glued to the little memorial the usher had handed her on the way in. But now, as the minister finished the eulogy and began the final prayer, she looked up, glancing around uneasily.

Most of the people in the church had their heads bowed, but here and there she saw eyes watching her.

Cyndi Miller was staring right at her. But at least when she looked at Cyndi, the other girl looked quickly away.

Ellen Stevens, on the other hand, glared at her, and it was Melissa herself who immediately shifted her eyes from Ellen's accusing gaze.

But I didn't do anything, she told herself once more. I was just walking along the road.

Or had she been?

She still couldn't remember anything at all, not from the time she'd put the wig on until the blast of the Porsche's horn had sounded in her ears.

What if it *had* been D'Arcy?

She had to put the question out of her mind, had to stop thinking about it. If she didn't, she'd go crazy.

Unless she already was.

But she didn't feel crazy, most of the time.

Suddenly she felt Teri nudging her, and came out of her reverie. Ahead of her the row of people were already on their feet, moving slowly into the side aisle and walking up toward the front of the church where the open casket sat on the catafalque.

Melissa felt a chill of panic creep over her.

Did she have to do that?

Did she have to look at Jeff's face?

Next to her her father stood up, and she numbly got to her feet.

I won't look, she told herself. I'll go up there, but when I pass the coffin, I'll close my eyes.

She edged sideways, following her father into the aisle, and a moment later felt a twinge of panic as more people crowded in behind her. She glanced around, searching for a means of escape. But the side doors were all closed, with an usher standing in front of each of them, and she couldn't bear the idea of scurrying across one of the empty pews, then running down the center aisle.

She was at the front of the church now, and she could hear the people ahead of her sighing softly, or muttering a quiet good-bye as they looked down into the coffin.

And then she was in front of the coffin herself.

Instead of closing her eyes, as she'd silently sworn to do, she gazed down into Jeff Barnstable's face.

He didn't look dead at all.

His eyes were closed and his face wore a peaceful expression, as if he were merely sleeping. Instinctively, she reached out and gently touched his face.

His flesh was hard, and cold as marble.

She gasped, and the panic that had been building inside her burst forth. "Nooo," she moaned. "I didn't mean to—I didn't—"

Her tears overwhelmed her then, and she buried her face in her hands. Instantly, her father's arm slid protectively around her and he hurried her down the aisle, threading his way quickly through the crowd of people.

The crowd of people who were staring at her.

Staring at her, and whispering among themselves.

She could almost hear them, accusing her.

"No!" she screamed. "I didn't do it! It was D'Arcy! It was D'Arcy who did it!"

A moment later she was out of the church, in the bright sunlight of the summer afternoon. She blinked and looked up to see her father gazing down at her, his eyes sympathetic, his gentle hand stroking her hair. But then she saw her mother.

Though Phyllis said nothing, Melissa shuddered as she felt the fury that emanated from the angry slits that were her mother's eyes. Terrified by her mother's silent rage, Melissa didn't notice the small smile of satisfaction on Teri MacIver's face.

As her father gently steered her to the car, a wave of hopelessness swept over Melissa.

I've done it again, she thought. And this time, she'll never forgive me.

CHAPTER

23

"I don't understand how she could have done that," Phyllis complained. They'd arrived home an hour before, and after calling Dr. Andrews, Charles had gone into the village to pick up a prescription for a sedative. Now Melissa was upstairs in bed, where Charles had sat with her until the medicine had begun to take effect. When she'd finally dropped into sleep he'd come back downstairs to find Phyllis, her features set angrily, pacing restlessly in the library. Teri, still dressed for the funeral, was perched nervously on a chair.

"Well, it doesn't surprise me at all," Charles replied. "Frankly, I can't imagine why she went in the first place, the way she's been feeling."

"She went," Phyllis interjected, "because she knew it was the right thing to do. And it would have been fine, if she'd simply managed to control herself. But to make a scene like that . . ." Her voice trailed off and she shook her head hopelessly. Then, after glancing at the clock, she sighed heavily and seemed to pull

herself together. "I suppose we'd better get going. The graveside
service should be over, and—"

"Going?" Charles stared at his wife, almost unable to believe
what she was suggesting. "You're not seriously suggesting we go
to the reception, are you?"

Phyllis met her husband's gaze for a moment, but turned quickly
away. "Of course I am," she said. "And the last thing I need from
you right now is an argument. What else can we do? After
Melissa's performance at the service, the least we can do is apologize for her. Didn't you see the look on Paula's face?"

Charles's jaw set. "I don't give a damn about Paula Barnstable,
or any of the rest of them. Right now all I care about is my
daughter. If you think I'm going to leave her alone now—"

"You're not," Phyllis broke in. "Teri says she'll stay with her."

Charles shifted his gaze to his older daughter, who smiled at
him sympathetically. "I really think Phyllis is right, Daddy," she
said. "I saw the way some of the people were looking at Melissa.
And if none of us goes to the reception, won't it just make things
look worse?"

Charles cocked his head. "Nothing happened except that Melissa got upset," he began, but frowned as he saw Teri and Phyllis
exchange a quick glance. "Is there something I don't know about?"

Teri shifted in her chair, as if reluctant to speak. "I—Well, a lot
of the kids are talking about Melissa," she said at last, her eyes
studiously avoiding her father's. "They—Well, some of them
think she's kind of—" She hesitated a moment, as if searching for
the right word. ". . . well, they think she's kind of strange."

"You mean they think she's crazy," Charles said bluntly. "I
know how kids are—I was one myself once."

"I didn't say that," Teri hastily replied. "But—Well, I just
think Phyllis is right. Wouldn't it be better if you went and
explained that Melissa was just upset, but that she's all right now?
I mean, if none of us goes, it's just going to make it worse for
Melissa, isn't it? Everyone will think we were afraid to leave her
alone."

Charles was about to protest once again, but then changed his
mind. Teri, after all, was right—all that had happened, really,
was that Melissa had burst into tears. If he let himself overreact to

it, in the long run it *could* only make things worse. In fact, he could almost hear the kids talking now:

"They had to take her home and lock her up. She was so hysterical no one could even leave the house."

"I knew she was weird, but at the funeral she went completely nuts. They had to put her in a straitjacket."

None of it would be true, of course, but that wouldn't stop the kids' talk. If he and Phyllis went to the reception, explaining that Melissa had simply gotten upset but was fine now, it might put a damper on the worst of the wagging tongues. "All right," he said at last, still not completely certain he was doing the right thing, but having no stomach for a further argument with his wife. "We'll go." He went over to Teri and put his arm around her, giving her a quick hug. "You sure you don't mind staying with Melissa?"

Teri shook her head, her lips compressing into a sad smile. "I—I really don't like funerals. I'd rather stay here with Melissa."

Ten minutes later, after checking once more on his younger daughter and finding her fast asleep, Charles hurried down the front steps to the car, where Phyllis was waiting impatiently.

From the porch, Teri waved good-bye.

Twenty minutes later Cora tapped at Teri's door, then pushed it open. "I'm goin' into the village," she said. "I'm gonna make a lemon pie for Melissa, and there's a couple things I need."

Teri glanced up from the magazine she was reading. "So?"

Cora's lips compressed into a tight line as she heard the insolence in Teri's voice. "So I just wanted to know if there was anything you needed." Then, realizing that Teri was still wearing the dress she'd put on for the funeral, she shook her head in disapproval. "You're going to ruin that dress, lying around in that way. It's linen, you know."

Teri shrugged. "If it gets wrecked, I can buy a new one. We're not poor, you know."

Cora took a deep breath, the temptation to give Teri a lecture on the value of money rising inside her. But then she changed her mind. She'd been watching Teri closely over the last few weeks and come to the conclusion that Polly's daughter wasn't quite what she pretended to be. In fact, she'd decided she didn't really like Teri very much. She was certain it had been Teri who decided to get Melissa all dressed up as D'Arcy for the costume party, and a fine mess that had turned out to be. And despite Teri's words of sympathy for Melissa, Cora had a distinct feeling that she was actually enjoying Melissa's unhappiness. "Fine," she said now. "Suit yourself. I'll be back within the hour."

A few minutes later, after she heard Cora's car grind down the drive, Teri got up and finally took off the dress, dropping it in a heap on the floor. Stripping off the rest of her clothes, she put on a bathing suit and wandered down to the swimming pool. She was about to dive into the cool water when she saw Tag.

He was standing twenty yards away from her, his head cocked oddly, staring at something.

The pottingshed.

Teri froze for a moment, thinking quickly. Then, dropping her towel on one of the chairs that surrounded the pool, she crossed the lawn. "What's wrong?" she asked. "What are you staring at?"

Tag glanced at her, sniffing at the air. "Do you smell something?" he asked.

Teri inhaled, and a rancid odor filled her nostrils. "Yuck," she said. "Where's it coming from?"

"I think maybe it's the potting shed," he said, moving forward. Teri fell in beside him, and together they approached the crumbling shed behind the garage. The closer they got, the worse the smell became. "Jesus," Tag said, wincing at the foul odor. "It smells like something died in—" He fell silent as he heard his own words. "Oh, God," he breathed softly. He hurried forward and pulled the door open, reflexively backing away from the cloud of flies that boiled out of the shed. But a moment later, holding his breath against the putrid odor, he stepped inside and glanced around. Except for a rusty shovel, the place was empty. But as he scanned the floor, he spied the loose boards. He let his breath out, then gagged as he took in a lungful of the fetid air that drifted up from beneath the floorboards. Coughing, he darted out of the pottingshed, took another lungful of the fresher air outside, and held his breath once more. Going back in, he reached down and lifted one of the loose floorboards.

His gorge rose as he gazed down into the space below the floor. Blackie's body, bloated with rot and crawling with squirming white maggots, was barely recognizable, but despite the putrefaction, Tag knew instantly what it was. He recoiled from the sight of the corpse, his eyes moistening with tears. "It's Blackie—" he gasped, turning to Teri so quickly she didn't have time to erase the twisted smile that had come to her lips as she watched Tag discover his pet. His eyes widened as he saw the cruel smile, and he stepped back. "You!" he breathed. "I was right."

"Don't be stupid," Teri said, her smile vanishing as she fixed her eyes contemptuously on the boy. "Why would I want to kill your dog? Don't you see? Melissa must have done it!"

Tag shook his head. "She wouldn't have. She loved him even more than I did." His mind raced, and suddenly he remembered Saturday night, when he'd gotten up late and looked out the window. He'd seen Teri, moving around in the house. A light had gone on in the attic, then gone out again, and a few minutes later come back on. Then it had gone out again, but after that he'd seen Teri moving back and forth between her room and the bathroom she shared with Melissa.

"What are you doing?" he asked. "What are you doing to Melissa?" But even as he spoke the words, he knew. "It was you," he breathed. "It was you she saw in the attic Saturday night. And you killed Blackie, too."

As he took a step toward her, a look of pure hatred came into Teri's eyes and she hurled herself forward, shoving Tag backward. He staggered under the force of the shove, tripping on the steps that led to the pottingshed stoop. Flailing wildly, he tumbled over backward. He reached out with his left arm to break his fall, but his hand dropped through the space that had been occupied by the missing floorboard and sunk deep into the moldering corpse below. He tried to roll over, his right hand searching for something to grab onto, but it was too late.

Teri, her eyes glazed over with hatred, seized the shovel that leaned against the shed's wall, grasped it with both hands, and raised it high.

A second later its blade flashed down, smashing into Tag's face.

He felt a searing stab of pain as the shovel's blade crushed his nose, and instinctively he tried to roll away from the next blow, but it was too late.

The shovel rose again, then smashed down on the back of his head. He twitched for a moment, then lay still.

Teri, breathing hard, stared at Tag's body for a moment, her mind already working. She hadn't really meant to kill him, she told herself. If he'd only accepted her story that Melissa had killed the dog, it would have been all right. But then he'd remembered Saturday night and figured out what he'd seen.

So she'd had to kill him—he hadn't given her any choice.

Instinctively, she scanned the grounds beyond the pottingshed door, but saw no one. And why should she? Everyone would be at the Barnstables' except for Melissa and Cora.

Cora wouldn't be back for at least forty more minutes.

And Melissa was in her room, sound asleep.

Asleep.

As she repeated the word to herself, she knew what she was going to do.

She knelt down and gingerly touched Tag's neck. For a moment she felt nothing at all, but then a pulse beat weakly under her fingers.

He wasn't dead after all.

At least not yet.

She rolled him over and looked at his face. Blood was oozing from his smashed nose, and his eyes were closed. She could hear his breath now, an uneven rattling sound in his chest interspersed with coughing as his own blood threatened to choke him.

Leaving him where he was, she ran back to the house, hurrying up to the attic, where she took the old white dress out of the trunk in which she'd hidden it late on Saturday night. Taking it with her, she went back outside, but instead of going back to the pottingshed, she went into the garage where the gardening tools were kept.

There, leaning against the wall, was the machete she'd seen Tag using to hack away the ivy on the north wall of the house. Smiling to herself, she picked it up.

Back in the pottingshed, she removed more of the floorboards and rolled Tag over once more, letting his unconscious body drop onto the decaying corpse of the dog. Then she gripped the machete, raising it high. Without so much as a second's hesitation, she brought the enormous blade down, feeling a slight shock as it struck Tag's skull, split it, then pierced through to the corruption below. Jerking the machete free, she hacked at Tag's body twice more, then finally put the machete aside.

Using the ancient white dress as a rag, Teri wiped up as much of the blood as she could from the floor, then reached down to sop up more from the body below. Standing up, she shook the dress out and smiled contentedly as she saw the red stains that now covered its front from the bodice to the hemline.

She folded the dress carefully, then put it aside while she once more replaced the floorboards over the joists. Flies hovered over the floor, and even as she watched, a few of them crept down through the cracks to feed on the feast below. But with Tag's body now covering most of Blackie's corpse, the vile odor seemed to fade away.

Taking the dress with her, Teri returned to the house and went once more to the attic, where she returned the bloody dress to its hiding place.

Cora let herself in the kitchen door, glancing at the clock. She'd been gone a little over an hour, but she still had plenty of time to make the pie for Melissa and get the Holloways' roast into the oven before going home to start supper for herself and Tag. She unpacked her bag of groceries, put away everything that she wasn't going to use immediately, and was about to start preparing the pie when she realized that neither Tag nor Teri had shown up even to say hello to her, much less to offer her a hand with the groceries. Not, of course, that she expected any courtesy from Teri.

She frowned, pursing her lips as she thought about it. She remembered Tag saying something about going out to look for Blackie some more, but what about Teri? Surely she hadn't gone off and left Melissa by herself.

She pushed through the swinging door to the butler's pantry and called out. "Hello? Anybody home?" There was a brief silence, then she heard Teri's voice.

"I'm in the library."

With a small sigh of relief that at least she hadn't left Melissa alone in the house, Cora plodded through the dining room and across the entry hall, then down the short corridor to the library.

Teri, clad in a pair of jeans and a white blouse, was sprawled on the red leather sofa watching television, her sneaker-clad feet propped up on one of its arms. "I can't believe your mother didn't teach you not to put your feet on the sofa," Cora commented, but Teri ignored her. "Is everything all right?"

"Of course everything's all right," Teri replied. "Why wouldn't it be?"

"Well, you might have come and offered me a hand with the groceries."

Teri shrugged. "I didn't hear you come in. Besides, it's not my job, is it?"

Cora, her jaw setting angrily, said nothing, but left the library and started up the stairs, nearly certain that anything could have happened to Melissa while she'd been gone and Teri would neither have noticed nor cared. But when she got to Melissa's room, the girl was still curled up in her bed, sound asleep. Feeling mollified, Cora returned to the kitchen and began putting together the pie.

Twenty minutes later, with the pie in one oven and the roast in the other, she went out the back door and crossed the lawn toward her own house. She stepped into the little entryway and called out to her grandson, but there was no answer. "Tag?" she called once again. "Where are you?"

She listened again, then glanced at the heavy man's watch that was strapped to her wrist. It was past six, and Tag was never late coming home. She moved down the short hall to the kitchen and searched for a note, but there was nothing. Puzzled, she finally returned to the main house and went once more into the library.

"Have you seen Tag?"

Teri reluctantly tore her eyes away from the television screen. "Why would I have seen him?" she countered. "Was he in the house?"

"If I knew that, I wouldn't be askin', now would I?" Cora replied tartly. "But he's not home, and I was just wondering if you might have seen him."

Teri shook her head. "Maybe he went off to see his friends," she suggested.

Cora sighed heavily. "He said he was gonna look for Blackie—" she began, but cut off her own words as Teri rolled her eyes scornfully. "And his best friend is Melissa," she went on a moment later. "Seems to me he might have come in to see how she was doing, that's all."

Now Teri groaned audibly. "If his best friend's Melissa, he's even stupider than I thought."

Cora's ruddy face grew even redder. "Some people," she said, "sure aren't anywhere near as nice as they make themselves out to be, are they?" she asked.

Teri smiled with exaggerated sweetness. "And some people," she said, deliberately mimicking Cora's tone, "might not be working here anymore if they don't show some respect for their betters."

The two of them stared at each other for a long moment, but in the end it was Cora who finally looked away. Turning abruptly, she left the room, pulling the door closed behind her with a loud thump.

Teri, snickering at the housekeeper's impotent fury, turned her attention back to the television.

Melissa woke up an hour after midnight, her mind still fogged by the sedative she'd taken that afternoon. For the first few moments she felt confused, but then it all began to come back to her.

She'd gone to Jeff Barnstable's funeral and felt everyone watching her.

And when she'd looked into the coffin, and touched him . . .

Even now she shuddered at the memory, and instinctively drew the covers closer around her. But it was all right, she told herself. She was home, and in her own bed, and her mother hadn't tied her down.

Nothing bad had happened.

She rolled over and felt something tangled around her legs and feet. For just a second she felt a moment of panic—had her mother tied her down after all?

But no—her hands and feet were free! It was just the sheet.

She jerked at the bedding, trying to kick it loose, and the sheet pulled away from the foot of the bed. But her feet were still tangled in something.

Turning on the lights, she sat up and threw the bedclothes back.

And there, tangled around her legs, was the dress.

D'Arcy's dress.

The dress she'd worn on Saturday night, when Jeff Barnstable had died.

And now, on the day of his funeral, it was in her bed, wrapped around her legs.

And covered with stains.

Bloodred stains.

She gasped, her heart pounding. It wasn't real—it was just another nightmare. It had to be.

She closed her eyes tight, then opened them again with a vain hope that the dress would have disappeared.

It was still tangled around her feet, and the stains seemed to have spread even in the moment she'd closed her eyes.

A squeal escaped her throat, but she clamped her hand over her mouth. And then the door to her bathroom opened and Teri, wrapped in a bathrobe, came in. "Melissa?" she asked. "Are you all—" She stopped speaking as her eyes came to rest on the bloody dress. "Oh, Melissa," she breathed. "What have you done now?"

Melissa's eyes widened and she cowered back against the headboard, finally managing to kick free from the folds of material. "N-Nothing," she whispered, her voice reflecting the desperation she was feeling. "I just woke up. I felt something, and—" She tore her eyes from the dress and looked beseechingly at her half sister. "Teri, what's it doing here?"

Teri crossed to the bed and picked up the dress. Holding it almost gingerly, she turned to face Melissa. "Don't you remember?" she asked.

"R-Remember?" Melissa stammered. "Remember what?"

Teri closed her eyes for a moment, shaking her head sadly. "Oh, God," she breathed. "I thought you were awake. But you weren't, were you?"

Panic rose inside Melissa. It wasn't possible, was it? Surely she hadn't been sleepwalking again. "What are you talking about?" she begged. "I've been asleep."

Teri dropped the dress and sat down on the edge of the bed, taking Melissa's hands in her own. "You went out," she said, her voice taking on a pleading note. "You must remember—you *have* to!"

Melissa mutely shook her head.

"It was—I don't know—maybe an hour ago," Teri told her. "Tag was outside, calling you. He woke me up, too. I told him you were asleep, but then you came out the back door." Her eyes flicked to the dress, then back to Melissa. "I thought you were wearing your bathrobe. You know—the white terry-cloth one? But—But . . ." Her voice trailed off. "Where did it come from?" she asked. "Where did you get it?"

Melissa shivered, despite the warmth of the night. "I don't know," she wailed. "I thought it was gone—I thought you got rid of it."

"I did," Teri lied, her eyes meeting Melissa's. "I took it out to the trash. I thought it was gone, Melissa. They came and took the trash away this morning."

Melissa swallowed. If Teri had thrown it away, how . . . Her mind reeled. It wasn't possible—it had to be some kind of a nightmare. None of it could be happening.

"You went off with Tag," Teri said. "I thought you must be going to look for Blackie."

"No," Melissa moaned, covering her ears as if she could shut out Teri's words. "I was asleep! I didn't go anywhere!"

"But I *saw* you," Teri insisted. "If I'd known you were walking in your sleep, I'd have come and gotten you. But I thought you were awake. Whatever happened, it's my fault, too."

"H-Happened?" Melissa echoed. "What—"

"The blood," Teri said. "It must have come from somewhere. . . ."

Melissa buried her face in her hands, willing herself to wake up from the nightmare. But when she looked up again, Teri was still sitting by her bed. "Wh-Where . . . ?" she breathed. "Where did we go?"

Teri shook her head. "I don't know—you were going out behind the garage."

"But there's nothing there," Melissa moaned. "Just the old potting shed."

Teri stood up. "We'd better go see," she said. "Where's your flashlight?"

Melissa shook her head. "No—I don't want to. I—"

"But we have to," Teri insisted. "We have to find out what you did. Don't you see? If you've done something—"

"No," Melissa wailed again. "I couldn't have—"

"But you *must* have," Teri pressed. "Come *on!*"

She pulled Melissa off the bed and helped her into her bathrobe, then turned off the light after she'd retrieved Melissa's flashlight from the drawer in her night table. Silently, she led her half sister downstairs and out the French doors onto the terrace. The night was bright, with the moon high, and Teri instinctively ducked into the shadows close to the house. They skirted their way along the terrace, then dashed around the pool behind the bathhouse. A few seconds later they stood in front of the pottingshed.

"Oh, God," Teri whispered, sniffing at the air. "It smells like something died in there."

Melissa's eyes widened and she felt a chill pass through her, but when Teri pushed the door of the pottingshed open and stepped inside, she followed, almost as if in a trance. Closing the door behind them, Teri turned the flashlight on and shined it around the little room.

The beam caught the machete, its blade still glistening with blood.

Melissa gasped as she saw it. "Wh-What's it doing in here?" she breathed. "Tag keeps it in the garage."

Teri shifted the beam of light and played it over the floorboards, where more bloodstains showed. "Look," she said softly. "They're loose."

Dropping down to her knees, she lifted one of the floorboards and shined the light into the space below.

A scream rose in Melissa's throat as she saw Tag's body sprawled out beneath the floor, his head split open, maggots already nibbling at the dead tissue of his brain. But then, before any scream could erupt into the quiet of the night, she felt Teri's hand clamp over her mouth.

"Don't scream," she heard Teri say. "If anyone hears you, there won't be anything I can do. They'll know what happened, and they'll send you away."

The scream died away in Melissa's throat, to be replaced by a wrenching sob. It was all impossible—Tag couldn't be dead—it was all just a horrible dream, and she'd wake up.

She'd wake up and be back in her room and everything would

be all right. She wrapped her arms around her half sister, her sobs overwhelming her.

"I didn't mean to do anything," she sobbed. "It wasn't my fault. I wouldn't have hurt Tag. I wouldn't have . . ."

Teri, smiling in the darkness, gently stroked her half sister's hair. "It's all right," she crooned. "I'm here, and I won't let them do anything to you. I'll think of something. You'll see. I'll think of something to get you out of this. Besides," she added, her voice dropping even lower, "it wasn't really you that did it, was it?"

Melissa, startled by the words, gazed up at Teri, her breathing still choked by her sobs.

"Don't you understand?" Teri asked. "It wasn't you at all. It was D'Arcy."

And suddenly it all came together in Melissa's confused mind, and she understood what had happened.

D'Arcy had come to her once again, come to her while she slept.

Come to her, and possessed her.

And this time, while she had slept, and trusted D'Arcy, D'Arcy had killed her best friend. Her anguished sobs overcoming her once again, she sank back into Teri's embrace.

But it was going to be all right. Teri was with her, and Teri would figure out what they should do.

Teri would save her.

CHAPTER

24

Cora stirred restlessly in her chair, and a moment later her eyes blinked open. She felt disoriented for a moment, but then realized where she was. She'd been sitting up, waiting for Tag to come home, but must have dozed off. The book she'd been reading lay open in her lap, and her small living room was lit only by the reading lamp behind her chair, which she'd turned on as the evening light began to fade.

She felt stiff, all her joints aching from the hours she'd spent in the chair, and she slowly began stretching her limbs as the last vestiges of sleep released their hold on her. At last she peered at her watch.

Almost one A.M. She must have slept for nearly four hours.

She hauled herself to her feet and started toward the stairs, but then stopped.

The house had an empty feeling to it. She was almost certain that Tag still hadn't come home.

The knot of worry that had been growing within her all evening now congealed into fear—Tag had never stayed out this late, and certainly never disappeared for so long without telling her where he was going. And surely, if he'd come home, he'd have seen her in the chair and wakened her.

Maybe not, she told herself, refusing to give in to the panic she could already feel creeping furtively around the edges of her mind. Maybe he saw me and just decided to let me sleep.

She climbed the stairs, one hand pressing against her left hip, which was sending a sharp stab of pain all the way down to her toes with every step. Perhaps, she reflected, it was time for her to move downstairs. She could convert the little dining room, which she and Tag never used anyway, into a bedroom, and at least be done with the stairs here. Not, of course, that it would help with the stairs in the big house . . .

She came to the landing and reached for the light switch, but knew even before the brilliant light blinded her for a moment that Tag was not up here.

The door to his room stood open, just as it had been when she'd come upstairs a few hours ago. Still, she moved on, checking both bedrooms and the bathroom.

She went back downstairs, going automatically to the kitchen, where she put a pot of water on the stove to make a cup of coffee. Then, as she waited for the water to heat, she tried to decide what to do.

Her first impulse was to go to the main house and wake up Mr. Charles. But if she did that, she would awaken Phyllis as well, and even as she stood at the stove, she could see the look on Phyllis's face and hear her words.

"You woke us up simply because Tag didn't come home? Really, Cora, I can't understand how you could be so inconsiderate! I've had a terrible day . . ."

And it would go on and on, until finally Mr. Charles put on a robe and the two of them went downstairs together. But tomorrow Phyllis would still be angry at having her sleep interrupted, and she wouldn't take it out only on Cora.

She would take it out on Melissa, too.

No, talking to Mr. Charles would have to wait until morning.

What about the police?

She almost grinned as she imagined their response. They'd think she was turning dotty, reporting a teenage boy as missing when he'd actually only been gone a few hours and it was still only a little after one in the morning.

And maybe they'd be right—maybe there really wasn't anything to worry about. After all, how many nights had Tag's father stayed out all night when he was the same age as Tag was now?

She couldn't even remember, it had happened so often. And usually he came home—if he came home at all—so drunk he could barely stand up.

The teapot began to whistle, and she put a teaspoon of instant coffee into a mug, then filled the cup with hot water.

Maybe all that was happening was that Tag was finally growing up, she told herself. Maybe he'd just decided it was time for him to go out and have some fun.

But even as she tried to convince herself that was all that had happened, she knew she didn't believe it. Tag wasn't at all like his father, and never had been.

She stirred the coffee, then took a sip, wincing as the nearly boiling fluid scalded her mouth.

Taking the mug with her, she went back into the living room. Completely alone in the house for the first time in nearly fifteen years, a strange feeling came over her.

She felt lonely. Lonely, and vulnerable.

She glanced around uneasily; the black rectangles of the windows seemed to gaze back at her, and she suddenly had a crawly feeling that there were eyes outside, watching her. Setting the mug down, she moved from one window to the other, closing the drapes.

Her eyes went to the wood laid in the hearth for a fire, and she toyed with the idea of lighting it. But it was midsummer, and the night was already warm. Though the flames themselves might make her feel better, the heat of them would quickly become unbearable.

She went back to her chair and picked up her book once more. Perhaps if she could concentrate on reading, she could put her worries out of her mind. But as she tried to focus her eyes on the words, she only became more and more conscious of the emptiness of the house.

And she also had a strange feeling that something was wrong outside the house.

She tried to assure herself that she was letting her imagination get the better of her, but the harder she tried to ignore the uneasiness, the stronger it got.

"You're a foolish old woman," she finally muttered to herself as she got once more to her feet. "You've got yourself all worked up over what's probably nothin' at all, and now you're going to scare yourself half to death, imagining things that aren't there." But despite her words, she moved to the front door, switched on the light, and stepped out on the porch.

The blackness of the night hung all around her, seemed to close in on her, and the uneasy feeling blossomed inside her. Her first instinct was to go back into the house and lock the door behind her, but she determinedly put her fears aside.

If something was wrong, a voice inside her whispered, it almost surely involved Tag.

She stepped off the porch and out of the bright circle of light from the lamp next to the door.

Teri stared at Melissa in the dim moonlight that streamed through the pottingshed door. Her eyes were open now, and fixed once more on the grisly corpse beneath the floor. But she'd stopped crying, and a calm seemed to have come over her since she'd uttered her strangled plea for D'Arcy to help her.

Suddenly Teri understood. It was just like that night when she'd found her half sister strapped to the bed, gazing blankly at the ceiling. And now it had happened again. Melissa's own personality had shut down, to be replaced by the "friend" she'd invented to shield herself from the reality of what was happening to her.

It was perfect.

Even more perfect than Teri had hoped.

A light suddenly came on—the light on Cora's porch—shining brightly in the night, and Teri instantly snapped off the flashlight and drew back into the deep shadows of the shed. A moment later she saw the silhouette of a figure against the brightly lit wall of the housekeeper's cottage.

Cora—still awake, still waiting for Tag. If she came this way . . .

But it was all right; Cora seemed to be going the other way, circling around her house.

"Wipe the machete off, Melissa," she whispered as loud as she dared.

Melissa remained where she was, unmoving, as if she hadn't heard Teri at all. And then Teri remembered.

"D'Arcy?" she asked. Melissa's head moved slightly and her strange, vacant eyes fixed on Teri. "You want to help Melissa, don't you? Isn't that why you're here?"

Melissa's head slowly nodded.

"Then clean off the machete," Teri whispered again. "Pick it up and wipe the blood off the blade."

As she watched, Melissa obediently reached out and took the weapon in her hand, wiping at the blood with a rotting rag that was lying in a corner of the floor.

"That's right," Teri whispered. "Now drop the rag in the hole."

Moving like an automaton, Melissa obediently dropped the rag onto Tag's body.

"Now help me," Teri went on. "We have to get the boards back in place."

She picked up the end of one of the floorboards and shifted it into position over the hole in the floor, and Melissa silently repeated her motions at the other end. Seconds later all the boards were back in place, the gap in the floor had disappeared, and the machete was once more leaning against the wall of the potting shed.

"You have to go back to the house now, D'Arcy," Teri whispered. Her eyes scanned the pool of light in front of Cora's house, but the old woman was still nowhere to be seen. "You have to take Melissa back to her room and put her back in bed." Melissa said nothing, but again her head bobbed obediently. "Go around the bathhouse, so if anyone sees you, they won't know where you're coming from."

She searched the darkness once more for any sign of Cora, then nudged Melissa gently through the door. Melissa, her eyes staring blankly ahead, moved through the darkness toward the bathhouse.

Teri herself, after checking the potting shed one more time, hurried back around the garage, ducked into the deep shadows by the walls of the house, and slipped through the French doors, locking them behind her.

*   *   *

Cora finished her circuit of the house, having seen nothing, and was about to go back inside when a flicker of movement near the pool caught her eye. She shaded her eyes against the glare of the porch light, then reached inside and flipped the switch. A moment later, as her night vision returned, the figure by the pool emerged clearly out of the darkness.

A figure, clad in white, moving slowly toward the back door of the house.

A gasp escaped Cora's lips as she instinctively remembered all the tales she'd heard of D'Arcy. A moment later her reason returned, and with it, the certainty that she knew who the figure was.

Leaving the porch still dark, she moved quickly down the steps and crossed the lawn, slowing as she approached the pale figure. She could see it clearly now, and nodded to herself as she realized she'd been right.

It was Melissa, her eyes open, her arms hanging limply at her sides, moving toward the house.

Moving toward the house, but sound asleep.

Instantly, Cora remembered the instructions she'd received when Melissa's sleepwalking had first begun.

"The doctor says the most important thing is not to frighten her," Charles had told her. "It'll probably never happen, but if you ever have to deal with it, try not to wake her up. She might wake up anyway, and if she does, just tell her she's all right, explain what happened, and get her back to bed. But you might be able to get her back to bed without waking her up at all. Just speak softly to her and try to guide her back to her room."

Taking a deep breath, Cora caught up with Melissa and gently took her arm. "It's all right, darlin'," she whispered. "It's just Cora, and I'm gonna get you back to your bed."

She paced herself to match Melissa's somnolent stride, gently restraining her for a moment at the back porch while she fished in her pocket for the key to the back door. As she opened the door and guided Melissa inside, she reached for the light switch, but stopped herself just in time, realizing that the sudden brilliance of the kitchen lights would be sure to awaken and frighten the girl.

She guided Melissa across the kitchen to the butler's pantry door, as familiar with the layout of the house in darkness as she was in broad daylight.

"That's right," she crooned. "Through the dining room now, and up the stairs."

They skirted the dining room table, moving into the foyer, then started up the stairs. At the second-floor landing Melissa paused, then started down the corridor in the exact opposite direction of her room. Cora's brows knit into a puzzled frown for a moment, but then she understood.

The attic.

As she had so many times before in her sleep, Melissa was heading once more for the tiny chamber beneath the eaves of the house.

"No, darling," Cora whispered. "Not tonight."

She moved around to block Melissa's way, and the girl stopped, staring at her vacantly. Then, as Cora gently turned her around, a puzzled look came into her eyes.

"It's all right," Cora assured her once more. "You're safe inside, and nothing bad is going to happen to you now."

Melissa's lips moved and a word, barely audible, drifted from them. "Safe?"

"Yes," Cora whispered. "You're perfectly safe. Your mother's sound asleep, and no one knows what happened."

A sigh escaped Melissa's lips, and then her eyes closed. For a moment she stood perfectly still, and then her knees buckled under her and she collapsed onto the floor. Instantly, her eyes flew open, and when she looked up at Cora, the dim glow of the night-light illuminating her face, the old woman could see the panic in her eyes.

"C-Cora?" Melissa stammered. Her eyes flicked around the corridor like those of a hunted animal searching for an unseen predator. For a moment she felt completely disoriented, and then a memory surged up in her mind. A memory of being in the pottingshed, and looking down into a hole in the floor, and seeing . . .

She choked back a sob as the rest of it came back to her. But what had happened? Why was she in the hall?

Why was Cora with her?

How had she gotten here?

Wordlessly, she stared up at Cora.

"It's all right, sweetheart," Cora told her, reaching out to help her back to her feet. The old housekeeper's mind raced. She could see how terrified Melissa was—if only she'd kept sleeping another minute, she'd have had her back in her bed.

"Wh-Where . . . how did I get here?"

"Hush, child," Cora said, her mind still working, searching for a way to keep from frightening Melissa any more than she already was. "It's all right. I—I just couldn't sleep, so I thought I'd have a glass of warm milk. And wouldn't you know, I'd run out. I came into the kitchen to get some, and heard you tramping around up here." She forced a chuckle. "Lord knows, you were loud enough to wake the dead. But your mother didn't hear you, so it's all right. We'll just get you back to bed. All right? Or maybe you'd like to come downstairs with me. We could both have a glass of milk." She knew she was rattling on, knew that if Melissa thought about it, her words wouldn't make much sense. But as she looked at Melissa, she wasn't sure the child had even heard her. Her frightened eyes had taken on a puzzled look, as if she were still trying to figure out what had happened.

"You were walking in your sleep again, darling," Cora said now, gently taking Melissa's arm and steering her toward her room. "I think you were going up to the attic again. But it's all right. I caught you in time, and no one need be the wiser. Let's just get you back to bed."

They were in front of Melissa's door now, and suddenly Melissa froze.

The dress.

She and Teri had left the bloodstained dress lying on the floor of her room. And when Cora saw it . . .

Cora pushed the door open and snapped the light on, and Melissa's eyes instantly went to the spot where the dress had lain.

It was gone.

Numbly, she allowed Cora to guide her into her room and help her out of her robe. Barely aware of what was happening, her mind still whirling with confusion, she let herself be put to bed, felt Cora tuck the covers around her. "There," she heard the housekeeper whisper. "All back in bed, all safe." She felt Cora's lips brush her cheek, felt her gentle fingers stroke her brow. "Just go back to sleep," Cora told her. "Everything's all right now."

A few minutes later, after Cora had gone, Melissa got out of bed and went to the window. Outside, barely visible, she could see the corner of the pottingshed sticking out from behind the garage.

Had she really been out there? Or was it possible that the whole thing had been a dream?

No. The memory of it was too vivid, too real. She and Teri . . . Teri.

Teri had gone with her. It must have been Teri who retrieved the dress.

But there was still that gap in her memory, from the time she had seen the horrible sight beneath the floor of the pottingshed, when she had called out to D'Arcy—called for her friend to come and help her—to the moment she had come awake in the hall outside her room.

It was gone, a blank void in her mind, gone just as surely as if it had never existed at all.

Turning away from the window, she slipped into the bathroom between her room and Teri's, then tapped softly at the door to Teri's room. When there was no reply, she turned the knob and gently pushed the door open. In the dim moonlight she could barely make out Teri's sleeping form, sprawled on the bed, covered by a sheet.

Hesitantly, almost shyly, Melissa crept across to the bed and knelt down. "Teri?" she whispered. "Teri, are you awake?"

There was no response from her half sister.

Melissa reached out and touched Teri's shoulder. Teri moaned softly and rolled over, turning her back to Melissa.

Melissa's heart raced. How could Teri be this sound asleep so quickly? Only a few minutes ago they'd both been out in the pottingshed.

Unless . . .

Inhaling sharply, she grasped Teri's shoulder and shook her. "Teri!" she whispered loudly. "Teri, wake up!"

Teri rolled over and sat up. Her eyes blinked a few times, then she squinted at Melissa in the dim moonlight.

"Melissa?" she asked, her voice sounding thick with sleep. "Wh- What time is it?"

"I—I don't know," Melissa stammered.

"Well, what are you doing in here?" Teri asked. "Why aren't you asleep?"

Melissa's eyes widened in the darkness. "The—The dress," she said, her voice faltering. "What did you do with it?"

Now Teri reached over and snapped on the lamp on her night-stand. Melissa shied away from the brilliance of the light, but in a few seconds her eyes adjusted to the illumination and focused on Teri's face.

Her half sister was gazing at her, her expression puzzled. "What dress?" she asked. "What are you talking about?"

Icy fingers of panic reached out to Melissa. It was impossible— it couldn't have been a dream—it *couldn't* have! "The white dress," she whispered. "The one from the attic, that I wore to the dance. It was in my room tonight!"

Teri frowned and shook her head. "It couldn't have been," she said. "I threw it away that night, after we brought you home."

"But you couldn't have," Melissa insisted. "Don't you remember? You saw it tonight. And we went out to the potting shed."

Teri's frown deepened. "Melissa, what are you talking about? We went out to the potting shed? When?"

Melissa's eyes flooded with tears. "Just a little while ago. We—We found Tag out there. D-D'Arcy did something to him. . . ."

Teri shook her head once more. "Melissa, I don't have the slightest idea what you're talking about. Just tell me what happened."

As best she could, choking back the sobs that threatened to overwhelm her, Melissa pieced the story together. "But after I saw Tag," she finished, "I—I don't remember anything else. The next thing I remember is waking up in the hall. C-Cora said I was going up to the attic."

Teri groaned and flopped down on the pillow. "Oh, for God's sake, Melissa, why don't you grow up?"

Melissa drew back from her half sister. "But—"

"It was a nightmare, Melissa," Teri declared. "Isn't it obvious? You had a nightmare and started walking in your sleep, and Cora found you!"

"But it *wasn't* a nightmare," Melissa insisted. "You were *with* me!"

Teri shook her head. "I haven't been anywhere, Melissa. I went to bed a little after ten, and I've been asleep ever since." Her lips twisted into a scornful smile. "If you can't even tell when you're dreaming, maybe you're as crazy as the kids say you are. Now go back to bed and let me go back to sleep, all right?" Without waiting for a reply, she turned the light off again and rolled over once more, pulling the covers up over her head.

But when Melissa was gone, she kicked the covers off, flopped over onto her back and clamped her hands against her mouth.

The last thing she needed right now was for Melissa to hear her laughter.

CHAPTER

25

"Missy? Honey, it's time to wake up." Charles Holloway shook his daughter gently, and finally she rolled over and opened her eyes, closing them instantly against the bright morning sun that flooded through the windows.

"D-Daddy?" she asked. "What time is it?"

"Almost nine, sweetheart," Charles replied, sitting down on the edge of the bed and taking Melissa's hand in his own. "I've got to go back to the city, but I didn't want to leave without saying good-bye to you."

Melissa barely heard the words, for as she came fully awake, the memory of the night before leaped into her mind. She felt a cold chill of panic run through her and sat up, her arms snaking around her father's neck. "N-No," she begged. "Don't go. Please?"

Charles hugged her close for a moment, but then gently disengaged himself from her embrace. "Hey, it's only for today. I've got a couple of things to take care of, and I'll be back tonight." He grinned at her encouragingly. "It's only a few hours. I'm going to fly down, go to a lunch meeting, and fly back. And if I don't get going, I'm going to miss my plane. Okay?"

Melissa, her mind still filled with the horrible images from the previous night, stiffened. She wanted to tell her father what had happened, beg him to go out to the pottingshed with her right now and look under the floorboards.

But then she remembered the night she'd seen Blackie in the attic, and the night D'Arcy, standing at the top of the attic stairs, had flung her hand down at Melissa's feet.

Both times, when she'd insisted that one or the other of her parents go and look, there had been nothing there.

And the memories of what she'd seen those nights were every bit as vivid as the memory of seeing Tag's body in the dim moonlight that had shined through the pottingshed door.

Could it have been nothing more than a nightmare?

It must have been, for the next thing she could remember after staring at the carnage in the pit was waking up in the house.

In the house, only a few feet from her own room.

And even now she could remember Cora's words.

"You were walking in your sleep again, darling. I think you were going up to the attic again."

Cora had been in the house—she'd been downstairs. If she'd really been outside, wouldn't Cora have seen her come back in?

It *had* to have been a nightmare.

"Y-You won't be gone all night, will you?" she asked, her voice trembling.

"Of course not," Charles assured her. "I told Dr. Andrews I'd take more time out here, just to be with you, and I meant it. But I just can't get out of this meeting. You understand, don't you?"

Melissa managed a nod, but as her father stood up, she clung to his hand. "I—I had another nightmare last night, Papa," she breathed.

Charles hesitated, then sank back onto the bed. "Another one?"

"T-Tag was dead," she said, her voice quavering and her eyes moistening with tears. "He—"

Charles's arms went around his daughter once more and he cradled her head against his chest. "Hush," he crooned. "It was only a dream, Missy. I'm sure Tag's all right—"

Melissa gasped and pulled away from her father, her eyes wary. "Isn't he here?" she asked.

Charles wished he'd thought before he'd spoken. "He went off somewhere yesterday afternoon," he reluctantly admitted. "And he hasn't come back yet."

A tiny wail escaped Melissa's lips. "Wh-What if—" she began, but her father silenced her by pressing a finger to her lips.

"Now just stop that," he told her. "You had a nightmare, and that's all there was to it. You were pretty upset at Jeff's funeral yesterday, remember? I wish I hadn't let you look at him at all. God knows, looking at dead bodies is a barbaric custom, and I don't know why anyone still does it. I remember the nightmares I had when I was your age and had to look at my grandmother after she'd died. For the next week, I woke up every night, sure that I'd seen her. She was dead, but her eyes were open and she was staring at me. Just watching me, as though I'd done something to her. And that's all that happened to you—you saw Jeff Barnstable's body yesterday, and in your dream it got changed to Tag's. But it wasn't real, honey." His eyes met hers and his voice dropped slightly. "You have to start understanding what's real and what's not," he told her. "Dreams are just that—dreams. Some of them might mean something, but it still doesn't make them real."

Getting to his feet once more, he smiled fondly at her. "Tell you what," he said. "Why don't you just stay in bed today and take it easy. And then, when I get home, you and I will spend the whole evening together. Just the two of us—we'll go out for dinner, and maybe go to a movie. Does that sound like fun?"

Melissa nodded automatically, though she'd barely heard the words.

If Tag was gone . . .

No, she told herself once more. *It was just a nightmare.* But no matter how hard she tried to convince herself, she knew she didn't believe it had all been a dream.

An hour later, still lying in bed, Melissa heard the familiar crunching of the gravel on the driveway as Cora backed her car out of its stall behind her house and left the estate on her way into the village. Cora had brought some breakfast up to her a little while ago, but the tray still sat untouched on her vanity. She'd asked Cora about Tag, but although Cora had tried to assure her that he'd probably be back any minute now, Melissa could tell the housekeeper didn't believe her own words. She'd started to tell Cora about her nightmare, but Cora had refused to listen.

"I don't want you even to talk about it," she'd said. "You should just forget about bad dreams. If you let them get you all upset, they'll just come back over and over again. They're like demons, that's what." She'd chattered on, but Melissa had stopped listening. She could not force her mind away from the horrible images she'd seen the night before.

Now, with her mother and half sister long since gone to the club to play tennis, and the house completely empty, she finally got out of bed, pulled on a pair of jeans and her favorite T-shirt— the one Tag had given her—and shoved her feet into a pair of worn sneakers. Though she still had no appetite, she forced herself to drink the glass of orange juice Cora had brought her, then took the tray downstairs.

The house had a strange silence to it, an oppressive emptiness that made Melissa want to run outside. She started to do the dishes, but as she ran some water into the sink, she suddenly knew she could stand it no longer.

She had to go out to the pottingshed and look for herself. If what had happened last night had truly been only a nightmare, at least she would know, and finally release herself from the terrible fears that had held her in their grip since the moment she'd awakened.

But if it hadn't been a nightmare . . .

She put the thought out of her mind.

Abandoning the dirty dishes and leaving the sink half filled with water, she opened the back door and stepped out into the sunlight, but even the heat of the morning couldn't penetrate the cold knot of fear that had settled into her belly.

She crossed the terrace and skirted the pool, unconsciously retracing the path she'd followed the night before, while lost in the sleep to which D'Arcy had sent her.

At last she came to the pottingshed, and a wave of trepidation broke over her as she examined its broken door. She felt her legs tremble and for a moment wanted to turn back. But she knew she couldn't.

She had to know.

She forced herself to move forward, and reached out to push

the door open. The first thing she saw, the morning sun glinting brightly on its blade, was the machete.

Her eyes fixed on it, willing it to disappear, to return to its accustomed place against the wall inside the garage.

It remained where it was, silently accusing her.

And then she noticed the scent.

The sickly sweet fumes of decaying flesh assaulted her nostrils, and as her lungs filled with the noxious odor, the images leaped back into her mind with a new clarity.

With shaking hands she reached down and lifted one of the floorboards.

Her mind reeled at the sight she beheld.

Flies covered Tag's corpse, a black undulating mass of feeding insects that swarmed upward as the floor opened above them. Beneath the flies were the maggots, feeding on the ragged edges of Tag's wounds.

Her gorge rising as her eyes fixed on the grisly scene, a stream of vomit spewed from Melissa's mouth, but she was unaware of what was happening to her body, for her mind—stretched finally too taut—was at last beginning to rend asunder.

Silently, she screamed out for help, screamed out to the only friend who had never abandoned her, never failed her. *Help me, D'Arcy. Please help me . . .*

She felt the familiar blackness closing around her, felt all the sights she could no longer bear to witness fade away.

Sleep.

She had to sleep.

And this time she hoped never to wake up again.

This time she wanted to fall away into the black abyss and simply remain there, submerged forever in the soft darkness of forgiving sleep.

No one was there to see the change that came over Melissa now, no one witnessed the strange transformation as the personality of D'Arcy emerged once more, coming for the first time into the light of day.

Her eyes, only a moment ago clamped shut against the horror at her feet, now opened, and she gazed steadily, almost curiously, at the carnage beneath the floor.

Teri's words, words that in her memory had been uttered only a few minutes ago, drifted into her mind.

". . . it wasn't really you that did it, was it?"

Why was she here?

She had gone back to the house.

She'd gone back to the house to put Melissa to bed.

But someone had sent her away.

Someone had started talking to her, and Melissa had finally heard them and awakened.

And now she was back in the pottingshed, and Teri was gone, and somehow it was daylight.

She gazed once more at the corpse beneath the floor. Had Melissa done this?

She didn't know. But she had never known *why* Melissa was in trouble. All she'd ever known was that when Melissa was being punished, it was up to her to take care of her.

And if Melissa had done this, surely she would be punished.

D'Arcy knew what that meant.

She turned away from the gaping hole in the floor and walked slowly back to the house. Ignoring the dirty dishes in the sink, she passed through the kitchen to the old servants' stairs and climbed quickly to the second floor.

Emerging from the door at the end of the guest-wing hall, she walked down the length of the corridor until she came to the master suite. She opened the door and went inside, going directly to the cedar chest in Melissa's father's dressing room.

In the bottom of the third drawer, hidden beneath a stack of sweaters, she found what she was looking for.

At last she went to Melissa's room and pulled back the covers on the bed.

She began attaching the thick nylon straps of the restraints to the frame of the bed, and, when she was done, took off her clothes and slipped into a pair of Melissa's pajamas.

At last she got on the bed, stretched out her legs, and began fastening the leather cuffs to her ankles.

When she was finished, she used the fingers of her right hand to fasten another cuff to her left wrist.

At last, the final strap, the one she'd been unable to fasten to her arm, held firmly in her hand, she lay stretched out on her back.

Once more she would endure Melissa's punishment.

Tom Mallory unconsciously tapped the eraser of his pencil against his front teeth as he scanned the report Cora Peterson had filled out. At last, dropping the pencil on his desk, he shifted his eyes from the report to Cora herself, perched nervously on the hard wooden chair on the other side of the desk. "Well, if it was anybody else but Tag," he observed almost reluctantly, "I'd have to say there isn't much we can do for another twenty-four hours or so. But I don't know . . ." He sighed, leaning back and folding his hands over his stomach. "I guess I tend to agree with you. Tag's never given anybody in this town a speck of trouble, and ever since he was knee-high to a grasshopper, he's been more grown up than half the men we got on the force here."

For the first time since Tag had disappeared, Cora felt a little of the nervous tension ebb from her body. "Then you'll look for him?" she asked anxiously.

Mallory nodded. "I'll have all the boys keep an eye out, and get copies of his picture made." He held up the snapshot of Tag that Cora had brought with her. In the picture, Tag was grinning happily, wearing a baseball cap that Tom Mallory himself had given to him only last summer. Mallory shook his head sadly. "I just can't see anyone wanting to hurt Tag," he mused almost to himself. "There isn't a soul in town who doesn't like that boy."

Cora nodded. "That's why I can't understand it. He was right in the middle of his chores when I came to town yesterday. And when I got back, he'd just vanished."

Mallory shrugged. "What about that dog of his? It ever show up?"

Cora shook her head. "But that's different. Dogs run off all the time."

"Well, I think the first thing we better do is have a few people check out the woods around the cove, and maybe that stretch of rocks up north. If Tag was out hunting for the dog, he could have had some kind of accident. If he was trying to climb some of those rocks . . ." He let his voice trail off as he saw the color drain from Cora's normally ruddy face.

"He wouldn't have done that," she said. "He knows how dangerous the bluffs can be. He—"

"Now, take it easy, Mrs. Peterson. I didn't say anything had happened to him. But it seems to me that right now the best thing we can hope for is that he fell somewhere and maybe broke a leg. And if he did, he'll be all right. We'll find him."

But Cora still wasn't convinced, and now she shifted uneasily in her chair. There was something she'd left out of the report, something she hadn't yet told Tom Mallory about. But it had been gnawing at her ever since yesterday. All night—as she'd lain awake listening every minute for Tag to come home—she kept thinking about Teri MacIver. But even now it seemed . . . well, it seemed just plain disloyal to talk to the police about Charles Holloway's own daughter.

Mallory, sensing her sudden discomfort, leaned forward once again. "Is there something else, Mrs. Peterson?"

Cora took a deep breath and made up her mind. "Well, yes," she finally admitted. "I—I hate to even bring it up, really. It— Well, it's Teri. Teri MacIver."

Mallory nodded. "Beautiful young lady. Looks just like her mother."

"Well, she certainly doesn't *act* like her mother," Cora observed tightly. Now that she'd finally broached the subject, her words tumbled from her lips in a swift torrent. "Nothing's been the same since that girl came into the house. Oh, she acts just as sweet as pie when anyone's around. Acting like she's Melissa's best friend, and all. But I don't believe it, and neither did Blackie!"

"Blackie?" Mallory echoed.

Cora nodded emphatically. "The minute he saw her, he backed away from her. Oh, she tried to make up to him, but he always snarled at her. A dog can tell about people, you know. If a dog doesn't like someone—" Realizing she was starting to ramble, she cut her words short. "Anyway, Tag saw her kick Blackie once. And ever since she's come, Melissa's problems seem to get worse and worse. The nightmares, and the sleepwalking . . ." She shook her head, her tongue clucking sympathetically. "I just can't help thinking Teri's doing something to her. I—"

Mallory held up a hand. "Hold on," he said. "Are you saying Melissa walks in her sleep?"

Cora paused, flustered. She hadn't meant to say that, hadn't meant to at all. But now that she'd made the slip, she couldn't take it back. Reluctantly, she nodded.

Mallory frowned deeply. "How come nobody told me that Saturday night?" he asked. "Could that be why she didn't remember going up to the road? When the Barnstable kid had his accident?"

Cora gazed at him uncertainly. "Well, I don't know," she said. She thought back to that night, when Melissa, all dressed up in her costume, had come through the kitchen on her way to the club. Now that she thought about it, Melissa's eyes *had* looked strange. In fact, they'd had that same strange vacant look as last night. "But now that I think of it," she went on, "there was something a little peculiar about her that night. She was acting kind of odd. I thought maybe she was just, you know, sort of pretending to be someone else, the way you do when you put on a costume."

"All right," Mallory told her. "I'll tell you what I'll do. I'll have some of the guys start looking around, but I also want to come out to Maplecrest myself. Just to talk to people—find out when the last time they saw Tag was—that kind of thing." And I also want to find out what's going on with Melissa Holloway, he added to himself. Saturday night, when he'd been talking to the whole family, not one of them had mentioned that Melissa had a problem with sleepwalking. Instead, they all—especially Phyllis—had insisted that the shock of the accident had simply caused a loss of memory.

But if it was something else . . .

Was it possible that she had, after all, caused the accident, rather than simply witnessed it?

He didn't know, but he intended to find out.

It was close to noon when Phyllis and Teri finally returned from the club. As soon as they came into the house, Phyllis went to the kitchen, her jaw setting angrily as she saw that Cora had only just begun to prepare lunch. "Really, Cora," she said. "I told you we'd be back by noon and that I expected lunch to be ready. If you can't follow the simplest—"

"It's almost ready," Cora broke in, pulling a platter of sliced melon from the refrigerator. "Won't be more than ten or fifteen minutes. I had to go into the village to tell the police about Tag."

Phyllis's eyes rolled toward the ceiling. "Cora, he's barely been gone twenty-four hours! He's a teenager, for heaven's sake. You know how kids these days are."

"Not Tag," Cora declared, turning to face her employer. "And Tom Mallory agrees with me. Fact is," she added, a rare feeling of spitefulness rising within her as she shifted her gaze to Teri, who had followed her stepmother into the kitchen, "he'll be coming out here to talk to everyone." She kept her eyes on Teri, but remained uncertain whether the girl had reacted to her words at all. "He'll be wanting to know—" And then she caught herself. Why let Teri know what the police were going to ask? "Well, he'll just be wanting to talk to people, that's all."

Phyllis shrugged dismissively. "Well, I'm sure he's welcome to talk to us," she said. "But what could any of us possibly say? None of us has any idea where Tag went."

"Maybe," Cora said, her eyes still on Teri. "And maybe not." This time she was almost certain she saw a flicker of apprehension in the girl's eyes, but then Teri smiled warmly.

"Where's Melissa? Is she up yet?"

Cora shook her head. "Her papa told her she could stay in bed, and I guess she's doin' it. I haven't seen her since I took her breakfast up this morning." She nodded toward the dishes that were still stacked on the sink. "Some people," she added pointedly, "at least help me tidy this place up sometimes."

But Teri was already on her way out of the kitchen. "I'll go up and see if she's awake," she called back over her shoulder.

Upstairs, Teri tapped at Melissa's door, then let herself into the room. Melissa lay on her bed, her eyes wide open, staring at the ceiling. And then Teri saw the straps.

Frowning, she stepped into the room and went to the bed, knowing the instant she looked into Melissa's eyes that she was seeing D'Arcy.

"D'Arcy?" she whispered. "Is that you?"

Melissa's eyes shifted, focusing on Teri's face.

"She went out to the pottingshed, didn't she?"

Melissa's head moved in a barely perceptible nod.

"Do you know what happened?"

Silence.

And then, from the open window, Teri heard the sound of tires crunching on the gravel drive. She turned away from the bed and hurried to the window.

A black-and-white police car was coming up the drive, disappearing a moment later as it pulled around to the front of the house. Teri's mind raced.

She had to find out what D'Arcy remembered; how much she knew of what had happened in the pottingshed. And after she found out, she had to turn D'Arcy's knowledge against Melissa herself.

She hurried back to the bed and looked down once more into her half sister's strangely vacant eyes. "You want to help Melissa, don't you?"

Again, that almost imperceptible nod.

Working quickly, Teri began removing the cuffs from Melissa's left arm and her legs. Then, grasping her arm, she pulled her half sister up. "Come on," she said. "If you really want to help Melissa, I know how you can do it."

A few seconds later, in the attic, Teri began helping Melissa into the dress once more.

"You have to tell them what you did," she whispered softly. "If you don't, they'll blame Melissa. You don't want them to blame Melissa, do you?"

Melissa shook her head slightly.

"Then you know what you have to do, don't you?" Teri crooned, fastening the last of the long row of buttons on the back of the dress. "You have to take the punishment, so they won't blame Melissa."

She heard Phyllis's voice calling up the stairs to her, and pulled the wig from its hiding place in the steamer trunk. Placing it on Melissa's head, she smiled softly.

"Wait," she said. "Just wait here, until I come for you."

Leaving Melissa standing silent and motionless in the attic, Teri hurried down the stairs.

CHAPTER

26

"Is this going to take much longer?" Teri asked. She was in the library, sitting on the sofa next to her stepmother, the nail of her right forefinger picking nervously at a crack in the red leather with which the couch was covered.

Tom Mallory glanced up from his notebook. Over the last half hour, as he'd talked with both Phyllis Holloway and Teri MacIver, he'd had a hard time making up his mind which of them he disliked more.

Phyllis had been barely civil to him, making it eminently clear that as far as she was concerned, his visit was an invasion of her home and her privacy. "I really can't understand why you want to talk to us at all," she'd said after keeping him waiting in the library for more than ten minutes before finally appearing. "I have a great deal to do today."

"I'm sure this won't take much of your time, Mrs. Holloway," he'd broken in. "But the fact of the matter is that Tag Peterson is missing."

Phyllis's brows rose skeptically. "Don't you think Cora is

overreacting to all this? The boy hasn't even been gone twenty-four hours."

Mallory had shaken his head. "There're quite a few kids I can think of that I wouldn't worry about if they took off for a day or two. But Tag's not one of them, Mrs. Holloway. Now, if you could just try to tell me when the last time you saw him was . . ."

Phyllis shrugged helplessly. "Well, I really don't know, Lieutenant."

"Sergeant," Mallory automatically corrected.

Phyllis's eyes narrowed slightly. "Sergeant," she repeated as if the word were distasteful to her. "Of course. At any rate, I'm not sure I could tell you the last time I saw Tag. He's just simply around, you know. We pay him for odd jobs he does, of course, but he's Cora's responsibility, not ours."

"If you'd just tell me when you last remember *seeing* him, Mrs. Holloway?"

Phyllis had sighed heavily. "Well, I suppose it was after the funeral yesterday. I seem to recall he might have been working on the lawn, but I can't be certain. Yesterday," she added pointedly, "was a difficult day for all of us, you know."

A few minutes later Teri MacIver had come in, and when he'd posed the same question to her, she'd simply shrugged her shoulders helplessly. "I'm not sure, really." She'd paused, and then frowned as if trying to remember something. "Actually," she went on, "I was in here most of the time Daddy and Phyllis were gone. But it seems to me I remember hearing him calling Melissa."

"Melissa?" Phyllis repeated. "But she was in her room, sound asleep."

Teri had shrugged once more. "Well, I didn't really see him, and I might be wrong. But I'd almost swear he was calling her. I thought they might be talking through the window, or something."

Cora Peterson, who had been listening silently from the doorway, eyed Teri suspiciously. "Seems to me you might have gone to take a look," she observed. "I mean, knowing Melissa was supposed to be asleep and all."

"Where is Melissa?" Mallory had asked then, shooting Cora a look that clearly said he could take care of the questions himself.

"She's asleep," Phyllis replied a little too quickly, giving the policeman the distinct impression she didn't want him to talk to her daughter. Sensing her mistake, she did her best to recover. "She had a very bad day yesterday. I'm afraid she became a bit hysterical at Jeff Barnstable's funeral. The doctor's recommended that she get a lot of rest."

"But she's not ill?" Mallory pressed.

"W-Well, no, not exactly," Phyllis stammered.

"Then if you don't mind, I'd like you to wake her up, Mrs. Holloway. It won't take but a minute or two, but if she *did* talk to Tag, I'd like to know what was said."

Phyllis had vacillated, as if weighing her options, but finally left the room. The moment she was gone, Teri's attitude had changed drastically. "I don't see what the big deal is," she had complained. "I mean, so Tag's gone. So what? Kids take off all the time, don't they? And it's not like Tag had any friends here. All he ever did was mow the lawn and trim the hedges, and he didn't even do that very well. He probably just got fed up with it."

"Now you see here, young lady—" Cora began, but Mallory silenced her with an upheld hand.

"Now let's all just take it easy, okay?"

That was when Teri had fixed him with angry eyes and demanded to know how much longer the interviews were going to take. "I have a couple of friends coming over to go swimming."

Cora's eyes narrowed. "Today?" she demanded. "It seems to me you might have thought about how your sister's feeling."

Teri smiled at her with exaggerated sweetness. "Maybe I did," she said. "And maybe I thought it might be nice for her to have some company."

"And maybe you didn't think at all," Cora grumbled, but before she could go on, Phyllis appeared in the library door.

"She's not in her room."

"But she has to be," Teri replied, her insolent smile instantly replaced with a look of grave concern. "I was just up there and she was sound asleep—" She cut her own words off and her hand flew to her mouth, but then she quickly dropped her hand to her side.

"What?" Phyllis demanded. "She *was* there, wasn't she?"

"Y-Yes," Teri said. Then, as if repeating a thought that had just popped into her mind that instant, she went on, "But—Well, she came into my room last night. She—She said she'd been sleepwalking." She turned to Cora. "She said you found her going up to the attic."

Cora licked her lips nervously, her mind working quickly. "Yes," she said. "That's true. But what—"

"Well, maybe she did it again," Teri suggested. Her eyes went to Phyllis. "I mean, it wouldn't be the first time, would it?"

An expression of grim anger came into Phyllis's eyes as she realized her daughter's problems were about to be aired in public. Cora, at least, had never talked about Melissa to outsiders. But now, she felt dizzy as she imagined the field day this policeman would have with the story: "The kid's crazy as a bedbug—wanders around the house in the middle of the night—hallucinates—the whole ball of wax. They shoulda locked her up years ago."

And he'd be right, too, Phyllis reflected darkly. It made her furious the way Burt Andrews had simply brushed aside her suggestion that Melissa be sent away. But if he'd only listened— and if Charles had only listened, too—Melissa wouldn't even be here now.

"I—Well, I suppose . . ." she floundered.

"Why don't we go up and take a look around, Mrs. Holloway," Tom Mallory suggested, then firmly took Phyllis's arm and led her out into the hallway.

Less than a minute later the four of them were gathered at the foot of the stairs to the attic. "But this is ridiculous," Phyllis protested. "It's the middle of the day. She's never—"

Her words were cut off by a sound from above.

It was a footstep. A second later, it was followed by another.

And then, as the four people gazed up toward the door at the top of the stair, the door itself opened and a figure appeared.

It was Melissa, clad in the white dress, her eyes glazed over.

She paused for a moment, and then her head moved slightly and her vacant eyes stared down at them.

"I did it," she said, her voice hollow. "It wasn't her fault. I did it."

She started down the stairs, and as the light from below finally fell on the folds of white material, they saw the bloodstains for the first time.

From the bodice to the hem the dress was stained a dark reddish brown.

Phyllis gasped as she stared at her daughter in shocked horror, and her hand instinctively grasped Teri MacIver's arm.

Cora, her eyes fixed numbly on the grotesque figure descending the stairs, felt her knees give way and would have collapsed to the floor except for Tom Mallory's quick movement to support her.

Teri MacIver simply smiled quietly to herself.

"I still don't see why Teri wanted me to come, too," Kent Fielding said. The two of them were on the beach, heading up toward the Holloways' house. "You're the one she likes."

Brett Van Arsdale grinned mischievously at his friend. "Maybe she's decided to set you up with Melissa," he replied. But then his smile faded as he remembered Jeff Barnstable. "What do you suppose really happened the other night?" he asked. "I mean, how could Melissa have walked all the way from Maplecrest and not even remember?"

Kent shrugged. "She's nuts, that's why." Then a thought occurred to him. "Hey, remember after the bonfire, when Cyndi and Ellen claimed they saw D'Arcy wandering around in the woods?"

Brett nodded. "I've been thinking the same thing. But she acted so scared when I was telling the story."

"Yeah, but she was really pissed off when Teri spilled the beans about her thinking she's friends with D'Arcy. Man, that's just too weird. But maybe she went home and put on that old dress, then went out trying to scare people."

Brett chuckled. "Well, if she did, it sure worked. Or maybe," he went on, "Ellen and Cyndi weren't lying. Maybe they really did see D'Arcy."

Kent glanced at Brett out of the corner of his eye. "Oh, come on. Nobody actually believes that old story. And after what happened to Jeff, you know it had to be Melissa the girls saw."

"Wouldn't you think they'd finally figure out she's a nut case and lock her up?" Brett mused. "I mean, even if she didn't remember what happened, she looked so scary, you can't blame Jeff for going off the road. Shit, I would've lost it myself."

They turned away from the beach and started up toward the big shingled house. "You sure you want to come?" Brett asked, turning to snap his beach towel at Kent, then backing quickly away before the other boy could retaliate. "I mean, what if Melissa gets a crush on you like she did on Jeff?"

Kent's brow furrowed into a dark scowl. "Jesus, Brett, that's really gross. I mean, whatever happened, I just can't believe she meant for him to—" And then his voice trailed off as his eyes, looking beyond Brett, caught a glimpse of a strange figure coming out the back door of the Holloways' house. "Holy shit," he breathed. "What the hell's going on?"

Startled by the sudden change in Kent's voice, Brett turned around to see what his friend was staring at.

Even from where he stood he knew immediately that the figure in white, with long blond hair streaming down over her shoulders, was Melissa.

"What the hell's she doing?" he whispered. "She's got that stupid costume on again."

Both boys broke into a trot, hurrying across the lawn toward the house. But they stopped short when they suddenly saw that Melissa wasn't alone. Behind her, watching her silently, were Tom Mallory and Phyllis Holloway. And behind them, emerging from the house just as they came to the steps to the terrace, they saw Cora Peterson and Teri MacIver. The boys froze where they were, uncertain what to do. And then Kent saw the stains on the front of the dress and nudged Brett.

"Look at that," he whispered. "It—It looks like blood."

Tom Mallory was the first to spot them. Instantly, he left Phyllis's side and hurried over to them. "Get out of here," he told them, his voice low but carrying an unmistakable note of authority. "Right now. Don't say anything, and don't move fast. Just back away."

Brett and Kent glanced at each other, and Brett's mouth opened, but then he changed his mind. Grasping Kent's arm, he backed away from the strange spectacle of Melissa, who seemed not to have noticed them at all. She was moving across the terrace now, heading toward the swimming pool.

Mallory, their presence already all but forgotten, turned away and caught up with Phyllis.

"What'll we do?" Kent whispered as the bizarre procession moved across the terrace, then turned to follow Melissa around the pool toward the bathhouse.

"Well, I'm sure not leaving," Brett replied. "Whatever's going on, I'm gonna see it."

They moved forward again, staying well behind the group following Melissa, but not letting them out of their sight. "She looks weird," Brett whispered a moment later as Melissa, her pace slow and stately, turned around the corner of the bathhouse and started toward the garage. "She looks like she's sleepwalking or something."

A moment later Melissa came to a stop in front of the old pottingshed. She stood perfectly still for a moment, and then her right hand came up and she pushed the door open.

A few flies were hovering in the air inside the shed. As the door opened, a foul stench drifted from within.

Though the others instinctively drew back from the odor, Melissa seemed not to notice it at all.

She stepped inside.

And once again her right hand came up.

This time the forefinger of her right hand pointed directly at the loose floorboards.

"There," she said.

The word seemed to hang in the air for a moment, and then Tom Mallory moved inside, knelt down, and pulled up a floorboard.

"Jesus," he whispered, closing his eyes for a moment against the sight of Tag's mangled body sprawled out beneath the floor. He paused for a moment, regaining control of his churning emotions, and then stood up.

Ignoring Phyllis and Teri, he went directly to Cora and put an arm around her shoulder. "It's Tag," he said softly. "I'm sorry, Cora. I'm so very sorry."

He turned and strode toward the house, already mentally organizing his investigation team.

Not, of course, that the team would have much to investigate.

Melissa, after all, had already confessed.

CHAPTER

27

Burt Andrews pulled his BMW up in front of Maplecrest, sliding it into a narrow gap between an ambulance and one of the police cars. There were three black-and-whites there now, plus an assortment of other vehicles, ranging from a dirty Volkswagen with a press sticker on the windshield to a Rolls-Royce Corniche convertible with New York license plates that read simply LENORE.

Leaving the BMW, he hurried up the steps and walked through the open door into the foyer. For a moment he had an eerie feeling that the house was empty, despite the number of cars in the drive, but then he saw a cluster of people on the terrace behind the house, and more scattered in small groups on the lawn that rolled away from the terrace toward the woods. From where he stood, it appeared that half the population of Secret Cove had already gathered here. He was about to step through the French doors when a voice from the stairs stopped him.

"Dr. Andrews?"

He looked up to see a tall blond woman, clad in a white blouse and brightly colored cotton skirt, gazing down at him. Despite what had happened here, she had an air about her of perfect control. As she came quickly down the stairs, she extended her hand toward him. "I'm Lenore Van Arsdale," she said. "I'm a friend of the Holloways."

Andrews took the proffered hand for a moment, but quickly released it, his eyes automatically shifting to the stairs. "Where are they?"

"Phyllis is in her room," Lenore Van Arsdale said. "Teri's with her, and Melissa is in the library, with Dr. Chandler. They wanted to take her somewhere, but when Teri told me about you, I suggested they wait."

Andrews's brows lifted a fraction of an inch, a gesture Lenore Van Arsdale didn't miss. She smiled thinly. "I have a reputation for being indomitable, and today I decided to use it." The smile faded away. "Melissa seems to be in a state of shock. I'm not sure she has the slightest idea of what's happened, or even where she is. It seemed to me there was no point in taking her anywhere until you got here."

Andrews nodded, starting toward the library, and Lenore fell in beside him. "What about Charles?" he asked. "Has anyone gotten hold of him?"

"He's on his way," Lenore told him. "He's the first person I called. He chartered a plane out of LaGuardia. He called a while ago from the airport in Portland. He's driving out right now."

"What about Phyllis?" Andrews paused outside the library door and turned to face Lenore.

For just the slightest moment he thought he saw a flicker of hesitation in her eyes, but then they cleared and she shook her head. "She's upset, of course," she said. "But I have a feeling that what's upsetting her most has nothing to do with what's happened here. She—Well, she keeps asking what people are going to think." Her voice took on a note of icy disapproval. "I'm afraid her main concern is whether this is going to ruin her socially. But then it's always been my opinion that she never really cared much about Melissa, or anyone else."

This time Burt Andrews's brows arched high. "You don't like her much, do you?"

Lenore shook her head. "I never have, and I never will. I'm civil to her because I grew up with Charles and I feel sorry for him. And I feel sorry for Melissa, too." She sighed heavily. "Maybe—Well, perhaps all of us here should have done more. We knew the pressures Phyllis put on Melissa—"

"Let's not blame anyone just yet, Mrs. Van Arsdale," Andrews interjected. "Until we know what happened."

"But we do know," Lenore broke in. "Apparently, Melissa confessed."

Andrews shrugged. "Didn't you just say she doesn't seem to know what's going on?"

For a split second Lenore Van Arsdale's cool facade seemed to crack, but she recovered herself. "You're right, of course," she said. Then: "Can I get you anything?"

Andrews shook his head. "I think I'd better have a look at Melissa." Lenore Van Arsdale lingered for a moment, almost as if she expected to accompany him into the library, but she finally turned away. Andrews let himself into the library, closing the door behind him.

Melissa, still wearing the bloodstained dress, sat stiffly on the edge of the sofa, her hands folded demurely in her lap, her eyes fixed on the fireplace. Fritz Chandler, a silver-haired, slightly overweight man of fifty-odd years whom Burt Andrews had known for better than a decade, heaved himself to his feet as the psychiatrist entered the room.

"Burt," he said, automatically dropping his voice to the level he habitually used when making rounds at the local clinic. "Let me tell you, I'm glad to see you. I've seen some strange things in my life, but this one . . ." His voice faded away as he shook his head helplessly.

"Have you given her anything?" Andrews asked. "Anything at all?"

"Not a thing. I've checked her over, and I'm telling you, Burt, I just don't get it. Looking at her eyes, I'd have said she was in shock, but she doesn't show any other symptoms. Pulse, blood pressure, reflexes—everything's normal. But she hasn't said a word. She was still outside when I got here, just standing by that goddamn pottingshed, like she was waiting for a bus or something. Jesus . . ." His eyes, which had been fixed on Melissa, suddenly moved to Burt Andrews. "Have you been out there?" Andrews shook his head. "Well, let me tell you, buddy, it's one hell of a mess. It's not just the Peterson kid, whose head was damned near split in two with a machete. There's a dead dog, too, which has been rotting in the heat for about a week, near as I can make out." His eyes shifted back to Melissa. "And she was just standing there, as if she didn't notice any of it."

Andrews nodded, his own eyes fixing on Melissa now. "What happened when you brought her in here?" he asked. "Any problems?"

"None. All I had to do was tell her what to do. I know she hears me, and I know she understands what I'm saying, but she hasn't said a word."

"All right. Let's take another look at her."

He crossed to Melissa and knelt down in front of her. If she even saw him, she gave no sign at all. Her eyes remained fixed on the empty fireplace, her face expressionless.

"Melissa?" Andrews asked. "Melissa, it's me. Dr. Andrews. Can you hear me?"

There was silence. Andrews took her wrist in his right hand, his fingers feeling for a pulse. He'd expected to find her skin cold and slightly clammy, but instead it felt perfectly natural.

Except that she seemed totally unaware of his touch.

As Chandler had told him, her pulse was perfectly normal.

He examined her quickly, rechecking for the symptoms Chandler had expected to find, but as the older doctor had said, they simply weren't there. Were it not for the vacant look in her eyes, and her total silence and stillness, Melissa would have appeared perfectly normal.

Except, Andrews began to realize as he studied her face more closely, something else had changed.

He knew he was looking at Melissa's face; all her features were perfectly recognizable. But somehow, in some subtle way he couldn't quite put his finger on, those features had changed.

And then he understood.

It wasn't Melissa he was looking at at all.

"D'Arcy?" he asked. "D'Arcy, can you hear me?"

Melissa's head swung around and her eyes gazed at him with no sign of recognition at all.

"I'm Dr. Andrews," he went on. "I'm a friend of Melissa's. Has she ever told you about me?"

Something changed in Melissa's eyes. Andrews was almost certain he saw a hint of a smile around the corners of her mouth. But still she said nothing.

"Where is Melissa, D'Arcy? May I talk to her?"

For a moment the girl simply sat staring at him. Then, very slowly, she shook her head and uttered a single word. "Asleep."

"Melissa's asleep?" Andrews asked.

Melissa nodded.

"Can you wake her up?"

Melissa shook her head once more. "She doesn't want to wake up. She never wants to wake up again."

Andrews took the girl's hands in his own and leaned closer. "D'Arcy, do you know why she doesn't want to wake up?"

Melissa smiled. "She's afraid. She's done something bad, and she's afraid she'll be punished."

Suddenly the door to the library opened and Charles Holloway strode into the room. When he saw Melissa sitting on the sofa in the bloody dress, he stopped short, the color draining from his face. "M-Melissa?" he breathed.

Andrews stood up quickly, and as Charles started once more toward his daughter, the doctor put out a restraining hand. "Don't try to talk to her, Charles. There's something I've got to explain to you first."

Charles started to brush past the psychiatrist, but as his eyes fixed on Melissa's face, he paused a second time, for he, too, could see the change that had come over Melissa's features.

He stared at her for a moment, and then his eyes shifted back to Andrews. "What is it?" he asked. "She looks—she looks different."

"She *is* different, Charles," Andrews told him gently. "This isn't Melissa at all. This is D'Arcy."

Charles Holloway's eyes widened with shock. "D'Arcy?" he repeated. "What the hell are you trying to say? There isn't any D'Arcy."

"But there is," Andrews explained. "D'Arcy is another personality that Melissa's been using to protect herself. And this is she. She says that Melissa's gone to sleep and doesn't want to wake up."

His legs suddenly threatening to collapse beneath him, Charles sank onto one of the wing chairs. "Wh-What does it mean?"

he asked, though he had a sick feeling deep inside that he already knew.

"It means we have a lot of work ahead of us," Andrews told him, resting a sympathetic hand on the distraught man's shoulder. "Somehow, I'm going to have to find a way to reach Melissa. But if she doesn't want to be reached . . ." He fell silent, leaving the words hanging in the air.

Cora Peterson stirred on her bed and heaved herself into a sitting position. Elsie Conners, who'd come over from the Fieldings' the minute she'd heard what had happened, got up from the chair next to the window and moved to the bed. "Now you just take it easy, Cora," she said, using the tone of voice she ordinarily reserved for disciplining her employer's son. "The doctor said you should lie down."

"Well, I'm not going to lie down, Elsie," Cora retorted, swinging her feet off the bed and standing up, automatically smoothing the wrinkles out of her dress. "I've lost both parents and a husband without coming all apart, and I don't think Tag would want me to start fallin' apart now."

"But the doctor—"

"Doctors don't always know everything," Cora groused. "Now, if you want to help me, fine. But if all you're gonna do is jaw at me, you might just as well get on back to the Fieldings'." She went into the bathroom she shared with Tag and reached for her hairbrush, but as her eyes fell on Tag's own brush and comb set—the one she'd given him just last Christmas, with his initials engraved on the back of the brush—she felt a sob rise within her.

Now, none of that, she told herself. Firmly checking her emotions, she ran her brush through her hair, then quickly washed her face. The cold water felt good, and when she was finished, she took a deep breath. For the last hour, while she'd been lying on her bed fighting off the sedative Dr. Chandler had given her, she'd been thinking. And the more she thought, the more convinced she'd become that something was terribly wrong.

Over and over again she'd tried to imagine Melissa killing Tag, and no matter how she put it together, she couldn't make herself believe it.

She hadn't seen Tag yet—someone had taken her away from

the pottingshed right after Tom Mallory had told her what he'd found beneath the floorboards. But now, she knew, she had to look at him, no matter how painful it might be for her.

She had to know what had been done to him, had to see for herself the wounds that had been inflicted.

Had to make up her own mind whether Melissa could have done it.

She started down the stairs, with Elsie Conners fluttering after her. "Cora, where are you going? There's no reason for you—"

"I'm going to see my grandson, Elsie," Cora told the Fieldings' housekeeper. Elsie gasped in horror at the very idea, but Cora silenced her with a look. "Don't argue with me, Elsie Conners. I know what I'm doing. And there's more than Tag to think about. There's Melissa, too."

"Melissa!" Elsie burst out, her voice quivering with outrage. "Cora Peterson, have you gone clean out of your mind? Melissa Holloway killed Tag! What are you thinking about, worrying about her? If it was up to me—"

"It's not up to you," Cora snapped. "And thank God for small favors."

She pushed open the front door, pausing abruptly as a memory of the night before came into her mind.

Melissa, walking in her sleep.

Walking from . . .

The pottingshed?

It was possible. She chewed thoughtfully at her lower lip, reviewing every detail of the previous night.

Melissa had been wearing her bathrobe.

A white terry-cloth bathrobe.

And there were no bloodstains on it.

Today, Melissa had been wearing the old dress from the attic, and it had been covered with blood.

She took a deep breath and started down the steps, then began threading her way through the clusters of people who had gathered on the lawn. She heard words of sympathy being offered to her, but never paused even to acknowledge them, let alone respond. Finally, after what seemed to her an eternity but could have been no more than half a minute, she came to the pottingshed.

A gurney had been set up in front of the crumbling shack, and even as Cora arrived, four men came out, carrying Tag's body, which had already been discreetly covered with a sheet of opaque plastic. For a moment Cora's resolve weakened, but then she stiffened her back and moved closer. Behind the four men, who were now placing Tag's body on the stretcher, was Tom Mallory. He paused in surprise when he caught sight of her.

"Cora, there isn't any reason for—"

"I want to see him, Tom," Cora said, her voice steady. "I want to see my grandson."

Mallory shifted his weight uneasily. "There's no reason for you to put yourself through that, Cora."

"I have my own reasons, Tom. I want to see him."

Mallory hesitated, scanning the old woman's face for signs of hysteria. But her gaze was steady as she looked back at him, and he felt the determination emanating from her. "All right," he said quietly, nodding to the man at the head of the stretcher.

As Cora approached, the medic folded the sheet of plastic back and Tag's head was exposed to her view. She gasped as she saw his smashed nose and split skull, but then once more regained control of herself. "All right," she breathed, shifting her eyes quickly away from what she'd seen as the man once more covered Tag up.

"What happened, Tom?" she asked.

Mallory shook his head. "Cora, you don't need to put—"

"Tell me, Tom."

A sigh escaped Mallory's throat, but he reached into his back pocket and pulled out his notebook. Flipping through the pages, he found the information he was looking for. "There'll be an autopsy, of course, but it looks like he got hit in the face first. His nose was broken and there was a lot of bleeding, which wouldn't have happened if he'd already been dead. It looks like he lay on the floor for a little while, and then she split his head open with the machete."

"Who?" Cora asked. "Who hit him? Who split his head open?"

Tom Mallory gazed at the housekeeper in bewilderment. "Melissa," he said. "Melissa Holloway."

Cora shook her head. "No," she said softly. "I don't believe that."

"Cora, you were there. You heard her. There really can't be any doubt. I'm sure when we examine it, we'll find her fingerprints all over that machete." He reached out to touch her, but Cora stepped back.

"I don't care what she said. I don't care what you find," she told him stolidly. "I know Melissa. I've known her since she was a baby. And Tag was her best friend. She wouldn't have done that to him—she couldn't have, Tom. She doesn't have a mean bone in her body."

Turning away, she started toward the house, once again ignoring the people around her, who were now staring at her in shocked disbelief at the words she'd just uttered.

She came into the house just as they were bringing Melissa down from her room, where her father had taken her a few minutes before. She was out of the hideously stained dress now and wrapped once more in the bathrobe she'd been wearing the night before, when Cora had found her out by the pool. Cora watched her silently as she came down the stairs, her eyes searching the robe for any signs of blood.

There were none.

Only a few smudges of dust or dirt, which could have come from anywhere.

As Melissa came to the bottom of the stairs, Cora hurried toward her and put her arms around her. "It's all right, baby," she murmured. "I know you didn't hurt Tag, and I won't let anything happen to you." Then, feeling the strange lifelessness in Melissa's body, she drew back slightly and looked into the girl's face.

D'Arcy's empty eyes stared back at her.

"Dear God," Cora gasped, turning to Charles, her eyes finally flooding with tears. "What's wrong with her? What have they done to her?"

Charles slipped his arm around the elderly woman. "They haven't done anything to her, Cora," he said. "She—She's had some kind of a breakdown,"

"But—But she didn't *do* anything," Cora insisted.

Charles squeezed Cora's shoulders. His own eyes were red-rimmed with tears. "It's all right, Cora," he managed to say. "They're not going to hurt her. They're taking her to a hospital. Nothing's going to happen to her. They're just going to make her well."

Through it all Melissa stood completely still, her unseeing eyes staring ahead, her face expressionless. The two doctors, one on each side of her, led her unresisting form toward the front door. But suddenly, as one of the ambulance attendants opened the door, she turned, her eyes fixing on her father. Her face contorted, as if some kind of internal struggle were going on within her. With a flood of tears streaming down her face, she uttered one more word.

"Pearls."

Everyone in the room stared at her in silence. Then Charles suddenly understood. "Her necklace," he said. "She wants her necklace."

Bolting up the stairs, he went into Melissa's room, pulled open the drawer in which she kept the necklace he'd given her the previous Christmas and fished around under her sweaters until he found it. A moment later he was back downstairs. Very gently, he fastened the string of pearls around his daughter's neck, kissed her on the cheek, then spoke softly to Burt Andrews.

"They're her favorite thing," he said. "Will they let her keep them at the hospital?"

Andrews hesitated, then nodded. "I'll see to it," he said. "It's a good sign that she asked for them." Charles gazed uncomprehendingly at the psychiatrist. "It was Melissa who spoke just now," he went on. "Couldn't you see the change in her face? She wanted the pearls so badly she was willing to wake up for them. And if she'd wake up once, we'll find a way to wake her up again."

But as they led his younger daughter out of the house to the waiting ambulance, a desolate thought came unbidden into Charles's mind.

Why? Why wake her up at all?

Why not just let her sleep?

A sob rose in his throat as he realized he might never see his Melissa again.

It was nearly midnight, and Maplecrest was silent. Cora had long since gone back to her little house beyond the pool, quietly refusing Charles's offer to her to spend the night in the big house.

"I don't expect to sleep tonight," she'd said. "But at least I can be in my own house, and feel Tag around me." She'd looked up at

Charles, her eyes dampening once more. "I don't rightly know what I'll do without him," she'd said. "I can't remember ever living in an empty house before. But I'll get used to it, I suppose. A body can get used to anything, if it has to." She'd reached out and taken Charles's hand. "And don't you worry about Melissa," she went on. "Deep in my heart, I know she didn't do anything to Tag. She loved him just as much as I did."

Charles didn't try to argue with her—he still wasn't sure how to explain to Cora what had happened. Indeed, he still hadn't grasped the full meaning of it himself. That there could have been another individual—a whole separate personality—living within Melissa, was almost beyond his comprehension.

"I'm not sure we'll ever know exactly what happened," Andrews had told him after they'd taken Melissa away. "Right now, the D'Arcy personality seems to be in full control of her, and until I can make contact with Melissa again, I can't even begin working on trying to integrate the two of them. But I might be able to find out more about what's been happening to Melissa over the years. There will be things that D'Arcy knows that Melissa isn't even aware of. And if I can get D'Arcy to trust me enough to talk to me—well, this isn't the time to be talking about that, is it?"

Eventually, the house had emptied out entirely, the neighbors returning to their homes, the police investigators finishing their jobs. At last there had been only the three of them left.

And now, at midnight, Phyllis and Charles had finally gone to bed. Teri MacIver was the only one still up.

She moved around the darkened rooms restlessly, experiencing each of them as if for the first time.

For now, tonight, with Melissa finally gone, Maplecrest truly felt as though it belonged to her.

She lingered on the first floor, putting off the moment she was most looking forward to. Finally, she could wait no longer.

Going silently up the stairs, she paused outside the closed door to the master suite, listening for any sign that her father and stepmother were still awake.

She heard nothing.

At last she went back to the other side of the house, but instead of going into her own room, she passed it by, opening Melissa's door instead. She slipped into the darkened room, closed the door behind her, and switched on the light.

The bloodied dress, which had been lying on the floor only a few hours ago, left there when they'd taken it off Melissa, was gone. Cora must have taken it away.

Or perhaps the police had taken it, to be sure the blood on it was really Tag's.

Not that it mattered. Melissa was gone now, and Teri had no further use for the dress.

It had, after all, served its purpose.

She lay on the bed, stretching out across its luxurious expanse, and began visualizing what she would do with the room.

Melissa's things—all of them—would go up in the attic. And then the room would be redone. She looked at the wallpaper with distaste. Maybe she'd have it done in silk. She'd seen pictures of silk walls, and always, when she'd lain in bed in the house in San Fernando, thinking about Maplecrest, she'd pictured her room here with silk brocade on the walls. Emerald green, with white trim.

She tried to visualize it, and just the image of it made her smile. She snuggled deeper into the soft mattress and felt a comfortable sleepiness come over her. She gazed up once more at the ceiling, picturing the little room above it, tucked under the house's eaves. "Thanks, D'Arcy," she said, snickering quietly to herself. "You've been a big help."

As she drifted off to sleep a few minutes later, a sound drifted into her ear, almost unidentifiable

Maybe it's D'Arcy, she thought. Maybe she's laughing, too.

CHAPTER

28

It was the kind of perfect afternoon that the members of the Cove Club had come to expect as their due on the day of the August Moon Ball. Through July and most of the following month, a stultifying heat had lain over the coast, and the pace of life had slowed to a crawl. By nine o'clock on most mornings the tennis courts had been all but abandoned, while the few souls who braved the morning sun gathered around the pool to huddle under small patches of shade offered by umbrellas over the tables. The luncheon buffet was set up every day, but as the heat increased, more and more people chose to remain in the cavernous cool of their own homes, leaving the food in the club's dining room untouched beneath its net coverings. Only in late afternoon would the members of the Cove Club finally venture forth to sit on the terrace around the pool, sipping tall drinks and solemnly swearing that the weather patterns were changing, and by next year Maine was going to turn into Miami.

But finally, toward the end of the month, the heat wave had broken, and today—the Saturday before Labor Day—the weather was perfect. The sky was clear, a soft blue dome that seemed to insulate the cove from the outside world, and even the humidity appeared to have taken a day off. A freshening breeze was wafting in from the ocean, and a tingle of excitement had replaced the lassitude of the last eight weeks.

Even the tragedy of Melissa Holloway was fading into little more than the major memory by which this summer would be marked. The Barnstables were gone—only a week after the funeral, Paula had insisted on putting their house on the market. Despite the fact that it was the first house on the cove to become available to "outsiders" in three generations, it hadn't sold yet, and there was talk of turning it into a historical museum.

"Who would buy it?" Lenore Van Arsdale had asked Eleanor Stevens only a couple of weeks ago. "After all, everyone on the East Coast knows we're inbred to the point of degeneracy. We've become an anachronism."

"We can't be too degenerate if we can still use words like that," Eleanor had observed, but still a sigh of resignation had come to her lips. "But you're right, I suppose. Who would want to come in here at this point, and listen to all of us reminiscing about the good old days, three generations back?"

Kay Fielding had chuckled hollowly. "Can't you just hear people fifty years from now? 'Oh, them. They bought the Barnstable house the year of that terrible business with Melissa Holloway. Maybe next year we'll vote them into the club.' "

They'd all laughed softly, and yet they all knew it was true, and privately most of the members of the club had begun to consider the idea of spending their summers elsewhere. There had been a rent in the fabric of their lives this year, and rather than mend it, they were all considering simply replacing it with something new.

But a sense of normality had slowly begun to come back to them, and today the air was alive with excitement about the ball. All day florists' trucks had been arriving, the doors to the dining room remaining closed, the curtains drawn over the windows. The theme of the party, known only to the committee, had remained a secret, although practically everyone had done his best to worm it out of one of the members.

Early this morning a large unmarked truck had arrived, and all day a crew of men had been working, but none of them were willing to answer a single question. Now, lying on the patio around the pool with Brett Van Arsdale and a few of their friends, Teri was still trying to figure it out. She glanced up at the truck still parked in the lot next to the clubhouse and groaned with exasperation. "Hasn't your mother said *anything*?" she asked Brett for at least the third time that day. "I mean, what's she wearing?"

"How should I know?" Brett replied, not even turning his head to look at her. "Why don't you ask Phyllis?"

Teri rolled her eyes. "I have," she said. "Every day for the last month. But she won't say a word. I even tried to get her to tell me what color dress to look for, but she just told me to suit myself."

Brett snickered. "I'll bet she wouldn't have said that to Melissa."

Teri's smile faded and a frown creased her brow. "That's not very nice. It isn't Melissa's fault she cracked up." Ever since the day they'd taken her half sister away, she'd carefully defended Melissa against any criticism, insisting that whatever had really happened, it wasn't Melissa's fault. "Anyone can have a breakdown," she'd steadfastly insisted. And though she'd never given any sign of it, she'd thoroughly enjoyed the admiration she received for her loyalty to the half sister she'd only known for a few short weeks.

"If she really did," Brett replied, voicing the idea that had been whispered around the Cove over the last few weeks. "I mean, maybe she's just faking it so they won't put her in prison for the rest of her life."

Teri rolled her eyes impatiently. "That is so stupid. If you could see her—"

"I know," Kent Fielding groaned, quoting everything he'd heard at least a dozen times before. " 'She doesn't say anything at all. She just sits there, staring at nothing.' " He shuddered exaggeratedly. "She sounds like a zombie to me."

"Well, at least we don't have to worry about D'Arcy anymore," Cyndi Miller giggled. "If she's busy possessing Melissa, she can't bother us tonight."

"Oh, please," Teri complained, "can't we talk about something else? Come on, Brett, let's go in for a swim."

She got up from her chaise and started down toward the beach.

Brett followed, catching her hand in his as they reached the bottom of the steps and started across the sand.

"It's just talk," he said by way of an apology. "No one really means anything by it."

"Well, it's mean," Teri grumbled.

"So it's mean," Brett replied, shrugging. "But everyone isn't as nice as you are. I mean, no matter how weird Melissa got, you always took her side."

Teri looked up at him. "And I always will," she said. "She's my sister, and no matter what she did, I'll always love her. So now can we just drop it?" Letting go of his hand, she ran down the beach and into the water, ignoring the shock of the cold against her skin. Finally she plunged through a wave, surfaced, and rolled over onto her back. "Come on, chicken," she yelled to Brett, who was still on the beach. "It's great!"

"It's cold!" Brett yelled back, but finally took a deep breath, steeled himself, and dove in after her. He swam toward her underwater, but at last his breath ran out and he surfaced.

Teri, laughing, was twenty yards away.

Brett set out after her again, falling into the steady rhythm of a strong Australian crawl, but Teri proved to be a stronger swimmer than he'd thought, and it took him almost five minutes to catch up. Finally, coming abreast of her, he began treading water. "Hey," he gasped. "What gives? When you first got here, you could barely swim at all. Remember how I had to pull you out that first day?" But as Teri grinned at him, a thought came into his mind and he cocked his head, squinting at her in the sun. "Or were you faking that day?"

Teri's lips curved up into an enigmatic smile. "I guess you'll never know, will you?" she asked. Then, as Brett grabbed playfully at her, she kicked away from him and started back toward shore.

Phyllis, dressed in a pair of khaki pants and a white blouse—smudged here and there with blotches of paint—stood back and surveyed the banner that was finally ready to be put up over the orchestra stand at the far end of the dining room. She ran a hand through her hair, remembering too late that there was still some wet paint on her fingers. But instead of feeling a flush of humiliation as she saw the smile on Lenore Van Arsdale's face, she only chuckled ruefully. "Maybe I better call the hairdresser and have him stock up on paint thinner."

Lenore, almost to her own surprise, found herself joining in Phyllis's laughter. Three months ago, she was certain, Phyllis wouldn't have been in this room at all—or if she had, she'd have shown up dressed for a formal luncheon and imperiously handed out orders to the workmen. But for the last three days Phyllis had been there with the rest of them, working hard to make the room exactly as they wanted it for tonight. All day yesterday, and through this morning, she'd painstakingly worked on the banner, determined that every letter, executed in a brilliant red edged with gold, be perfect. "My father was a sign painter," she'd explained when she'd announced she'd do the lettering herself. "From the time I was in kindergarten, he taught me everything he knew. In high school, when all the other girls were working as waitresses, I was painting signs. I hated it, but I was good at it."

The other women had glanced at each other in surprise, for even after almost fifteen years, this was the first time any of them had found out what Phyllis's father had actually done for a living. "He was in advertising," was the most she'd ever said before, then quickly changed the subject.

But a lot about Phyllis had changed over the last weeks. In the first days after the doctors had led Melissa away, she'd barely been seen at all, staying behind locked doors, emerging from the house only to drive to the hospital where Melissa had been taken. But after a week—a week in which Teri had told Brett that all Phyllis was doing was brooding in the library all day with the curtains closed, Lenore had finally taken pity on her and gone to talk to her.

"I don't know what to do," Phyllis had reluctantly admitted. "I know everyone thinks it was all my fault, that I was too hard on Melissa, but . . ." Her voice had trailed off and her eyes filled with tears. Lenore's years-old grudge against the woman had melted away in the face of Phyllis's self-recrimination.

"Nonsense," she'd replied, though privately she believed that most of what Phyllis had said was true. "I'm sure you did the best you knew how, and no one can blame you for what's happened. If you sit here in the dark for the rest of your life, you won't have much of a life left and you'll never be of help to Melissa or anyone else. Now let's get you dressed and go have some lunch."

"But I couldn't," Phyllis protested. "I couldn't face anyone. What will I say? People will stare at me!"

"People will certainly stare at you if you try to turn into a hermit," Lenore replied. "Now, come on."

She'd taken Phyllis upstairs, gone through her closets and selected a deep maroon suit and a simple blouse. "Wear this. It's not gaudy, but on the other hand, if you wear navy blue or black, it will look like you're in mourning."

Phyllis had winced. "I—I feel like I am," she'd stammered.

Lenore sighed heavily. "Well, you're not. Everyone in town knows what happened, and they know Melissa isn't dead. So you can't act as though she is. It will only make things worse than they already are."

Phyllis had echoed the sigh. "I suppose so. At least that's what Teri's been telling me. But I just haven't known *how* to act."

Lenore, for the first time in her adult life, had spoken literally without thinking. "Well, she's absolutely right. Let's face it, Phyllis—you've *never* known how to act. You've spent a whole decade trying to pretend to be something you're not, and it hasn't worked. So why not give it up and just try being yourself?"

And over the last weeks it seemed that was exactly what had happened. Phyllis had begun showing up at the club again, but more and more often it was with Teri. And instead of pushing their way into whatever group happened to be there, Phyllis and Teri had usually taken a spot by themselves.

Inevitably, people had begun to drift over to speak to her, at first simply out of adherence to the Cove Club Crowd's strict sense of duty, but eventually because they discovered that Phyllis had changed.

She was quieter, and seemed to listen more, and, somewhere along the line, had lost her sense of desperation. She seemed to have mellowed.

Perhaps, out of Melissa's tragedy, the people of Secret Cove decided, some slight amount of good had emerged.

Now, giving a few final instructions to the workmen, the two women emerged from the dining room just as Teri was approaching the door. "Caught you," Phyllis told her. "Thought you could sneak a look, didn't you?"

Teri grinned at her stepmother. "Well, you can't blame me for trying."

"I can, but I won't," Phyllis replied. "Come on. We're going to be late for our hair." She turned to Lenore. "How about if we meet you there?" she asked. "Charles is going to the hospital, and I have something I want him to take to Melissa."

Lenore's countenance softened into an expression of sympathy. "How is she? Has there been any change?"

Phyllis compressed her lips into a resigned smile. "I wish I could say there has," she said. "But Dr. Andrews seems to think it could take a long time."

Lenore shook her head sadly. "If there's anything I can do—"

"I wish there were. But it seems as though there's nothing, really, that any of us can do. And who knows? Perhaps she's better off just the way she is. I know it's a horrible thing to say, but if she *does* get better, what's it going to be like for her? The things she'll have to face . . ." Her voice trailed off, but then she straightened her shoulders. "Well, I simply cannot dwell on it, can I? After all, I have Teri to think about, too. And you," she added, turning to her stepdaughter, "have a lot to do tonight, or Brett's going to wind up going to the ball alone."

"Oh, no he's not," Teri assured her. "The one thing I am is prompt."

The two of them said good-bye to Lenore and started away. Lenore watched them leave. It was remarkable, she thought, how well stepmother and daughter got along. For each of them the other seemed to have replaced the person they'd lost this summer, and both seemed to be better for it.

Perhaps, after all, she and her friends had been far too hard on Phyllis over the years. Perhaps, after all, Phyllis hadn't been pushing Melissa too hard.

Perhaps Melissa's madness had been there all along, and Phyllis had only been doing her best to keep it under control. It must have been awful for her, all those years, coping with a child whose grip on reality had been so tenuous.

Yes, Lenore decided as she got into her Corniche, it had probably all ended the only way it could have. In all likelihood, Phyllis was right.

Perhaps it would be better if Melissa never remembered what

had happened at all. Perhaps it would be better if she simply stayed in her world of fantasy and let everyone else's scars heal as best they could.

As they walked along the beach toward Maplecrest, Teri reached out and took her stepmother's hand. "How's it going?" she asked. "Are you all right?"

Phyllis was silent for a moment, but finally smiled at her stepdaughter. "I'm fine," she assured her. "And you were right— they'll do anything for you, as long as they think you need help. All those years I tried to be just like them, and they treated me like dirt. But now I do what I want and say what I want, and they'll forgive me for anything. It's as if they've decided I'm a saint."

"Well, aren't you?" Teri asked, her voice reflecting perfect innocence. "I mean, I just don't see how you did it all those years. With Melissa getting weirder and weirder, and you doing your best to help her. It must have been even worse for you than it was for her. I mean, she didn't *know* she was going crazy."

"Well, I didn't either, really," Phyllis replied. She began talking, letting herself ramble on. It was so easy talking to Teri—Teri always seemed to understand how she felt about things.

Especially how she felt about Melissa.

After that day when they'd taken Melissa away, she hadn't known what to do. She'd been certain everyone in town was talking about her, and all she'd wanted to do was hide. But then Teri had begun talking to her, explaining that none of it had been her fault. "You didn't know what was happening to her," she'd insisted. "No one did. So how can anyone blame you?"

"But they do," Phyllis had replied. "They've always thought I was too hard on her."

Teri had shrugged. "Then tell them *that*," she suggested. "Tell everyone you see that it was all your fault. And see what happens."

And to Phyllis's surprise, it worked. All she'd had to do was summon up a few tears for Lenore Van Arsdale, and suddenly a woman who'd snubbed her for more than a decade had turned into her best friend.

And the rest of them—all the people she'd thought were so smart—had fallen right into line.

She smiled silently to herself. All those years, when Melissa had humiliated her in front of everyone . . . Now, with Melissa finally out of her way, she was at last getting the recognition she deserved.

And, in Teri MacIver, she had the daughter she deserved as well.

Her life, finally, was turning out exactly as she'd planned it that first day she'd arrived at Maplecrest and recognized Teri as the perfect child she'd always wanted.

Now they were together, the two of them, and life was just the way it was supposed to be.

She squeezed Teri's hand affectionately, dismissing Melissa from her mind.

Everyone, after all, was better off with Melissa gone.

Charles Holloway pulled up to the Harborview Clinic and nodded to the guard, who pressed a button that allowed the large wrought-iron gate to swing slowly open. At either side of the gate a cyclone fence, discreetly screened with tall shrubs, stretched away into the distance. The fence completely surrounded the fifty landscaped acres on which the clinic sat, but as Charles drove up to the mansion that housed the insane patients within, he had no sense of being in a prison. Rather, the clinic still looked exactly like the estate it had once been, and though he'd been shown the security systems installed when it had been converted to a private mental hospital, they'd been so cleverly concealed that he could see none of them now.

Charles parked the Mercedes on the apron in front of the main building and hurried up the steps. The receptionist, sitting at a small antique desk just inside the front door, smiled welcomingly at him. "We can always count on you, can't we?" she asked.

Charles nodded an acknowledgment of her words, but his eyes shifted immediately to the day room. The receptionist's smile faded as she understood what he was looking for.

"Not yet," she said. "They brought her down again this morning, but she did the same thing she always does. She seems to feel safest in her room."

Charles felt the faint hope he'd been nursing all day die within him, but he made himself smile. "Well, maybe tomorrow." He mounted the stairs to the second floor, where a duty nurse sat at another desk—almost identical to the one downstairs—placed at right angles to the wall on the landing.

"You can go right in, Mr. Holloway," the nurse told him.

Charles strode down the west corridor, pausing outside the third room on the left. He peered through the small window in the door and, just as he had yesterday and the day before, saw Melissa sitting in a chair by the window, her hands in her lap, staring straight ahead.

Staring at nothing.

No, Charles told himself as he turned the knob on the door and went inside. She sees something. She's looking at something she only sees in her mind—something she can't understand. But she'll figure it out, and when she does, she'll be all right again.

"Melissa?" he said, pulling a straight-backed chair close to his daughter. "Missy, it's me. Can you hear me?"

There was no response from Melissa at all. It was as if she hadn't heard his words, wasn't even aware of his presence.

"But it doesn't necessarily mean she doesn't hear you," Andrews had assured him only last week. "Melissa's personality is still there, even though we don't see it." He'd paused for a moment, searching for a simile. "Maybe you should think of it as a game of hide and seek. You can't see Melissa, and you can't hear her, but she's somewhere nearby, and she might very well be listening to you. You have to remember that she's a very frightened little girl, and it's quite possible that she's so terrified of what might happen to her that she simply won't expose herself."

"But D'Arcy says she's asleep, doesn't she?" Charles had asked.

Andrews had nodded. "But D'Arcy probably doesn't know the whole truth, any more than Melissa did. Melissa knew D'Arcy existed, but had no knowledge of what D'Arcy experienced. We have to assume D'Arcy's the same way."

"Has D'Arcy told you what happened?"

Andrews shook his head. "As I said, it's quite probable that she doesn't know. All I can say for sure is that she's protecting Melissa. Or at least she thinks she is."

It had taken Charles several weeks simply to adjust to the reality of his daughter's dual personalities, and though he'd finally been able to accept it enough to discuss D'Arcy with Andrews, he had been unable to bring himself to talk to the strange and silent girl who seemed to have simply appropriated Melissa's body.

And so on his daily visits he sat next to Melissa, holding her unresponsive hand in his own, talking quietly to her, sometimes telling her about what he'd been doing, but more often reminiscing about the past, about the good times they'd had together.

Today he stayed with her for nearly an hour. Finally, he glanced at his watch. "I have to go now," he said apologetically. "It's a big night at home. Your mother's been spending all her time getting the club ready, and she hasn't even told me what the theme of the party is. But from the look on her face the last few days, I'll bet it's going to be something special."

He leaned forward, taking both Melissa's hands in his own. "I wish you could be there," he said softly. "Remember what I always promised you? The summer you turned thirteen, I'd take you to the August Moon Ball and dance the first dance with you."

For a split second a flicker of interest seem to spark in Melissa's eyes, and he felt his heart suddenly race. "Missy?" he asked. "Missy, did you hear me?"

But as quickly as it had come, the spark died away. Charles reluctantly got to his feet. Kissing her gently on the forehead, he left the room, but even after he closed the door, the image of that strange brief light in her eyes stayed with him.

He turned back and gazed once more through the glass panel in the door.

Melissa, though, sat as she'd been sitting before, her eyes staring at nothing. Then, just as he was about to turn away, her right hand came up and gently fingered the string of pearls around her neck.

Charles's eyes flooded with tears as he remembered her words when she'd opened the box containing the necklace last Christmas.

"I'll wear them to the August Moon Ball," she'd breathed.

But she wouldn't be going to the ball. Not tonight. Perhaps not ever.

Wiping the tears from his eyes, Charles turned and hurried away.

CHAPTER

29

Teri tightened her arm around Brett Van Arsdale's neck and let her head rest against his chest. Her eyes were closed, the slow music of the last dance of the evening enveloping her in its gentle melody. All around her other couples were moving just as slowly, as if by slowing their steps they could prolong the perfect evening.

And it had been a perfect evening, ever since the doors to the dining room had been thrown open at precisely eight-thirty. By then most of the club members had gathered in the large foyer, and when Phyllis Holloway and Lenore Van Arsdale had finally stepped forward to unlock the huge double panels of polished mahogany, the crowd had unconsciously held its breath.

Collectively, they gasped in amazement as the doors were thrown open to reveal a nearly perfect re-creation of the dining room as it had been a century ago. Temporary panels had been placed against the walls, covered with a red-flocked wallpaper that was the closest anyone had been able to find to the original. The chandeliers—never replaced over the past century—had been freshly gilded for the occasion, and new bulbs put in that imitated the flickering of the original gas jets.

Along the walls, mounted to the temporary panels, were real gas sconces, their flames lending the room a glow that seemed to wipe away the passage of time.

Potted palms filled every corner of the room, and on the orchestra stand there were no microphones. Tonight, the orchestra would play without amplification. Above the orchestra the banner that Phyllis herself had so carefully lettered, announced the theme of the ball.

Full Circle
Back To Our Beginnings

And, indeed, the whole evening had felt as if the intervening century had never taken place at all.

Phyllis had thought of everything—each of the women had a dance card, tied around her wrist with a velvet ribbon. The music, all of it, was from another era, the orchestra playing from yellowed sheet music that had been culled from almost every attic in Secret Cove.

Pictures were on display—faded daguerreotypes from another era—but nearly everyone who had been at that first August Moon Ball a century ago had a descendant present at the party tonight.

Brett, after absorbing the spectacle, had swept Teri out onto the dance floor, and pulling her close, whispered into her ear. "It's almost creepy. You don't suppose D'Arcy is actually going to show up, too, do you?"

A chill had run through Teri. She'd quickly shaken it off, and yet, for the first hour of the dance, it seemed to her that the same thought must have crossed other people's minds, for time after time she saw people glancing furtively toward the door, then reddening slightly as they realized what they were doing.

But as the hours had passed, the crowd had relaxed, and now, as the last strains of the final waltz faded away, a ripple of applause passed over the room.

The guests began drifting toward the doors, all of them pausing to congratulate Phyllis and Lenore on the success of the evening. Phyllis listened to the compliments, the words of praise sounding far sweeter than the music itself could possibly have been.

At last Teri and Brett, their hands entwined, approached the door. Teri leaned forward to kiss her stepmother's cheek. "It was perfect, Mother," she murmured.

Phyllis, her eyes dampening at the word Teri had just used for the first time, pulled back slightly, wondering if it had been a slip of the tongue.

But Teri was smiling at her. "It's how I feel," she said. "I just feel as if you've always been my mother. And I think you're as perfect for me as the ball was for everyone else."

Phyllis felt her heart swell with pride. "And I feel the same way," she whispered, holding Teri close. "I feel just as if you're the daughter I always wanted. And now I have you."

A few moments later Teri and Brett stepped out into the night. It was warm and balmy, as if the weather itself had conspired with Phyllis to make the evening perfect, and when Brett started toward the parking lot, Teri stopped him. "Let's walk," she said. "Let's go home the way they would have that first night."

They descended the steps to the pool, then on down to the beach, Teri pausing to remove her shoes before stepping onto the cool sand. The moon was high, the sea glittering with silver light, and as they walked, Teri slipped her hand back into Brett's.

She sighed. "Wasn't it just wonderful?" she said. "Sometimes I wish I'd lived back then. I mean, when everyone had a big staff, and all the houses were full of guests all summer. Don't you think it would have been fun to live then?"

Brett made no answer, but slipped his arm around her waist and pulled her closer. They walked silently, coming at last to Maplecrest. When they were on the porch, he put his other arm around her and pulled her close, kissing her. "Why don't you invite me in?" he whispered. "Your folks are at my house, and won't be back for at least a couple of hours."

Teri said nothing for a moment, instead pressing herself close to him and kissing him once more. But then she drew back, shaking her head, a tiny smile playing around the corners of her mouth. "Not tonight," she whispered. "It's a hundred years ago, remember? Nice girls didn't do that kind of thing."

Before Brett could protest, she'd slipped out of his arms and through the front door, closing it silently behind her.

The lights in the foyer had been left on, and Teri paused in the entryway for a moment, resting her weight against the front door, feeling the house surround her.

It felt like home.

As each day went by, the past slipped farther and farther into the recesses of her memory, until now she could almost believe she'd never left here at all, never been taken away from the casual luxury of these immense rooms to grow up in the cramped confines of the tiny house in San Fernando.

Suddenly, unbidden, an image of the fire that had been the first step to bring her here leaped into her mind. She shuddered involuntarily before quashing the memory, locking it away with all the other memories of the things she'd done.

None of it, she told herself, was real. The only reality now was that she was back in her rightful home, with people who loved her.

Or who at least loved the image she had so meticulously built and so carefully presented to the world.

She sighed contentedly, slipped off the thin silk wrap she'd bought especially for tonight, and climbed the stairs to the second floor. Going into her room at the end of the hall, she hung the wrap in her closet, then dropped down into the chair in front of her vanity to admire the room once more.

It was exactly as she'd always pictured it, every trace of Melissa finally removed. Cora had packed up her half sister's things, storing them away in the attic, and then the decorators had come in—the same decorators who had rolled back time at the club tonight.

They had rolled back time for her, too, giving her the room she'd dreamed about since she was a little girl, the room she still felt a tiny thrill in every morning as she woke up. The walls were covered in an emerald moiré that was the exact shade she'd envisioned, and more of the shimmering material was swagged around the four-poster bed she and Phyllis had found in an antique shop in Portland. Melissa's chest was gone, banished to the little room beneath the eaves. That had been Teri's own idea, to put Melissa's bureau in what Melissa herself had thought of as D'Arcy's room. Now an ornate hand-carved armoire stood in its place, with its matching night tables flanking the bed.

All of it exactly as she'd imagined it.

She was absorbing it all in the mirror when she heard the first faint sound from upstairs.

She frowned slightly, then shrugged it off. Surely the noise had been nothing more than a branch brushing against the walls.

It came again.

A soft, whimpering sound.

As if someone were crying.

Teri's frown deepened and her pulse beat more quickly. But then the nearly inaudible sobs died away and the house was silent.

Until the footsteps began.

She heard them distinctly, moving across the ceiling above her with a slow and stately tread.

She thought she heard a door open, then close again with a soft click.

Then silence.

She listened, her flesh tingling, the fine hairs on the back of her neck standing on end.

She was imagining it. The house was empty—she knew it! She'd seen the lights in Cora's living room, even seen the old woman herself dozing in her chair.

She had begun to relax when she heard the steps again.

Now they were on the same floor she was on, moving slowly down the hall toward her closed door.

Gasping, she hurried to the door, twisted the key in the lock, then went back to her vanity.

The footsteps grew louder, and now she could sense a presence just outside her door.

Her heart was beating furiously, and icy fingers of panic were reaching out toward her.

Once more she insisted to herself that it was nothing, that it was only her mind playing tricks on her, as she had played tricks on Melissa, making her half sister believe she saw things that weren't there.

Her lock on her memories suddenly snapped and all the images of what she'd done poured forth, looming before her, horrifying her.

Was this how the rest of her life was going to be?

These terrible visions of her own guilt sneaking up on her, leaping out of their hiding place to torment her?

She turned away from the door, but the images in her mind followed her, mocking her. She closed her eyes for a moment, but then, as she heard the sound of a key turning in a lock, her eyes reopened, and she stared into the mirror.

Behind her the door that had been locked only a moment ago, the door she'd locked herself, stood slightly ajar.

Trembling with fear but unable to resist, she turned around.

As she watched, transfixed, the hinges groaned and the door swung slowly open.

A figure in a white dress, its face veiled, stood framed in the doorway, staring at her. Though she could see nothing of the face beneath the veil, her own terrified mind filled in its features.

Polly MacIver's features—her face contorted in a mask of death as she lay in the driveway after having fallen from the second-story window.

Tom MacIver's features—the flesh of his face burned away, the hollow sockets of his eyes gazing accusingly at her.

Tag Peterson's face—the features bloody and crawling with maggots. Tag was hidden beneath the veil, too, and she could see his eyes clearly, watching her, gazing at her as if he could see right through her. She'd had to kill him—there hadn't been any choice! He'd known what she was doing, and he was going to stop her.

Even Jeff Barnstable's face—he was there, too, and now, in this terrible moment of clarity, in which all her victims had risen from the dead to confront her, she knew that she'd killed Jeff as well. Perhaps not with the cold deliberation of the others, but in the end, the responsibility for what had happened to him was hers.

And finally, gazing at her almost pityingly through the heavy mesh of the veil, she was certain she could see Melissa Holloway.

Melissa, whom she'd hated for years before she'd ever met her.

Melissa, whom Teri had finally succeeded in exiling from her life and her home.

She could see them all in the veiled figure, and as the cold hands of her own guilt closed around her, she knew that whatever this figure demanded of her, she would do.

The figure raised its left arm to point at her accusingly.

But there was no hand at the end of the arm.

Only a bloody stump, the flesh and tendons curling back from the severed bones, so that it was white, glistening bone that pointed at Teri.

She rose, knowing already what she had to do, and followed the grisly figure as it turned and led her from the room.

In her room at Harborview, Melissa came slowly awake in her bed. Even before she opened her eyes, she sensed that she was not in her room at Maplecrest. No, she was somewhere else.

A hospital.

She was in a hospital where they'd brought her after . . .

Her eyes flew open and she sat straight up in bed as the floodgates of her memory suddenly opened.

The memories tumbled over one another as they struggled to capture her attention.

Some of them were familiar—familiar, and horrible.

The vision of Tag, his mutilated body lying under the floor of the pottingshed.

And Blackie, a string of pearls around his neck, hanging from a rafter in the attic.

Some of them were strange.

She saw an image of herself in the shower, scalding water pouring over her skin while her mother scrubbed her roughly, screaming at her.

Lying in her bed through endless nights, the cuffs around her wrists and ankles chafing at her.

Teri, her face looming over her in the darkness, talking to her.

No—not talking to *her*.

Talking to D'Arcy.

Talking to D'Arcy . . .

Her mind shifted suddenly, and she remembered the night of the costume ball. But now she remembered all of it. She remembered putting on the wig and going up to the attic. She remembered going down the servants' stairs and moving through the strangely unfamiliar kitchen.

And the path that seemed somehow to have changed.

All the blank spots in her memory were suddenly filled in, and for a moment a great fear filled her.

Instinctively, she called out to D'Arcy.

There was no reply.

There was no reply, for D'Arcy had gone away.

No, not gone away, not exactly.

Rather, D'Arcy had become a part of her, finally adding her own memories to Melissa's.

She sat still in the bed, looking around the room. There was nothing strange about it; indeed, she found that she knew every nook and cranny, every slight imperfection in the wallpaper. And yet it was also as if she'd never seen it before.

Her eyes wandered to the night table and the string of pearls that lay on it. She picked them up, feeling the familiar texture of them in her fingers.

But something was wrong.

One of the pearls—the third one from the end—should have had a slight imperfection in it, just the tiniest bump that you could barely feel.

Frowning, she examined the pearls more closely, and her eyes fell on the necklace's golden clasp.

The clasp that was engraved with her initials, in letters so tiny and fine they were hardly legible.

She brought them close, straining to read them, looking for the familiar M.J.H.

But what she found were other initials.

T.E.M.

Teresa Elaine MacIver.

But it was impossible. They were *her* pearls! Her father had given them to her last . . .

And then she remembered.

These were the pearls she'd removed from Blackie's neck the night she'd found him hanging in the attic.

For a long time she sat perfectly still, absorbing the meaning of what she'd found on the necklace's clasp.

The memories—all of them, hers and D'Arcy's—began to fit together and take a logical shape.

At last, as tears flowed down her face—more of pity for the people who had died than for herself—she pressed the buzzer that would summon the night nurse.

Charles and Phyllis let themselves into the house, and Phyllis impulsively threw her arms around her husband and hugged him.

"Wasn't it wonderful?" she asked. "How could it have been more perfect?"

It would have been perfect, Charles silently thought, if Melissa had been there. But for tonight he wouldn't mar Phyllis's joy with his own sadness. He would let her enjoy her moment of triumph, let her go on basking in the glow of her success. Time enough tomorrow for her to begin dealing with reality once again.

For he knew she'd been avoiding it, was all too aware of the excuses she was making to escape having to visit Melissa in the hospital.

But Melissa was still her daughter, and she still had a responsibility to her, no matter how distasteful that responsibility might be.

As if sensing his thoughts, Phyllis released him from her embrace, her happy smile fading away. "Couldn't you put her out of your mind even for one night?" she complained.

Charles shook his head. "I'm sorry," he said. "But I can't. It hurt so much not to have her with us tonight. She'd been looking forward to it for so long."

Phyllis sighed with impatience. "She doesn't even know she missed it, Charles. Dr. Andrews says—"

Charles held his hands up in a gesture that pleaded for peace. "Not tonight," he said. "I didn't even mean to bring it up. Now, why don't you go up and say hello to Teri. Her light's still on, and I can't believe she's gone to sleep yet. In fact, why don't you bring her downstairs? I'll fix us a nightcap, and she can have a Coke or something."

Her momentary anger forgotten as quickly as it had welled up inside her, Phyllis hurried up the stairs. The moment she reached the landing, she knew something was wrong.

Something in the house didn't feel right.

"Charles?" she called. "Charles, come up here!"

Charles hurried up the stairs to find Phyllis staring at the floor. His own gaze following hers, he saw a trail of dark red staining the hardwood floor.

He frowned, following it to the open door to Teri's room.

With Phyllis following him, he hurried down the hall. "Teri? Teri, are you okay?"

The room was empty, but lying in the middle of the floor, a

shapeless crumpled mass of brilliant green material, was the dress
Teri had worn to the ball that night.

He stared at the dress uncomprehendingly, then quickly crossed
to the bathroom.

It, too, was empty.

Leaving the bathroom, he strode out of the room and followed
the trail of blood in the opposite direction.

Phyllis, her breath already coming in choking sobs, stumbled
after him. At last they came to the base of the attic stairs.

That door, too, was open. Charles, with Phyllis clutching at his
arm, stared up into the darkness above. At last, taking a deep
breath, he started up the stairs, but Phyllis's hand tightened on
his arm.

"N-No," she whispered. "I—I don't want to."

Charles's voice rasped through his clenched jaw. "We have to,"
he said. "If she's up there . . ."

He left the sentence incomplete, hanging in the air, and once
more started up the flight to the attic.

He came to the top, his hand grasping his wife's, almost pulling
her along behind him. Then, when she was standing beside him
on the landing, he reached into the dark cavern of the attic and
switched on the light.

They both saw it at the same time.

Fifteen feet away, Teri, clad in the bloodstained white dress
that Melissa had worn the day she'd led the police to Tag Peterson's
butchered corpse, was hanging from one of the rafters, a thick
rope knotted tightly around her neck.

The dress itself glistened redly in the harsh light of the naked
bulb. There was a pool of blood beneath Teri's feet.

Her left arm, ending in a stump that was still dripping fresh
blood, hung at her side. On the floor, directly below Teri's lifeless
form, gleamed the blade of a meat cleaver.

Phyllis stared at Teri's contorted face, the eyes bulging outward
to gaze at her accusingly, a grimacing smile of death twisting her
lips. Then, screaming once, she collapsed to the floor, sobs rack-
ing her body.

Charles, stunned for a moment by the grisly sight, felt his gorge
rise inside him, but then seized control of his roiling emotions.
Turning away, he bolted down the stairs and ran to the master

suite and the telephone on the bedside table. Grabbing the phone with one hand and turning on the light with the other, he started to dial the emergency number.

And froze.

The phone dropped back onto its cradle as his eyes fixed numbly on the object on his pillow.

It was Teri's severed hand. In its blood-soaked fingers was clutched a string of pearls.

The pearls, he slowly realized, she'd sworn she never received.

He was still staring at them a moment later, trying to absorb what they meant, when the phone jangled loudly at his side.

He wanted to ignore it, to shut the insistent buzz out of his mind while he tried to comprehend everything he'd seen in the last minutes.

But the phone kept ringing, and finally he picked it up.

"H-Hello?" he asked, his voice shaking so badly it was barely intelligible. There was a momentary silence, and then a voice, a whispered voice almost as shaky as his own, spoke from the other end.

"P-Papa? This is Melissa."

EPILOGUE

Melissa felt a shiver run through her, but wasn't certain whether it had been brought on by fear or anticipation. Though she said nothing at all, Charles Holloway sensed his daughter's sudden unease and glanced over at her from his position behind the wheel of the Mercedes. "It's not too late to change your mind, honey. There's no reason we have to do this at all."

Melissa shook her head. "There are all kinds of reasons, Papa," she said. "We can't just pretend nothing ever happened here."

It had been five years since either of them had been back in Secret Cove, and when she'd first suggested to her father that they go to the August Moon Ball this year, his reaction had been a flat-out refusal.

"I can't imagine why you'd want to go, nor can I imagine anything in the world that would make me go," he'd told her. But she'd just grinned knowingly at him.

"How about if I asked you?"

And so they were here. Cora had stayed in New York, shaking her head dolefully when they'd told her where they were going. "Not me," she'd said. "If you two want to go stir up all those memories, I don't suppose I can stop you. But I've had my share of grief, and it's all tied up with that place." Her old eyes had fixed on Charles. "And that place never brought you much happiness, either."

But Melissa had been adamant. "I want to see it," she'd insisted, trying to find the right words to explain her feelings about both Secret Cove and herself. "I don't want to live at Maplecrest again—I don't think I even want to spend a night there. But I want to know that I *can* go there. I hid from too much for too long. I don't want to hide from anything anymore. And," she added, "believe it or not, I still want to go to the August Moon Ball. So you have to go with me, because you promised to dance the first and last dances with me, remember?"

And so here they were, pulling into the village for the first time since that terrible summer five years earlier.

Now Charles lifted his right eyebrow a fraction of an inch. "We both managed to pretend nothing was happening for years," he observed. "So why not go on?"

Melissa reached out to squeeze her father's hand affectionately. "If you don't want to go, you don't have to," she said. "I can drop you off in the village and go by myself. I'll look at the house, and go to the ball, and you can sit in a bar and drown your troubles in booze."

Charles put on an exaggeratedly aggrieved expression. "I never did that, and you know it."

"Well, you had a right to," Melissa replied. "How you could have stayed married to Mother all those years—" She cut her words short. They'd gone through that too many times to bring it up again. The subject of her mother was still painful enough for both of them that they rarely mentioned her anymore.

Now, as they passed through the village, Melissa gazed curiously around. "It never changes, does it?" she asked.

Charles shook his head. "That's always been its appeal. Something to count on in a changing world."

Five minutes later they pulled up in front of Maplecrest, but neither of them made any move to get out of the car. Instead they simply sat silently staring at the house in which both of them had spent every summer of their lives until five years ago. But unlike the village, Maplecrest had changed.

It had the look of abandonment peculiar to all unused houses, a look that went beyond peeling paint and unkempt grounds. There was a lonely aura to the structure, as if it was consciously aware that no one wanted to live in it anymore. At last they got out of the car and let themselves into the house itself. They wandered silently through the stuffy rooms whose furnishings had long ago been covered with sheets, each of them preoccupied with their own memories. At last Melissa went upstairs to the room that had been her own.

But it was hers no longer. The furniture Teri had chosen was still there, and nothing about the room seemed familiar to Melissa. And that, she decided, was just as well. If she ever came back to Maplecrest again, at least this room wouldn't haunt her, wouldn't bring the past too close for her to deal with.

The things of her childhood were gone, stored away somewhere in the attic, she knew. Perhaps some other time she would return again and go through them. But not today.

Today it was enough to know she could walk into the house without a sense of fear and foreboding.

The memories were there, but the past was dead and buried.

At eight-thirty that evening Charles pulled the Mercedes up in front of the Cove Club, hurrying around to the other side to help Melissa from the car. In the lobby several people were gathered in front of the open doors to the dining room, talking quietly among themselves. A silence fell over them as they recognized Charles and Melissa Holloway.

Charles had changed little over the past five years—his hair had grayed at the temples, and permanent creases were etched into his forehead.

Melissa, however, had grown up in the years since these people had seen her last.

She was as tall as her father now, and her figure was slim and elegant, the puppy fat of her childhood long gone. Her face had an enigmatic beauty to it, with high cheekbones and a jaw that was wide and strong. But it was her eyes that people always remarked upon. Large and dark brown, they sparkled with curiosity and good nature, yet there was a depth and wisdom to them that was far beyond her years.

Tonight, clad in a deep red dress that complemented her coloring perfectly and accentuated her figure to its best advantage, she could feel people staring at her.

Staring at her, but not laughing at her.

She felt her father's hand tighten on her arm. "Are you all right?" he asked, his voice so low that only she could hear it.

She smiled at him. "I'm fine," she said.

An hour later she knew she truly *was* fine. The first few minutes after she and her father had entered the ballroom and the silence they had expected had indeed fallen over the crowd, she had felt a few misgivings. But, determined not to back away from the mass of surprised faces, she had moved forward, her hand extended, smiling warmly. And it had been all right.

Now, as the first strains of a slow waltz began, she felt a presence behind her and turned to see Brett Van Arsdale, even handsomer in his twenty-first year than he'd been when she'd last seen him. He was smiling at her uncertainly, and when he spoke, there was a slight tremor to his voice. He feels the way I used to feel, she thought. He doesn't know if I'm even going to speak to him. But as he almost shyly asked her to dance with him, she nodded immediately and slipped gracefully into his arms. He moved her into the crowd and for a few minutes said nothing at all. Finally, he pulled away from her slightly, just enough so his eyes could meet hers.

"I don't know how to tell you how sorry I am," he said, his voice trembling once more. "I mean, it's not just me—everyone feels terrible about the way we used to treat you. I know it's too late to make it up to you, but—"

Melissa pressed a finger against his lips. "It's not too late," she said. "And I know how everyone feels. I've seen it in everyone's eyes all evening. But we don't need to talk about it, Brett. The past is the past, and all the ghosts are gone."

Brett was silent for a moment, but then his head cocked. "Would you tell me something?" he asked.

Melissa smiled mischievously. "Maybe. What is it?"

Brett hesitated, then finally spoke the words that had been in his mind for five long years. "It's about D'Arcy. Do you think . . . well, do you think she was real?"

Now it was Melissa who was silent for a long time. At last she nodded. "For me she was. She was part of me. And in the end, I think she was real for Teri, too."

Brett frowned. "But Teri killed herself."

"Maybe she did," Melissa said, her voice solemn. "But maybe she didn't. Maybe D'Arcy killed her."

They danced on, letting the strains of music envelop them, and then, as they slowly walked off the floor when the dance was over, Brett asked one more question. "What about your mother?" he asked. "What happened to her?"

Melissa felt a slight chill come over her for a moment, but quickly shook it off. "I don't know," she said, her voice firm. "And I really don't want to know, either." And it was true. Finally, tonight, the last of the past was truly behind her.

Three thousand miles away, in a mansion high in the hills west of Los Angeles, Phyllis Holloway sat nervously on the edge of a chair, watching the young woman who was even now reading over the last of her references. As the woman looked up, smiling, Phyllis breathed a silent sigh of relief. It was going to be all right.

"Well, everyone certainly seems to be happy with your work, Mrs. Holloway," she said. "And I think you're exactly what we're looking for. Shall we go upstairs and introduce you to our baby?"

Phyllis's heart fluttered with anticipation. From the moment two hours ago when she'd first walked into this house, it had felt right. Large and airy, it occupied two full acres on the very crest of the hills, with a panoramic view of Los Angeles on one side and the San Fernando Valley on the other. There was an Olympic-size swimming pool and a pair of tennis courts, along with perfectly tended formal gardens that reminded her of home.

Home.

Except that Secret Cove and Maplecrest weren't home anymore, would never be home again. Indeed, she'd had to promise never to return to the East Coast at all, in exchange for Charles's agreement not to prosecute her for child abuse.

As if she'd abused Melissa! Just the thought of it was still enough to make her blood boil.

All she'd *ever* tried to do was teach Melissa proper behavior. And what had she gotten in return? Not a trace of the gratitude to which she was entitled. Far from it—she'd been dismissed from the house as if she were no more than a servant, divorced with a settlement that hadn't been enough to support her for more than a year, and forbidden ever to see Melissa again.

But she was a survivor, and this job, with a middle-aged lawyer and his young wife, was perfect.

She would have her own suite of rooms on the second floor, right next to the nursery, and live here as a member of the family.

And eventually, when the marriage inevitably failed . . .

She put the thought out of her mind as the woman—what was her name? Emily!—as Emily opened the door to the nursery. A soft gurgling sound emerged from the crib that stood next to the open window, and Phyllis strode across the room, crouching down to look at the baby about to be entrusted to her care.

A pair of dark brown eyes, large and serious, stared up at her from the crib. The tiny face was almost perfectly round, but with a deep dimple in the center of its chin. "Well, aren't you just the most precious thing I've ever seen," Phyllis crooned. She lifted the infant out of the crib, cuddling it close.

Almost instantly, the child began to cry, and Emily hurried across the room to take it from Phyllis. But Phyllis turned away and shook her head. "No, no—she's got to get used to someone besides her mother holding her. And it doesn't hurt a baby to cry now and then, you know. It's perfectly natural." Her eyes shifted back to the sobbing infant in her arms, and she snuggled it closer. "But you'll be all right, won't you? You're going to love me as much as I love you, and pretty soon, you'll be just like my own child."

The baby kept crying for a moment, and then, as if sensing some sort of unseen danger, turned silent. But its eyes, wary now, remained fixed on Phyllis.

Phyllis smiled reassuringly at the nervous young mother who was still hovering a couple of feet away. "You see?" she asked. "It's going to be fine, and you aren't going to have to worry about a thing. I'll treat her just as if she were my own." She was silent for a second or two, then spoke once more, barely audibly, almost to herself. "Yes," she said. "I'll treat her just as if she were my second child."